Yesterday's Gone

Yesterday's Gone

CINDY WOODSMALL
& ERIN WOODSMALL

Tyndale House Publishers
Carol Stream, Illinois

Visit Tyndale online at tyndale.com.

Visit Cindy Woodsmall online at cindywoodsmall.com.

Tyndale and Tyndale's quill logo are registered trademarks of Tyndale House Ministries.

Yesterday's Gone

Designed by Libby Dykstra

Edited by Sarah Mason Rische

The Author is represented by Ambassador Literary, Nashville, TN.

Scripture quotations are taken from the *Holy Bible*, King James Version.

Yesterday's Gone is a work of fiction. Where real people, events, establishments, organizations, or locales appear, they are used fictitiously. All other elements of the novel are drawn from the authors' imaginations.

For information about special discounts for bulk purchases, please contact Tyndale House Publishers at csresponse@tyndale.com, or call 1-855-277-9400.

Library of Congress Cataloging-in-Publication Data

A catalog record for this book is available from the Library of Congress.

ISBN 978-1-4964-7256-4 (HC)
ISBN 978-1-4964-5422-5 (SC)

Printed in the United States of America

28	27	26	25	24	23	22
7	6	5	4	3	2	1

From Cindy:

To my longtime friend Kay, who believed in me before I dared to tell others of my desire to write, passing me novels to read and assuring me I could write one day too if I believed in me as you did. Whether my life is being overly joyous, desperately grievous, or something between, you steady me and encourage me, and I thank you from the depths of my heart.

From Erin:

To my husband, Adam: above all the unexpected and no matter what path life takes us on, I'd choose you in every timeline. And to our baby Iris, our "Penelope," who we lost before birth: our time together was but a breath, but aren't all our lives in comparison with eternity? You matter and exist, and writing this book was part of my promise to you.

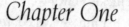

Chapter One

Sweat rolled down Eliza Bontrager's neck as she carried her youngest sibling on one hip and a plate of sliced bread in her hand. Stale bread, and the last of it. The mountain air hung thick with the familiar July aromas. But was there a hint of stench in the air from the feed mill where *Dat* worked? Surely not. Despite how foul that odor was, it stayed in downtown Calico Creek, rarely meandering this far into the rural part.

"*Kumm,*" Eliza called. "*Es iss Zeit esse.*"

The moment she said it was time to eat, excited voices filled their little nook of the Appalachian Mountains. Four children, not looking at all as if she'd hauled water and bathed them last night, scurried to the picnic table. The old wooden benches and marred table wobbled as the little ones clamored to a spot. Despite grubby hands snatching up bread, she couldn't help but chuckle. They were just too cute.

The little one on her hip squawked, reaching for a piece of bread. She passed him a slice, and he bounced up and down.

Four-year-old John shoved a big bite into his mouth. *"Denki,"* he mumbled. Even as he ate, his brown eyes were glued to the remaining three slices of bread, the ones meant for Ruth, Moses, and her, but John stayed so hungry of late, and one slice wasn't likely to fill his stomach.

Eliza did what she could to bring money into their home. Her skill was textiles, mostly weaving fabrics on a small loom from cotton and wool she purchased when she could. She also made quilts and blankets from scraps. But she hadn't been able to purchase threads for the loom in a while, and thick blankets were a hard sell during the dog days of summer. The good news was Dat would be home in a few hours, and today was payday. But without a working flue for the cookstove, they couldn't bake bread, and buying store-bought was out of the question. There was nothing quite as difficult as baking bread using a wood-burning cookstove during the hottest summer months, but it had to be done at least once a week.

She shooed flies away from the bread in the little ones' hands. Most days keeping food on the table was hard work but rarely this difficult. Between the broken flue and Dat's last paycheck being short due to missing more work than he had paid days off, the last week of feeding the family had been more challenging than most.

Cicadas buzzed loudly, a constant song during the hottest months each year. A summer breeze kicked up, and she lifted her head to enjoy it. A familiar screeching sound let her know someone had opened the screen door. She turned to see her sister Ruth coming outside. Ruth was the smart one, and she currently held the spot of a teacher's assistant at the local Amish school. Unfortunately, it only earned about four thousand per year, which was only three hundred a month. Ruth wouldn't look for anything else because her dream was to become a full-time teacher when she turned eighteen, and her best chance of that was to faithfully stay working as a teacher's assistant. She walked to the picnic table, carrying a pitcher of water and three cups. The little ones always had to share . . . plates, cups, beds, clothes, bathwater, and the few toys they possessed.

"*Gut!*" John clapped. "*Jah?*"

He knew the water would help fill his aching belly. Eliza bent and kissed the top of his head. He was always grateful for every kindness that came his way.

Ruth poured water and passed it out before grabbing a slice of bread. "Where's Moses?"

"He's trying to fix the flue, but something broke, and he said he knew what to do, so he put a bridle on Tank and rode off bareback toward Ebersol land."

"Think he can fix it?"

Moses had a good heart, but he was only thirteen. He needed someone older to help him. Most of the menfolk in these parts were at the plant working or sleeping because they'd worked third shift. It wasn't a very Amish way to make a living—or an uplifting way—but it's what was available.

Eliza shrugged. "I'm equal parts hopeful and doubtful. *Mamm* said we should plan on cooking over a campfire again tonight."

Ruth glanced around. "Where is Mamm?"

"She's in the henhouse, prayerfully looking for enough eggs to make a decent meal with." It was always tough growing a vegetable garden on the ridge, but this summer was the worst. "She got a few ears of corn, some cucumbers, and several tomatoes for tonight's supper."

They might not have their fill, but no one would go to bed fully hungry.

The little ones, all except John, had left the table and were beneath a shade tree, scratching sticks across the soft dirt. Eliza's stomach growled as she handed him her piece of bread.

His brown eyes grew large as he threw his arms around her waist. *"Ich lieb du."*

"I love you too." She patted his back before he released her.

Three horses with riders topped a nearby hill. One was Moses. She squinted, trying to make out the others.

Jesse.

Her heart crashed against her rib cage, threatening to leap out of her chest.

How had he slipped back into Calico Creek without her knowing? Oftentimes of late he only made it home every three to four months. It took three hours by car to get here to visit. At apprentice pay and with the cost of living elsewhere, he didn't have money to hire a driver to go that distance and back, so he had to wait until someone he knew was coming this way. Her heart raced, and it was hard to breathe.

Moses rode toward the old barn. She recognized Ben, Jesse's cousin, and he followed Moses.

Jesse. He rode tall and powerful in his saddle these days, three years since he'd moved to Hillsdale to work for Frank

Mulligan, a home builder. Jesse was full grown now, twenty-one years old, and dating women in his new Amish community who were fascinating, she was sure. Women who weren't dirt-poor.

Would he forget in a few years that they'd ever been close friends while growing up? Had he even noticed on his visits home that she'd grown up too? She trailed behind him three years, but still, she was grown now.

He rode to the picnic table before stopping. "Ruth." He nodded at her.

Ruth? Why was he addressing her little sister? Eliza's chest burned.

He got off the horse, his eyes meeting Eliza's. "Hi."

Speak, Eliza! You're friends for goodness' sake! But she couldn't find her voice.

He pulled a burlap bag off the side of the horse. "It's two pounds off a smoked ham, a bag of green beans, and half a loaf of Italian bread."

Had his dat been paid in groceries again? Unlike most of the men around here, his dad didn't work at the feed mill. He was a handyman, able to fix almost anything. But it was just as likely that Jesse brought food home to his family and was sharing it with Eliza's family. She wouldn't ask.

He turned to Ruth again and held out the sack. "You need to take it to your mamm to put up."

"Denki." Ruth took the sack and clutched it tight. "I got to say it twice: denki." She smiled at him. "When did you get back?"

That was what Eliza wanted to know. Staying quiet wasn't like her. What was going on?

Jesse's eyes moved back to Eliza. "About twenty minutes ago." He patted his horse. "Levi," he called.

Eliza's eleven-year-old brother hurried to them. Jesse held out the reins. "You know what to do, right?"

Levi frowned, looking as if he'd rather go play. Ruth held up the food. "A tasty, filling dinner. Jesse brought it."

Levi's face lit up. "Uh, jah, I knew about tending to a horse before I's born." Chuckling, Levi took the reins and walked off with the horse.

Jesse had nine younger siblings, including a set of four-year-old twin brothers, and he was comfortable putting any of the older ones to work helping.

"You here for the whole weekend?" Ruth asked.

"I am. Until Monday morning when my boss will pick me up, and I'll return to Hillsdale."

Ruth sent a knowing but wary look Eliza's way. Her sister understood how Eliza felt about Jesse. But Mamm and Dat forbade any romantic notions with the likes of Jesse Ebersol. "Well, gut," Ruth said.

But it seemed to Eliza that when Jesse did come home and they got time to talk, he was most interested in telling Eliza what she needed to do about attending singings and dating. He insisted she do both, and then he'd leave again.

Moses and Ben strode out of the barn.

Moses was carrying a slightly rusty piece of an old flue. "Jesse had this in his smokehouse. Said we could have it."

Eliza nodded, finally finding her tongue. "That's very kind, Jesse. Denki."

"*Nee.*" Jesse shook his head. "It's nothing."

He probably felt that way because he was a giver, but it

wasn't nothing. Every piece of scrap mattered in these parts, whether it was metal, rope, boards, or food. All the Amish around here struggled. No wonder Jesse stayed away. How much more time would pass before he stopped coming to visit like this? The only things the Amish of Calico Creek weren't in short supply of were love and respect for each other, work ethics, and children.

When their Amish ancestors settled in these parts hundreds of years ago, they'd thought the mountains would be good farmland. They were wrong. The valley was some of the best farmland, but the ridges were mostly crop-resistant shale and sandstone.

Hard living aside, Eliza was sure God felt like she did about all the children—that nothing was more important than the joy and hope each child brought to this fallen planet.

"Whew." Ben made a face as he sniffed the air. "Country fresh air, but you would not believe what it smells like in downtown Calico Creek. Today's a particularly stale one."

"I thought I smelled the plant a bit ago."

"I guess it's possible," Ben said. "Maybe Andrew is right that someone should investigate if this stench is safe to breathe."

Ruth held the burlap bag against her as if concerned she might lose it. "Since Andrew is the first person I've heard of who seems to think it's a problem, he should be the one to check into it. Who's Andrew?"

Ben removed his straw hat. "You have to know Andrew. He's my best friend. Surely you two have met."

"Maybe. I don't recall it," Ruth said.

"He lives in the next district over, like me. I guess maybe

it makes sense that you Calico Creek Ridge Amish don't know all the Calico Creek Glen Amish. Same bishop, but different Amish school, different preachers. Still, how do you not know him? He's our age."

"Ah." Ruth grinned. "So at sixteen years old, he's got lofty, suspicious ideas and nothing he can do with them. It most likely stinks because feed for pigs, poultry, goats, and numerous other animals is being processed and cooked twenty-four hours a day, seven days a week at the mill."

Ben shrugged. "Probably so."

Moses held up the old flue segment. "Kumm, let's get this done for Mamm."

Ruth, Moses, and Ben headed for the run-down house. Eliza paused, hoping for a moment with Jesse, hoping he'd tell her something interesting or funny that happened in his world recently. But when she looked into his beautiful greenish-blue eyes, she saw that something was troubling him.

"You're home for a reason," she offered.

He nodded. "Jah." He cleared his throat. "We need to talk, Eliza. Can you find time later today or tonight?"

Her excitement at his being home fled and nausea churned. He'd found someone. She was sure of it, and she didn't want to hear about it. "Just say it, Jesse."

He pulled a flat, round rock from his pant pocket. "Maybe we could walk to the creek after we get the cookstove fixed."

She didn't want to skip rocks as if time with her mattered. Then again . . . why would she refuse them having some fun? Why not make the most of their time? If he'd found someone, this was likely their last romp in the woods. Could she change his mind? Would she dare even try when he was a fine catch and she was . . . well, nobody?

Besides all of that, they were forbidden. "Tonight, at our old spot by the creek, after my chores are done."

Jesse shifted, lowering his hand a bit. "Sounds gut."

Eliza's heart pounded. She snatched the stone from his palm. "I'll win." She tossed it slightly into the air, ready for it to land in her hand.

Jesse reached in and grabbed it before it hit her palm. "Jah?" Smiling, he slid the rock into his pocket.

"Definitely." Could she win what really mattered? Would she even be able to make herself try?

Chapter Two

Jesse's nerves danced across his shoulders, tightening the muscles. Hard conversations weren't for the faint of heart, but for better or worse, it was time he came clean with Eliza. He fidgeted with the rock in his pocket as he watched her wade into the creek.

She'd reached into the shallow, clear water and picked up a palm-size stone. She bounced it in her hand. Jesse peeled out of his shoes and socks. He eased into the water.

They'd been neighbors all of their lives and friends for more than a decade. She was the ideal friend, the best one anyone could have. But he wanted more, far more. His gut said she did too, but even so, it wouldn't solve all that was stacked against them. As much as her parents liked and appreciated who he was, and his parents felt the same about her, they would be dead set against them dating. To them, a union between the Ebersol and Bontrager families was offensive and unthinkable.

Eliza turned to him. "Throw yours, Jesse. Let's see what you can do."

He pulled from the heaviness and set aside his concerns. "I need a minute to mentally prepare," he teased.

"Jah. Take all the time you need." She shrugged. "But it won't help."

He chuckled. "*Ach*, so much confidence."

"Yep." She took a deep breath. "Smell the mountain laurel."

"Jah."

It grew along the riverbanks, and year-round, this little gorge held a bounty of aromas she loved.

He'd waited months for time with her again, and he took it all in. The sun waned behind the trees that lined the mountains, and tree frogs joined the cicadas in song.

It'd taken her longer than expected to get everything done for the day. Her list of responsibilities seemed endless. It might drive a lot of teens to rebellion, but her love for her siblings seemed to cause any workload to bring her joy. Since she was eighteen and the chores were done, she had freedom to disappear for a bit on a Friday night—not for long, but hopefully long enough.

"Before it gets dark, Jesse Ebersol? Or is the plan to wait until we can't see the number of skips your rock makes? Then you can declare it skipped a dozen times."

"I hadn't thought of that, but it's not a bad plan, except it'd make me a liar." He slung the flat rock. It skidded across the surface, bouncing eight times. He laughed. "Wow. I didn't expect . . ." He cleared his throat, choosing to tease instead. "I mean, no way can you beat eight jumps. I'm the winner today." He reached into the water and picked up another stone.

"Ha. Watch as I seal my victory." Eliza wrapped the small rock in her apron and rubbed it, wiping off water and muck.

"Oh, I'm watching . . . as you clean a rock that's about two skips from sinking into the mud again."

Truth was he had a hard time not soaking in her every move. Did she know how well their personalities and hopes for the future fit together? He was reasonably confident in how she felt about him, which was likely only a small fraction of all he felt for her, but would she give in to it and give them a chance? The community typically honored the romantic wishes between any Amish couple. She could be with anyone who wasn't an Ebersol, and everyone would celebrate it. The same was true of him and anyone but a Bontrager. Would she be willing to withstand the pressure of her family and the ministers frowning at this relationship?

"Before it gets dark, Eliza Bontrager? Or is the plan to wait until we can't see the number of skips your rock made? Then you can declare it skipped a dozen times."

Her laughter filled the air and she moved in closer to him. "That would make me a liar. Are you calling me a liar?" Her brown eyes danced, and his heart went wild with hope.

He smiled down at her, longing to touch her hand. Her face. Her lips with his. "No. I think lies would be afraid to tempt you, afraid you'd kill them dead. Therefore, I would believe you no matter how absurd something sounded."

"Gut. I'll hold you to that." She smiled before something in the woods caught her attention. She eased an index finger against her lips and nodded over his left shoulder.

Jesse slowly turned his head and torso, spotting a doe and her fawn. The deer didn't seem to notice them as they made their way down the bank to the edge of the water. As the doe drank just a few hundred feet from them, the fawn pranced and ran around excitedly. Eliza was enjoying every moment, but Jesse's thoughts continued to churn.

Most of the Ebersol and Bontrager families on this Appalachian ridge—including his and Eliza's—were descendants of Amish who'd fled Germany due to religious persecution, lived in Switzerland for a while, and then come to America on the same ship in the early 1740s. There were ten families with different surnames who were descendants too, but marriage in combinations of any surnames other than Ebersol and Bontrager wasn't a problem. The Amish in these parts were dead set against any marriage between an Ebersol and Bontrager who were direct descendants from the original 1740s ancestors. Each time the two families married, it caused serious problems within the Amish community. His grandfather had a written record somewhere of the specifics from those difficult marriages. To say their families would frown on them getting married was an understatement.

He studied Eliza, his heart pounding. She was the only one for him. He knew that, but he also knew the history that was stacked against them.

The worst union he knew of was from a marriage that took place back in 1953, between Omar Ebersol and Verna Bontrager. The story went that within six months, the marriage was hurting, causing grief to the entire community. It was said that five years later, in the late 1950s, their marriage was a total wreck. Since the Amish don't believe in divorce, the ministers and community did their part in helping them stay together. But the couple refused weekly counseling or having private Bible studies with the ministers, and they also refused to allow any couple with a healthy marriage to move in with them to show them how things should work between a godly couple. They were shunned for not submitting to the Amish way of making a marriage work. Omar and Verna left the Amish and divorced. As far as Jesse knew, no one had heard from them since. Every Amish parent was responsible for making sure their children understood that any marriage between the Ebersol and Bontrager descendants was cursed.

But none of that had been able to stop his heart from wanting what it wanted. He'd been studying the Bible of late, and the word *curse* meant that a person or family wasn't under the full blessings of God. That seemed like a common occurrence for mankind. Wasn't the remedy staying close to God? Wasn't that what the Bible was all about—how to be under His blessings?

The doe startled, and she and the fawn ran up the hill and out of sight.

Eliza grinned. "That was a treat."

The joy of being alive seemed to radiate from her and splash onto him. He nodded and gestured toward the stone in her hand. "Before or after dark, Eliza?"

She clicked her tongue, mocking anger before she turned and fired off her stone. One skip, two, three, four.

Feeling reminiscent of childhood days, he slung his rock, and it hit hers, stopping the skips after the seventh one.

She whirled around to face him, her skirt whooshing as it skimmed the creek water. "Hey, cheater!"

"Who, me?" He shrugged, looking skyward for a moment. "Actually, I think I should get some bonus points for managing to hit your rock. That's way harder than skipping a stone. I couldn't repeat that if I tried."

She dipped her hands in the creek and scooped as much water as she could in his direction. He laughed and returned her splashes.

Minutes later, they were still laughing while sitting on the grassy riverbank.

Eliza squeezed some water out of her skirt. "Ruth is not going to be happy if I come inside dripping since cleaning floors is fully her responsibility."

It was time to say what was on his mind. Jesse leaned an elbow on his propped-up, wet knee. "I think a cabin would go well right over there." He gestured up the hill to an open spot in the green valley on his family's side. "Then we wouldn't have to walk far from the creek to be home."

He studied her to see her reaction to his use of the word *we*. Her expression revealed nothing except curiosity. "A cabin, like a hunting lodge?"

"Like a home." He spread his arms. "A decent-size log cabin with a wide front porch and a wood swing built for two, with one of your quilts draped over it. You make such nice quilts."

She looked at the area he meant. "Jah, that sounds lovely."

Jesse wiped creek water from his brow, sat up straight, and slid his hand over hers.

She stiffened and eased her hand from his. "Trying to keep me from throwing another rock, and that would show I am the winner."

Did she not have any clue how he felt? Or how she felt about him? Would the whole curse issue make her run from the idea of being together?

"Eliza." He drew a breath. "Um, I've been thinking about the future. Thinking a lot, actually. What I'm gonna do and all."

"You mean something besides building houses and cabins for Mulligan Builders?"

"I intend to keep that up for a while yet, but I want to eventually work for myself and bring the business here to Calico Creek." Amish men of all ages needed better jobs in this area, but part of what weighed on Jesse was the number of boys who'd soon be grown, including his six younger brothers, and would need decent jobs. Otherwise they'd either raise their own families in poverty or move elsewhere in hopes of a better life. He wanted so much more for his people of Calico Creek.

Eliza gazed at him. "Ah, so that's why you're thinking of building a cabin, sort of as a model home, but maybe one you live in?"

"I hadn't thought of using it as a model home, but that's a good idea. What I do know is *Englischers* love owning a cabin in the mountains. They're simple enough to build, as far as homes go. I'd make most of the pieces in a workshop—prefab—then go with an *Englisch* tractor trailer driver to deliver parts to the homesite and put them together there. I'd need a team on some projects, but others I could do on my own. Frank Mulligan's a good guy, and he's all for me learning the trade and bringing it back to this community once my contract is up with him. If I can pull this off, I could have my own business and bring opportunities for employment into our community."

She beamed. "Ebersol Cabins. How exciting."

"Ebersol Cabins?" He wasn't sure he should use his name. Was that too vain? "Maybe Deer Run Cabins."

"Maybe, but the business will have your heart and your craftsmanship. I think it should have at least part of your name."

"Okay, Ebersol Cabins it is."

"I can't even tell ya how much I like the sounds of this business in Calico Creek. Scratching out a living around here is just too hard."

"I don't know if it's even feasible for me to dream of saving enough money to buy the lumber that will be needed to get started, but that's my goal."

"First, begin by building your credit so you can get a small business loan."

"That's not our way."

"I know. The Amish way is for fathers and grandfathers to loan or give the younger generation money to start a business, and usually they have a business to pass down, but none of our people have that kind of money. You're going to have to think differently to attain your dream." Her eyebrows went high, and he knew she'd had another idea. "Then let the Amish who have good groves of trees give you those in exchange for a share in your business."

"I hadn't thought of that." He knew she was smart, but he hadn't realized just how much natural business know-how she had.

"Add to that, Mr. Jordan owns hundreds of acres with virgin timber. Maybe you can barter with him or make a deal that pays him a little along."

"He'd be a hard nut to crack, Eliza. He's never sold to a logging company, and to put it politely, he's none too partial to the Amish."

"Well, we've got time, and I'll pray about it every day. How long do you think you'll need?"

Every word from her mouth confirmed what he already knew to be true—they could be a powerful team.

"It'll take at least three years to finish my apprenticeship contract with Frank, and then another two or three to build my own business here. During a good portion of that, I'll be gone more than I'm home."

She squared her shoulders. "You won't be home much, but it'll be worth it, and that's what counts, right?"

It was time. What if she said no? How could he manage the weight of all he wanted to do without her help? "Goodness, why am I so nervous?"

A faint smile crossed her lips. "You're making me nervous too. Maybe it's because that kind of a commitment and dream is bound to be a bit scary."

He wanted to put his hand over hers. "Jah, but probably not for the reason you think." He fidgeted with his suspenders, trying to find the right words. "Eliza, I need to tell you something."

Was that disappointment on her face? She shook her wet

apron at him, spraying him with droplets of water. "It sounds as if you've found someone, and I think I might be jealous. I keep doing as you've said, attending singings, even going for buggy rides home afterward with guys who ask. I've had more than two years of it, but I can't make myself find one of them interesting."

"There's a reason for that."

"Jah? Is it because I don't want to be there, but you've been insisting that I attend singings and go for a ride with whoever asks?"

"There's a reason for that too."

"Is there a reason you're keeping all of the reasons to yourself?"

"Everyone—the ministers, my parents, the whole dad-blame community—says we're taboo. I . . . I thought if I left here and dated other girls that I could find someone. I knew she wouldn't be like you, but . . ."

Her face drained of emotion. "Wh . . . what are you saying?" She sounded offended, and it shredded his confidence. Still, he had to speak his mind.

He shifted, staring into her eyes. "I love you. I have for a long time." His heart pounded.

She stared at him. "You . . . love me?"

He nodded. She held his gaze, not even a hint of a smile. Lowering her eyes, she plucked grass from the ground. "But . . . you've been seeing other girls."

"Jah, I went to every singing I could in other Amish districts. I've been desperately trying to stop loving you. I prayed about it, asking God to set me free of wanting a life with you."

"But you told me to date other guys."

"Of course I did. If you found someone, that would help me move on. But you haven't, and I'm tired of ignoring the one thing I want more than anything else in life . . . you. I've been acting as if it didn't make me sick to my stomach when you went out with other guys every Sunday night."

"I thought you were being honest with me."

He held up his hand. "I know, but I thought I was doing the right thing because it's what the preacher, bishop, deacon, Mamm, Dat, your parents, and everyone says is the right thing." He said nothing else, giving her some time to catch up.

"I can't believe you're in love with me. I'd dreamed of it, but I never actually believed it possible."

"Undeniably in love, Eliza, but is that enough with the church, parents, and so many others against us?"

"I . . . I don't . . ." Her voice faded as she stared at the creek.

His world blurred as he waited on her to absorb what he'd said and then tell him her real thoughts.

She plucked a piece of grass and tossed it. "There are so many other girls who are smarter and prettier."

There it was. Her belief that he was somehow better than her. He'd seen it before, and no doubt, he'd see it again. "Two things: I've never found one, and I looked. I never will, because you're the one for me . . . if you'll have me." What would it do to them, to *him*, if she realized she didn't care for him enough to stand against their families and community?

Tears welled in her beautiful brown eyes. "It's terrifying to think of going against what everyone believes in these parts.

They feel so strongly about it, and there's got to be good reason for that."

"It's a superstition, Eliza. Nothing more."

She tilted her head, her eyes searching his. "You're sure that's all it is?"

"Darkness falls away when light shows up, and a curse falls away when blessings show up, so I have no doubts at all."

A moment later she nodded. "I trust you."

"Jah?" His heart flittered. "Gut."

"I thought you were going to tell me you'd found someone, and I was trying to work up the courage to try to change your mind." She laughed and put her hand on her chest. "Tell me again, Jesse."

He chuckled. "This time I'll ask, you love me?"

She bobbed her head. "You know I do." Her face radiated delight, and his heart sang. "One thing about your plan, Jesse. Since it'll be years before we marry, we'll have plenty of time to pray that God softens our families' and community's hearts, jah?"

"Jah. But our waiting has nothing to do with their superstitions."

"I get it. We've seen what poverty is." She put her hand in his. "We know what it means to be dirt-poor, for parents to struggle to feed and clothe their young'uns. We wait because we want to change that . . . for us and for the Amish of Calico Creek."

"It'll take time and patience and enduring a long-distance relationship, although I'll come home as often as I can. The good news is when we marry, I'll be able to support you and a houseful of children. Will you marry me, Eliza?"

She stared into his eyes. "You know the answer to that, don't you?"

"I've been hoping I did."

"I can't believe you love me. That alone will take me a year to adjust to." She laughed. "Jah, I'll wait, and I'll be here for you, helping you however I can from this day until the day I die."

"You've made me so happy." He leaned in, caressing her face. "May I kiss you?"

"I . . . I'm not sure I know how. I've never kissed anyone."

He blinked. That was an unexpected turn.

She smiled. "You could make me date those guys. No one could make me kiss them."

Jesse leaned in, his warm lips enveloping hers.

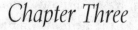

Chapter Three

FIVE YEARS LATER

Ruth spilled a bit of coffee as she passed the mug to the preacher. The brown liquid ran down her starched organza apron. She snaked through the throng of people to the kitchen. There were two hundred guests here today.

It was finally Eliza and Jesse's big day. Everyone inside this cabin that Jesse had built mattered to him and Eliza. During the last five years, it seemed as if the whole world had changed drastically while her sister and Jesse worked endlessly and waited patiently for today.

So . . . where was Jesse?

She grabbed a clean washrag, dampened it, and ran it down her apron. The wedding should've started two and a half hours ago.

Ruth turned, seeing her mamm at the island. Mamm's newest baby, Noah, was in a front carrier, and two-year-old Becca held firmly to the hem of Mamm's dress. Her parents had two more babies during Eliza's engagement. Mamm had been twenty when she had her first child. At forty-three she gave birth to her tenth one. As much as Ruth loved her brothers and sisters, she hoped her mamm's childbearing years were now over, but only time would tell.

Mamm added a few thinly sliced carrots to a tray of food. She held out the tray of cheeses, crackers, and slices of various veggies to Ruth. "Take this to the wedding party."

"I just finished getting fresh coffee for the ministers, and I want to be with Eliza. She needs me."

Mamm grimaced. "If Jesse doesn't arrive, she will need you for a very long time. But right now you can help her the most by tending to her wedding party and chatting with them so she doesn't have to put on a brave front. They've been here since 6 a.m. helping prepare for a wedding, and they need a little tenderness and care." Her mother's voice was heavy, and her eyes reflected a deep sadness. "Still, the two of them not marrying may be the most merciful thing that could happen here today."

"Mamm," Ruth snapped, disbelief ringing in her soul. After five years of Eliza and Jesse waiting to marry, handling their lives in ways becoming of Christ, this was how Mamm felt? She knew the families still had reservations, but this teetered on the edge of a cruel attitude, didn't it?

Mamm pushed the tray toward Ruth. "The stress is making me think and feel things I shouldn't, and I need to mind my tongue. Now go."

As Ruth turned, she caught a glimpse of her sister through the packed rooms. Eliza stood vigil, looking out the front window of the cabin. Jesse should have arrived home last night before the fresh blanket of thick December snow covered everything and the high winds knocked the phone lines out.

Jesse had called Eliza from North Carolina yesterday morning, saying everything was going smoothly and that he'd be home before dark. It wasn't unheard of for him to run later than expected, but with the lines down, he couldn't even call to say he was safe . . . if he was safe.

Ruth watched Eliza. There was something eerie about her sister dressed in her Amish wedding attire, every piece newly sewn by Eliza—blue dress, white organza apron and prayer *Kapp*—waiting for, praying for her love to return.

Ruth pulled from the ghostly thoughts and went to the living room. "Food?" She held out the tray to several people who took items.

Ben came to her and took a few crackers. "I just checked on the youth in the barn. Everything and everyone looked on the up-and-up."

"Gut. Denki."

The cabin couldn't hold two hundred people milling about for hours, so the youth decided to take their energy to the barn. That included Moses these days since he was eighteen. About an hour ago, she'd gone out to the phone shanty to check the lines again, something she was doing often for her sister. To her shock and dismay, Moses was by the side of the barn, drinking liquor from a flask. She confiscated it, saying they'd talk about it tomorrow. Then she told Ben what was going on so he could help her watch the youth.

Ben munched on a cracker. "I saw you and Andrew talking a bit earlier this morning, and I think you two have a lot in common. You're both really smart and read nonstop. Since you're paired with him for the wedding, maybe you should take the time to really get to know each other." He motioned at Andrew, who was across the room. Andrew nodded and walked toward them, easing his way around others.

Any Amish wedding party consisted of all single people. It was the Amish way of helping to matchmake, hopefully being the cause of another wedding or two. But thoughts of Eliza pressed in hard. Ruth longed to slip outside to check the phone shanty again. How could she stay there and chat with guests, even ones as well-liked as Ben? Despite what her mamm wanted, Ruth should be at Eliza's side, whether people had hosts to talk with or trays of food to snack on or not.

Ruth touched Ben's hand. "We'll need to pick up this conversation later, okay?"

Understanding seemed to enter his eyes. "Oh, jah. Of course."

As she started for the back door, Andrew stopped in front of her, looking ready to strike up a conversation with her and Ben. Before he spoke, his attention diverted to something behind her. "There's an elderly woman waving her hand in the air and pointing this way. Is it you she wants?"

Ruth turned. "That's my great-aunt." She held up her index finger to her aunt, letting her know she'd be right there. "My grandfather's sister who's been single her whole life. I better see what she wants or there'll be a high price to pay. Independent-minded women are *not* to be ignored. Trust me."

She hurried toward Auntie Rose. After tending to whatever it was her great-aunt needed, Ruth would check the phone lines again.

Eliza's fingers trembled as she traced them along a smooth pine board of the log cabin windowsill. She studied the snowy horizon, willing Jesse home. Nausea stung her throat. If she didn't have a cabin full of guests who had driven here hours ago, she'd be tempted to think the mountain roads in December might be too bad for him to get through. *Jesse, kumm Heemet. Come home.* She couldn't imagine a future without him. It would be bleak beyond measure.

"Eliza." Ruth's warm hand touched her back.

Eliza kept her eye on the driveway. "You checked the phone shanty again?"

"I did. The lines are still down."

Eliza had woken early and hurried to her mamm's kitchen table, where Jesse always took the time to leave a note for her when he arrived home during the night. Then he'd go to the home he shared with his parents and sleep for a while. But there'd been no letter, so she'd slid into her clunky old barn boots, wrapped a half-finished quilt around herself, and hurried to the phone shanty near the barn. The answering machine—probably two decades old but reliable—held no message to her. Jesse didn't have a cell phone, although the ministers would allow him to have one due to his work and traveling. But they were costly, and every penny earned had gone into his business and building this home.

Ruth rubbed her back. "Inhale and count to ten."

Eliza did.

Searching her heart, Eliza tried to sense if he was hurt and needed her to find him or if he was even alive. She shuddered at the thoughts. The ball of anxiety resting in her chest blocked any hint of intuition. What could possibly have kept him from returning home when their wedding was today— supposed to have started more than two hours ago?

"Gut. Now do it again."

Eliza did.

Ruth put a comforting arm around Eliza's shoulder. "Now take note of your surroundings. Listen to the murmuring voices. Study the logs and windows in the cabin."

Eliza focused on the wood beneath her fingers.

How many years had the tree grown strong in the sunshine and rain of the Appalachian Mountains before being used in this amazing cabin? Jesse had chosen each piece of lumber so that their home would last for generations to come. She could still see sweat running down his face, filthy clothes, and calloused hands as he worked ceaselessly every spare hour for a year and a half.

"Gut, Eliza. Try not to let your mind trick you into assuming the worst. Maybe come up with a special thought to hold on to."

One of Eliza's favorite memories danced in her mind and she turned toward the window. The winding creek had a winter haze, and the banks were covered in a light dusting of snow with flurries swirling about. Today's weather was the opposite of the day Jesse proposed, but she could see it clearly in her mind.

She'd been a wisp of a girl at eighteen that day. Jesse, three years older, was full grown . . . or seemed so at the time, five years ago. Everything about that evening had been perfect, including her bare feet in the cool water as she wiggled her toes in the sand to steady her footing. She'd been completely content just to be with Jesse. She smiled, remembering trying to beat him at skipping rocks. Then . . . his sweet, vulnerable, patient proposal. Warmth surrounded her at the thought of it.

"Your shoulders relaxed a bit. Feeling calmer?" Ruth asked.

"Jah, denki." She had her good thought that would hold her for a bit, hopefully until Jesse arrived home.

"Well, I'd love to tell you it was all for you, but I have an ulterior motive."

Eliza laughed, and it caught her off guard. "What do *you* need on *my* wedding day, Little Sister?"

"Glad you asked." Ruth grasped her hand. "Auntie Rose needs to see you."

"Not now," Eliza whispered. Until today, she'd loved every minute with Auntie Rose. In some ways, she was a very odd bird, but she always felt more like a beloved grandmother than a great-aunt.

Ruth tugged on Eliza's hand. "She has something on her mind that is for your ears only, and she wouldn't take no for an answer. Trust me, I tried."

"Okay." She turned from the window. Her eyes stopped at the wall hanging she'd sewn. It had two tall, barren oak trees intertwined. The trees were at the center of the fabric and the entwined trunks had her and Jesse's names. Today's date was stitched on the bottom of it. The branches of the trees were left blank, leaving room for Eliza to add the names and birth dates of all their children. What a dream it would be to fill all ten spaces. But she needed her love to return so they could begin their married lives.

Ruth looped her arm through Eliza's as if they were going for one of their strolls. "I had a long talk with Auntie Rose this morning, and she helped fill some gaps in my genealogy research. I wrote down two—" she held up a couple of her fingers—"family stories I'd never heard before. One from all the way back in the 1920s when she and her siblings—including our grandfather—were children." Ruth pulled her palm-size notebook from her pocket.

How many of those small books had her sister filled with family stories throughout the years?

Trying to remain calm inwardly and outwardly, Eliza followed Ruth. Dozens of women were squeezed into the various rooms, bits of their conversations drifting to Eliza as she passed by.

"Did you see this woven rug Eliza made?" a guest asked someone nearby. "Her aunt Bette had a large antique loom transported here for Eliza as a wedding gift."

Eliza wanted to pause long enough to remark about the gift, to let them know how thrilled she was to have received it, and to thank the giver if she was close by, but her throat seemed sealed shut. Besides, they weren't talking to her, just chatting as she went by them.

Aunt Mary, Dat's oldest sister, held out her hand. "Girls, this isn't right. What is going on?"

She was a stickler for tradition and procedure.

Ruth kissed her cheek. "Jesse's been held up. The wedding will start soon."

Aunt Mary pursed her lips and nodded.

Eliza continued following Ruth through the cabin. "We're going to the washhouse?"

"To the laundry room, as Englischers call it, but jah," Ruth said. "I think you should call it that too because it's a really nice room Jesse built for you."

When they entered the room, Auntie Rose was in a chair with her eyes closed, resting. Ruth had provided their great-aunt with the chair before going to get Eliza. Auntie Rose had one quilt covering her legs and another folded in her lap.

Ruth knelt near her, and their great-aunt opened her cloudy blue eyes. "You were right, Auntie Rose. She is worried and out of sorts."

The frail old woman gave a slow nod, then took Eliza's hand. "Don't fret, *Liewi*."

Eliza made herself smile. "It's hard not to. But I know God will protect him." If she *knew* that and wasn't just saying what she thought she should, why was she in knots despite the good thoughts she was hanging on to?

"Jah." Auntie Rose sat up a little straighter and turned to Ruth. "Can I trouble you to bring me a cup of coffee? Your mother is making a fresh pot."

"Of course." Ruth left, pulling the door closed behind her.

Auntie Rose tugged on Eliza's hand. "Kneel down with me, my girl. I have something to tell you that I don't want to spread to anyone else. Only a few in this world would understand."

Eliza knelt, trying to focus on what her great-aunt was saying.

Auntie Rose pulled Eliza's hands into her lap and on top of the folded quilt. "This is my wedding gift to you. It's been in our family since our ancestors came to this country. It has been prayed over for centuries, and it holds power unlike anything you've seen before."

Eliza studied the quilt. She didn't recall seeing it before today, which seemed odd. The beautiful intersecting stripe patterns were in every color—rich earth tones of all kinds as well as the colors of wildflowers, from deep to light. Although it had a slight yellow tint, it was in remarkable shape to be that old. She wanted to simply thank her, but Eliza couldn't muster a word.

Auntie Rose leaned closer, her lips almost touching Eliza's ear. "If you ever need it, you can use this quilt to go back in time once and fix an event. All you have to do is take this quilt to the old log cabin in Hunters' Woods and restitch one of the threads to go back to a previous moment in your life. My aunt went to the cabin and restitched the quilt to keep her brother from being killed while cutting a tree. Her brother was my dat. She went back in time before he was killed, insisted Dat take help with him, and because of that, Dat was never hurt."

Eliza sat back a few inches, trying to absorb her great-aunt's words. She gently squeezed the old woman's hand.

Clearly Auntie Rose was suffering from some sort of momentary dementia to think anyone could go back in time.

But there was an old log cabin in Hunters' Woods, one of the first Amish homes built in these parts when their German ancestors settled in Calico Creek—one room, dirt floor, rock chimney, huge hearth with a cooking crane where meals were made. That much of what Auntie Rose had said was true, but no one could undo an event that had taken place. Still, Eliza wouldn't hurt her great-aunt's feelings by refusing the quilt or correcting any part of what she'd said. "It's lovely and incredibly generous. Denki. I'll take good care of it."

Auntie Rose grabbed Eliza's hand. "Remember, you can only go back to a specific event once, and briefly, so be wise and cautious before using it. My sister Verna wasn't so careful."

Verna Bontrager Ebersol, who had left the Amish and divorced Omar Ebersol. Eliza didn't want to hear about Verna, not on her wedding day.

She kissed Auntie Rose's cheek. "I'll be careful with it." She held the quilt close as she stood. Movement through the washhouse window caught her eye. "Excuse me." She eased closer to the frosty, foggy window. A horse and rider were coming down the winding path. *Jesse. Please let it be Jesse.*

Auntie Rose stood, also looking. "Hold steady, sweet girl. It might be Jesse."

"It might be someone arriving with news of Jesse."

"Either way, child—" Auntie Rose put the quilt around Eliza's shoulders—"go."

Eliza hurried through the cabin and out the front door. The cold air hit her like jumping into a lake, and she was grateful for the warmth of the quilt. Her feet never stopping as she flew down the porch stairs, she hit solid ground and broke into a run.

The rider picked up the pace as he galloped closer, and she saw him clearly. Jesse! *Denki, Gott.*

He dismounted a few feet from her and enveloped her in his arms. Warmth and relief melted through her, and a song of joy and love flowed from her heart. He was here. He was safe.

"I'm so sorry, Eliza." He squeezed her tight before he pulled back from their embrace enough to kiss her. He rested his forehead against hers and cupped her cheek in his gloved hand. "Unavoidable things happened, and the lines are down, and—"

"It doesn't matter. You're here now."

He grinned. "We did it, Eliza. I closed the deal. We own the cabin business and workshop." He pointed at their cabin. "We can fill that home with as many kids as God allows, and we'll never struggle with feeding them."

"Ebersol Cabins . . . finally we begin." Her face seemed unable to stretch far enough to accommodate the smile she wanted.

"Owning the business outright means we can put more money into the pockets of the workers in this community, not into paying off a loan. We can hire any Amish man that wants to leave the feed mill, and first on that list is your dat and Moses."

"Jesse, that's amazing."

"I thought we'd finish the deal by noon yesterday, but it ended up being four by the time we wrapped up everything.

Then on the way home, the bus I was in broke down. We waited hours for a crew to come fix it or for another bus to arrive, but around midnight I gave up and walked twenty miles until I came to an Amish farm. The family fed me and insisted I rest a few hours before riding homeward."

If only they each had a cell phone! Eliza would've paid a lot to be able to get in touch with him this morning. But the ministers wouldn't allow her to have a cell phone since she didn't have a job that required her to need one, and she understood the strict rules, but landlines were too unpredictable during Pennsylvania winters.

"You made it home and that's all that matters." She pulled the quilt closer around her shoulders.

He scanned her. "Your wedding dress!"

She glanced down at her new blue cape dress. She'd sewn it last week, and after today it would become her best Sunday dress. The hem of it was wet with smatters of mud and snow.

"It doesn't matter. If the stains won't come out, they'll always remind me that you arrived safe." She grinned. "And still in time to marry me on our wedding day. That's good stuff, jah?"

He chuckled. "It is." He reached back to pat the horse on the head. "I have to return this good girl who had such sure footing going through the mountain trail."

She narrowed her eyes at him, teasing. "I believe there's supposed to be a wedding first."

"I suppose there is." He laughed, sounding relieved to be here.

Moses hurried from the barn. He reached for the reins. "I'll take care of her for you."

Jesse released the reins. "Denki."

Moses tipped his hat at Eliza. "I'll be in before all the folks are seated."

She nodded, and he hurried toward the barn while throngs of young people moved from it to the house.

Jesse pointed at the multitude of their friends' and family members' buggies surrounding the cabin. "It looks like everyone is here."

"Just waiting on the groom." Eliza cradled his face, so very grateful he was home. "Know anyone interested?"

He kissed her in a way he'd never kissed her before, long and deep. "Oh, boy, do I."

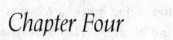

Chapter Four

Ruth was on a bench, studying the room and soaking in the joyous celebration that vibrated throughout the packed house. People filled every corner, some sitting, some standing. The wedding had been simple, as befitted an Amish home, but it was deeply heartfelt by so many, especially Jesse and Eliza. The wedding meal was over, and the beautifully decorated main cake, as well as all the other cakes, had been cut and passed out to the numerous guests.

Jesse was still in the groom's seat at the table next to his radiant bride as he began a song. Soon the beautiful harmony of a cappella singing that Amish were known for filled the room. Laughter erupted so often Ruth couldn't keep up with what was funny. Joy definitely overflowed in this home, and she knew Jesse and Eliza's love would serve them well in life.

Ben came in the back door. He'd gone out to start fires in the fifty-five-gallon burn barrels that had been prepared with paper and kindling. They'd use that to burn the trash collected later today during cleanup. He stopped near the fireplace, and Ruth grabbed a plate with a piece of cake and a fork and headed that way. She'd thought everyone had been given a slice of cake, but had Ben?

She wove around guests. The volume in this home was a bit overwhelming. She'd been to a lot of Amish weddings in her life, probably at least three a year since she was born, but none compared to the celebration happening here today. Relief that Jesse had arrived safe was part of the excitement. Part of it was from the news Jesse brought with him—poverty and plant jobs would soon be behind this Amish community. Part of the excitement was the sheer joy everyone felt because this couple, who loved the community more than themselves, were finally wed.

"Ben, did you get a piece of cake?"

He looked at the plate in her hand. "I did, but, uh, I wouldn't mind having another."

She passed it to him. "Burn barrels going?"

"Jah." He gestured toward his cousin. "But I was hoping to return inside to find you and Andrew talking."

"We talked some earlier." Her eyes moved to Andrew as he studied a letter written in 1810 that she'd framed. Slivers of the tattered pulpwood paper had broken off, and other parts were no longer readable—too faded or smudged. She'd found the letter in an attic while researching her family history. It was written by a bishop in the valley and addressed to Amish of Calico Creek. "We have several things in common.

The most important of which is neither one of us has any desire to get married."

The surprise on Ben's face said it all. "Not ever?" His Adam's apple bobbed as he swallowed hard. "You want to spend your whole life single and being an Amish school-teacher, just like Rosanna?" He sounded dumbfounded.

She chuckled. "Jah, pretty much just like Auntie Rose." Ruth as well as Eliza had been particularly close with their great-aunt all of their lives, and not once in all that time had Auntie Rose hinted at any regret over remaining single. On top of that, Auntie Rose had loved being a teacher in a one-room Amish schoolhouse throughout the decades.

"I wouldn't want to stay single. That's for sure."

"Most feel that way," Ruth said. "Nothing wrong with that. But maybe in order to improve your odds, you should stop talking to me and go talk to the attractive young woman you were paired up with for the day."

He shook his head. "I gave it my best shot, and we can't find one thing to talk about. That says it all, don't it?" He shrugged. "Probably just as well about you and Andrew, him being another Ebersol like Jesse and you being a Bontrager."

"True." For years Ruth had been sure that Jesse and Eliza would never convince their families that their fears were really just superstitions that needed to be set aside.

Andrew faced the room, searching. His eyes stopped when he spotted Ruth. He pointed at the framed letter and mouthed, *"Wow."*

She couldn't help but grin and nod. "Kumm." She motioned for Ben, and the two of them wove around people to get to Andrew. She started talking before she came to a stop near him. "I asked permission from a lot of Amish to go through their attics and old barns before I found that treasure in a home that once belonged to my great-great-grandfather. The house had been passed down from generation to generation by overlapping occupants." Not all Amish called it *overlapping occupants*, but she was sure he knew what she meant. For hundreds of years a younger married couple moved in with an established couple, often one of their parents, usually sharing the home for several decades, raising their children, before the older couple passed away, and then one of the children would marry and move in with the *new* older couple. Typically that meant that out of respect, certain items were never cleaned out of an attic, just pushed back into far corners.

"Was this in an attic or old barn?" Andrew continued to study the letter.

"Attic. Amish attics in old homes are the best treasure keepers. If you've never searched one in your area, you should. I think this letter originally belonged to what I believe is my ninth great-grandmother."

Andrew looked at her. "You're unsure of the DNA or the generational mathematics?"

Ben put both hands on his head. "I didn't even understand that question." He lowered his hands. "Ruth, did you?"

"Perfectly." She nodded. "He's asking whether my lack of certainty is based on doubting my genetic relationship to the woman or a genealogical mathematic issue."

"What?" Ben looked from Andrew to Ruth and back again. "It's as if you're talking in code here."

Ruth gave Ben a reassuring smile. "It's a genealogy thing."

"Or a researcher's thing." Andrew put his hand on Ben's shoulder. "But apparently it's not your kind of thing, which is perfectly okay."

Ben laughed. "Ah, now I get it."

Andrew lowered his hand and focused on Ruth. "And?"

"I know she's a biological great-grandmother. I verified the bloodline and marriages through tracing in multiple books, but she could be my eighth, tenth, or eleventh great-grandmother, rather than ninth."

"Mathematics, then?"

"I don't think so. The issue seems to be following the actual lineage. Women's genealogy is always harder to trace than men's. Women change their surnames when they marry, and two hundred years ago, a woman might easily be widowed two or three times. Add to that how many Amish women in a family have the same first name, and it's hard to pinpoint an answer."

"Jah, I can see that . . . though I'd never thought of it. I don't do much of that kind of research, but when I do, I follow the menfolk, so nothing as confusing as changing last names."

His tone held respect for the issues of trying to trace one bloodline of grandmothers, and she appreciated it.

"Andrew is trying to get on staff with the *County Times*," Ben said.

"Really?" Ruth's interest soared. Did Andrew intend to ignore the Amish way and go to school to earn a degree? Did the *County Times* have a position for an Amish man's take on certain things?

"*Trying* is the key word." Andrew shrugged. "I log a lot

of hours helping my dat run his business of ABCC Amish Buggy Rides on the square of Calico Creek, and I probably make more money there than I would at the paper, but I want to write."

"Wait." Ruth held up her finger. "Let me guess at ABCC—Amish Buggies of Calico Creek or something close to that."

Andrew laughed. "That's it. We're the best Amish buggy ride tour in town. Of course, we're also the only one, but still . . ."

Ruth chuckled, enjoying his sense of humor. She circled her finger backward, toward herself. "Returning to the original topic, what's keeping you from getting on at the paper?"

"I need a way of proving myself to the newspaper by writing a story no one else can or has thought of, and so far the stories I've uncovered just don't hold enough interest."

A memory flashed through Ruth's mind. "Did you ever check into whether the stench connected to the feed mill is toxic to residents?"

Andrew's eyes widened. "How'd you . . . ?"

"Ben mentioned it about five years ago, back when you were way too young to do anything about those concerns."

"Ah." Andrew nodded. "The dreams and abilities of teens are star-crossed lovers."

"That's true." Ruth chuckled. "But we're no longer teens, although I'm not sure if we have much more power at twenty-one than we did back then."

"Exactly, Ruth," Andrew said. "But I've already researched it the best I can and came up with nothing. The problem is I can't uncover anything without access to internal documentation. Without proof that something is amiss, no judge would allow me access to that."

He must've done a lot of legwork to know he needed a judge to give him access. She wouldn't have known that.

"Jah, I see what you mean." Ruth tried to think of possible ways he could get access to internal documentation.

He shrugged. "Maybe it's just a stench and nothing toxic is going on."

"Maybe." Ruth rubbed her forehead. "You know . . . a health survey of residents in downtown Calico Creek might be helpful. Compare that to public records of the health of the general population in other towns in this state. If there is toxicity in the air or waterways, wouldn't it make the people living near the plant more sickly than people outside of that area?"

"Good grief, Ruth." Ben shook his head. "Do you have any idea how much work that would take?"

Andrew's eyes reflected a very different set of thoughts from Ben's. He pointed at her, shaking his finger. "That's a great idea. Why on earth haven't I thought of it?"

Ben blinked. "Seriously?"

"We should brainstorm on types of questions you need to ask," Ruth said. "You could send the questionnaire out via the mail, but for the addresses that don't respond, I imagine a smart-looking Amish man knocking on doors and asking questions will get all the info he needs."

"Smart-looking?" Ben asked. "So who is Andrew supposed to hire for that?"

They laughed. Ruth saw someone from her peripheral vision and turned. "Auntie Rose." Ruth moved through the crowd and looped a supportive arm under Auntie Rose's. "Kumm. Sit." They went toward the chair near the framed letter Andrew was so enthralled with.

With a bit of help from Ruth, Auntie Rose eased into the chair. "I've been holding out on you, Ruth. But it's time you heard the story behind the quilt I gave to Eliza."

"Oh, I would love that." Ruth sat at her aunt's feet.

"May I listen in?" Andrew asked.

Auntie Rose grinned, nodding. "In the 1600s, in the old country, our people had fled from Germany to Switzerland, fleeing religious persecution. They were safer in Switzerland but still persecuted, so by the early 1700s, a group of Plain folks, headed up by some Ebersols and Bontragers, started making plans to set sail for America. In the old country, our matriarchal ancestors were skilled at weaving on looms and at making clothes and quilts. They made a lot of items to sell to help pay for the voyage across the seas."

"Was the quilt you passed to Eliza made by those women?"

"It was, and I'm going to tell you the heartaches and hopes they went through while making that particular quilt. I believe that quilt has been prayed and wept over more than any Bible that crossed with them during that same time."

Andrew's eyes met Ruth's, and she knew he was every bit as interested in hearing this oral history as she was. Would her aunt tell stories she'd never told before? If so, why had she held on to the stories until now, especially since Ruth was always searching for any kind of Amish history? She set those questions aside.

"Ayla Bontrager and Bytzel Ebersol were strong, able women, determined to survive in a new land, but mostly they were armed with a loom and fabrics from the old country. . . ."

Ruth hung on every word, wishing she hadn't set her notebook and pen in the kitchen a little bit ago. But surely she'd remember more of the story by listening intently rather than taking notes. She was grateful Andrew was listening too. He could help her remember the details.

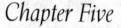

Chapter Five

Eliza leaned toward the center of the kitchen table and gently pulled two daisies from the bunch of flowers in the milk-glass vase. Piles of produce waited on her kitchen countertops: corn, green beans, sweet red peppers, onions—the last of the garden's summer bounty. She studied the two delicate white blooms in her hand. Two flowers for the two who would've been her babies. She rested her other hand on her round belly. The little person inside seemed to notice and gave a squirm. Hope for the future rose in her chest. *Soon,* she told her little one.

But right now, she had canning to do, although what she really wanted was to walk to her favorite tree and place these two flowers.

A clatter of metal on metal startled her, causing her to look in that direction. Ruth was coming in the back door with a pile of canning lids and rings, some of the rings still bouncing across the floor.

"Oops. Sorry. Don't worry. I'll resterilize these."

Eliza had been canning since June—and it was now late September. Apparently she'd planted a much bigger garden than she had the energy to keep up with this year. She set the flowers to the side. "Denki, Ruth." Eliza scooped up several rings and lids. "Let me help you."

"Nope. Stop right now. I'm here to help *you*. You're going to sit and put your feet up."

Eliza looped several rings around her fingers and rattled them. "Does sitting with my feet up sound like something I've ever wanted to do?"

Ruth dropped a bunch of lids and rings into the sink before she turned on the tap and began filling a large pot of water. "All the more reason you should do it."

Eliza rubbed her protruding belly. "It's not like this *Bobbeli* is going to be my last, and the work won't stop when I'm expecting future ones."

"That's true, but I finished grading papers last night so I could be here to help today, and you will accept it without a fight. Sit, breathe. You need to save your energy for the real labor that'll start soon."

Eliza raised a brow. "You're being a little pushy, but I'll indulge you and enjoy doing so." She grinned and picked up the two daisies. Her sister was a treasure. "I'm going for a walk."

Ruth put her palm against her forehead. "Eliza."

"Just to my favorite tree. I want to pray and thank God."
The screen door creaked as it opened, and Jesse walked in.

"Talk to your wife." Ruth motioned at Eliza. "She needs to sit, not go for a walk."

Jesse put his warm arm around Eliza's shoulders. "I'll go with her."

Eliza turned toward her husband, and he lowered his head, kissing her on the lips. His love wrapped her from her head to her toes. Thoughts of him holding this little one thrilled her. The midwife had said labor could begin anytime now. How many more days would it be?

Ruth put the pot of water on the stove's eye. "I suppose that's acceptable."

"Thanks for permission, Mamm." Eliza winked at her little sister.

Ruth stuck out her tongue.

Eliza chuckled and grabbed Jesse's hand, still holding her two flowers in the other.

"Did you want to grab that quilt to sit on?" Jesse pointed to the back of the recliner where Auntie Rose's quilt lay. A bit of sadness hit Eliza's heart. She missed her great-aunt and her stories. If only she had lived another year to see the first in the next generation of children be born.

"Sure." Eliza grabbed it.

They walked out the front door and down the porch steps. A few yellow leaves drifted across the gravel driveway in front of them. Jesse lifted the folded quilt from her and draped it over his arm.

He slid his hand into hers. "I'm officially on leave from work until after this babe is born."

"Starting today?"

"Jah. Moses is going to do a fine job taking care of our clients. He's great with Mr. Jordan. The elderly man really enjoys Moses, and your brother assures me it's a mutual thing between them. I'm not sure I'd have the patience to have long chats with Mr. Jordan each time I stepped on his property to get work done, not like Moses does. But Ebersol Cabins owes Mr. Jordan and his virgin timber a lot. *You* opened that door."

"God did. I just happened to be on the road late one night when his barn caught fire, and the rest is history."

"You were far more instrumental than that. As a matter of fact, your faithful prayers and gentle effort saved him and—"

"Enough of that." She held out her hand in a stop position as if she were a crossing guard. She knew the real deal, and Jesse gave her far too much credit. "Tell me more about Moses."

"Okay, I hear you." He lifted her hand to his lips and kissed it. "He even has a lead on a huge custom project for this wealthy Englisch couple. We'd build the whole home on-site rather than in our factory. Moses surprises me with his skill and focus."

Her brother had really taken to this job with Jesse's company. After he'd been caught drunk time and again, Eliza had feared he'd never stop. She'd seen it happen to other young Amish men, and it was breaking their mamm's heart. Eliza had felt powerless to stop it.

"That sounds great. Your beautiful cabin designs plus Moses' people skills are a winning match. He really needed you to give him that chance to work in the cabin business."

"Sometimes people need a second chance. Besides, he's

doing so great at work, and I owe him more than he owes me. It's been almost three years, and he hasn't let me down yet."

Leaves crunched under their shoes as they meandered down the familiar path. How many times had Eliza walked in these woods?

The sprawling branches of her favorite oak tree seemed to welcome her to the grove. It was her spot to sit, pray, and dream. The edges of a few leaves had turned red and gold, with green in each leaf's center, promising beautiful color in a few weeks. The trunk was at least four times the size of its neighbors. How many hundreds of years old was this tree? She'd found it years before she and Jesse were married, although it was part of his family's land before his family gifted this portion to Jesse.

Eliza released Jesse's hand and laid both daisies at the base of the tree. When her first two pregnancies didn't make it past fourteen weeks, she'd buried what she could here next to the oak. Were those two little souls watching her?

Jesse put a hand on her shoulder. "I wonder about them too. Who they would've been." He rested his other hand on her belly. "I look forward to learning who this little person will be."

"Jah." She put her hand over Jesse's, and the baby kicked.

They laughed, and Jesse kissed her forehead. "It's been a long, hard journey to get to this place."

She closed her eyes, thinking of all the sadness they'd endured after losing each baby just barely into the second trimester. But even when their hearts were broken, their hope and faith were not.

Soon, she told her little passenger once again. *Soon.*

Ruth breathed in the aroma of a freshly cleaned barn mixed with the scents of late fall that came through the open windows and doors. The bale of hay beneath her was a bit prickly as she sang. Two dozen other youth, also sitting on hay bales inside the barn, sang along as she desperately tried not to glance *his* way.

Last weekend, she'd helped Eliza finish canning for the year, and this weekend, until this Sabbath day, she'd graded papers and prepared new lessons for her students. Andrew glanced at her, and she couldn't keep herself from grinning. This evening promised to be nothing but fun for her and Andrew. Since the wedding, they'd spent time together here and there, mostly at the public library researching important-to-them topics. Slowly their time together kept increasing, just as friends. They enjoyed each other's company—whether researching, doing crossword puzzles, or reading news articles and discussing them.

The bishop began a new song, clapping out a beat this time. He nodded at her, smiling. What was that about? No clue, but she and the others followed his lead, singing and clapping.

After years of meeting at the library most Friday evenings, she'd been surprised by Andrew six months ago when he drove his rig from the other side of downtown Calico Creek, up the mountain to her district, and came to a singing. It was his first time to attend a singing since the purpose of these Sunday evening gatherings was finding a mate. Since that evening six months ago, he hadn't missed coming to a singing. Her heart pounded whenever she considered what that might mean. Was he interested in her as a possible spouse?

She cared for him. A lot. But enough to get married? Her head said *no*. Her emotions said a lot of things, including *jah*.

Although marriage hadn't been on her mind, she'd been going to singings since she was sixteen. They were fun, and at the end of the festivities, she enjoyed gathering up a group of girls whom no one had asked to go for a buggy ride and going on their own ride, talking and laughing until her sides hurt. But none of that had taken place since Andrew showed up. When it was time for everyone to go home, he took her for a buggy ride.

Something hit her shoulder and she yelped. A rumble of soft laughter came from the men's side of the barn, and she looked that way.

Andrew held up his hands, showing innocence as he mouthed the words *"Not me, but sorry."* Without pausing in song, she saw the culprit—her brother Moses. He was still laughing. She wagged a finger at him.

The singing continued, moving from one song to another, only interrupted by occasional laughter when something went awry, like the bishop starting a song out using the wrong words or a fly buzzing too close to open mouths or someone not paying attention to when a song was coming to the end and continuing to sing. Some of the silliness was on purpose, and the bishop usually played along, laughing as much as the young people, especially during the last month or so.

"Sell iss gut." The bishop held up his hand, bringing the singing to a close. *"Loss uns bede."* He bowed his head to pray and waited for the room to quiet.

Finally. The end of singing. It'd been going on for over an hour. As the bishop prayed, Ruth's mind wandered.

How was Eliza feeling this evening? Maybe after the bonfire, before she and Andrew meandered through back roads for hours while talking, they should drop by to see Eliza and Jesse. Labor hadn't begun this morning when Ruth left for church, but Jesse wanted Eliza to stay home and take it easy. Typically the church frowned on anyone missing church without good reason, but they gave Jesse the freedom to do as he saw fit concerning Eliza, probably because of the losses.

Ruth had offered to stay with her and let Jesse attend the Sunday meeting, but her sister insisted Ruth get out and socialize. *"You're not the one having a baby, so you should get out for a bit,"* Eliza had said.

Oh, Ruth had gotten out. Church in the morning, then the after-service meal, then a long, fruitless afternoon of interviewing family members. How could she have spent that much time asking questions but gleaned no new material? Now the singing, but soon everyone would be set free to enjoy festivities on the Miller property before going for buggy rides.

The bishop ended the prayer. *Finally.* She was a patient woman, but she'd waited all week to get time with Andrew. Almost immediately everyone started talking and laughing. Andrew helped gather hymnals. She wasn't volunteering to help with one more thing today. She'd washed dishes for nearly two hours after the meal.

Ruth eyed the exit, excusing herself as she ducked around her chatty peers. She stepped outside into the cool darkness of the late-September air. She listened to a few stray chirps of katydids and crickets. First frost hadn't hit yet, but by the feel of the night air, it would soon.

What a gorgeous evening to spend with Andrew.

Ruth looked through the barn door to scan the crowd. Andrew caught her eye.

He passed the hymnals to someone else, stepped around a few people, and hurried through the door. "It was a long singing tonight, huh?"

"Jah." Lately, all she wanted was more time with Andrew. Maybe a lifetime with him. She'd only kept her desire to remain single until the youthful age of twenty-four. How had Auntie Rose never desired to marry?

Andrew looked skyward. "It's a beautiful night for s'mores and then a buggy ride."

She nodded, grinning. "You've convinced me."

"Gut."

"We might need to take a shorter buggy ride tonight than usual." She made her hands look like binoculars over her eyes. "Baby watch."

"Sure. No problem." Andrew reached into his pocket and pulled out a newspaper folded up longways. "I brought you a copy of this week's *Die Bericht*. I know it's too dark to read right now. Maybe you could read it to Eliza later if she's bored."

She took it from him. The Amish paper, *The Report*, had become so much more interesting since Andrew had taken a part-time position as reporter and editor. When they spent all those Friday nights at the public library reading information, she realized that Andrew had a strong intuition for when a business was trying to cover up information, what was simply lazy writing by the journalist, and what was a well-researched and thorough piece.

She opened the paper, looking for his name in the byline. It still gave her goose bumps to think about when he'd pursued what was happening to the environment because of the feed mill, Calico Feed Nutrition, which took six months of diligent investigation on his part. He'd unearthed dangerous issues that probably saved dozens of lives. A journalist, Rick Bluestein, took Andrew under his wing, writing the piece with him for the *County Times*. It was a huge success.

His and Rick's piece in the *County Times* had caused the plant to do environmental cleanup, and the residents of downtown Calico Creek were healthier because of it. Calico Feed Nutrition was responsible for their medical bills and workdays missed due to illness caused from working at the plant or being a resident near the plant. Dat and others had received full recompense for all the days missed due to "unexplained illness." In truth, her dat and others had been sick and missed a lot of workdays because of the toxic fumes he breathed in while at the plant.

Once that story broke, Andrew didn't need a degree to be on staff for the *County Times*. He also enjoyed writing for the *Report*, covering day-to-day things like Amish meetings and how the weather was affecting planting or harvesting. Sometimes he wrote a poem. What a mind for words! Even though she constantly gathered true stories from her family and had stacks of notebooks of events written down, she couldn't imagine being able to write an article or a poem, let alone either being good enough to be published.

She shook the paper at him. "Maybe I should get your help convincing my family to talk."

He tilted his head. "It didn't go well today?"

Ruth folded the newspaper back, looking forward to reading his article. "Nee, it didn't. I don't know how I'm supposed to write the history of the Bontrager family since we immigrated to the United States if people have conflicting stories or no stories at all."

"Jah, it's tough gathering stories that go that far back. It's tough enough to get all the pieces of information correct on current events."

Ruth moved out of the doorway and took a few steps closer to the barn wall as several of her peers passed her on their way to the backyard, probably to make the bonfire. She wasn't ready to share her time with Andrew with the others. The two of them could talk uninterrupted for hours on any topic, but once they joined the bonfire crowd, their deeper conversation would have to be put on hold until their buggy ride.

Ruth propped her hands behind her against the barn. "Maybe that's the wall I'm hitting, but I'm beginning to think there are a few skeletons in the family closet that no one wants to talk about. I'm not sure whether I should keep pursuing the information."

"That's a question every reporter asks from time to time. Only you can answer it."

"Reporter, huh? You going to hire me?"

He laughed and ran a hand through his dark hair. "Yeah, I don't actually have hiring capabilities. Wish I did. Maybe one day."

"It's okay. I love teaching, and I really need to take care of my own family's story first."

The bishop came out of the barn. He'd probably been

stacking hymnals or shifting some of the hay bales back to the right spots. He turned and nodded with a smile. *"Hallo."* He was the bishop for both of their districts, so he knew each of them well. "It's so good to see that you two decided to move from weekly library meetings to join us for singings. I mean Ruth's been attending them for years, but it's nice that you're both here."

Her heart skipped a beat. "You knew about the library?"

"I did. I was deeply concerned at first because you are a Bontrager and Andrew is an Ebersol, but Jesse and Eliza have been nothing but blessing after blessing to this community—during their long engagement and since their union—so my reservations have been put to rest."

"You knew about the library?" Ruth repeated.

He laughed. "It takes a lot of traveling between the two districts to do my job as bishop, so I get around, me and old Charlie Brown. He's the best horse for navigating the roads on this mountain ridge and in the valley of downtown. I never told a soul I saw your rigs there, but I've sure done lots of praying."

He'd probably feared that they were dabbling in too much of the Englisch world, especially after Andrew became a writer for the *County Times*. She had a lot of respect for the bishop for keeping that to himself. He started for the backyard. She could wager money on his next move. Everyone else had gone to the Millers' backyard. As a chaperone of the event, the bishop would want them, even at their age, to be within eyesight. He motioned. "Kumm."

Yep, she knew it.

Andrew chuckled. "Time to join the crowd again, Ruth."

"Apparently so." She could understand the bishop being watchful over the teens, but few singles were as old as Andrew and Ruth. They'd both turn twenty-five in a few months. Still, the bishop's heart was in the right place.

Ten minutes later they were shoving marshmallows onto straightened wire hangers while chatting and laughing with friends. The bonfire crackled with heat.

Andrew's shoulder rubbed hers as he leaned in closer. "Any chance you'd like to go to the Ebersol family reunion–slash–fall festival next month?"

Her heart thudded madly. He wanted her to go to a family reunion? That was a big invitation. As of now, only a few close relatives knew they were dating. The chaperones and hosts for singings were bound to secrecy concerning who was flirting with whom and who accepted a buggy ride with whom . . . because in a small, tightly knit community, young adults deserved a little privacy. Plus, adults weren't supposed to meddle in the romantic leanings of the singles—with the exception of Ebersols and Bontragers, which might, thanks to Eliza and Jesse, be a nonissue moving forward.

Andrew wanted her to go to his family reunion?

She should play it cool. "You better ask my new niece or nephew."

He laughed. "The baby's going to give me permission to take you?"

She stifled how amused she was by him. "No, I have to give that permission. But my ability to leave my sister's house is fully dependent on what that little one needs."

He tapped his chin. "Hm. Well, in that case, I'll just move the whole gathering to your sister's house."

She nodded. "Okay."

His eyes widened, and it was hard not to laugh at his confused expression.

He fiddled with his marshmallow. "I, um, can't really do that."

She laughed. "Maybe you should consider these things before offering."

"I guess so, because—"

"Ruth! There you are." Her brother Levi ran to her, out of breath. "Eliza needs you. I have to get you to her now."

Her heart leaped, and she turned to Andrew, dropping her marshmallow stick. "The baby must be coming!"

"Nee." Levi removed his hat.

"No?" Ruth studied her brother. "No to what?"

"You can't rush in all excited to see Eliza."

Her heart threatened to stop. "Is something wrong?"

"She delivered." Levi winced. "Had a baby girl. But something was wrong. The baby only drew a few breaths before passing away."

Tears filled Ruth's eyes. Not again. *Dear God, please, not again.*

Chapter Six

Jesse laid a hand on his daughter's soft head of dark hair. Even swaddled in a blanket, she was tiny.

Jesse wanted to rage, scream, even break things. Why their daughter? Why them?

Instead, he kept calm. He had to be strong. His wife needed him.

Eliza lay in the now-clean bed she'd given birth on, propped up on pillows and staring at their still little girl. She touched the baby's cheek. "I think we should call her Penelope. It was our first choice, and it seems wrong to call her anything else."

He nodded. "Our daughter Penelope." Tears misted his eyes. He had to hold it together. "It's beautiful, just like she is." He didn't know if any Amish had the name of Penelope, but Eliza had loved the name for a few years. He felt it was befitting for the name to be so unusual. His and Eliza's life was also unique among the Amish.

Another knock sounded on their cabin door. He'd answered it several times this evening.

He wiped his eyes and stood from the chair beside the bed. "I'll be right back, my love."

Eliza gave a slight nod, an almost-imperceptible movement. Ruth continued tidying up the bedroom, making Eliza sip on orange juice every few minutes.

No one knew what to do. No one ever talked about what happens after a newborn dies. He wasn't sure when the midwife had left. Time had become a blur, an unbearable, confusing blur.

Jesse walked through the cabin hallway toward the front door. His feet were so heavy he could hardly move them, yet they didn't seem unattached to his body or the movement of walking. His head swam. How was this even real?

Jesse opened the door. An Englisch man stood there, along with Leah, the midwife who had delivered their baby.

Leah gestured toward the man. "Jesse, this is Dr. Morgan."

The doctor held out his hand. "I'm with the Special Children's Clinic, and I've been partnered with Amish and Mennonite communities for the last few years. I'm so sorry for your loss."

The words *thank you* stuck in Jesse's throat. He couldn't thank anyone right now. But he nodded and managed to shake the man's hand. "I . . . I don't understand why you're here. We have no need of a doctor." His heart clutched, and the nightmare threatened to swallow him whole. He turned to Leah. "Do we? Is something wrong with my wife?"

"No, Jesse. Eliza is doing well. Physically. But when a baby dies like this, a doctor needs to see the little one."

Jesse's head roared with confusion, and the doorway of the cabin seemed to be spinning. "Dies like this?"

Leah motioned into the house. "Would you like to sit? Maybe have a drink of water?"

He didn't budge, but he wasn't sure whether that was a decision or if his body simply refused to move. "Dies like this?" he repeated.

Leah put her hand on his arm. "It's her third loss, Jesse. The doctor needs to swab the inside of the baby's cheek with a Q-tip. Then he can run some medical tests that will give him very helpful information."

Jesse couldn't imagine what the doctor wanted or what they hoped to piece together.

"I know this doesn't feel like the right time," Leah said. "You're confused and exhausted. But I'm asking you to trust me enough to allow him inside to see your newborn."

"Our." He choked on the word as his eyes welled with tears.

"I'm sorry?" Leah studied him.

"You said, '*Her* third loss.' She didn't lose our daughter. *We* lost her. I will not allow the loss to be laid at my wife's feet. Do you understand?" Where was this angry resolve coming from? He'd felt inklings of it when they lost the two others. When pain was as thick as snow after a winter storm, no one could word anything right.

But for the Amish, having children was everything, the most important blessing of all. Moreover, a woman's value had unbreakable chains fastened to her ability to give her husband children. He wouldn't allow those shackles to wrap around Eliza.

"Yes, you're right," Leah said. "And I apologize."

Again, he couldn't say the words *thank you*, and this time, he couldn't nod either. "What are you looking for, Doctor?"

"If I'm correct in my hunches, I think the information I'll have to share will help give you and your wife some hope and peace of mind."

Jesse didn't want that kind of hope. There was no hope for his daughter, and she wasn't spilled ice cream. Dip up another cone and forget the one you dropped. He wanted his daughter alive and well, and no one could fix that. He longed for his wife's heart to not be shattered from the loss of love and broken dreams only Penelope could fulfill. What good could this doctor do them? The most he could offer would be hope for future children, and they weren't ready to even think about that.

"Please, Jesse," Leah said.

Perhaps any amount of hope, no matter how small, would be like a drink of water in a parched desert to Eliza. "Come on in." Jesse stepped aside so the two could come in the cabin. Was that the sun coming up over the mountain? Everything felt so unreal. Penelope had been born before sunset, and no one had slept since.

He closed the door behind the visitors. "My wife is . . . still holding her."

The doctor took out a small notebook and pen. "Could you tell me what happened in your words?"

Jesse nodded, and they moved to the kitchen table. Leah got a glass out of the cabinet and filled it with water. She set it in front of him. He took a drink and his mind reeled back to about twelve hours ago . . .

He remembered kneeling beside the bed, next to his wife's face.

Tiny burst blood vessels from pushing surrounded her eyes; her hair was messy and prayer Kapp askew. She'd never looked so beautiful.

"Almost there." He squeezed her hand. "I'm so proud of you. I love you so much."

He'd looked at the midwife sitting between Eliza's feet. Leah, a woman of about sixty, smiled and nodded at him. He'd been saying the same thing to Eliza for the past twenty minutes, and it seemed it was finally true. The labor had happened so fast at the beginning he wasn't sure if Leah would get her items fully unpacked, but she had. She didn't complain about Jesse being there or try to make him leave. Most Amish didn't stay with their wives during labor. But he wouldn't leave his Eliza. He couldn't.

He smoothed a few strands off his wife's forehead. "We're so close to meeting our baby. You're doing an amazing job."

Eliza clenched his other hand tightly as the powerful contraction tightened her entire body.

The midwife reached under the propped-up blanket. "There's your baby's head!"

Jesse couldn't see what Leah saw, so he kept his focus on his wife's face. Her sweaty brow was knit in concentration.

A baby's cry. The best sound in the world.

He let out a breath he hadn't realized he'd been holding.

The midwife held up the squirming, red newborn where both could see. She had a head of dark hair and her cute face was scrunched up. "Congratulations, Eliza! You have a girl!"

A daughter. Eliza's eyes met his, holding pure relief and bliss. He kissed her lips. Was it possible for a heart to actually burst with love?

Their kiss broke, and Eliza held her arms out to the midwife, asking for the baby. But Leah had put the infant on the bed and was looking her over. Her face looked . . . panicked?

Eliza pushed herself to sit straight up. "What's wrong?"

Leah held up a hand. "Don't move yet."

Eliza lay back down.

"Now, I don't want to alarm you, but we need to call a doctor for the baby. And possibly an ambulance. Although I don't know what they'll be able to do." The midwife put both hands on the infant, closed her eyes, and murmured a prayer. The baby kept squirming and fussing. Wasn't that what newborns were supposed to do?

Time seemed to stop. Jesse couldn't even breathe. Leah looked at Eliza and Jesse. "I've seen this before."

What had she seen before? He'd wanted to ask but couldn't utter a word. What did all this mean? Eliza's eyes widened with disbelief.

He had to fix this! He'd take whatever was wrong to God. Just like he'd always done. God would provide. He would. Jesse held his arms out to Leah. "Let me hold my daughter."

The midwife quickly wrapped the baby in a receiving blanket and gently handed her to Jesse. "I'll step out of the room to call someone. Then I'll be back to tend to Eliza and the afterbirth. Leave the baby's cord attached." She sprinted out of the room.

Jesse cradled the precious small bundle where he could examine her closely. The baby was crying, a little less loudly now, but she was obviously breathing. What on earth could be wrong?

He placed her in Eliza's arms and knelt beside the bed so they could study her together. A head of dark hair, a button nose, and a tiny pink mouth wide-open and crying.

Eliza shook her head and snuggled the baby close. "She's perfect. The midwife is wrong."

His poor wife. She was still out of breath from pushing. She should be soaking in this precious moment. Why would Leah do this to them?

Jesse traced his fingers down the baby's body, moving the blanket. Something looked . . . off. The baby's ribs went inward where they shouldn't, in a shape like an hourglass. Like a band had been tightened around her chest in the middle.

Eliza wiggled her thumb inside the infant's balled fist. "Jesse, she has six fingers on this hand." She gasped, but her inhale stopped when she saw their baby's chest.

Horror churned in the pit of Jesse's stomach. The baby's forehead had taken on a bluish hue. Her tiny chest rose and fell in extremely shallow breaths.

No!

Jesse closed his eyes and prayed with everything he had.

But before the ambulance arrived, their daughter had stopped breathing.

Jesse choked on the last word as he recounted the story. He'd almost gotten through without breaking down. *Calm down. Finish telling him.*

He took a few steadying breaths. "I turned the paramedics away. Was that the right call? I don't know. I just couldn't see letting them take Eliza to the hospital when they couldn't do anything. And . . . I was afraid they'd take the baby."

Jesse covered his face with his hand. These people didn't need to see him cry.

Dr. Morgan put a hand on Jesse's shoulder. "You did everything right. Can I meet your wife and daughter now?"

Wife and daughter. Another pang of sadness hit his chest. It was too late to really meet them both. His daughter was already in heaven.

He wiped his eyes. "Jah."

He led Dr. Morgan to the bedroom, knocked gently, and cracked the door open. His wife didn't seem to notice. She held Penelope close, whispering. Maybe she was talking to her or maybe praying, but the scene frightened him.

"Eliza."

She looked up.

"There is a doctor here, a Dr. Morgan. He wants to talk to us about the baby. Is it okay if he comes in?"

"Jah." Her voice sounded as if it were rooms away, and the pain in her eyes broke his heart anew.

He opened the door. She looked so beautiful holding a baby. The unfairness of the situation kept hitting him over and over.

He walked in and motioned for the doctor and midwife to come in. "This is Eliza, her sister Ruth, and . . . baby Penelope."

"Do I need to step out?" Ruth asked.

"No, stay." Eliza motioned for Ruth to come closer. Jesse

sat on the end of the bed and stroked Eliza's knee through the covers.

Dr. Morgan sat in the chair next to the bed. "She's beautiful. Do you mind if I take a look at her?'

Eliza pulled the baby closer for a moment before slowly relinquishing the tiny bundle. Jesse swallowed back tears. They didn't have much time left to hold Penelope. Eliza knew that.

Jesse took his wife's hand while the doctor laid the baby on a blanket on the dresser, his back to them as he examined her. The midwife passed him something from his bag, probably the Q-tip she had talked about.

Dr. Morgan swaddled the baby again and handed her to Eliza. "Jesse, Eliza, you are dealing with one of the hardest things in the world—the loss of a child. I'd like to give you a little information to help you make sense of everything. Leah feels it might help."

Leah nodded.

The doctor continued. "First off, I want you both to hear me when I say this: what happened to Penelope is no one's fault. There's nothing you could've done differently in your pregnancy, nothing you ate or drank that caused this, and no way you could've known her body wasn't developing in the typical way, unless you'd gone in for an ultrasound, a scan of the baby before birth. But even if you had gotten a scan, it wouldn't have changed anything other than knowing ahead of time what would happen." The doctor opened his mouth as if he had more to say, but Eliza's sobs seemed to stop him short.

Jesse put his arm around her shoulders. Ruth laid a hand

on Eliza's leg. Eliza closed her eyes, regained her composure, then looked up at the doctor. How could she be so brave?

Dr. Morgan gave them a sad smile. "I'd need a full gene sequencing panel to confirm what I think happened, but based on what I'm seeing here, we're looking at a genetic syndrome called Ellis-Van Creveld. This is something I've observed before in your community."

Genetic? He'd learned something about that in the one-room Amish school years ago when studying how plants and animals passed down traits. "Our daughter got this . . . from us? How? Neither of us have any physical issues."

"That's a good question. This syndrome is what's called recessive. Meaning Mom and Dad are carriers who are healthy and have no symptoms. Upon conception, both of you can pass on 'bad' copies of a gene and end up with a child who doesn't develop in a healthy way, although some children with this condition survive. Having said all that, your chances of conceiving unhealthy babies are relatively small."

Eliza shivered and turned to her sister. "I need Auntie Rose's quilt."

Ruth grabbed a quilt off the rack at the foot of the bed.

"Nee. I want the one Auntie Rose gave me on our wedding day."

Jesse didn't understand why it mattered which quilt, but he doubted if Eliza knew why either. She'd loved her auntie Rose deeply, so maybe the quilt the old woman had given her brought comfort no other one could.

Ruth went to the closet. She came back with the quilt and placed it over Eliza.

While she held Penelope so gently in one arm, she clutched

the quilt tight before looking straight at Dr. Morgan. "I've been pregnant three times and not given birth to a healthy child yet. That's not a small chance. That's 100 percent."

Was Eliza saying they lost the other babies because of this same issue? "Our other losses happened before birth. Could those have been for the same reason?"

"I can't say for sure about the cause of previous losses, but it's likely. Going forward, the odds for your future babies are on your side. I'd like to use a word picture. Dice means more than one die. You're familiar with dice?"

They nodded.

"With recessive conditions like this one, think about it like rolling a four-sided die. On three of the four sides, your baby inherits at least one healthy copy of this particular gene and is unaffected. But on one of the four sides, he or she inherits the two unhealthy copies. Now that you have rolled the 'bad' side at least once—maybe up to three times— chances are your next will be healthy. One-in-four affected are actually good odds. Other genetic syndromes are a one-in-two risk."

Eliza's fingers turned white as she clutched the quilt. "But for all you know, we could have another syndrome. Or something worse. Something that takes every child we conceive."

The doctor seemed taken aback. "Anything is possible, but it's highly unlikely. We could test early next time for Ellis-Van Creveld and also screen the both of you for the one hundred other most common carried conditions. Set your minds at ease."

"Could you change the outcome?" Ruth asked.

"Well, no. But—"

"I've heard enough." Eliza's face became vacant. "I need you to go, please."

Jesse stood and gestured toward the doorway. "Thanks for your time. I don't doubt your intention, but nothing you've said has been helpful."

The doctor nodded. "I'm sorry again for your loss. I'll be able to clarify more when the test results come back." He dipped his head and left, the midwife going with him.

Jesse studied his wife. Her eyes were on their daughter. With one hand she continued to hold the quilt so firmly her knuckles remained white.

How were they supposed to move forward after this? Were they ever going to be whole and happy again?

Chapter Seven

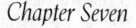

The branches of the oak were wide and welcoming. *Come rest,* they seemed to be saying. Eliza stared up at the huge hundreds-of-years-old tree. Some of the beautiful leaves of red, gold, and brown were falling in the late-September breeze, drifting over the tiny, freshly dug plot. Her children would all be tucked in a beautiful fall blanket. But their rightful place was in her empty arms.

God, why? Why them? Why her? If she had any strength left, she'd scream, not caring who thought what. She'd done that a few times at home. But now all she could do was stand there, quietly staring at the ground.

Their family surrounded Jesse and Eliza at the tree, filling the forest opening. Some people stood among the other trees. A sea of men in white shirts and women in their Sunday-best dresses. These same people had been at their wedding, plus others they'd met along the way. Some had traveled from out of state. With this many people who loved them, why did she feel so empty?

She'd been embraced by countless women, but not one bit of the warmth of those arms could penetrate the frost that covered her heart. No one could fix it. Nothing could ever fix it. They'd lost three babies. Three for three. Despite the doctor's opinion, she knew it could happen every time. Would it?

Bishop David cleared his throat and opened to a page in the *Ausbund*. "'Eternal Father in heaven, I call to You from my innermost being,'" he read from the old German hymnal. "'Do not let me turn away from You, but keep me in Your truth until the end. Oh, God, keep my heart and my mouth. Watch over me every hour. Do not let me turn away from You because of anxiety, fear, or distress. Keep me steadfast in Your joy.'"

Steadfast. That's what Eliza needed to be. Her body ached and her knees threatened to buckle. She'd given birth three days ago. They'd waited for today, giving relatives time to get the news and travel here. What a blur time had been these few days. She looked at her husband beside her. Jesse had his eyes closed, praying. He seemed to be able to be steadfast. But she kept falling apart. She stood taller and closed her eyes. She would make it through this funeral. She had to. She owed it to Penelope.

She thanked God for sending a bishop kind enough to allow them to bury their daughter here instead of at a graveyard. At least now Eliza could visit often and in privacy.

Tears welled again as the hymn recitation ended, so she began silently praying the Lord's Prayer.

"Our Father which art in heaven, hallowed be thy name . . ." She knelt and kept praying it silently, over and over.

She heard all those friends and family start to walk back to her home. She went back to an earlier part of the prayer. *"Forgive us our debts."* Was this her fault? Had she done something that had brought this awful genetic curse upon them?

Was this what the warning was about—that the Ebersols and Bontragers got along but didn't marry? Was there some hidden past sin between the families? Her mamm hadn't wanted her and Jesse to play together at first. But Eliza had ignored all that. Was it selfish?

Maybe this was her fault.

She prayed the entire prayer again. And again. And again. And then prayed asking Jesus to tuck Penelope in heavenly blankets. And then asking for forgiveness. Time seemed to cease flowing.

She opened her eyes, her face wet with tears. The only ones still at the gravesite were Jesse, Ruth, Mamm, Dat, and Bishop David.

Eliza's knees hurt, and her body complained in all sorts of ways. Jesse gave her a hand up, and she stood and dusted off her black dress. She wiped her face on her apron. How long had it been since the end of the service?

She couldn't bear to go back to the house, so full of people yet so empty. Her baby was here. Why should she be anywhere else?

"I'm not ready to go to the house yet. Can I . . . have a few more minutes to talk to God alone?"

Bishop David gave her a small smile and nod. His kindness was a gift, but her stomach turned at the looks of pity from him and everyone else. "Of course."

Jesse put a hand on her shoulder. He looked uncertain. "I'll . . . attend to the visitors and then come back for you."

"Don't worry about anything, Eliza. We'll handle the guests." Ruth's eyes were puffy and red from crying.

"Denki." She nodded at them. Just a minute more and she'd be alone. No one there to watch her fall apart.

Through a mist of tears, she watched them walk off down the trail toward the house. When they were far enough away to not see her, she let out a held breath, flung herself onto the freshly dug dirt, and wept.

Just a few feet separated her and Penelope now. Why had Eliza been anxious for the end of the pregnancy? If only she could put her baby back. Back close to her heart. Back to feeling those precious feet kick.

Everything about this was wrong. If someone had to go, why couldn't it have been Eliza? If she was the one who did something wrong, why did an innocent baby have to pay the price?

"Eliza, my love. It's getting dark."

She sat up. Jesse stood beside her. How had time slipped away from her again?

He brushed off her face. She felt pieces of mud fall. "I'm not asking you to come in yet. I just want to sit with you. Let me help you up for a second."

She did, and he spread out the quilt Auntie Rose had given her.

Wasn't there something special about this quilt? Some

story she couldn't quite remember? This quilt was comforting for reasons she couldn't understand. Her brain was so fuzzy these days. When was the last time she slept? Or ate? It didn't matter. The midwife said her hormones were running amok inside her, making everything harder. Her breasts produced unneeded milk. The midwife had given her a shot of something that was supposed to help with that.

Jesse sat on the soft surface and beckoned her to do the same.

She eased onto it, feeling all the aches of having given birth just three days ago and having flung herself onto the grave earlier. She lay down, ignoring the achy complaints, and curled around the area where Penelope was buried. Jesse lay behind her. Being here like this was so right and so wrong at the same time.

"You can use this quilt to go back in time once and fix an event."

The words stole her next breath. Wasn't that what Auntie Rose had said on their wedding day? If only that were true.

But going back to before Penelope was born wouldn't help anything. She'd have to go back . . . She pondered the situation.

To when?

She held the quilt close, praying, seeking God. Was she imagining things or being nudged to understand the power of the quilt, a power she'd dismissed when Auntie Rose told her of it? She'd completely discounted what her aunt had said without a second thought . . . until now. Was there a God-given power in this quilt from so many Amish women through several centuries praying over it, crying out with pure love and unbearable grief? Maybe she was going insane to consider this quilt had the power to change her life, but she held firm to the fabric, determined to join her foremothers in devoted faith and fervent prayer.

If she could go back and change one event, what would she change?

Andrew poured three circles of pancake batter onto the griddle and waited. He looked through the open kitchen window of his parents' home. Birds flitted and chirped. Sunlight streamed through the golden leaves of the American elm. Children ran ahead of their parents, hurrying down the sidewalk toward downtown Calico Creek, laughing.

He flipped the hotcakes.

It seemed so odd how the earth could be completely out of sync with one's reality. Ruth's heart was broken. He was sure the long, dark of night consumed everything about Eliza and Jesse—their thoughts, their emotions, even their hope and faith. He'd gone to the funeral four days ago, and the Bontragers and Ebersols were in the eye of a destructive storm. They couldn't see past the dark skies and hard rains right now. Yet the blue earth spun with sunlight rippling, children laughing, and life bustling along.

"What are you up to today?" Mamm asked.

"Ben's coming by and we're going in search of something to lift the spirits of a friend of ours, maybe to the antique store." Surely they could find something meaningful for Ruth.

"That sounds good."

A group of Englischers passed in front of the house,

hurrying down the sidewalk toward the square. Was something special happening downtown?

During his great-grandfather's time, this house sat on twenty-five acres, pretty removed from town life. But over time Calico Creek had spread farther out. This home and barn sat on a little over two acres. They were allowed to keep horses on the small tract they owned because of laws that grandfathered in his family as well as most other Amish families this close to the downtown square. Over the years they'd sold small parcels of the original acreage to family members and to the city, but that wouldn't happen again. They needed every inch of the land they still had.

Andrew ran a spatula under each pancake and stacked them on a plate. He put a couple of pieces of bacon beside the short stack and set it in front of his mamm.

She peered over her mug of coffee. "Denki, Son." She slathered butter on the hotcakes. "It's not like your dad to miss out on your Saturday morning breakfasts. I'm not even sure where he went, but he left an hour or so ago."

"My guess is it has something to do with the business."

She slid her fork into the stack, cutting another bite. "These are so good. If you ever decide to marry, she will be one very blessed woman."

He refreshed his mamm's coffee cup. She was beating around the bush, hinting at what she wanted to know—if he was seeing someone. His parents were aware that for the past six months and for the first time in his life, he left on Sunday evenings and came home late, which could mean he was attending singings, but it might mean something else entirely. He poured himself a cup of coffee and took a seat.

He had no interest in eating. What he wanted was a way to make Ruth feel better, but how?

Mamm took a bite of bacon. "You've seemed out of sorts this week."

He could tell her a little bit. "Someone I care about is grieving, and it's as if I can feel her pain."

She studied him for a long moment, probably deciding whether to ask questions or not. "It works that way sometimes if you're close."

He sipped his coffee. It surprised him how close he felt to Ruth these days. They'd slowly moved along, being friends for years. Then all of a sudden, his heart was invested as if they'd been in a committed relationship for a long time. Other than enjoying each other's company and being friends, how did she feel about him?

"Have you known her long?"

Mamm sounded nonchalant, but he knew she was aching for information. She also wanted hope that he would one day marry and have a family. In his mind, he was only twenty-four, turning twenty-five soon, but all eight of his siblings had married by the time they were twenty. His youngest sibling, Katie, married at eighteen, and before the year was out, she had her first child. She and her husband lived with his folks about a mile from here. He wished the Amish encouraged their children to slow things down a bit. For the sake of entering marriage with some adult maturity and knowing one's self, shouldn't people wait until they were at least twenty-one or so to marry?

His mamm kept studying him, and he felt it was time to tell her a few things.

"We've been friends for years and seeing each other for six months."

Mamm's eyes grew large. "Are you serious?"

He nodded. "Jah, I am." Maybe over-his-head serious. "I've invited her to next month's Ebersol family gathering."

"What?" She was glowing now. "Ach, my heart." She patted her chest, grinning and flushed. "This is incredible news. Congratulations!"

"Um, let's slow it down a bit, please, and you tell no one."

The screen door to the kitchen opened. Dat stepped inside carrying a folded newspaper under his arm. "What aren't we telling anyone?"

Mamm ran her index finger and thumb across her lips, feigning that she was zipping them.

Dat moved to the coffeepot and filled a mug.

Andrew stood. "You ready for some pancakes?"

Dat shook his head. "I had to go into town to get a linchpin for a buggy wheel, and I ate at the diner." Dat took a seat, putting the folded copy of the *County Times* in an empty chair beside him. He stirred his coffee, probably waiting for Andrew to answer.

Andrew fidgeted with his mug, keeping his eyes on the black liquid. He could inform his parents. Telling his siblings was totally different. They would push him to hurry up and marry, give endless advice, and worry that the world might fall apart before he wed. But Andrew wanted him and Ruth to know how they felt before others started telling them how they should feel and what they should do.

He lifted his eyes to meet Dat's. "We're not telling others that I'm dating someone, someone really special."

The serious look on Dat's face slowly eased into a warm smile. "I'm so glad you're seeing someone. It'll help me stop feeling as if you'll leave the Amish one day."

Andrew had never talked to Dat about leaving the Amish. He'd never said a word to anyone except Ben, and Ben wouldn't have told anyone that. But when younger, Andrew had felt tempted to leave. Most young people felt that way at one point or another. His dat must've picked up on how he was feeling back then.

"This is great, Son." Dat took a sip of coffee. "How serious? Like nice-wall-clock-type serious?"

He chuckled. A lot of Amish men gave beautiful wall clocks with moving parts and music as a gift when they asked a woman to marry them. Since Amish were allowed wall clocks, they could get the kind that had multiple moving parts and chimed music. He didn't think Ruth would enjoy that kind. Her style was more traditional Amish than that.

"Well, Dat, I'm not planning on giving her one this month, but jah, that's part of my hopes for the future."

"Wow," Dat whispered. "So what's she like?"

"She's amazing. She actually helped me with the research on my first article in the *County Times*, the one that caused the feed mill to clean up the toxins and give restitution to workers. But she doesn't want people knowing her part in it."

"So she's amazing and humble," Dat said.

Mamm pushed her plate to the side. "She's also going through a sad time. Lost someone, I think, and Andrew is hoping to do, find, or buy something today that would make her feel better."

Dat nodded. "What's the most important things to her?"

"Family and the Amish history of family and community . . ." Andrew pondered that and knew what he and Ben should do today. "I've got it." He smacked the kitchen table. "I need to go through the attic and find an old letter or diary or farming record book." Maybe he'd find an old clock while up there.

Mamm blinked. "It's a huge mess."

"Exactly what I need," Andrew said. "Dat, you care to help?"

"I'm game. An Ebersol has lived in this house for over a hundred and fifty years. We know we won't find old baseball cards or comic books like the Englisch do, but I imagine we'll find something valuable your girl would like."

Mamm shrugged. "Okay. But after you pick out something for her, I get second dibs on anything of interest."

"Deal." Andrew glanced at the clock over the stove. Ben would be here in about an hour. Andrew longed to leave the table right now and get started, but he knew Dat wanted something else from him. Andrew held out his hand.

Dat moved the newspaper from the chair to the table and slid it toward Andrew.

Andrew unfolded it. "Something in particular you're interested in?"

"At the bakery, I overheard someone mention that an inquiry in Congress is widening."

Andrew read the various headlines. He'd been fifteen when he realized his dat couldn't read. Andrew's earliest childhood memories were of his older siblings at the table reading the paper or the Bible aloud. He'd loved growing up in a home where reading out loud and then having a discussion at length was a part of their daily lives. Mamm could read, but it was a vulnerable thing to be unable to read, and Dat was most comfortable with someone besides his wife reading to him. He was a smart man, and Andrew was sure if Ruth had been his teacher, even though Dat was dyslexic, he would have learned to read. She would've made sure of it in the most encouraging, respectful way possible.

But it seemed to Andrew that Dat had taken his most painful vulnerability and made it work on his children's behalf by having them read aloud and talk about subjects so they were well-informed. Andrew and his siblings always made the best grades in school.

Andrew saw the headline about a congressional inquiry. "It says here . . ."

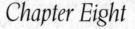

Chapter Eight

ONE MONTH LATER

Get ready, get ready. Jesse moved his body weight from one foot to the other while standing on his toes. The muddy hay squished underneath him. Barnabas tossed the ball—well, actually a Hacky Sack since they'd busted the family's original cornerball two years ago—up and down in his hand as he narrowed his eyes at Jesse. Why had Jesse beaned his cousin in the head so hard during last year's game? It was funny at the time, but now Barn's moment of revenge was here. If he could catch Jesse first.

Jesse's mom and sisters cheered and laughed from behind the fence. Where was Eliza? They'd stuck together during most of his family's annual fall festival, but he'd lost track of her after cornerball began. It'd been a month since Penelope's death—was that too soon for Eliza to be at a gathering like this? It'd felt so good for him to laugh with his family and play games. The grief didn't leave during the laughter. It simply got a little lighter, a little more in perspective for a few minutes. But was Eliza also feeling lifted? Or was she stifled by the large number of people here?

Keeping one eye on Barnabas, Jesse scanned what he could see of the Ebersol family gathering. The crowd around the cornerball pen made it hard to see much of the rolling gold-and-green hills of his parents' property. Whiffs of delicious funnel cakes made by some of the women wafted from the outdoor fryer, almost overpowering the smell of trampled hay and mud. Was Eliza preparing food with his aunts?

Barnabas lifted his arm to lob the ball at Jesse. Barn flung an overhand throw that should've hit him in the gut. Jesse leaped backward, but his heel caught in the soft mud and he toppled to the ground, flat on his back.

Where was the ball? Ah, the first throw had been a fake-out! Barn raised his hand again and Jesse flipped himself into a push-up position. His cousin threw the Hacky Sack like he was skipping a rock, and Jesse pushed himself up hard. He put a foot under his body, but Barn's hand never finished the throw. Another fake.

Barn reloaded his throw and flung the ball hard. He would've hit Jesse—if Jesse had followed through on standing up. Instead, he dropped back to the ground, smacking his chest and chin on the muddy hay. The ball whooshed by above his head. That one would've smarted.

That was it—Barn had used his throw.

The crowd around the fence cheered with Jesse's team. Barnabas made a noise of frustration, but Jesse could hear him laughing along with the rest of the men and boys in the cornerball pen. He sat up and picked bits of hay and mud from his beard. So worth it.

He scanned the group at the fence again. There was Eliza. The rest of his extended relatives squished in around her, but she'd made it to the fence line. The quilt Auntie Rose had given her was draped over her folded arms. She'd said they could spread it out and sit on it during the evening singing, but he knew there was more to it than that. Something about that quilt comforted her.

He winked at her. She gave him a half smile before turning to walk away. Had she seen his amazing dodge followed by that face-plant into the mud and hay? Surely that was worth some amusement.

His teammates clapped him on the shoulder as he hurried after his wife. He slid an arm around her and they kept walking across the grassy field. "Mamm made chicken potpie for dinner. Doesn't that sound good?"

Eliza shook her head. "Nothing really sounds good anymore." She fidgeted with the stitching of the quilt she carried. "I . . . don't think I can sit through a meal with everyone tonight. I'll probably just walk home."

He breathed in deep through his nose. It wasn't the first time he'd heard her say nothing sounded good or the first time she'd skipped out on a meal. "You gotta fuel your body so you can recover. The midwife said it's important."

Her shoulders tensed at the word *midwife*.

He'd said too much. He stopped walking, wrapped his

arms around her, and pulled her close. "I'm sorry. I'll have Mamm pack us some food to go, and we'll head home."

She pulled back enough to look him in the eyes. "Weren't you looking forward to talking to the family who came here from elsewhere, ones you haven't seen all year? If you're worried about me being alone, I can take Ruth with me."

He shrugged. "There will be other times to visit, and we had fun playing cornerball. I'm not sure I want to sit across from Barnabas anyway. He'd probably kick me in the shin under the table." He smiled down at her, wanting to be brave for her and keep trying to make her smile too.

The pain in her eyes made his heart hurt. Every day he prayed for healing to her spirit. He'd tried to give her time. But he was more than ready to see a hint of progress.

Eliza winced and closed her eyes. "How do you do it?"

"Do what?"

She looked at the ground. "Pretend everything is normal. It's not. Penelope *died*. I should be carrying *her* in my arms right now, not this quilt."

Jesse cupped her chin, angling her face toward his. "I know. Losing her is hard to accept, and I want her here with us too. It grieves me that we had to say goodbye so soon. But I have to trust that Jesus is holding her until we can."

She pulled away. "You seem to be coping just fine. It's like you've completely moved on."

Anger flared in his chest and he struggled to smother the flames. She was speaking out of hurt. But to even imply that he didn't love Penelope as much as she did . . . "Do not assume that because I'm better at acting normal, I don't love her."

"There it is. You're doing *better* than I am. Well, I'm

doing the best I can! I'm sorry I'm not acting normal enough for you."

"That's not what I meant." Jesse sighed. "I'm trying to help you."

A cool breeze kicked up, and fall leaves tumbled across the ground.

"I shouldn't have come." Eliza shivered as she turned away. "Watching Annie with her baby boy, who was born on Penelope's birthday, is more than I can bear. I'm grateful he's here and healthy, but seeing a mom and her newborn is just too painful. And I can't stop wondering why we've been so cursed."

"We're not cursed." He put a hand on her shoulder. "Shouldn't we trust God? He's never failed us, even when we don't understand His ways. And there isn't any indication that all our children would die. I won't believe that for a moment."

She pulled free of his hand. "I can't trust like that. I'm sorry if that makes me a bad Christian. I feel like I'm in a pit, and I'll never break free of this."

Jesse swallowed. She was suffering worse than he thought. It was as if she hadn't left that night or the bedroom where Penelope had died.

She clearly wanted space from him. What could he do to help her? "I'm sorry, Eliza. I love you."

She nodded. The wind kicked up again. If she was going for a long walk, he was glad she had the quilt with her.

"Would you like for me to go find Ruth?"

She nodded again, perhaps only because she wanted him to go and knew he wouldn't leave her out here by herself in this state of mind.

Chapter Nine

Ruth held the mallet, trying to line up a perfect hit. A burnt-orange leaf from a sugar maple rolled across her path, stopping when it came in contact with her mallet. She exaggerated a huff, picked it up, and shoved it into her hidden apron pocket. "No leaf will stop me. Well, at least not that one. I'm about to roquet."

Andrew propped his mallet against his shoulder. "I'll believe it when I see it."

Ruth laughed. "Jah, me too, but you gotta admit—" she swung her mallet, hitting her ball but missing Andrew's— "the word *roquet* is fun to say."

He grinned, moving in closer. "It is fun to roquet while playing croquet, but you're better at talking about it than doing it." His eyes clung to hers. "You are something else,

Ruth Bontrager. I knew it when we talked at Eliza's wedding three years ago."

She playfully pushed him away. "Did not."

"Without even trying, you knew what I needed to do to get the ball rolling for the investigation into the feed mill. I'm not saying I wanted us to date, not then. Neither did you. I'm saying I knew you were a very gifted woman, and the more I get to know you, the more I realize how very true that first impression was. Half of my reasons to meet you at the library had more to do with getting to know you than with what we accomplished through research, and what we achieved was huge. You make my life more than it is, Ruth. I . . . want you to know how I feel about you, about us."

Her heart skipped a beat before it soared, but no words came to her. In her deepest grief over Penelope, he'd brought her the most amazing gift from a storage chest in his attic—a diary written by his great-great-great-grandfather, containing nearly a lifetime of names and dates of weddings, births, and deaths of all Amish in Calico Creek. It also listed the weather on each day and the particulars of planting and harvesting for a farmer. The man had jotted down almost nothing of his thoughts or emotions, and yet she could catch glimpses of overwhelming love and grief throughout his lifetime. She wasn't sure what the best gift was: the journal itself or Andrew's dedication for her sake in finding it.

He focused on the ball and smacked it good, sending it through two wickets. "Did I say too much?" He studied her.

She shook her head, still unable to think of what to say.

"It's a lot to put on a budding relationship."

"Maybe so, but I have to be honest—"

"Ruth?" Jesse called as he strode toward her. "Eliza needs you. She's by herself at the edge of the wood, and she'd like you to walk with her."

Long, meandering walks were the only thing that seemed to help Eliza these days, that and carrying the quilt from Auntie Rose. Ruth's heart lurched. It wasn't good for her sister to be alone right now.

"I'll find her in no time." She passed her mallet to Jesse and hurried off through the grassy field toward the woods.

Soon enough she spotted her sister right before the tree line. "Eliza, wait."

Eliza turned, and Ruth sprinted to her. They stood there for several minutes as Ruth caught her breath. She looped her arm through Eliza's, and they walked in silence as they entered what they used to call the hundred-acre wood. In reality it was probably only forty acres.

The deeper they went, the more narrow the path, and soon Ruth was following her sister. Her thoughts returned to Andrew, and she cringed to realize she never finished her sentence. He'd made himself vulnerable to her, and then she ran off. She'd wanted to tell him that she felt the same way about him—that her heart belonged to him, and God seemed to be pleased with it.

She tripped over a root and grabbed on to a tree to regain her balance. How long had they been walking?

Eliza paused, looking as if she was unsure which way to go. She shivered, and Ruth lifted the quilt from her sister's arms and put it around her shoulders.

Everyone at the Ebersol family gathering had feasted all afternoon, but had Eliza eaten anything? What time was it now?

"Maybe we should start for home."

"I guess." But Eliza didn't move.

Ruth looked at the forest around her. Light was beginning to fade. They'd spent half their childhood in these woods, but she didn't have her usual sense of bearings. "Um, I don't recognize where we are. Did we get turned around?"

Eliza kicked at a root. "Jesse and I had a fight. Well, sort of a fight." She leaned against a big oak tree and faced Ruth. "It's my fault. Every single thing that's said feels like a personal attack."

"I'm sorry. But disagreements are a normal part of marriage—even between Mamm and Dat. And Jesse understands."

"Even he can only take so much. Everything I say is selfish and filled with self-pity. I can see it, but I can't manage to stop it before it spews out of my mouth."

"You're grieving. It's only been a month. Be patient with yourself."

"I have so many questions of late. Why is it so hard for an Ebersol and Bontrager marriage to be blessed? Why have so few of those couples stayed in Calico Creek?"

"A lot of Amish left these parts before Jesse made a successful go with Ebersol Cabins. But most of those couples having left makes it hard to know very much about their offspring."

"What happened to Omar Ebersol and Verna Bontrager, to their marriage, that they left all family behind in order to divorce and completely disappear?"

"I don't know. But no one in these parts has been good at writing down events."

"Apparently no one wants to talk about it either, or we'd have heard stories."

"I've asked for details, but no one will give more than the simple answers we've always been told. Some of the elders told me that marriage between the two families 'just wasn't done.'" Ruth stretched her arms behind her back. "I'd chalk it up to old people and their superstitions. They can take almost anything out of the ordinary and call it a curse."

"Maybe it's the only word that describes what happens. Or maybe the 'curse' is a genetic disease. I'm not sure there is a worse thing than dooming an entire family of children to die before they get a chance to feel love and comfort and joy."

"Eliza . . ." Was this what she and Jesse had fought about?

"What if those elders knew more than we did when we married? Maybe Jesse and I, as much as we love each other, are cursed, and all of our children will die."

Ruth pulled the quilt tighter across Eliza's shoulders. Her sister's grief was clouding her mind and making her jump to worst-case scenarios. "But the doctor explained it as a one-in-four risk."

"Those aren't the real odds. He was sugarcoating the truth. Maybe for some it's a one-in-four risk, but clearly not for Jesse and me. Is this what happened to Omar and Verna and no one spoke of such things back then? It would explain why they were married for five years without having any children." Eliza stared into the barren treetops. "We *are* cursed."

Ruth started to reply but decided to keep her mouth shut. There were some things a person had to figure out on their own. Besides, she could see where Eliza was coming from.

It wasn't logical, but who could expect Eliza to have strong logic right now?

Ruth smoothed her apron. "I visited several older women in our family last week. I asked if any of them had lost babies. Most had, sometimes early, sometimes at birth or a few months beyond. They each had different ways of coping with the losses. But none of them knew about Ellis-Van Creveld. Losing Penelope to it was a lightning strike, a tragedy that hit your family but seems unlikely to happen again."

Eliza rubbed her temples. "I wish with all my heart you were right, but Jesse carries half. I carry the other half. Why was everyone so set against Jesse and me dating and marrying? There was a hidden curse, one that only shows up when an Ebersol and Bontrager marry."

Ruth sighed. "You are not cursed. You and Jesse have a beautiful home, friends, family, and a very successful business. I can't think of where our community would be without you two living and working as a couple."

"Jesse would be able to do all that without me." She took Ruth by the hands, staring into her eyes. "Listen to me, Sister. I know you really care for Andrew, but have you considered that you and Andrew might end up dealing with the same thing as Jesse and me?"

Her heart froze in place. "Nee."

"Please, think about it carefully." She released Ruth's hands. "I'd do anything to set Jesse free of this."

"Eliza . . ."

A puff of smoke visible through the tops of the trees caught Ruth's eye. She pointed. "There's fire inside our forest?"

Eliza stood straight, looking in that direction. "We should check it out."

"Are you sure we're still on Ebersol or Bontrager land?"

"Bontrager. Positive. You should be too. We know these woods forward and backward."

"It's been a while, and right now it's all looking the same to me—trees and underbrush that goes on forever." But Ruth trusted Eliza's sense of their land. She'd been going for long walks day and night for weeks. "You been coming this far when walking?"

"Nee." Eliza ducked under a partially fallen branch. "But this is part of Hunters' Woods. Kumm."

Ruth followed her sister through underbrush in the direction of the smoke.

They came to a clearing, full of shadows as sunlight waned. Their ancestors' small, primitive cabin came into view. It had been a decade since Ruth had laid eyes on this old place. Eliza continued toward it. Ruth hesitated a moment, then followed.

White smoke puffed out the stacked-stone chimney. The rest of the building was made of untreated split logs with a thatched roof. Rocks were stacked at the corners of the cabin, being used as the foundation. No one built like this anymore, unless as a replica of settler days. She and Eliza used to play here sometimes as children, either when Mamm was nearby, berry picking, or when they were old enough to come this far on their own.

Eliza glanced back at Ruth before facing the cabin. "Hello?" she yelled.

A moment later the wooden door opened slowly and a Plain woman stepped onto the stoop. "Kumm." She motioned.

Eliza strode toward the cabin. "Ma'am, you shouldn't be here."

The woman tilted her head, looking serene. "But weren't you looking for me? After all, you brought my quilt."

Ruth blinked and rubbed her eyes. The woman looked to be in her sixties, but she resembled a younger Auntie Rose. Ruth had once found a picture of her great-aunt as a younger woman, the forbidden image hidden away in a box with old papers. The resemblance to that photo was striking.

"Are you a . . . ?" Ruth couldn't make herself say *ghost*. That was sacrilege. She and Eliza should get out of here. But if they left now, wouldn't they wonder forever what was going on?

"Auntie Rose?" Eliza went up the steps.

"My name is Mercy." She moved back a foot or so from the entryway. "But I am part of your family that came over from the old country. Do you not recognize me? As little ones playing here, you called me your guardian angel."

Chills covered Ruth from head to toe. As an adult, whenever she had memories of seeing a guardian angel, she'd discounted the experience as the vivid imaginations of children.

Eliza hesitated at the cabin door.

This was too spooky. "Eliza, please," Ruth begged. "Let's go home."

Her sister touched the wooden frame. Was she as unsure if this was actually happening as Ruth was?

Mercy beamed, the skin around her eyes crinkling in smile

lines, making her look even more like Auntie Rose. "It's okay. Whenever I meet someone for the first time, they're always surprised. But soon everything makes sense to them. I have the teapot on to boil. Kumm, sit with me."

Eliza followed her through the door. Ruth peered inside.

The cabin looked the same as when they were little— a one-room home with a stacked-stone fireplace and an over-size hearth with a black teakettle hanging from a crane. No beds or stove. The only difference between now and when they were little was a fire blazed in the hearth and steam rose from the spout of the iron teakettle.

What was happening?

Her heart pounding, Ruth reached for her sister.

Chapter Ten

Eliza stared at Ruth's hand on her arm. This didn't feel real. It was like something out of a dream. Her gaze slid to the quilt, the one Ruth had draped around her shoulders—the one Mercy said was hers. The multicolored intersecting stripes looked more vibrant than usual.

Mercy traced her finger along one of the stripes. "You know, the women in your family were quilters even before they were called Amish. They brought quilting and other fiber crafts with them to this new world, working on this very quilt while on the ship that brought them to this new country."

This at least rang true. There wasn't a woman in her family who didn't do some sort of weaving, sewing, or quilting for more than just the clothing they and their families wore.

"The women on that ship prayed night and day as they sewed on this quilt, grieving over loved ones who died before setting foot in America, holding fast to faith despite what beset them. That first year in this new land was unbearably difficult. Soon Ayla realized that before boarding the ship, she'd made a wrong decision—thinking the men had enough guns and ammunition, she removed her flintlock revolver and the cartridges from a pocket in the folds of her skirt and traded it for dried meat that went bad before the journey across the sea was half over. That decision had her family, their beloved Ebersol friends, and the settlement on the verge of starving. Once she unwound all the decisions it took to get to this land, she realized the moment of her mistake, and we prayed over that fervently."

We? Had Mercy been a woman who crossed over to this land with the other women or a guardian angel who'd joined her faith with Ayla Bontrager's?

Mercy smiled. "I asked God to give Ayla a few minutes to go back and fix that one decision—to choose the best thing, a gun and cartridges to keep with her so it wouldn't be swept downstream as they crossed rivers. A sole remaining gun in the bitter winter of 1742 was their only chance at survival. While weeping and praying, she snipped a thread on the quilt, and all were saved because of it."

Wait, did Ayla actually go back and fix *the decision she'd made in the past?*

"Now I'm here to offer you the chance to go back and fix something in order to move forward without unbearable pain. But know this—there is always pain. That is unavoidable on this planet."

Ruth took another tentative step into the cabin. "How . . . how can this be?"

The woman tilted her head. "Didn't your relative who passed this to you explain?"

Ruth's brows furrowed. "Auntie Rose told me beautiful stories about the quilt. She even spoke of Ayla but told different accounts than you've shared. She said nothing about the quilt having any kind of power, and she never breathed a word about time travel."

Eliza removed the quilt from her shoulders. "On my wedding day, she said I could use it once to go back in time, but I thought . . ." She shrugged. "I . . . didn't believe her. I didn't think of her words again until after we lost Penelope." Even now she felt unsure exactly what had been said. Her mind reeled back to her wedding day. She and Auntie Rose were alone in the washhouse, and her beloved great-aunt passed Eliza an unfamiliar, heirloom quilt. What were Auntie Rose's exact words? *If you ever need it, you can use this quilt to go back in time once and fix an event. All you have to do is take this quilt to the old log cabin in Hunters' Woods and restitch one of the threads to go back to a previous moment in your life.*

She met the woman's clear blue eyes. "Have I gone mad?"

Mercy smiled. "Today is happening, child. I'm here; so are you. Come sit and spread out my quilt. I'll pour the tea."

Eliza walked toward the large table, Ruth at her elbow. She pulled out one of the wooden high-back chairs and took a seat. Her sister did the same with the chair next to hers, sitting on the very edge.

Ruth's leg bounced under her skirts. "Eliza, I'm curious too, but this is getting weird. We should go."

Eliza couldn't recall ever feeling so strange, but she shook her head. "What if this is exactly what I've been praying for? I can't leave now."

Mercy placed an earthen clay mug in front of each of them and one for herself at the empty spot at the table across from Eliza.

Eliza shook out the quilt and spread it across the center of the table. Mercy poured steaming hot liquid in each of the cups, and the fragrant smell of black tea filled the small space.

"So if I restitch one of the threads, I can go back in time?"

Mercy sat in the chair across from Eliza and lifted her mug, blowing at the steamy drink. "That's right. Do you know what you want to change?"

Eliza picked at one of the white threads with her fingernail, fiddling with it but not breaking it. "I want my daughter to live."

Mercy gave her a sad smile. "I'm afraid it doesn't work that way. Her fate was already written when she was conceived. There's nothing to change in the past that would let her be born without the disease and still be *her*. You could go back and try to have a different child."

Eliza's heart sank and it was hard to breathe. "If I did that, we'd still have the curse between us." Her mind churned with rolling thunder and thick clouds. Hundreds of thoughts pelted her like drops of heavy rain, but one stood out above the rest. "I have to go back to the creek the day I told Jesse I would marry him and say no to his proposal."

Ruth seemed to be yelling *no* at her, but it was muffled as if a pillow covered her mouth. Mercy pulled a soft, solid brown cloth from the bib of her apron. The fabric seemed to be wrapped around something.

"Eliza." Mercy put the cloth in her lap and leaned in. "I want you to listen to me. Hear my words. If you do this, it's done."

The word *done* hit Eliza like a bolt of lightning in the storm of her mind.

Mercy studied her. "You can't restitch the same thread again. You'll have to continue on, traveling your new path, and it'll be as if this life never existed. Are you sure?"

Eliza looked at Ruth. Her sister had grown quiet, as if she was no more than an observer now. Eliza could spare all of them so much pain—Jesse and Penelope. Ruth and Andrew. Her parents. Jesse's parents. How could she choose anything different than to save all of them from their pain? To save herself? She was drowning in the grief and it would never be okay again.

Eliza touched the thread. "I'm sure."

Mercy put the cloth on the table and opened it, revealing its contents. It held two sewing needles and a pair of old scissors. She held out the rusty scissors. "Then break the thread, Eliza."

Was that all there was to it? Eliza took the scissors and plucked the now-glowing white thread, breaking it.

"Eliza!" Ruth grabbed Eliza's arm, her face horrified. "No! What are you doing?"

"What I need to do." She *had* to take this chance of fixing things.

Ruth's objections muted to a murmur Eliza couldn't make out, as if her sister were far away.

Mercy held out a needle. Eliza took it.

The two sides of the fabric were coming apart now. What would happen when she put them together? She put the thread that was attached to the quilt through the eye of the needle to restitch what she'd broken. Odd, but the thread was long enough to be able to restitch that same spot. How was that possible? The needle didn't look that different from the usual needles she used, save for a slight glowing gold color reflecting from the thread.

She plunged the needle through the two pieces of fabric.

In an instant, Eliza was standing in a creek. She blinked. The evening light was jarring after coming from the dark inside of the cabin. Cool water flowed over her bare feet and she wiggled her toes.

She looked up to see a young man skipping stones in the creek. Her breath caught. Jesse. Mercy was right? Eliza was really back in time.

He grinned and leaned in close. Wow, he looked so young. No beard, and his eyes didn't show him carrying the weight of the world yet. She'd do anything to keep it that way.

"No way you can beat eight jumps. I'm the winner today."

These moments were so etched in her memory. Maybe her most cherished memory other than their wedding day, and she was about to break it.

"Jah, guess you are."

He jolted, blinking. "I'm surprised, Eliza. Usually you're way more competitive. But I'll take the win." He winked at her, and the familiarity of the gesture threatened to knock her over. How long had it been since they teased each other like this? And after today they never would again. "Would you care to sit on the riverbank with me?"

Her stomach lurched, every part of her rebelling against what she had to do. How was she going to turn him down? "Sure."

When they did this the first time, they'd been soaking wet and laughing. Now neither of them spoke as they moved to sit on the riverbank.

He cleared his throat. "I think a cabin would go well right over there." He gestured up the hill to an open spot in the green valley on his family's side. Their cabin site. Would he end up building anything there without her? "Then we wouldn't have to walk far from the creek to be home."

She licked her dry lips. "You should build a cabin there for you and your future family."

He gave a short laugh. He was so adorable when he was nervous. "Well, I've been thinking about the future. Thinking a lot, actually. What I'm gonna do and all. You know that I've been working the job with Frank over in Hillsdale."

She hated herself more with every word he spoke. But she had to do it. She *had* to. Even if it hurt him now.

"I want to bring the business here to Calico Creek. Englischers love the cabins, and they're simple enough to build, as far as homes go." He continued on about building cabins, just like the first time, but she couldn't hear him for the roar in her head and heart.

He tapped his fingers on his knee. "It will take at least three years to apprentice with Frank and then several more to build my own business here in Calico Creek. During a good portion of that, I'll be gone more than I'm home." He glanced at her and she tried to keep her face neutral.

"Any woman would be blessed to be with you. You're incredible, but I—"

"I'm just going to say it," he blurted out as he turned to face her. "Eliza . . . I want to build a life with you. No one else. I love you. I have for a long time. Maybe I always have." He swallowed. "Marry me?"

Her chest hurt. It was time for her to lie to him. Every part of her mind rebelled at doing this. But what else could she do? *I love you, Jesse.* "I'm sorry."

His face darkened.

"I can't be with you like that, and I can't marry you. You're my friend, but that's all. You know that our families can't marry."

He grabbed her hand. "Eliza . . . the weird superstition that some of our family members have doesn't matter. The only ones this is between are you, me, and God, and I've prayed about this for years. We'd be great together. We'll build a strong family."

If only that were true. "I'm sorry. It hurts to say it, but my mind is made up. I can't."

He dropped her hand and turned away to look at the stream. "Was it . . . all in my head? I thought you felt the same about me."

Tears gathered in her eyes. *Stop it!* She had to follow through, break the thread, and close this door. "It's not been in your head. We've both thought things and felt things at times. We've allowed daydreams, and I apologize if I led you on. I care for you as a friend, but nothing more." The lie tasted sour as it came from her mouth.

"I . . . see." He stood. "I'm going to go home now."

Wait! Her heart was screaming at her to stop him. She wanted to stand, spin him to face her, and give him their first kiss. She bit down on her tongue as her heart pounded. *Stay the course.*

Jesse slid his shoes on his wet feet, not even stopping to clean any dirt off, and then walked toward his family's home.

Eliza flopped backward on the riverbank, tears flowing. She closed her eyes. What now?

It felt as if she were being spun around. She opened her eyes, and she was sitting in the old chair in the cabin, the quilt and a steaming mug of tea in front of her. That was it?

Ruth shook her shoulder. "Eliza? What happened?"

Eliza's tears dripped onto the quilt. The seam she'd ripped was now closed by a glowing thread, the needle still in her hand.

"I'll finish that for you." Mercy's voice was gentle. She reached out for the needle and Eliza gave it as quick as she could. Her mind reeled. That had been awful. She'd never imagined what it would be like to boldly lie to Jesse or the confusion and hurt such a lie would cause him. But she'd been gentle in her about-face turn, hadn't she?

"Ruth, I did it. I went back in time." Eliza followed each of Mercy's movements as she tied off the glowing thread, using every bit of the thread. Had the thread grown and then shrunk according to their need of it?

"How? We've been sitting here. I feared something

would happen, but you simply sewed that quilt and started weeping."

"Trust me. I went back. I felt and saw everything. I turned Jesse down."

"What?"

Mercy removed a small needle case from her pocket and opened it. "You'll feel a shift too, Ruth, as soon as you leave this cabin." With slow care, Mercy placed the needle in the case and closed it. "I've never had two people come to me at once. But I'm glad you're here with your sister. I have a feeling she's going to need you."

Eliza touched the newly sewn stitch. "What will our lives be like now?"

"You'll have to go and see. You changed a big event from many years ago. This is a first for me too. Every other woman who changed something chose a more recent memory."

Whatever it was, it had to be better than subjecting Jesse and Penelope to the pain that'd been their lives before. She'd deal with the consequences.

Ruth stood, her palms facing out. "That's *real* reassuring."

Mercy tucked the needle case back into her pocket. "I wish I could tell you more. Your lives will be whatever you put into motion."

"Let's go, Ruth." Should she take the quilt? It'd been in the family for hundreds of years, and perhaps another Bontrager woman would need it one day as Eliza had. She put it around her shoulders, leaving as she'd arrived—cloaked in the soft, powerful fabric. She took a deep breath, stood, and walked to the cabin door. Time to see what her new life was.

Ruth pinched the back of her hand. "Maybe this is all some weird dream."

Eliza shook her head. "This is as real as anything I've experienced. Mercy . . . thank you. For this chance."

"I hope it brings you the peace you're searching for, child."

Ruth offered Eliza her hand. "I'm still hoping this is a shared imagining."

Eliza took Ruth's hand and together they stepped out the cabin door and down the steps. Eliza's head spun.

Ruth stumbled, grabbing on to a tree to stay upright. "What was that?"

"The shift, I think." Mercy was right—*shift* was the best description.

Eliza looked around. The woods still surrounded them, and the cabin was still there.

Ruth rubbed her temples. "I feel . . . different."

"Me too." Eliza's hand drifted to her stomach. It felt flatter, like how she remembered it prepregnancy. They stood in silence as Eliza gathered her thoughts and emotions. Finally she was ready to sort a few things out. "Ruth, what do you remember from our lives before the cabin?"

Ruth lowered her hands. "I still remember you marrying Jesse . . . and Penelope dying. But now there's other stuff too. It's like I have two sets of memories now, although some of them are fleeting, like butterflies I can't catch."

"Me too. I think right after I turned Jesse down, I moved to Ohio to live with Auntie Bette in her home on the square of Apple Valley."

"It seems—" Ruth studied her hands as if they didn't feel real—"that I joined you in Ohio about a year later."

Eliza rubbed her forehead. "That sounds right. Remember how part of Auntie Bette's home was set up as a small shop for selling textiles? I'm pretty sure we've done a lot of weaving on her loom, making cotton and wool fabric and sewing quilts and scrap blankets."

"Jah, I kind of remember that too. But I'm pretty sure you've been running that store and making textiles while I've been teaching at the Amish school. I think a teaching position opened there for me when I was seventeen, and that's why I moved to Apple Valley."

Eliza's thoughts were a thick fog as memories of parallel lives she'd lived ran through her mind. "That seems right to me too."

Ruth looked at the ground. "I don't think Andrew and I are together here."

That would make sense because in this timeline, Ruth had been living in Ohio, so how would she and Andrew have met? "I'm sorry, Ruth." It was for the best, though Ruth couldn't understand that right now. Her sister and Andrew didn't need to chance going through what she and Jesse had with Penelope and the two losses before her.

"Ruth, did we tell Auntie Bette we were coming home for a bit? I know we've come home from Ohio fairly often on Saturday night before a between Sunday, so I didn't bump into Jesse at church, but did you tell the head of the school board that you'd be gone for a few days, or do you have to be back for the next school day?"

Ruth lifted her shoulders to shrug, but she didn't lower them. "I don't even know what day it is."

"I think it's Saturday, the same year, month, and day we were on when we went to the cabin with Mercy."

Ruth looked as displeased as she was confused. "That makes sense, I guess."

Her sister shivered and Eliza reached for the quilt around her shoulders to give it to Ruth. But it was gone.

"The quilt." Eliza looked behind them, searching where they'd walked, but saw no sign of it.

Ruth glanced at Eliza's shoulders before also searching the ground. "Wait." Their eyes met. "You didn't marry Jesse, so Auntie Rose never gave it to you."

Eliza nodded. "Maybe so."

Ruth took a deep breath. "Let's go home, to our parents' house. I'll call Auntie Bette and nonchalantly see what she knows of our plans. If need be, I'll call the school board person, whoever that is. But right now, we need to go home to Mamm and Dat's and figure all of this out."

"Not yet. I need to see something first. If the cabin Jesse built for us is gone, then I'll know I was successful."

A fresh start. No more grief and pain. Could it really be possible?

Eliza closed her eyes. Her heart still felt like it was breaking in two for missing Jesse and Penelope. Would that ever fade?

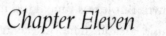

Chapter Eleven

Jesse slid his shoes off beside the creek. It'd be freezing this late in autumn, but after being on his feet all day during the busy gathering at his family's home, the cold water sounded like a balm. He touched the stream with a toe. It was like ice. He smiled. Younger him wouldn't have hesitated. He plunged his feet into the dark water speckled with yellow and brown leaves.

"This is a long hike from your parents' place. You sure you want to build all the way out here?" Martha stepped over some briars, the thorns catching on her dress. She pulled it free with a hard yank.

"Jah. It's the right spot." He picked up a smooth, flat stone, tested the weight by tossing it in his hand, and then skipped it across the top of the water. How many times had he done this as a child? It'd been so long though. Since Eliza turned him down. But it was time. He'd moved on. Now he intended to build a cabin here, just as he'd always wanted to do.

A memory floated to the surface—him and Eliza as children, play-fighting in the water before going to their separate homes and getting in trouble. It never stopped them though. He shook his head. He'd never understood why Eliza cut all ties to their friendship so abruptly and then left Calico Creek, never responding to his letters or phone calls, but . . . whatever.

That wasn't the only thing that hadn't worked out for him. Owning a construction company that built prefab cabins hadn't panned out either. He'd hit too many roadblocks, including the ongoing health issues of too many men in Calico Creek. But with Frank's financial backing through Mulligan Builders, Jesse had built four cabins in the area, bringing some temporary work to his community. He and Martha would rent one of those cabins until Jesse got this cabin built.

Jesse breathed deep, taking in the sounds and smells of the mountain. It'd taken him a while to learn the most important life lesson: being flexible with his hopes and dreams was the key to everything that mattered.

Lose the girl of your dreams? Grieve for as long as necessary. Accept it. Move on. Although, in truth, he had a grudge against Eliza that he'd appreciate being able to voice if given the chance. Still, anything positive about that relationship as well as anything grief-filled was water that had gone under the bridge long, long ago.

Don't own a thriving construction business as hoped? Do the next best thing: work for a wealthy general contractor who deeply respects you. Jesse had worked his way up to being Frank Mulligan's right-hand man, and he had the title and pay of a construction superintendent. It wasn't his construction business, but he built good, solid homes for a living, and that was a large part of his dream.

Haven't started a family by twenty-nine years of age? Find a beautiful, amiable young woman and ask her to marry you.

Martha leaned over the bank, looking at the rocky stream. "I can't believe you're standing in that cold water!"

He pulled from his thoughts. "It feels nice. Care to join me?"

She grinned. "Since I don't want my toes to fall off my feet, no, I think I'll keep my warm shoes on." She lifted her skirt slightly and wiggled a foot in the air. Too adorable. They didn't know each other very well yet, but he knew marrying her was a good choice. He'd thought he'd known Eliza really well and look how that had turned out. Now three of his younger siblings had already married ahead of him. It was time.

He stepped out of the creek to join Martha on the bank, pointing to the clearing. "I can do it. I'll build us a cabin here. Though I won't be able to finish it before our wedding next month." Why had he waited so very long to build? It wasn't that he didn't have the money. He had a good job and lived at home in the small apartment he'd added on to his dat's workshop. He gazed at the spot for the cabin. "It'll be done by the end of summer."

Martha nodded. "If it's too much to add to your workload,

we're in no hurry. The cabin we'll rent will suit us just fine for an indefinite amount of time. Most of my friends who are getting married this fall are living with one set of parents." She shrugged.

He sat and slid his socks and shoes back on. She seemed content with whatever worked out in the way of living arrangements. But he liked the idea of building a cabin here. At twenty-nine, the only thing written in stone to him was it was time to marry. Past time, really. He didn't want to be single and thirty years old next year.

"Oh, hello." Martha waved at someone.

Jesse pushed to his feet. Had someone wandered over from the family gathering?

Eliza. She was walking up to the clearing Jesse had been pointing to, her sister Ruth trailing behind her. Eliza froze like a doe in the field as her and Jesse's eyes met. How and why was she here? She'd moved off to her aunt Bette's in Ohio eight years ago. He was sure she returned to Calico Creek from time to time, not that he'd seen her. But why would she choose to visit home during his family's reunion? Her mamm or dat would've told her the Ebersols were having a gathering this weekend—and why of all places did she come to the creek? This wasn't her family's land. She had no reason to be here. Annoyance rose, and he fought to push it down.

"Can I help you, Eliza? Did ya forget the woods after so many years away and get lost?"

She flinched. "Uh, no. I'm sorry. Just going for a hike."

"Lots of other places to hike."

She studied him as if trying to see things inside him

that were none of her business. He bristled. "Cat got your tongue?"

She closed her eyes, looking hurt. "Okay." She looked at him, smiled, and nodded. "I hear you, and I'm sorry I bothered you." She grabbed her sister's hand and hurried off in the direction she came from.

Good.

Was he out of line to have no patience with her? Declining his marriage proposal was one thing. Ending their friendship and treating him like he was a plague was another. Eight years since he asked her, and this was the first time they'd come face-to-face. She'd responded to his proposal exactly as her folks and the ministers would've wanted her to. It'd been his greatest concern for them come true.

"Who was that?" Martha studied his face.

He forced what he hoped was a peaceful look. "My old neighbor. Amos and Dorothy's oldest daughter." His heart pounded with anger. She'd not responded to his letters or returned his calls about them remaining friends. Who did that? Someone who needed to be set straight, that's who.

"Jesse?" Martha touched his face, bringing him back to her. "What's going on?"

He drew a deep breath. "Sorry." He cupped his hand over hers. "I didn't mean to make you feel awkward. Eliza and I . . . well, I thought we'd be more, and so I pursued her, and she rejected me."

"Hm, sounds like her loss then." She smiled at him. "And my gain."

He grinned. "Denki. Guess things worked out better for all concerned."

Ruth's head rushed with disjointed thoughts as she pondered what had just taken place at the creek. Jesse with someone else. Him barely civil to Eliza.

Andrew. Her heart thudded with panic. What would become of them? Had he found someone else too? Eliza sobbed, and Ruth rubbed her back as anger warred with her desire to comfort. When would Ruth get a chance to sob and maybe scream? Eliza had turned both their worlds upside down with her restitching. *All* their worlds, even if Jesse didn't know it.

When they'd caught a glimpse of Mercy as children, they'd believed she was their guardian angel. What kind of "angel" let a grieving woman make such a drastic change? Maybe they'd been deceived by something much worse. Bewitched.

Eliza wiped her face on her apron. "He . . . didn't know who we'd once been." Her voice wavered. "His reaction to me was as if . . ." Her pupils were huge, much like they'd been each time she'd experienced the trauma of loss. "As if me turning him down really happened. I mean, I knew I'd said *no* to him all those years ago. I was there. I experienced breaking his heart. But somehow it still feels as if it never happened." She closed her eyes and drew a deep breath. "Above all else, it just feels wrong."

Ruth wanted to shake her. How could Eliza have chosen this? She and Jesse had worked for years to be together. "It feels wrong because it *is* wrong." She reached into her hidden apron pocket, hoping to find a tissue for Eliza. Instead, she pulled out the leaf she'd stuffed into her pocket while playing croquet with Andrew. She had to find a way to get back to that time, back to him. "We're in over our heads. We need to go back to the cabin. Or at least find someone in the family who knows something that can help us reverse this."

Eliza shook her head quickly, brushing tears from the corners of her eyes. "No. Remember, Mercy said when it's done, it's done. But if you dragged me back to cabin to see Mercy, I'd make the same choice. I would have to. Why can't you see that as hard as this is, it is the right thing for everyone involved?"

"Everyone?" Ruth pinched the bridge of her nose. "You can't possibly know that. We need to see what your choice has done before we can know that." Would it matter what they discovered? "I'd like to tell you what little I do know, except I can't tell anymore what memories are from this new time or from our previous lives."

Eliza straightened. "Jah. That's true for me too. Let's go home."

Dead leaves crunched under their feet as they went through the familiar forest, and the sound of movement from small animals in the underbrush filled the air between them. Songbirds sang as if history hadn't been rewritten. Nothing had changed here. The trees were still the gold, red, and brown colors of every October. The air still smelled of the familiar scent of the damp fall leaves.

Dat and Mamm's house waited in the valley in front of them, a puff of white smoke coming from the chimney. The scene was familiar, but it felt very different.

Andrew . . . She should've finished telling him how she felt, not that it would matter now. But she would've gotten it off her chest. Could she find him again? What if she found him and he wasn't still single? Ugh. What a mess.

"Eliza, you remember how I used to be really into reading newspapers at the library?"

"Jah." Eliza stepped over a fallen log.

"Once I read an article about this thing called the butterfly effect and chaos theory."

"What's that?" Eliza paused and turned to face her sister.

Ruth shaped her hands into butterfly wings and moved them up and down. "The butterfly effect means that if a butterfly flaps its wings in Chicago, the wind disturbance could be enough to cause a tornado in Japan."

Eliza blinked. "That sounds impossible." She turned and began walking again.

"Jah, so did time travel until today." Ruth followed her sister, wishing this were a dream and she'd wake at any moment. "Besides, the example I gave is more an illustration than literal. But the article explained that chaos theory has been proven, and science says that one seemingly insignificant change can have a ripple effect through *everything*, resulting in a huge difference."

"A ripple effect?" Eliza looked at her own hands before lowering them. "I don't think we're dealing with science here."

"Maybe not." Ruth stepped on a briar before it could catch the hem of her dress. "But we should be prepared."

"For what?"

They came to the edge of the woods and paused.

"For everything to be different."

Eliza gestured at the forest behind them and the sprawling valley in front of them. "It doesn't seem that different. The leaves still fall. The woods are the same." She motioned to a tattered rope of an old tire swing, hanging from one of their favorite trees. "And there's Mamm and Dat's house, same as ever."

Ruth rubbed her temples. Had it yet dawned on her sister that it wasn't just Mamm and Dat's house? It was now Eliza's house too. She no longer had a home of her own. "You didn't think all of this through."

Eliza hurried her pace toward their parents' house. "Everything is fine. You'll see. The only difference is Jesse will be happy. You saw him with another girl. He's moved on just fine."

"No beard. He's not married. And he didn't look that happy to me."

"Look, whatever happened during the last few years has to be better for him than three of his children dying and a future that follows that pattern until we're too old to conceive."

Ruth moved her tongue over her teeth, biting back some words that would only hurt Eliza. Her sister wasn't listening. They had to deal with whatever alternate present Eliza had made.

The rest of the walk went quickly, with no more conversation.

As their home came into closer view, reality pressed in on Ruth. Everything about the homestead spoke of poverty. Eliza kept going as if she hadn't noticed. Ruth picked up her pace, staying at Eliza's heels.

"Mamm?" Eliza called as she opened the creaky side door to the kitchen. Ruth followed her.

The kitchen looked . . . worse than usual. The paint on the wall peeled from ceiling to floor. Was the wood-burning cookstove the only oven they had? Dat had purchased a gas range and fridge a few years ago and had a large propane tank installed out back.

Mamm dried her hands on a threadbare dish towel. "Where have you two been?"

Eliza closed the door, the squeak echoing in the kitchen. "We went for a walk in the woods."

Something was wrong. Ruth studied her mother closer. "Mamm, have you been crying?"

Mamm sighed, wiping at her eyes with the back of her hand. "Is it that obvious?"

"What happened?"

"Moses came home after losing another two-bit job. He's passed out again in his old room."

Ruth's and Eliza's eyes met. Ruth's stomach sank as the right memory became clear. Moses had never gotten clean.

Chapter Twelve

The light from a kerosene lamp scattered the darkness. Eliza stood in front of the floor-length bathroom mirror in her underwear. Eerie strange. Yesterday her postpartum body had dark stretch marks, a rounded lower belly, and a belly button that never went completely back in. Now . . .

She eased her hand across her flat, unmarked stomach. She had a body that never carried a baby. As much as that made her insides ache, it was better for Penelope. Better that she'd never been born than to have suffered as she had, struggling to breathe, writhing about until her strength was gone and she drew her last breath.

Knowing Penelope hadn't suffered brought Eliza comfort. No doubt. But in this new time, her daughter had never existed, which meant Eliza and Jesse had never experienced the joy of her existence. They'd never shared the amazing, inexplicable bond that happened simply because they had created a being no one else on this planet could. Until this moment, she hadn't understood the depth of emptiness that she would feel because Penelope never had a moment of life inside her.

Yet there was nothing to grieve because Penelope had never existed.

The emotional overload was too much. She needed to keep focused on the pain she could prevent Jesse. Another wave of grief threatened to overwhelm her. To drown her. Jesse with someone else . . . Her heart broke at the thought, and cherished memories flashed through her mind. Long walks. Deep discussions that strengthened them. Hot meals shared. Nighttime treats snuck into the bed. Giggles. Laughter. His warm lips on hers . . .

"Stop," she hissed.

The new reality was she'd never lived that life. Whether the memories faded or not, she'd chosen this new path. She could do this. She *had* to do this.

Eliza dressed quickly. The sun had yet to rise. After securing her prayer Kapp, she took a deep breath and said a silent prayer. Today was a church day. She couldn't recall whose home the meeting would be held in, but she dreaded seeing Jesse and that young woman again as much as she hoped to sneak unnoticed looks at each of them, who would be on opposites sides of the room—the men on one and the women on the other.

She closed her eyes, steeling her emotions. She'd changed things for good reasons, and she needed to keep reminding herself of that. Time to wake Ruth and get to work setting to right anything that had been wronged through going back in time.

She picked up the lamp and padded down the hallway.

"Ruth." Eliza put the lamp on the nightstand, sat on the edge of the bed, and touched her sister's shoulder.

Ruth flipped away from Eliza and pulled the covers over her head. "Go away, Eliza. You've done enough damage."

Fair. But Ruth's anger wouldn't fix the situation with their brother. "We have to talk to Moses."

Ruth pulled the covers back and glared at Eliza over her shoulder. "I hardly slept last night, hoping that the whole thing was a dream, but even now, barely awake, I know I'm not that fortunate."

If it took years for Ruth to forgive her, it was still the right decision. But they had to get to work making things right with Moses. "I'm sorry you're struggling, and I hope to make it up to you soon. But Moses needs us to work together. I have a plan. We need to look at everything that's now different for the worse. Then we can apply the same solutions that worked in our original life. We need to figure out how to undo the poverty the community is stuck in, but the most pressing issue is Moses. Since working for Jesse is what helped Moses originally, I'm going to get him a job with Jesse again."

Ruth sat up, frowning at her. "Considering how he feels about you now, how's approaching him possibly going to help?"

Her sister's words caused fresh hurt. Did Jesse hate her? She steadied herself. "I'm going to make it work out. I can convince Jesse."

Could she?

Ruth shoved strands of hair behind her ear, radiance from the lamp glimmering against the natural highlights in her brown hair. "Right. Well, you'll be on your own with that. I need to see what pieces of my life remain."

Eliza hadn't banked on Ruth being this angry. But they were sisters, and they could work through this. Right?

"Okay. Did you get a chance to call Aunt Bette last evening?"

Ruth tsked. "Of course. She'd assumed we'd come home to Calico Creek, but she'd been unsure. Apparently we just disappeared on her, and in your eight years and my seven years of living with her, we hadn't ever done that. I apologized profusely, assuring her that you and I got our wires crossed, neither one of us realizing we were leaving without forewarning her. I told her we'd be here for a few weeks, maybe longer. She's sending us our wallets with our cash and debit cards that we forgot along with various quilts and blankets you'd told her you would take with you the next time you came to Calico Creek, to see if you could sell them in town."

"Where?"

"Don't know. She said you'd know, so I dropped it. And I called the deacon because I sneakily got Aunt Bette to tell me that he's the head of the school board in Apple Valley. I hate this game, Eliza. The one where I pretend everything is normal while trying to understand who I am in this timeline. Anyway, I told him I needed at least a month off in order to have some time with Dat, who isn't looking well."

"He doesn't look good." Eliza rubbed her forehead. "That

part wasn't a lie. Mamm told me that he had a bout with pneumonia this fall and hasn't been able to take off much time to get better. She says he's improving." She fidgeted with the wick raiser knob. "Listen, at least come talk to Moses with me."

Ruth grumbled as she got out of bed. She left the bedroom and went down the hallway in the dark. When she returned, she sat on the bed and fixed her long locks into a tight bun, and she readied herself without a word or glance to Eliza. Had Ruth forgotten that Eliza had lost three babies and was sure to lose more if she and Jesse remained married? Was the puppy love between her and Andrew all that mattered to Ruth? Well, *puppy love* wasn't a fair term. Still, compared to all the pain Eliza was sparing Jesse, it seemed that Ruth could try to put it into perspective.

They stepped out together into the hallway of Mamm and Dat's old farmhouse. The first rays of sunlight eased the darkness, and the sounds of younger siblings filled the air. When they went downstairs, Mamm was banging around in the kitchen and the two littlest ones—five-year-old Becca and three-year-old Noah—were on the tattered sofa. The preteens, John and Peter, were on the marred wood floor, playing with marbles. She didn't know where the teens—Levi, Annie, and Naomi—were. Maybe tending to the few animals they should have as an Amish family—the horse, milking cow, and laying hens.

Eliza had forgotten how worn and threadbare everything had been before Jesse brought good jobs to Calico Creek and Andrew's investigation caused the company to pay out restitution. Eliza couldn't think about all of that. Mamm had said last night that Moses was passed out in his old room. Time to get coffee and tackle this day.

Ten minutes later, Eliza carried a tray holding a mug of steaming hot coffee and a plate of warm scrambled eggs, buttered toast, and two extra-strength Tylenol. She'd go wake Moses gently, then tell him her plan. She could get him a job with Jesse, just like he used to have. And with that sense of purpose etched in Moses' heart, he'd be able to get clean, and she'd help in any way she could. He would be fine. Besides, if he were bringing money into the home, that would help solve some of the poverty issue Mamm and Dat were living with.

She balanced the tray carefully as she walked down the hall to Moses' room. Someone sighed behind her and she glanced back. "So you decided to help me, Ruth?"

Ruth frowned, following Eliza with her arms crossed. "Seeing Moses is part of my need to determine how bad life is now."

"Like I said before, I know how to get him clean. Trust me, he'll be fine. He has it in him."

Ruth glanced around the hall before stepping forward to speak in Eliza's ear. "We need to be focused on one thing and that's fixing the timeline. Find the quilt. Find Mercy. Though that name is hardly befitting of her. There *has* to be something we can do."

Whispers returned to Eliza: *"Eliza, I want you to listen to me. Hear my words. If you do this, it's done."*

The words brought little comfort this time. "No. Remember, she said it's done. For better and worse, we have to figure out how to make our lives work here."

"I can't give up yet. I have to believe there's something we can do to fix things."

"Ruth, I fixed the most important thing."

"Did you? Did you really? Look at this place. Our family is a wreck."

"There are events I didn't consider, but it can't be on me and my relationship with Jesse to fix everything and everyone else. We'll have to find other ways without me being with Jesse."

Arriving at Moses' door, Eliza balanced the tray between her left arm and hip. Ruth made no motion to help her. The knob didn't move. Shoot, it was locked.

Ruth banged hard on the door with her balled fist. "Moses, can Eliza and I come in?"

"Ngghh," came a muffled reply.

"Okay, I'm opening the lock." Ruth took a few brisk steps down the hall to remove a long and thin metal rod from the doorframe over the hall bathroom door, the opener that worked on all the old indoor locks in their parents' house. She walked back to Moses' door and used it to jiggle the lock to open, the door swinging wide. Ruth gestured for Eliza to go in. "All you, Eliza."

Eliza took a deep breath and gripped the tray firmly with both hands, stepping into the bedroom. "Moses. I want to talk to you about something. I brought you coffee."

Moses sat up slightly in bed, rubbing his head. "Eliza?"

"Ruth is here too." Eliza glanced over her shoulder at Ruth. Her sister was waiting in the doorframe, arms crossed again.

Moses smiled. "Glad you two are home. Mamm could

use the help on the house. Just let me know what you need, and I'll help you fix up whatever. Just give me a little time to wake up." His speech was slightly slurred. How long did alcohol affect the body?

Eliza sat at the end of the bed, setting the tray beside her. "Moses, this isn't you. I know you've been drinking. Mamm knows too. It hurts her to see you like this."

Moses looked away, scratching his head. "You've been gone a while, Eliza. It's not like that. I'm just tired, is all."

"I can smell it on your breath."

Ruth took a step into the room. "Moses, we're not *that* naive."

He looked from one girl to the other. "I appreciate my sisters' concern, but it's really none of your business. I'm just extra tired from my last job and sleeping it off at home."

Eliza touched his knee. "What is your job right now?"

Moses picked up the Tylenol and reached for the coffee. "It just ended."

"Mamm said you were fired."

He looked down, then at the ceiling, and then at the left wall. Anywhere to avoid her eyes, it seemed. "Abel Byler and I had a difference of opinion. I can't help it if he overreacted by ending my contract. I'll find something else."

"Moses . . . let me in. Let me help you. We used to be so close."

"Jah, a lifetime ago." He swallowed the pills with a gulp of coffee. "Thanks for breakfast, Sis."

"Really, I have an idea. You remember my, uh, friend Jesse? I can ask him if you can work with him on cabins. I think it would be really motivating for you."

"Who's he working for again?"

His question pierced her heart. "I . . . I thought he owned his own business building cabins."

"Nee. He built three or four cabins nearby somewhere, but he works for someone else."

Who *was* he working for? And why? She cleared her throat. That wouldn't matter as far as Moses getting help— just working with Jesse was what really put Moses on the right path before. It could happen again. It *had* to.

"I'll handle asking him. I just want your word that you'll do your best. No drinking, okay?"

"Of course. It was the last time. Promise."

Chapter Thirteen

Ruth stared out the window of the hired car. Rain droplets raced across the glass. The rigs belonging to her folks either leaked or didn't have working wipers. While deciding what to do, she'd gone through her closet and drawers, finding enough money to hire a driver to go to Andrew's parents' house with some cash left over. Her stomach churned and it wasn't due to car sickness, or even the unpleasant town smell that overpowered the fragrant, fresh bread sitting in her lap.

The financial well-being for Andrew would be the same, right? It wasn't like he'd depended on working for Jesse like Moses or her dat had. Andrew was a journalist who worked for the *County Times*. His dad operated Amish buggy ride tours on the town square. Andrew and his family should be untouched by Eliza not marrying Jesse. All Ruth knew for sure was that in this version of reality, she and Andrew never spent Eliza's wedding day paired as a couple, so they'd never gotten to know each other. Without that, they'd never spent time at the library researching, reading newspaper articles and talking about them at length, never played word games to see who could win, never worked crossword puzzles together. What if he had a girlfriend? Or was already married? Surely it wouldn't be that far-fetched. If he was, what would she do?

Yesterday, after church and following the after-church meal, Ruth had returned to Hunters' Woods and the cabin spot, looking for any possible clues that would help her undo this change of time. She'd scoured the cabin and grounds, but she'd come up empty-handed. No sign of the quilt or of Mercy.

The car slowed to a stop at a red light. "What's that smell?" Ruth asked the driver. Maybe if she struck up a conversation, it would ease her nerves.

The driver chuckled and glanced at her in the rearview mirror. "Calico Creek. Our fresh Appalachian Mountain air." His voice dripped with sarcasm.

"It's not the feed mill, is it?" It couldn't be. Calico Feed Nutrition had been forced to clean up their act years ago. Breaking the story of the feed mill's toxicity was Andrew's start in journalism.

"I guess you live way out in the country. 'Course it's the feed mill." He shrugged, accelerating as the light turned green.

"But they cleaned up."

"Cleaned up what? It smells the same as always. Today it's not as bad as usual. Rain clears the air, and that seems to help, but it stirs the smell that clings to the asphalt and such. It'll pass as we get off this street."

This wasn't good. After she and Andrew met at Eliza's wedding, he'd begun research into the feed mill. He spent untold hours per day for about six months doing the research that broke the story concerning the health of people who lived near the plant or worked at the plant. This meant Calico Feed Nutrition had done nothing to clean up the toxins, paid for no one's health issues related to the plant, and reimbursed no workers for the surplus of days they were out sick due to the toxins.

What about the ten or so people who'd developed lung disease and cancer? Who had footed their bills?

Thoughts continued to swirl in Ruth's head. Was Andrew even writing for the paper? What had changed that he didn't investigate the feed mill? Or maybe he did, and somehow it didn't have the same effect.

After the driver pulled into Andrew's family's gravel driveway, Ruth exited the car, holding her bread. She'd baked it before leaving, unwilling to show up empty-handed to his parents' house.

Hurrying because of the rain, she went up the wooden steps to the white front porch with chipping paint. Chaos theory in practice. And nothing had turned out better so far.

She tapped on the door.

A woman in her sixties answered. Andrew's grandmother, Sarah. Ruth had met her at the family gathering . . . the one she'd been at with Andrew before Eliza and Mercy altered everything.

The woman's eyes crinkled in a smile. "Good morning."

"Hello." Ruth returned her grin. "I'm one of Andrew's, uh, friends. I'm looking to speak to him." She had no way of knowing what all was different in Andrew's life, and all the introductions she'd practiced in the car had fled from her brain.

Sarah's smile fell, just slightly, before one side of her mouth curled up. "Are you now? Please come in."

Ruth stepped inside and wiped her shoes on the mat.

Sarah turned over her shoulder. "Lois, Deb, we have a visitor." She patted Ruth's hand. "You have to understand, we've been hoping a young Amish woman might come and ask about our Andrew. I'm Andrew's *grossmammi*, Sarah. It's been my prayer for years. I had a dream a young woman showed up."

Ruth tilted her head, asking nothing but needing to know so much.

Sarah winked at her. "See, I need someone to bring him back."

The words sent a jolt through Ruth. *Bring him back.* That meant Andrew had left the Amish. His grandmother wouldn't have worded it like that if he hadn't. Once he'd even told her how close he'd come to leaving. In this reality he really left? She didn't need to ask herself how so much had changed. The beating of the tiny butterfly's wings had become a hurricane that had wrecked the whole town. If Andrew wasn't Amish, that could explain why he never wrote the article that exposed the toxic conditions of the feed mill. How many more people were sick now because of it? She had knowledge no one here did—she *had* to help them!

Andrew's mother—Lois Ebersol—came into the room,

wiping her hands on her apron. "Oh, hello." She smiled at Ruth. No light of recognition entered her eyes. It dawned on Ruth how odd her relationship with Andrew had been. Since Eliza's wedding, Andrew and Ruth had met at the library off and on for years, but since they'd had no interest in marrying and meeting his family would've given the wrong idea, she hadn't met them until a few hours before Eliza went back in time and changed everything.

"Excuse my messy hands." Lois wiped her hands on her apron one last time. "We were just finishing up canning some apple butter."

Another woman Ruth knew, Lois's sister, entered the room—Deb. She looked similar in the eyes and facial features to Lois.

"I'm so sorry to drop in like this and interrupt. I'm Ruth Bontrager. I was hoping to get in touch with Andrew." She held out her offering of bread. "My family is neighbors to some of your relatives."

"Ah, one of the Bontrager girls. Your folks live on the ridge."

Ruth nodded. "That's right."

"I'm sure we've met at some point during one of the gatherings for both districts, but I don't recall it."

"My sister and I have been living in Apple Valley for the past several years."

"Ah, that's right. I remember hearing about that, so if we have met, I haven't seen you for quite a while."

Deb's and Lois's eyes met, and Ruth was sure they would ask how she knew Andrew.

Lois turned back to Ruth and took the bread from her.

"This looks delicious. We need a break anyways. Care to share some of this bread with us, topped with homemade apple butter?"

"That would be lovely."

Ruth followed the women to a large pine kitchen table. Rain still pattered against the windows. Sarah brought plates to the table. Lois and Deb made small talk while one sliced the bread and the other slathered each piece with fresh apple butter. Ruth was unable to fully focus on what was being said. Andrew had left the Amish . . . now what was she going to do? And not just for herself; she owed it to the people of Calico Creek who were sick. Could she help them without him?

Andrew's grandmother tapped her fingers together. "We need you to go to Penn State University and bring him home."

Wait. How much of what was being said had Ruth missed? She put her hands up in front of her. "I don't know if I could do that. I was just hoping to get in touch with him." *He probably doesn't know me.* The awful thought caused her heart to ache. But she couldn't reveal he didn't know her—or else it'd look too suspicious, her coming here asking to see him.

Lois gave a sad smile. "We know nothing is guaranteed, Liewi. But a mother has hope."

Deb nodded. "And an aunt has some funds."

Funds? "I can't take your money." This wasn't the conversation she thought she'd have.

Deb wiped apple butter from the corner of her mouth with a cloth napkin. "It's just a little we've all set aside to cover travel expenses to and from the university. It's a two-hour drive by car, almost a hundred miles from here."

What was the right answer here? If she agreed to do this, she'd probably be giving these women false hope. Andrew in this timeline had been at the university. Educated. How many years had he been gone from the Amish community? "What year is he in?"

The women looked at one another. Lois seemed to suddenly understand the question. "Oh, he started at Penn State two years ago."

No way on earth would he leave school in his second year to follow a random Amish woman back to a home he'd left for solid reasons. He could even have a serious Englisch girlfriend. That thought made her feel nauseated, and she set the unfinished slice of bread on the plate.

It was wrong of Ruth to lead these women on and say that she knew him. "Lois . . ." She swallowed. "I have to confess that Andrew doesn't know me."

Lois set her slice of bread on her plate. "Why are you asking about speaking to him, then?"

"I just . . . I can't fully explain it. If I tried, you'd think I was crazy. But I very much need to speak to him." It *was* a need. Something inside her was driving her forward, even to embarrass herself if she had to. If she spoke to him, perhaps she could get a few pieces of this world back on the right track.

Andrew's grandmother cleared her throat, staring at something in her lap. "I think she's the one."

Lois studied her mother. "From your dream?"

Sarah nodded and made eye contact with her daughter. They shared a smile, looking a bit hopeful.

Lois leaned in closer to the table. "It sounds like he really needs to speak to you also. Please, take the funds we set aside for this. Whether you fail or succeed in getting to speak to him, you can bring back anything you don't use. We insist. Here, I'll write down his dorm address and the address of the college. He's in the school of journalism. Someone on campus should be able to point you that way if you can't catch him at the dorms."

"Please don't give me money. I can pay my own way." Could she? She had found enough money in old purses this morning to pay a driver to come here. That's where her plan ended. She still had a little money, but until her wallet arrived with her ID and banking information, she had no way of getting money out of the bank, assuming she had money in this new life of hers.

Andrew's grossmammi reached out to take her hand. "We insist."

Andrew squinted at the LSAT study guide. The harsh lights in the library didn't help as the words started blurring together. He closed one eye and tried to reread the sentence. A second-year journalism student preparing to take the law school admission test needed to study for a crazy amount of time.

"Something wrong with your eye?" Anh tapped the eraser end of his pencil on the table.

Andrew sat up straight in his uncomfortable library chair

and rubbed his temples. "Nah, just getting a headache for some reason."

"Man, we've been here for three hours. Got here when it opened. I think that's reason enough. Time to give it a rest." Anh slammed his study guide shut, the pages making a loud smack that reverberated through the historic library. A girl at an adjacent table shot them a glare. Anh waved at her, and she rolled her eyes before turning back to her own book.

Andrew flipped through the pages of his hefty study guide. *Simple and Easy Prep* was definitely a misnomer. "To me, the test is coming up too soon. I'm not ready."

"Dude, your writing is awesome. You're gonna ace it."

Andrew shook his head. "Writing, I can do. Especially arguing on paper. It's the logic games section I'm stressed over. They're not the sort of puzzles you think about while growing up giving rides to tourists in Amish buggies. In fact, most of my life I had to ignore logic in order to stay focused on the practical."

Anh scratched his chin. "Um, I'm not sure it worked. We've been sitting in this smelly library on a beautiful Monday morning while being miserable. It's nearly noon, and I'm hungry. I very much question if *this* is practical."

Andrew chuckled. "Well, yeah, there's that." He gently closed his study guide and slid it into his book bag.

"You coming to the multicultural festival Kappa E is throwing starting this afternoon? My girlfriend's all excited about us each wearing cultural clothing. She'll wear an ao dai from our home country."

"Does she miss living in Vietnam?"

"Nah, I don't think so, but it's good to honor our roots. You could break out your Amish duds."

"Ah, no." Andrew put up a hand. "I don't think I'm ready for that. I'm glad to put that part of my life behind me."

Anh shrugged. "Sorry. Didn't mean to bring up anything painful. I just meant that everyone comes from somewhere. It's part of our stories. You'll be telling your origins when you become the first ex-Amish lawyer. And then senator."

Andrew pulled his book bag into his lap and zipped it up. "Ha. I'm positive I'm not the first. And I still don't know if I'm cut out for politics."

Anh stood, pushing in his chair. "You'd be a lot better than much of what we have now. You actually care about standing up for the little guys. Isn't that why you started here?"

"Yeah. I wanted to be a journalist. Then the reality of student loans hit me, and I realized I have to be able to make money to pay back those loans."

Anh grimaced. "True that. See you in psych class tomorrow?"

"See ya." Andrew stood, shaking one leg and then the other from so long sitting on the hard chair.

The girl who'd glared at his friend earlier gave him a shy smile and gestured to the empty chair in front of her. Maybe she'd overheard enough of his conversation with Anh to feel he might be interesting . . . or perhaps a lawyer one day. He nodded at her as if he hadn't noticed her invitation to sit. He wasn't interested. It'd taken enough to break out of the marriage-obsessed mindset he'd grown up in. He wasn't willing to step into that world among the Englisch. Still, he struggled, feeling isolated and out of place. Little things bothered him throughout each day, like rarely understanding the pop culture references in his textbooks. Anh understood them, and he'd spent half his life growing up in another country. But Andrew was fairly sure he felt miserably out of sorts and out of place because he missed Ben. All the time, actually. Here at Penn State, Anh was his closest friend, and yet he'd never met the guy's girlfriend or gone with him anywhere other than classes and study groups. That certainly wasn't very close to be his closest friend.

Maybe he should go to that festival.

Chapter Fourteen

Eliza knocked on the thin metal door of the mobile home, the office for Mulligan Builders. Finding out where Jesse was building houses had been easy. Dat had known that information. Getting to Brush Hollow *hadn't* been easy. Between the rain, traffic, and fighting to find this place, it'd taken her close to two hours by horse and buggy. She'd made several wrong turns along the way. Adding to those things was her challenge of driving here in a buggy that leaked and had bad wiper blades. She'd covered her coat and head with an old tarp to stay dry and sat on the edge of her seat to be able to see. But the rain had stopped about thirty minutes ago.

Did Jesse drive here and back each day using a rig? Did he hire an Englisch driver to get him back and forth from home in Calico Creek? Maybe he lived in Brush Hollow now.

Her heart ached over how little she knew about his life for the past eight years. Dat hadn't offered any info about him, and she feared she'd break down crying if she asked too many questions.

Could she hide her feelings while trying to get a job for Moses?

She drew a deep breath and was about to knock again when a woman's voice called out, "Kumm in."

Eliza opened the door and stepped inside.

The young Amish woman who'd been with Jesse at the creek held the handset to a tan landline phone to her ear. She held up an index finger, indicating she'd be with her in a minute. A large desk at the center took up most of the room. Various stacks of paper filled the corners of the desk. Office supplies as well as building supplies were leaning against the walls here and there. Eliza had never been in this office before, but it looked familiar. The messiness was definitely Jesse's office workspace. Although she couldn't see the items, she was sure she knew where his set of plans would be as well as the notes from contractors and the separate ones from the contracted home buyers.

An unfamiliar ache twisted through Eliza. Why? She drew a breath. Eventually the old memories would fade. It was good Jesse had found someone. Good for them both. No curses involved.

From what she could tell, Moses had listened when she'd confronted him about his drinking problem. He'd prayed with her twice yesterday and today and had helped Mamm around the home.

It was so weird living back with her parents. But she'd

figure out the rest of her life after she first fixed things for Moses. And maybe Ruth. Would Ruth ever forgive her? They'd barely spoken since early yesterday when they went to Moses' room. But over time, they could rekindle their sisterhood and closeness. She knew they could.

The young woman hung up the phone, smiling. "Oh, hello." She closed the gap between them. "You're Eliza, right? I'm Martha Peight."

"Jah. Good to meet you." Eliza forced a smile.

"Come on in. I was just organizing some of the paperwork in this office, if you can call it that." Martha winked and motioned for Eliza to follow her to the desk.

A few foldable filing cabinets were wide-open—that must've been what Martha was working on.

"I'm so sorry to bother you—and I know this sounds odd, but I need to talk to Jesse. It's about my brother Moses. See, I just came back to Calico Creek, and it's obvious Moses needs a job. I was hoping he could apply for a job here? Being around Jesse might help him . . . find himself again."

Martha nodded. "We do have a posting for a job, but it seems rather odd for a sister to ask about her brother getting a job. Does he want to work here?"

Eliza pushed a string to her prayer Kapp behind her shoulder. "He agreed to work here, and he's a good builder. Knows his way around tools from the time he was a little kid. He and Jesse used to build tree houses."

"It sounds good to me. Jesse is *so* underwater on this neighborhood. Have you seen it? Huge beautiful homes. Lots of work, and half of the crews are out sick!"

"I haven't seen it, no. But I think Moses could be a big help."

"Jesse is the man to see about any hiring with Mulligan Builders."

Why did Jesse still work for Frank Mulligan?

Martha grabbed a set of keys out of the desk. "I could go with you to find Jesse."

"That's kind of you and would be very helpful." It was going to hurt more than walking through fire. But she'd do it. She was the one who'd changed the path Moses was now on.

Martha pulled a sweater from a peg on the wall and slipped it over her dress. "He's out on lot forty-six. It's about a half-mile walk. I might could flag down a worker using a golf cart to drive us."

"Walking is fine with me." She and Jesse used to walk every day. Walking, talking, laughing, and dreaming . . .

Martha went to the door and held it open for Eliza. "Great! I'll point out some of my favorite houses as we walk that way. This subdivision was abandoned by the original builder back in 2008 when the economy crashed. One home had all the framing done when the builder walked off, leaving it to the elements."

Both women stepped out the office door. Eliza went down the steps of the trailer.

Martha locked up and joined her. "The lot the house sat on was great, but the framing was ruined with mold and rot from sitting in the elements all those years." She gestured to her right, and they walked in that direction. "Mr. Mulligan wanted to bulldoze the whole thing, including taking the foundation up, covering it with dirt, and making the lot a green space. The blueprints for the home that matched the layout of the foundation were gone, just another thing lost in the economic bust. But Jesse saw the potential, even with the erosion around the foundation. He poured everything he had into fixing the foundation and creating a set of plans that used that particular footprint. He felt the homeowners who lived here deserved someone to make right what the devastation of the economy did to their half-built community." Martha stopped. "This is the one."

Eliza studied the magnificent home with its tall columns, porticos, and glistening windows. She couldn't remember ever seeing a more beautiful place.

Martha motioned toward it. "I offered my two cents here and there when he was designing the floor plan. It's a private residence now or I'd take you through it." She sighed contentedly. "In another life, I think I would've liked designing house plans."

Despite the ache that threatened to swallow Eliza, she loved knowing that Martha enjoyed home building. A perfect fit for Jesse. Eliza smiled even as her heart lurched. "Maybe you and Jesse could do that for a living."

Martha shook her head and began walking. Eliza fell in step with her. Martha buttoned her sweater. "Well, unlike that one, the house plans come from Frank Mulligan, and Jesse sticks to the plans. Besides, Jesse and I know that after marriage, I'll be too busy to even consider a career. Lots of family expectations."

Yeah. Eliza knew. Ones that she had been unable to fulfill by having healthy babies. Pain twisted in her gut again for the loss of Penelope. Had Eliza ever gone a single hour without mourning her?

Martha fidgeted with the keys she carried. "We're getting married in three weeks. Not sure if you heard or not."

Eliza stopped walking, unable to breathe as new revelations or perhaps just a deeper revelation hit her. She'd grieve her losses endlessly—the loss of him, their marriage, their friendship, their dreams. Meanwhile, he would spend his years enjoying all of those things, never a day marred by the grief she had to live with.

Martha paused, looking at Eliza with such innocence. "Actually, to be precise, it'll be in twenty-four days."

Snap out of it! Eliza forced her feet to move so they could continue walking, but she couldn't make herself return Martha's smile. "Congratulations."

Why hadn't anyone told Eliza he was getting married in a few weeks? Then again, no one in her family would consider it important news. To them, she'd never gone on one date with Jesse. The echo of pain inside her threatened to make her knees buckle.

"I'm sorry—I didn't mean to be thoughtless or rude." Martha rattled the keys, mindlessly playing with them. "Jesse told me what happened between the two of you and how his feelings were not returned. I assumed that it wouldn't bother you that we—"

"Of course, Martha." Eliza put a hand on the young woman's shoulder. *Put your smile on.* "I'm sorry. It was just surprising, but I'm very happy for you and Jesse. Truly." She was. And she wasn't. In either case, she tried to mean her words. Martha was so sweet. She'd be great for Jesse.

No dead babies.

No heartbreaks.

"Jesse?"

Eliza's clear voice. He continued using the nail gun, popping nails into the half-finished wall. He wanted to tuck behind the cinder block wall he was attaching a frame around and avoid her altogether. But if anyone should be embarrassed, it should be her for trespassing at the creek during a family reunion. She had to have known he might be at the creek that day. Still, after eight years of never running into her, her presence had caught him off guard, and his knee-jerk reaction was rude. Could he muster an apology and a kinder response to whatever she needed? He had to try.

"Jah?" With the nail gun in hand, he stepped away from the wall. His eyes moved to Martha.

She grinned. "I thought you'd be at this house."

"As always, you have good intuition."

Martha giggled. "Or maybe I just knew what construction site needed you the most."

"Eliza." He straightened his black felt hat. *Don't look at her face. It'll hurt less.* "I only have a minute. We're down several people, so if you could make this quick, I'd appreciate it."

Goodness, how was that an apology or a kinder response?

Martha nodded. "Eliza is here about the job posting."

He blinked at his fiancée. "Eliza is going into construction? I suppose this could be interesting."

"Jah, give me a nail gun." Eliza held out her hand, smiling.

The hairs on the back of his neck stood. Should he play along? It felt like he was inching his way out onto a half-frozen lake. Which misstep would cause it to shatter and for him to yet again be over his head with her? He laughed and held out the cordless nail gun. "Sure."

She didn't take it. "Moses really needs a new job. He's even worked in construction before. I think you know how good he is."

He set the nail gun down and took in a deep breath. Moses was trouble. More so than Eliza probably realized. She'd been gone from Calico Creek for so long. There was no doubt that during family visits with Eliza, Moses was on his best behavior, but Jesse personally knew better. "Uh, I don't know."

"Jesse, you have the privilege to hire whoever, whenever, and we need people so bad."

Jesse looked at his future wife. "Martha, you're missing a piece of the puzzle. Moses has . . . some problems."

Eliza held up her hands. "I know. But he's going clean. He's prayed with me, and we'll keep that up. I'm helping him. He just needs a job."

Did she not know? "That's not all he needs, and I'm doubtful it's the first thing on the list of things he needs. His reputation isn't great. He's been seen drinking on the job, and he's stolen money from at least one of his jobs."

Concern crossed her brow. "I didn't know. I'm sorry that happened."

"You don't have to apologize for your brother's actions. But you can see why I can't hire him for the job, no matter how desperate we are."

Martha jiggled the keys. "If he's a drunk, he needs to join a group, like AA."

Jesse cringed for Eliza's sake. The phrase *a drunk* was a harsh one, but Martha had never met a word or subject she hesitated to discuss. If it crossed her mind, it left her mouth. Despite this awkward moment, he liked that about her.

"Martha." Jesse said her name gently, hoping she'd refrain from saying anything else.

"What?" She shrugged. "Ain't no shame in it. My dat used to be a drunk—not in my lifetime, but two of my three older siblings recall seeing him drunk. He's been clean for twenty years and still goes to meetings every week. He's not afraid to talk about the daily battle. I know he'd be glad to talk with your brother, help him find a group and a sponsor."

"Denki, Martha." Eliza's eyes closed for a moment. "That's very kind and helpful. I'm sure you're right." She stepped closer to Jesse, her brown eyes pleading as she looked up at him. "He also needs a job, not just any job, but one with you. I know I'm asking a lot, and you have no reason to want to go out of your way to help me. But I'm asking anyway. You remember Moses. He's *good*. He's just made some bad choices. I can't explain it, but I have this strong feeling that if he comes to work for you, he'll get back on his right path."

Jesse took a half step backward. She was right. This was a lot to ask. He glanced at Martha. She gave a little nod, wanting him to use his position to help someone he'd grown up beside.

He removed his hat and ran his hand through his hair. What was the right call here? It seemed that every other business around these parts had given Moses a chance. He'd left Corner Cabinet in a lurch by not showing up on a big job. Stolen money from a different company. Came in late so often that even a laid-back boss Jesse knew had fired him. But Eliza was putting herself out for her brother. Being vulnerable. Jesse couldn't crush her.

"For you, my childhood best friend, I'll offer him a job." He held up a finger. "With a few conditions. One, he has to come here this afternoon and interview with me himself. I need to see that he's not on anything that would impair his judgment. It can be dangerous work. Two, you have to babysit him until I know he's a safe hire."

Eliza raised an eyebrow. "Babysit him?"

"I can't be expected to keep my eye on him. I have dozens of men, numerous subcontractors, and several houses being built at once. He'll be given a task on one jobsite, and I move from home to home as needed. I can have a little peace of mind and faith in his staying out of trouble if you're watching him."

She nodded quickly. "Jah. Okay. I can do that."

"And lastly, Mamm and Martha could really use some help with wedding preparation."

A flash of what looked like pain twisted her face. "You . . . you want my help with your wedding?"

He shrugged. "I heard you took your skills and apprenticed with your aunt on weaving and quilting. Do you not still sew?"

"I do." She regained some composure, gave a really bad fake smile, looking as if she might tear up. "Of course I'll help."

Her behavior made absolutely no sense. She'd had no interest in him, so why would it bother her to help his mamm get ready for his wedding day?

He looked at Martha before turning his attention back to Eliza. "You know how many quilts each mamm is supposed to have ready to give the couple on their wedding day. Add to that the numbers of suits and new dresses for Dat, herself, and my siblings that she needs to make. She's really feeling the pressure."

Eliza glanced at Martha, then at the ground.

Martha gestured toward a set of makeshift steps that led to the second floor. "I think I'll take a quick look at the progress that's been made to the upstairs." She gave a little shrug and went up the steps.

"What's on your mind, Eliza?"

The strings to Eliza's prayer Kapp fluttered in the breeze, and she pushed them over her shoulders. "Listen, I know you're angry with me for leaving town like I did all those years ago. Before I left, whenever you came home, I spent every moment I could with you, and I shouldn't have. That's my responsibility, my fault, and I'm sorry."

He hadn't done anything wrong by asking her to marry him that day all those years ago. She hadn't done anything wrong to turn him down. But she'd nailed his issue with her—he was still angry that after turning him down, she fell off the face of the earth.

"How could you have known what my feelings for you were? I was the one who made sure you were dating others, the one who pretended to not care." He replaced his hat and drummed his fingers against an exposed wood board. "It's not your fault." Did their going separate ways mean anything to her? Maybe so, based on her face. It had undone him. He thought he'd never put himself back together. But maybe this wedding was also a new start for their friendship.

Martha came back down the stairs, her eyes meeting his.

He nodded at her before looking to Eliza. "I didn't mean to sound angry at the creek. It's all water under the bridge that flowed many years ago. We're adults. We can be friends again. It's okay." He stepped forward, put an arm around Martha's shoulders, and gave them a little squeeze. Then he offered his other hand to Eliza.

She shook it.

The moment her soft skin touched his, he saw flashes of . . . her and him. Laughing together and splashing each other in the creek, clothes soaking. Walking down well-worn trails in the woods, talking and dreaming of the future. Snuggled next to each other on a warm bed under an oversize quilt, mugs of hot chocolate in hand. Holding her tight while lying in their bed and breathing in the sweet lavender scent of her hair. These were all the dreams he'd had for them. Why did they suddenly feel so real? Almost like memories.

The thick ice he'd placed over thoughts of her was completely shattered, and he was already in too deep.

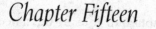

Chapter Fifteen

With a map of the campus in hand, Ruth stepped off the university bus and onto the busy sidewalk. College students milled around her. She swallowed. Wow. How was she going to find Andrew in all of this? Perhaps the journalism area of the university would be smaller. The building should be on this street, according to everyone she'd asked and the campus map she'd picked up at the visitors' center.

"Looking lost there, pilgrim." A blond young man wearing a Penn State sweatshirt grinned at her, his hands in his pockets and a book bag slung over one shoulder.

"I'm looking for the school of journalism. Do you know an Andrew Ebersol?"

He chuckled. "That's cute. There are nearly a hundred

thousand people on campus. Journalism building is up that hill, though."

A hundred thousand? It really was a needle in a haystack. She sighed. "Thanks."

Students crunched through the leaves gathered on the sidewalk. She followed them up the hill toward the journalism building.

This was pointless. Not only was she unlikely to find Andrew, if she did manage that miracle, he probably wouldn't have any time or desire to talk to her. He was at a university for goodness' sake. He'd intentionally left the Amish and their ways far behind him. Now a stranger from his hometown arrived with instructions from his family to try to bring him home. She didn't see this going smoothly.

Ruth squared herself in front of the journalism building. It wasn't the biggest building she'd seen on campus, but it must have a bunch of rooms. Classrooms, she supposed. And offices. She might be better off parking herself in front of Andrew's dorm to see if he came back in the afternoon or evening. It was near one o'clock, but that option was still available. She studied the map and then looked around. Where were the dorms?

"You're a time traveler."

She whirled around to see the same young man she'd asked directions from earlier. How could he tell? Maybe Ruth and Eliza weren't the only people this had happened to?

She stepped closer to him. "What do you mean?" She lowered her voice. "How could you tell?" Did other people know about this ability? Not that she had gathered in all of her time reading at the local library. Did they teach about it at universities?

He grinned wide and snaked an arm around her shoulders, leading her away from the building and back to the main sidewalk. "Dunno. Had a hunch. I'm CJ. What's your name, pilgrim?"

Pilgrim? "I'm Ruth."

"Yo, CJ, who's that?" Two other young men were snickering while walking toward CJ. One had on a red hoodie with symbols. Greek, maybe. The other wore a black jacket.

CJ squeezed Ruth's shoulders. He was acting awfully familiar. She didn't like it. "My new friend Ruth, the time traveler."

The young men's snickers turned into all-out guffaws. Were they all just messing with her? She frowned and stopped walking.

CJ stopped too. "Hey, don't laugh." He tightened his arm around her shoulder. "It's quite serious. The colonies could be in danger. I was gonna take her back to the Sigma house and teach her about the twenty-first century."

How could she be so stupid? These men—no, *boys*—were making fun of her, and she was letting them lead her straight into a dangerous situation. She ducked under CJ's arm, twisting away and stomping the instep of his shoe.

CJ yelped and hopped back on his other leg.

"I won't go anywhere with you!" Her voice rose as if it had a will of its own. "I know you're making fun of me and trying to prey on my ignorance, and I won't stand for it."

One of CJ's friends put his hands up like he was surrendering. "Whoa, whoa, no need to get upset."

The one in the red hoodie nodded quickly. "CJ likes to joke around, that's all. We live at the Sigma Chi house on Beaver Avenue. All he was going to do was bring you back to let you meet the brothers and hang out."

"That's a ridiculous suggestion, and you know it." Ruth walked away.

CJ hurried after her, grabbing her by the arm. "Wait."

Ruth flinched and yanked away. Who did this guy think he was to stop her by grabbing her arm? "Keep your hands to yourself!"

He looked at his hand as if confused that she was offended. "Come on. We're just—"

"Excuse me." A familiar tenor voice was a welcome sound in her ears.

Ruth turned to see Andrew walking toward her in a hurry. Her heart lurched, and it was all she could do to control herself from throwing her arms around his neck in a big hug. That comfort would feel divine right now.

He smiled and nodded at her. Did he recognize her after all? Were there memories from this timeline she hadn't received? She tried to focus on him, on anything that she could determine was real. She could still picture all their times together from their previous lives, but no new flashes sprang to mind. No, she was pretty sure they'd never met in this timeline. How was she supposed to explain any of this without sounding absolutely nuts? She wouldn't believe it either if someone had approached her with her own story last week.

But he still *looked* like himself, albeit in Englisch clothing with an Englisch haircut. Sounded like himself too. Could they connect even here when they had nothing in common? Would they even like each other?

Andrew crossed his arms as he faced the three fraternity boys. Anger boiled in his chest. The woman's Amish garb had caught his attention the moment he'd rounded the corner. He naturally headed her way to see if the outfit was part of the multicultural festival happening later today or if she really was Amish. Then he saw that the three guys surrounding her were laughing. He'd seen that scenario too many times in his life, been caught in it a few times himself—they were laughing at her because of how she was dressed. But when she walked off, the tallest guy physically stopped her while still laughing.

This kind of behavior was disgusting. "Just what do you think you're doing? You may be having fun, but she's *not*, so back off." He pointed at one of the boys' shirts. "You're all from Sigma Chi, right?" The guy nodded. Andrew shook his head. "Wasn't it founded on inclusivity?"

The student in the red hoodie said, "Man, chill. This really isn't a big deal."

Andrew looked them over, trying to memorize identifying features. "What's your chapter president going to think when I tell him you were picking on this woman because of how she's dressed? I know Steven. He's in my econ class."

The woman gestured toward the student who'd grabbed her arm. "That one is CJ. If that helps."

Her accent and clothes made it clear she'd been raised Old Order Amish. But there was no way she was still living Old Order with how she'd stood up to them. Any Amish woman he knew would've been intimidated and far more agreeable.

"Trust us, we were already aware it was time to back off before you showed up." The one in the red shirt smacked CJ with the back of his hand. "Let's go."

The frat boys hurried away. Would they have tried to physically stop him if he'd shown up at school in his old Amish clothing? Probably not. Sexist jerks. He'd definitely be bringing up this incident to Steven.

"Are you okay?" Andrew turned to the young woman, offering a smile. "I'm Andrew."

She smiled back, her brown eyes twinkling in the daylight. She was cute—no—beautiful, even in the Plain duds that tried to hide it. "Ruth. Denki for coming to my rescue."

He shrugged. "Pretty sure I rescued them from you. Don't you know these guys have fragile egos? They have a lot of money invested in school. I want them to be able to finish."

She laughed, and he liked the sound of it. Could he finally have found a friend here who understood his struggles of leaving his family behind?

"Not that you need help, but if you'd like, I'll walk with you. I take it you're looking for the grounds where the multicultural festival will take place later today? I never thought I'd meet another ex-Amish here."

Her smile fell and she blinked. "Ex? No, I'm now and forever Amish."

His heart dropped. "Oh. I see. Then why are you here?" Not just at the college, but in front of the journalism building where he took classes every day. He had a sinking feeling he knew the answer, but he held out hope that she was here as an authentic aspect for the multicultural festival, maybe to answer questions about Amish life.

Her brows knit as if she was considering what to say. "It's . . . complicated. Before I tell you, can you give me your word to simply hear me out?"

He'd heard enough. "No need. Good luck to you, Ruth." He turned and started walking toward the building. He should've known. How could he have not seen through it immediately? The women in his family were relentless. Sending a young Amish woman who was just his type—fearless and attractive. They probably paid her to come here.

"Hey, wait!" Ruth caught up to him. "Could you slow down, please?"

Andrew kept walking. No reason to even listen to her if she was sent by his family to guilt him into coming back. He waved her on. "You're not the first person they've sent. First it was the bishop. Next it was a cousin. Now they've sent a pretty girl."

"Ugh." She made a loud noise of frustration before rushing in front of him and holding her hand out straight, like a stop signal from a crosswalk attendant.

He paused.

She panted. "Look, I won't lie. Your mom and aunt sent me. They gave me money to get here and back home."

"Uh-huh." He sidestepped her.

"Please." She got in front of him again and did the same stop signal move with her hand. "Your family is *not* the real reason I came to find you. Yes, they gave me money, but . . ." She sighed. "It's complicated. Please. Just . . . have a coffee with me. Twenty minutes of your time. Please."

"No thanks." As he went around her outstretched arm, he brushed against her hand. A flash of . . . something . . . entered his mind. He and Ruth were playing croquet.

She laughed. "But you gotta admit—" she swung her mallet, hitting a ball—"the word roquet *is fun to say."*

He grinned, moving in closer. "It is fun to roquet while playing croquet, but you're better at talking about it than doing it."

What was that?

He'd never played croquet with this woman. "I . . ." He shook his head. His imagination was being overactive. "Fine. I'll hear you out. But I'll never go back to Calico Creek." No matter how interesting the ambassador his family sent was.

Chapter Sixteen

Eliza steered the rig onto her parents' long, gravel driveway. Today had been as successful as she could hope for. Yet it seemed hard to catch a breath or see beyond the darkness inside her.

Her body ached as she brought the horse to a stop just outside the barn, detached the buggy, gathered up the lead lines to keep them from dragging on the ground, and walked the horse into the barn.

Jesse was in love. Tears threatened, and she refused them.

After removing the tack, she used a couple of towels to wipe sweat from the horse and gave her a thorough brushing, the whole time trying to convince herself to feel successful concerning Moses. She put the horse in her stall, dumped feed in her trough, and gave her fresh water before hurrying toward the house.

She climbed the steps. "Mamm? Moses?" The tattered screen door clattered closed behind her.

Mamm waved at her from the kitchen. "He's up in his room."

"Has he been helping you today like he agreed?" He'd been agreeable enough since yesterday morning—when Eliza was with him. Then again, it'd been Sunday. Only unavoidable work, like tending the animals, was to be done, whether it was a church Sunday or between Sunday.

Mamm dried her hands. "He said he has a headache."

Eliza wasn't sure she had the patience for this, feeling torn between sympathy and wanting to jerk him up from his bed and scream at him. He was young and healthy. Why was he doing this to his life? "I'll go check on him." She hung her coat on the coatrack near the door and started for the stairs.

"Eliza, wait."

"Jah?"

"I'm concerned."

"Me too. It's why I'm trying to get Moses a job with Jesse. I think it'll really help him."

"Jesse from across the creek? Your and Moses' friend from when you were little?"

"Jah. He works for a construction company."

"Eliza, when I said I was concerned, I meant about you."

"Me?"

"I heard you sobbing last night."

It was true—she had been crying. How could she not be? The loneliness was unbearable. She missed her husband and best friend. Her sister, who'd been cold and distant. And the little passenger she'd carried in her belly for nine months.

"Mamm, I'm fine."

"You came back from your aunt's a shell of your former self. And Ruth is mad at you. What happened there?"

Could she try to tell her mamm? No—the story was too unbelievable. And worse, it could come across like magic or witchcraft. It wasn't. It was an answer to Eliza's unceasing prayers, a gift from God. But it wouldn't sound like it, not to Mamm.

Eliza shook her head. "Nothing happened. I've been focused." That was an understatement—focused on breathing while begging God to help her set Jesse free of a woman who could carry his offspring but couldn't give him a family. "As for Ruth, we just had a misunderstanding. We'll work it out."

Mamm took a few steps closer, studying her face. "I know this look. I've seen it plenty since you moved to Ohio, but never this bad. You're lonely."

Eliza broke her gaze. "I have you and all my family."

"Have you dated anyone?"

"Nee."

"Maybe you should consider it. Attend the singings. You'll be a little older but not too old yet. You never know who you'll end up meeting. It's quite a lonely life sometimes for unmarried women. All women have times of feeling it, married or not, truth be told. But we end up spending a large amount of time tending to little ones, which fills the soul in a way I can't explain."

Eliza had to get out of this room. "Please," she whispered, trying not to cry. "Not now, Mamm."

"The blessing of babies aside, there's nothing like having

a good man in your life, like how I have your father. Don't wait too long, Eliza. Date. Fall in love. Have babies."

She'd never date again. There was no one for her but Jesse. Her hands shook and her eyes stung as she fought to keep her composure. *Hold it together and escape.* "I'll consider it. Denki, Mamm." She forced a smile, turned, and ran up the stairs. *Focus on Moses and getting him well. One goal at a time. Next, get out of Calico Creek and back to Ohio.*

She shook her head, then her arms and hands, trying to make the overwhelming feelings leave her body. She crossed the hallway and knocked on her brother's door. "Moses?"

"Sorry, Eliza, I've had a bad headache this morning. Mamm said I could take the day off."

"That wasn't what we agreed on. Can I come in?"

Some rustling around in his room. "Just a sec. Let me brush my teeth and comb my hair."

Had he not even gotten ready for the day yet? It was 2 p.m. He'd have to be up and on time for this job from now on. And the days began *early*. She heard water running in the attached bathroom and more rustling around. After about five minutes, Moses' door opened. She released a breath of relief. He looked like his old self. Cleaned up, shaved, smelling fresh. He could go interview with Jesse looking like this.

"You're right. I'll come help Mamm now. What was it you wanted to tell me?"

"I went to a subdivision being built by Mulligan Builders. That's where Jesse is working. I spoke with him, and they could really use good help. You need to interview with him this afternoon, and if that goes well, you start tomorrow.

There's one catch though. I have to . . ." How could she word this without sounding offensive? "Accompany you."

Moses nodded. "So just like when we were kids, you're my babysitter. Got it."

Eliza winced. "Well . . . yes."

He gave a short laugh. "It's okay. I understand why. I don't blame 'em. I do got a question for you though."

"Yeah?"

"Why do you care so much? Why go through all this trouble for me?" He seemed unable to lift his eyes from the floor. Guilt was clearly pressing in on him, like he was a dog who'd been caught stealing food from the counter.

Had everyone given up on him?

"You're my brother, for one reason. I know your heart. I saw it the whole time you were growing up. Underneath the man who drinks, I still see that sweet, determined person I grew up with. The need for drink is a liar and a destroyer of dreams, but you are so kind and full of potential."

He drew a deep breath, his eyes never leaving the floor. "I'll just end up disappointing you. Everyone except Mamm has completely written me off."

She put a hand on his shoulder. "Moses, you're disappointed in yourself, and if anyone understands that, I do, although my life may not look that way to you. But I believe with all that's in me that we can dust ourselves off and do better from here forward. There's a woman you'll meet this afternoon, Martha, and her dad struggled with addiction years ago. He's been clean about two decades, and she says he'd be happy to tell you what he's learned. Happy to connect you with others who are determined to stay sober."

He said nothing.

"Moses, you can get clean. I know you can."

He gave a shrug, a slight smile playing across his lips. "I hope you're right."

"I am. I'm sure of it."

She could set this new time right for him. Just like she would for everyone she loved.

Ruth fiddled with the brown sleeve of the paper coffee cup containing liquid that was way too hot to drink. It was after two now, and she should be hungry, but she'd do well to be able to swallow this liquid once it cooled.

She and Andrew had taken a bus to the edge of campus and then walked several blocks to get to this quaint coffee shop. They were sitting at a small round table in the corner of the busy place. The air in here smelled intensely amazing—the fragrance of fresh-roasted coffee beans and baking pastries. College students formed a long line a few feet from them, ordering all sorts of caffeinated concoctions. After she and Andrew waited in that long line, the only item she knew she'd like was regular hot coffee. How did all these people even keep up with what they were ordering? Even with as many books and articles as Ruth had read, coming here into the Englisch world was like stepping into another country. Another culture. One Andrew was a part of and had no desire to leave.

She kept catching him staring at her, looking way too intense to be casual. His eyes darted away again. If he thought she sounded crazy thus far, what would he think once he heard the whole story?

He used the straw in his black iced coffee to stir the liquid, making the cubes clatter together, then took a sip. "I was a bit rude once I realized who'd sent you. I'm sorry."

At least that was a start. "It's okay. I appreciate you hearing me out."

Despite its heat, she took a sip of her coffee, giving herself a moment to gain some courage. Why was she here? Were her motives as simple as needing to see what his life was like in this new timeline and get some help concerning the toxicity of the feed mill? If that was her only intention, couldn't she go about this without telling him about time traveling?

"Ruth?"

"Jah." Her voice trembled. "I'm not sure where to begin or how much to hold back."

He drummed his fingers on the table. "Just tell the whole of it. Isn't that why you're here?"

She hoped her intentions were as pure as she'd thought when she chose to come here, because she knew all too well the result of someone meddling in others' lives. Would she ever be able to look at Eliza and not feel furious?

"I need your help."

"Mine specifically? Unless something's wrong with my memory, we've never met."

Why did he word it that way? Did he have a hunch that this timeline was wrong?

"Jah. You're the only one I *know* that can do it." Oh, boy, she was nervous. She put her hands in her lap under the table and clenched her fists together. "What I'm about to say will sound crazy on so many levels. But I'm hoping you'll believe me, at least enough to help."

He put his cup down and tilted his head a bit as he stared at her, looking intense again.

"About those guys who were harassing me . . . they got my attention because they called me 'time traveler.' And . . ." She took a deep breath. "I am. But not in the sense they were meaning. I come from *another* time. I knew another version of you. We . . . were close."

His eyebrows rose and he leaned back against his chair, a smile breaking across his face. "This is the strangest Amish conversion tactic I've *ever* heard. Please, do go on."

He didn't believe her. This was no surprise. She wanted to yell, *"I don't want to convert you!"* But she wasn't completely sure that was true. Everything inside her was a jumbled mess of longing, anxiety, and fogginess. She had far more thoughts and desires than she knew what to do with. Was this some of what Eliza felt when she shifted the timeline?

"Just listen. I met you at my sister's wedding. Afterward, we loved going to the library, doing research, playing word games together. You worked at *Die Bericht*, the local Amish and Mennonite paper. You also worked for the *County Times*."

He shook his head. "See, your story already has plot holes. The *County Times* doesn't hire anyone to report without a degree. No paper does, not even local ones. It's why I chose to go to school: to have more opportunities. Try again."

"They made an exception because of the validity of your research and the power of your writing. You used that research to convince one of their senior journalists, Rick Bluestein, to work with you. You did most of the work, but you were able to get him on board and join you. A professional journalist pulling for you with his superiors and helping guide the piece gave weight to your story, and together you broke a story that made national news."

He stared at the wall behind her; maybe he was looking at one of the strange multicolored melted-glass artworks hanging in the coffee shop, probably waiting for her to finish.

Ruth steadied her pounding heart. "You're not believing a word of what I'm saying, are you?"

He sighed. "Gotta admit, what you're saying is a hard sell, but I'm not walking out yet. You were outside the journalism building, so I'm sure my mom told you I'm a student. Maybe that's where you got the idea of me breaking a story in a newspaper."

She was in a losing battle.

He shrugged. "Tell me, how exactly did you time travel? Magic powers? You use some of that powwow stuff the really out-there Pennsylvania Dutch used to practice long ago?"

How could she explain the quilt? "Do you remember reading the old book *The Time Machine* by H. G. Wells? We used to sneak science fiction from the library and talk about the stories. I assume you still love books?"

"Everyone loves books."

"You and I both know that's not true. Did you read it or not?"

"Yeah, I read it. Snuck it from the library back when I was a teen, if you must know. Good guess."

"Okay, good. There's this quilt that's passed down in my family. It's really old, from the 1740s. I think it acts like a time machine—or something of the sort. My great-aunt Rose gifted it to my sister Eliza when she married your second cousin Jesse."

"Ah, so we're in-laws *and* dating. How very Amish of us."

She held up a finger. "I don't think I said we were dating."

"Don't you think it's kind of implied if we met at a wedding, were close enough to talk about forbidden library books, and played word games?"

Interesting. She grinned at him. "The wedding took place long before we began dating. Neither of us were interested in dating or marriage, so we only connected as friends for a little over two years before we began dating, often going to the library to research stuff and talk. But on the day that everything went wrong, we'd been dating about six months and were at an Ebersol family event together."

He studied her. "I need to be clear. I'm listening because I'm a journalism student, and the reporter in me knows I have to look at things from a neutral perspective. To accomplish that, I choose to both believe and not believe you at the same time. I'm trying to not outright disbelieve you, but any question I ask doesn't mean that I believe you. Okay?"

She nodded. "Jah, I understand."

He leaned forward, his elbows on the small table. "What happened that day?"

"The time travel day?"

He nodded.

She told him every detail she could remember.

"Where's your sister now?"

"In this new time, our brother Moses drinks a lot. We saw hints of it in the old timeline, but we'd helped him redirect his life through work. So she's trying to help him get a job and get clean again. She thinks that she can undo all the damage she did through changing that one event in time, and she aims to set things straight one person at a time. But that's impossible."

"Yes. You're getting into chaos theory and the butterfly effect."

"That's what I told her."

"How do you know about that stuff?"

"Sneaking science fiction, remember?"

"You're something else, Ruth Bontrager. If you're pulling my leg, points for originality. I never saw this coming."

"So do you believe me or not?"

"That's putting me on the spot with a *really* big story."

"Apologies."

He drummed his fingers on the table. "Even if I did believe you, what do you want *me* to do about it? Seems like it has to do with your family, not mine."

She nodded. "I know. I don't expect you to be able to fix the timeline. But I wanted to tell someone I trusted. Eliza is no help." *And I miss you, you idiot.* "But the pressing thing, and the reason I had to come see you, is about the feed mill."

"The story that made me famous?"

"Jah. You know that Calico Creek Glen, downtown especially, stinks."

"Yeah, that's one of the reasons I don't want to go back."

"There are people who don't have the capability to move. That's especially true for those stuck in generational poverty. They live next to that feed mill, have been getting sick, and can't do a thing about it. My dat and so many other Amish men work there, and it's wreaking havoc on their health. It's not right."

"Plants often stink. It's the nature of the beast. But that doesn't mean it's toxic."

"Do you recall thinking that someone should investigate the plant, just to be sure it wasn't toxic?"

His brows furrowed. "I don't remember that."

"Why do you want to become a reporter, Andrew?"

"I don't." He shrugged. "But I thought I did, and I'd wanted to seek the truth and tell people about it. The problem is there's not enough money in it to cover my student loan debt. I've had no financial support from my parents, and I already have so many loans from getting my GED and working on my bachelor's degree. I'm trying to get into law school now. It's why I'm so stressed and probably have come across as too snippy. Because of how little I started out knowing, I feel I need to stay focused on studying for my LSAT, even though I'm not taking a test for a while yet."

"LSAT? A lawyer?" She blinked. "I didn't know. That's a lot on your plate. I would try this myself, except no one will take me seriously as an Amish woman. Besides, you're the one with the skill to unearth missing information and piece it all together. Originally, you sent out surveys to all the homes within a mile radius, interviewed all who were willing to talk. You compared that information with public records of the health among the general population in other towns in this state. What you uncovered was that a disproportionate number of those living near the plant and working at the plant were sick with serious breathing illnesses and cancer."

He frowned. "Think about what you're saying. According

to you, I was Amish with no formal education at the time, and they listened to me. If so, then they'll listen to you as much as they would me."

It was painfully obvious he was struggling to accept anything she said as valid. She didn't blame him, not really. He probably also thought she was in need of serious psychological help, but at least he was being polite and kind.

"Look, Andrew, I can't piece all the research together like you can. I helped you, but I wasn't capable of doing what you did . . . what you can do."

"I'm sorry. I can't help you."

He didn't understand how serious this issue was. "There's more. When you blew the lid off the air pollution, the authorities also found a thirty-year-old boiler still in use, but it hadn't been serviced in years, so it was really unsafe. They fined the plant for it. If Calico Feed Nutrition has never been made to clean up, that boiler is an accident waiting to happen."

"Yeah. Okay. The time travel thing aside, I see your concerns. Everyone in Calico Creek Glen knows the plant is gross. But no one has ever done anything about it. Let me make some calls. Maybe ask some of my professors what they think. Okay?"

That was a start—he didn't turn her down. "Jah. Denki."

"I'm guessing you don't have a cell phone."

She shook her head. "My family has a phone shanty."

"Give me its number. I'll call you, okay?"

Would he? What would she do if he walked away from her just like he had done his family?

Chapter Seventeen

Jesse inspected what Moses had been working on. This place was an enormous ranch home. The frame was about 80 percent done. When this home was finished, it'd be a marvel, more than enough space for a family of ten. Of course, the intended Englisch buyers probably didn't have eight children. But he could see it—the bones of the home becoming real in his imagination. And the bones looked strong, including the work Moses had done today.

"Everything okay?" Moses asked.

"Jah. We have an entire afternoon of work in front of us, though. Hope your mamm doesn't need you home early."

"Schedule's wide-open." Moses tipped his hat at Jesse. "Just glad you gave me a chance to have a job here."

"Well, keep doing what you're doing, and you'll keep it.

The roofers are going to be at this address in five days and we're way behind. We don't even have all the skeletal walls up yet, let alone the framing for the roof. Then we have to deck that framing for the roofers." Jesse wiped his brow with the back of his hand. It still got warm in the afternoons, even in October.

"Lunchtime," Martha called.

Jesse peered out front and waved. She returned the wave, a picnic basket and blanket in her hands.

Lunchtime, finally. Today was only day one, and he didn't want to get ahead of himself, but so far Moses had been a welcome reprieve to his heavy workload. Jesse looked out front again. Eliza was still sitting on a large blanket, doing needlework while keeping an eye on Moses. She'd moved about a little, mostly outside the house, checking on her brother. But for the most part, she'd been on that blanket since arriving by horse and buggy at daybreak with Moses, working on some kind of scrap-quilt thing, pulling pieces of torn fabric from a soft basket and tying them together.

Apparently her skill for digging in her heels and not budging covered more than just stubbornness about talking to him after their day at the creek. Who could stay put for so long while piecing together a quilt?

Jesse removed his tool belt. "Moses, let's go eat."

"Sounds good." Moses popped a few more nails in the studs before setting the gun on the subflooring.

Martha was kneeling on the blanket beside Eliza, unpacking a basket of ham sandwiches, fresh fruit, and lemonade. An odd feeling jostled around inside him to see the two women chatting freely.

He and Moses walked down the construction-site gravel driveway toward the grassy spot where the girls were.

Moses gestured in Martha's direction. "I like her. How'd you find a good girl like that?"

Jesse shrugged. "Keep working hard, try your best to be a good man, and God will provide." Truth be told, he'd done nothing special. It was funny—from their conversations today, he had the impression that Moses thought Jesse had it all together. But no one had it all together. Seemed to him that most people who didn't fall apart were held together by faith, hope, and a determination to find healing and acceptance and stay in forward movement. That's what had held him together after Eliza disappeared and built a wall around herself. Faith in God. Faith in himself. Faith he could survive and one day thrive. It'd been a long, miserable journey, but apparently a necessary one. Even after all of that, Jesse often still felt like a kid trying to figure out life . . . and himself. Did a person ever feel like a true adult? Maybe after marriage he would.

Martha motioned at Eliza, and Eliza set her quilting to the side. Martha held out a plastic cup to her.

Eliza took it. "You even brought food and lemonade for Moses and me?"

Martha grinned and opened the jug. "Well, it's Moses' first full day. I thought we'd start with a picnic." She motioned to Jesse and Moses. "Come sit."

What was it about hard work that made food taste so good? They ate and chatted for a few minutes.

Eliza seemed oddly distant. She smiled when appropriate, thanked and complimented Martha on the lunch, but it was like her mind was elsewhere. What had happened to her?

As if she noticed his attention on her, she sat upright and turned to Martha. "Congratulations on your wedding. Next month, jah?"

Martha beamed. "That's right!"

"How did you two meet each other?" Moses swallowed a bite of sandwich. "I do enjoy a good first-met story between couples."

Martha sipped her lemonade, nodding. "It was very cute. He basically saved me."

"Oh?" Eliza's curious regard flitted to him, suddenly making him uncomfortable. It wasn't all that cute, and Jesse hadn't saved her.

"It was a hot summer day. I was driving a buggy with my family's most difficult horse, Mousse. You see, all the good horses were being used by my parents and siblings."

Moses held up a hand. "Hold up, your horse is named *Moose*? I love it."

"Yes, Mr. Chocolate Mousse, if you're being formal. So anyways, the other part I forgot to mention is that I hate driving a rig. Loathe it. I'd much rather hire a driver. But . . . I'd spent all my allowance."

"Ah." Moses nodded. "My mamm used to give me an allowance when I was a teen too."

"Well . . . this was last summer, and I wasn't a teen. I'm twenty-one."

Jesse cringed, hoping it wasn't showing on his face. He'd never put it together until now that Martha and Moses were the same age. The little kid, Moses, whom he used to babysit. But an eight-year difference between spouses wasn't unheard of. His parents had seven years between them.

"We talking last-year summer or this-year summer?" Moses asked.

"This year." She squinted at Moses and leaned forward on the blanket. "You are not making it very easy to tell this story. I met Jesse in June. We started dating immediately, and I started working here in July. Now we're engaged."

"In June?" Moses looked surprised.

Martha raised a brow. "For goodness' sake, four months is not *that* short when you know what you want."

"It's not too short at all," Eliza assured her. "Don't worry about him. I think he's just a little jealous." She winked at Martha. "Want to tell us the rest?"

"So Mousse and I were riding down Fox Trail Road, headed to town. You know how that road is really bumpy? Well, maybe you don't since you're not from Brush Hollow. Anyway, I guess I hadn't done a proper job securing the horse to the rigging, and the cragginess of the road jiggled things loose. I was at the top of a hill when the shafts came completely undone. And Mousse, that stinker, kept going!"

Eliza looked worried. "Were you injured?"

"Oh, my cart didn't go anywhere or roll backward. It just rolled to a stop—the shafts against the road acted like brakes, I think. And Mousse decided to get a snack on some plants, so it wasn't like he was gonna run off. I was just sitting there, blanking while trying to remember how to reattach things. That's when Jesse came driving by. He fixed me up and saved me from roasting in the hot sun. We got to talking and found out that we got along pretty well. I asked him out and he said yes."

Moses grinned. "And the rest is not-ancient-at-all history.

We gotta work on your storytelling though. Maybe 'I nearly rolled down a mountain in a broken rig after my unruly horse busted free.'"

Martha laughed. "That would add some excitement." She wiped her mouth with a cloth napkin. "Enough about me. You all used to play and build tree houses together as children? I want to hear about that."

Moses nodded. "Well, Jesse was the mastermind builder. He used scraps, repurposed old stuff, anything he could find. With him as our fearless leader, we managed to build some pretty impressive stuff. Eliza was his muse, inspiring all the ideas, and me . . . well, they let me come up with the secret code words. Riddles. All of that. I still like riddles."

Martha snapped her fingers. "Oh, so if I answer right, I can come into your clubhouse?"

Moses grinned at her. "You got it. Give me a second to come up with a good one." He scrunched his face. "Okay. This riddle is adapted from an oldie. But here goes. Three people buy a home from Jesse here."

It was nice to see that Moses was more or less the same as he'd remembered, personality-wise. Maybe he'd expected to see someone spun out on alcohol. "Why am I involved?"

Moses waved him off. "Just go with it. The home costs thirty dollars."

"Ha. We're talking a dollhouse, right?" Jesse made the shape of a dollhouse-size roof with his hands.

"Shush. So each buyer pays Jesse ten dollars. But upon tallying what he spent on building the home, he calculates and realizes that they overpaid. The home should've only cost twenty-five."

"Got it. It's not a dollhouse. I sold 'em a birdhouse."

Moses seemed to ignore him. "To fix this error, Jesse gives me five one-dollar bills to return to the paying customers. But as I'm walking to their house to give the people the money, I realize I can't split the five one-dollar bills evenly among the three people. Since they didn't know about overpaying and weren't expecting the money anyways, I keep two dollars as a tip and give each person a dollar back." Moses gestured at Martha. "Wouldn't you agree that each person paid nine dollars? They'd each paid ten initially, then got one back, so they each paid nine."

Martha nodded. "Yes, that sounds right."

"What's nine times three?"

"Twenty-seven."

"That's correct. Add the two dollars I kept, and you get twenty-nine. But remember, they paid thirty. Where's the missing dollar?"

"Wait." Martha bit her lip, looking deep in thought. "I . . . hm." She counted on her fingers. Then after several quiet moments, she stood and fished her hand into her hidden apron pocket. She pulled out a crumpled dollar bill, took a step closer to Moses, and pressed it into his palm. "There's your missing dollar. Let's never talk of this again."

Moses howled with laughter, slapping his knee. "Good answer. We gotta let her in the clubhouse, guys!"

Eliza was laughing too. Jesse had missed this. Being together with Eliza and Moses filled a hole in him he hadn't realized was still there. When Eliza disappeared the way she had, he'd missed her friendship, missed their laughter. While in Hillsdale working for months at a time, he'd missed looking forward to going home.

They finished their picnic, laughing with Moses as he brought up more memories of childhood and Eliza filled in the less-than-flattering pieces that Moses left out. Martha was eating up this time together. She fit right in with their group. Was it possible that after all these years, they could be friends again?

No, before he could trust in that again, he and Eliza needed to clear the air. Why did she leave so suddenly and never talk with him? It was one thing if she didn't see him as husband material, but their friendship had been so much more than a path to marriage.

They all were straightening up, putting trash into Baggies and cups and plates back into the picnic basket.

Jesse closed the basket. "Hey, Moses, will you walk Martha back to the office and carry the picnic basket for her? Then it's back to work."

"You got it, boss." Moses scooped up the picnic basket and gestured for Martha to join him.

"Did Eliza tell you about my dat?" Martha asked.

"A little." Moses shifted the basket. "Care to tell me more?"

Eliza started to follow them.

"Eliza," Jesse said.

She and Martha turned.

He gestured from himself to Eliza. "We need a minute."

Eliza's smile faded completely.

Martha looked from Eliza to Jesse and raised her index finger at him. "You be nice."

He tipped his hat. "Yes, ma'am."

Eliza stayed in place, watching as Martha and Moses walked away, chatting about something. "You made a good choice with Martha. It doesn't matter that you met her recently. Your relationship will grow and grow. I know she'll be a great wife and mother to your children."

"Um, thanks." The lighthearted laughter from the picnic had evaporated, and all that was left was awkwardness. "I enjoyed the picnic, and although it's too early to say if Moses will continue proving that he can be reliable, I'm really hopeful I can keep working with him."

"You were always so kind to me, and I really appreciate this with Moses more than I could ever say."

Were those tears in her eyes? Her demeanor, her voice, her eyes all seemed to say the same thing—that she was broken inside.

"Eliza." He stepped closer. He wanted to hug her, but that would be inappropriate, wouldn't it? "It seems we have a chance to repair some of the damage between us, but I'm not interested in going there without some honesty from you. Please. I have to know. Why did you leave? Why did you never talk with me again? I wrote you and you didn't answer. I called your aunt Bette's phone shanty, and you never returned my call. You left, and for eight years you've avoided coming home if there was any chance we might bump into each other at church or an event. It was as if you knew what weekends I'd come home, and you were never here while I was in town. When I learned where you'd moved to, I could've gone to Apple Valley, but you'd made yourself clear—you wanted me to leave you alone. I get that you didn't see me *that* way. You didn't think me worthy of marriage, and that's fine. But you fell off the face of the earth. We were good friends. You were my best friend, and then you were just gone."

She wrapped her arms around her stomach. "I . . . can't explain." Her voice cracked. "But I'm so, so sorry. Believe me when I say you *are* worthy of marriage. You're the best man in the entire world."

"Ach," he scoffed. "That's a little over-the-top."

"No. It's true."

"Then you're saying I wasn't the right one for you? Had . . . you found someone else in Ohio while I was away, traveling for work, telling you to date others? Is that why you moved there?"

She seemed completely baffled. "Didn't we cover this at the creek? That I had no one else?"

He sifted through his memories and shook his head. "I think I would remember that."

She nodded, looking as confused as he felt.

"So you moved to Apple Valley and then found someone, and that's why you refused to respond to my letters or call me?"

"No!" She seemed startled by her response before drawing a deep breath. "We've said enough, please . . . before I say too much."

"You'd have to say *something* before it could possibly be too much." He stared at her. "I'm tired of guessing at what happened and why. Surely you can understand that."

Compassion reflected in her eyes. "I need to live alone, live a life like my auntie Rose."

The single, elderly aunt who had lived about half a mile from Eliza's family? "Alone? Eliza, why?"

A few tears rolled down her cheeks. "I can't tell you. I'm sorry."

His pulse raced and a desire to pull her into an embrace and comfort her tried to overtake him. Instead, he brushed his fingers against her face to wipe the tears. As he touched her skin, images flashed in his mind's eye—marrying her, laughter inside a home he couldn't quite place, happiness filling his days and nights. Then the almost-memory-like thoughts shifted, and Eliza was in bed crying, heartbroken as Jesse held her, stroking her hair. He shifted her onto her back as he kissed her rounded stomach.

They'd . . . lost a child.

He shuddered, tears forming in his eyes. He pulled away.

Why would his mind come up with something that depressing? It was one thing to imagine what happy times they could've had together, but this was something else. Reasoning fled from Jesse, and desire to understand her consumed him.

He cupped her face with his hand. Would he see more? "Do you see that?"

She yanked away. "What?"

"The moving pictures of us together. They're so clear. Like memories. Sounds awful to say, but in the images, I'm holding you after we lost our child."

The color drained from her face as she backed away from him. "I . . . I don't know what you're talking about. I have to go." She hurried toward the horse and buggy.

Why was she running? Had he said something that frightening?

What about Moses? And she'd left her craft basket and

the quilts she was working on. Maybe this was just who Eliza was now. Someone who fled when things were awkward or difficult. But those flashes . . . they'd flooded his heart and mind and emotions. How could he ignore what felt so real?

Eliza's world spun as the horse made its way out of Brush Hollow, through downtown Calico Creek, and up the mountain. She was still breathless as she drove the rig as close to the tree as possible. *Her* tree. *Penelope's* tree. One beautiful, stoic tree that carried life throughout it, had branches that swayed with the wind, changed with the seasons, and hid her loss near its roots but never moved from its spot in the woods.

She brought the buggy to a halt, got out, and all but sprinted to it. In this new time, the trail ended, and the underbrush of the forest kept snagging her dress hem.

She must've looked like a crazy person leaving Jesse calling after her, leaving Moses to hitch a ride home with Jesse. But now that she was here, she was alone on the land. Just her and God.

Dear Gott . . . Her words were breathless. What should she even pray about? How had Jesse seen their memories? It seemed to happen when he touched her face. Why would he dare touch her skin? It had seemed like an instinctual response to her. Did he feel some part of the deep connection he'd had with her over the years? It was the only thing that explained him crossing the boundary of being engaged to one woman while wiping tears from the face of another. She *had* to stay farther away from him so it wouldn't happen again. Somehow she needed to keep an eye on Moses and yet avoid social interactions like the picnic. Be there for Moses only. In less than a month, Jesse would be married to someone else, and he'd never reach for her again.

A huge lump rose in her throat, and she longed to pray, truly seek God. But what should she pray for?

Coming here to this different time hadn't done what she'd thought, and now she'd lost more of her bearings than when Penelope died. She hadn't been thinking straight when she chose to go back in time. Her logic had been full of flaws and holes. Her thoughts again turned to Penelope's whereabouts. Where was she now? Did she still exist in heaven or had she never been conceived? Was it better to have suffered and gone to be with God or never to have suffered because one had never existed?

What did the Word say about babies before they were born? Maybe she could ask the bishop, as long as she didn't raise any suspicions.

She placed her hand on the rough bark of the oak. It felt sturdy. As wonky as this new place was, there were constants. God was here too. *Please, help me let go of what I lost. Let Jesse find happiness with Martha. Keep . . . Penelope safe with you.*

She knelt by the tree and prayed. For Jesse. For Ruth and her anger at what she'd lost. For Moses. And even for herself.

Finally she stood. How much time had passed? It was late afternoon. Had Jesse let Moses finish the workday? Had he sent Moses home early via a hired driver? Or did Jesse drive him home in his rig after work?

She was weary of herself, of her selfish, rash behavior. Was the constant fog she was in impairing all of her judgment and logic or just today's when she ran from Jesse?

One thing was certain: wherever she went, whatever time-line she scrambled, she was still there, as was her grief and fog. She sighed and wiped her tears.

It was time to go to her parents' place before they got concerned about where she was. If Moses wasn't there, then he was probably on the jobsite. He'd figure out what to do to get home. Tomorrow she'd apologize, and hopefully everything would go back to working like it had this morning. Was Martha aware she'd taken off after talking to Jesse? Disappointment in herself pressed in.

Something caught her vision. White among the brown fallen leaves. Were those . . . petals? Like the flowers she'd left for her babies. Eliza took a few steps back and ran toward home. She was hallucinating. Was any of this real? Could she trust her own mind anymore?

Chapter Eighteen

Andrew glanced at the LSAT guide sitting on the corner of his tiny dorm room desk. *"Read me, you dunce. What are you doing?"* the book seemed to say. Andrew groaned. He put his pen down. He'd been taking notes in a small spiral notebook after making calls regarding the feed mill back in Calico Creek. Why was he bothering? He couldn't lie to himself and say he didn't find Ruth interesting, but her story was so far out there it irked him.

He touched his iPhone screen to check the time. Fifteen minutes before five. His roommate, Tom, wasn't due to return until probably around seven. Tom usually spent as little time as possible in the tiny prison cell–like dorm room. Andrew could call Ruth, tell her the bad news, and be back to studying with plenty of time before his roommate returned and his concentration was broken.

He opened the contacts list, touched Ruth Bontrager, and then her phone shanty number.

It rang enough times that he was about to end the call, but then someone answered.

"Hallo?" She took a few breaths, as if she'd been running.

"Ruth?"

"Andrew! Jah, it's me. I've been listening for calls for days, running to catch each one. It's finally you."

Guilt weighed on him a bit. He didn't realize she'd been that intense about waiting for his call. Yesterday he'd done Google searches and made his calls to the plant and the newspaper.

"I'm sorry to keep you waiting." He touched the imprints his pen had made on the notebook paper. "And I'm really sorry that I don't have better news for you."

"What is it?"

"I did some searching into Calico Feed Nutrition. Looks like someone beat us to the story."

"What? No, that can't be. The plant hasn't cleaned up yet."

"But nonetheless, according to the byline in the paper, that Rick Bluestein you mentioned has investigated it and written a hard news piece for the *County Times*. The paper ran that news article concerning the plant and two short follow-up pieces. I can send you the links to the articles." Oops, no, he couldn't. "Uh, next time you go to the library, you can look them up."

"What does the main article say?"

"There have been two separate lawsuits brought against the feed mill in the past decade. Both times, the families accepted payouts to cover their medical bills."

"But other people will continue to get sick. And what about the faulty boiler I told you about? Unless authorities investigate, how will the plant be forced to fix it? There could be an accident."

"That's just how things are in small towns. Ever hear about Flint and their water supply?"

"Jah, but—"

"I'm sorry, Ruth. I tried. I even called the feed mill. They have proof of recent inspections and how their air pollution is within all legal limits." And he'd put up with lots of condescending attitudes from everyone he'd called.

"Listen, there's a key you're missing. I mentioned it at the coffee shop. You have to gather the data first before any newspaper will take you seriously. Last time you had a written survey for all the residents who live within a mile of the plant. You compared that information with public records to know the general health of the population in our state. Then you presented graphs to Rick representing how much higher the incidence of serious lung issues and cancer was for those connected to or living near the feed mill."

"That sounds like something you should try to do."

She was clearly passionate about this and even had ideas of what needed to happen. Why did she need him specifically to be involved? Other than this timeline thing she seemed to believe.

"Again, how am I supposed to get them to listen to me? I'm an Amish woman who can't hand them data because I don't know how to understand it or compile it."

"You're clearly smart enough to learn how to do those things." If she actually believed she was from a different timeline, and it wasn't a plot to get him to come back, then she would have all the information she needed to do it by herself.

"But I need you to—"

"This is really starting to feel like an excuse to get me to come to Calico Creek again. You and the women of my family can forget it. I'm never coming back. Since you know what you need to do, do it. You can even call me. I don't mind helping with what I can over the phone and assisting you on using the Internet to research."

She clicked her tongue, sounding frustrated. "It's not an excuse! And I'm so tired of you accusing me of that. I'm not asking you to join the Amish church or any church. I'm not asking you to stay and I'm not asking you to talk to any of your family members. I just need your support. The Andrew I knew wanted to help people. You seem to just have an angry chip on your shoulder. What happened to you? Why are you so different?"

"How am I supposed to answer that? I don't know the other version of me. You do. Supposedly."

Silence fell. "When did you leave Calico Creek?"

Should he tell her? "Two and a half years ago."

"That makes sense, because it would be after when Eliza's wedding was supposed to have been."

"I can guarantee my leaving had nothing at all to do with your sister and her wedding."

"I'm sure of that, but what happened?"

He drew in a long breath. "Have you ever had someone you love die? Like someone you really love?"

"Yes. My niece."

Did this happen in the fictional timeline? He wasn't going to ask. "It shakes you to your core. Nothing is ever the same again. *I'm* not the same. My friend died due to negligence and lack of education. That's the way of life in Calico Creek and all the towns like it. There are no jobs for the Amish anymore, no means of making a living that don't constantly risk your life and health. That's why my best friend died."

"Your best . . ." She gasped. "Ben? Ben Mast?"

It irked him that she knew who his best friend had been. It felt like he was being played, and he struggled to speak. "I'm guessing my mother told you after all."

"No, she didn't, I promise, but can you tell me what happened?"

A few heartbeats passed in silence. His face felt hot. Even after all this time, bringing Ben up was like opening a raw wound. Not that he ever talked with anyone about what happened. "There was an accident three years ago. He was using farm machinery he had no business operating with no oversight. He'd had no prior experience operating a gas-powered combine. He didn't understand the dangers, not the physics of how it worked or the operations to shut it down. His death wasn't quick. He was in the hospital, all these high-tech things keeping him alive. I prayed over him for days, unceasingly. I fasted. I called upon God to save him. He didn't. It was hard to have faith after that, but a little time made me realize that I still had faith in God and His Word. My faith had taken a hit, but it was still there to build on. I just didn't believe the way the Amish do, and I couldn't stay. I lost all faith in the Amish way of life."

"Oh, Andrew," she whispered.

He didn't want her pity. "Look, Amish faith is just another way used to keep us bound to the *Ordnung*. A way to keep the worker bees loyal to the hive and to perpetuate the population by creating a society that believes in early marriage and having every child God is willing to allow them to have. I had to leave. It took me months of wrestling through thoughts, reasons, and excuses to make my decision, but I knew that leaving was the only way I could ever find peace or be happy." It'd been his only way of finding real faith in God again, not that he was anywhere near where he should be when it came to faith. Faith in God was similar to any relationship—each day was a step closer to or farther away from the other person.

"I'm so sorry. But, Andrew . . ." She paused. "Ben is alive where I come from."

This was just cruel. "I'm hanging up now."

"I promise!" She was nearly shouting. "I'm not making any of this up. Ben works for Jesse at his prefab cabin business. A lot of young men do. Things are better."

"Right. Because this one magical business is going to save an entire town."

"It's a big part of the solution. Your investigative articles were a huge part of the solution too. I know other things helped make it better, but whatever else happened, we certainly are happier in the time I'm from. And the town doesn't stink."

Maybe it was time to bring up the other research he'd been doing. "Ruth, I don't doubt your sincerity at all, but I think you need to talk to a professional therapist. I can help you find one. The school has a program where they charge very little because it's part of psychology students' training.

I was doing some googling and you may be suffering from what's called Capgras delusion. It's where you think that people you know have been replaced by impostors. People with this delusion have also said that they think time has been warped, which is what you're doing, and they wish to change things back to what they perceive as normal." That didn't take into account him *sharing* her delusion at that one point when he saw the croquet game. But those memories could've easily been his imagination. He'd spent a lot of years playing croquet at family and community events before leaving the Amish.

What did Sherlock Holmes say? Andrew had loved those books. *"When you have eliminated the impossible, whatever remains, no matter how improbable, must be the truth."*

Well, time travel, timeline changing, and magical quilts were impossible. No question. So he'd imagined a croquet game with her. Imagined how life would be if he were dating her and still Amish. That's all that had gone on when he saw those images.

"You'll never believe me. Believing in someone Amish is just too hard for you. I'm wasting my time mourning over someone I used to know. The Andrew I knew had a zest for life. He helped people with serious issues like those who were sick from the feed mill. But not only that, he wrote articles that made people laugh—both Plain and Englisch. Here, it's like you're a shell of who I knew."

"At least a shell can be built upon, which is more than can be said about fairy tales of going back and forth in time."

"I'm so sorry you lost Ben. He was an exceptional person—warm, supportive, and funny. He was your second cousin you'd known your whole life, so he was more like a brother to you. He put his all into everything he did and made everyone around him want to be better. I can't imagine what losing him must've done to you."

"Don't talk about him like you knew him." Andrew ended the call.

No more. He was done with her no matter which it was—a psychological delusion or an elaborate plot to bring him back into the Amish fold.

But what about the plant? Was he dismissing something that was hurting a town of people, including family and friends? Not everyone had the opportunity to leave that area like Andrew had. But factories across the US stank. It came with the territory, and the levels of pollution those plants put off were safe for residents, despite the smell.

He sighed, staring at his phone. Should he dig a bit deeper into the situation? Maybe call that Rick Bluestein person to see what he knew? Rick's beat appeared to include any plant business in a five-county region. Andrew shook his head. Was he going to let Ruth pull him into her delusion?

Chapter Nineteen

Ruth slid the large chef's knife through the sweet potato. It was immediately stuck in the dense vegetable. *Stupid dull knife. Stupid stubborn man.* She banged the knife hard with her fist on the back of it, splitting the sweet potato. With the vegetable half as thick now, she made quick work of dicing it.

Mamm looked up from her rinsing. "Are you chopping wood or potatoes?"

"Sorry."

"Both you and Eliza have seemed off recently. Pardon your mother's prying, but I noticed you took a call before we started on dinner, and then you came inside looking upset. Is there anything you want to talk to me about? A boy?"

Ruth picked up the cutting board and slid the diced sweet potatoes into a large bowl. "A boy. He . . . doesn't feel the same. I can't make him."

Mamm gave a slow nod, shaking water off the lettuce in a colander. "I'm sorry."

"Thanks, Mamm. I'd rather not talk about him, though." If she shared more, she was liable to either scream in frustration or burst into tears over the loss of *her* Andrew. How had he given up so easily on the Old Ways? That type of behavior just didn't sound like Andrew.

They finished preparing the meal in relative quiet. Mashed sweet potatoes, a salad of only lettuce—both of which Ruth's little sister Naomi had managed to coax out of a raised bed—went along with a scant amount of chicken baked with half a bottle of barbecue sauce. Mamm's homemade bread was popular as ever, and thankfully that cost only pennies per loaf. Feeding everyone had been so much easier in the previous timeline. The day before Eliza restitched the quilt, Ruth, her parents, and her siblings who still lived at home had eaten grilled steak and cheese sandwiches cooked by John. They finished the meal with a choice of chocolate chip oatmeal cookies or a slice of pecan pie, made by Naomi. Store-bought milk, coffee, and butter had been easy to come by.

"Hey." Dat walked inside, clearly home from work. Ruth tried not to react to how he looked these days. He was sickly thin with an ashen face and an occasional cough that worried her. He grinned. "It smells amazing in here." He hung his hat on a peg by the front door. Mamm stepped out of the kitchen to give him a kiss.

They'd spent most of their lives scraping by, barely making ends meet, and yet still managed to stay in love. How was it fair that after they'd worked so hard to rise above poverty, they were now put back into this? Couldn't Eliza see how wrong that was?

"Dinner!" Mamm hollered.

Eliza joined Ruth in setting the table. By the time they had the food set out, her parents and all ten of their children were in their seats around the old table.

After a silent prayer, everyone dug in like grateful but ravenous people.

Three of her younger siblings were teens now—Levi, Annie, and Naomi. John would be a teen before the year was out, and Peter was less than two years behind him. The two youngest siblings, Becca and Noah, who'd been born between when Eliza was engaged and when she wed, would be turning four and six very soon. Ruth was sure that life became even harder on Mamm and Dat when she and Eliza moved to Ohio years ago. Eight for Eliza and seven for Ruth. In the old time, Ruth had always lived at home and helped out a lot. Eliza had lived at home for five years before marrying; even then she hadn't moved very far.

A few minutes after mealtime began, Ruth had finished over half of her food. She swallowed. "I've been working on some family history stuff."

Dat smiled. "Jah? That's great. Life just kinda happens, and before you know it, years pass and no one has written anything down."

"I was hoping I could ask some questions."

"Sure, kiddo. We'll do our best to help."

Eliza eyed her but said nothing.

"There was some sort of feud that happened between us and the neighbors, the Ebersols, right?"

Dat laughed. "Interesting place to start. Feud? Nah. I'm friendly with Leonard and his family. His oldest son, Jesse, used to help us out with stuff through the years. Moses has a job with him now, right?"

Moses cut his small piece of chicken with a well-worn knife. "He's been pretty nice to work with, gotta say. Strict though."

She needed to press harder. "There must've been *something*. Why do the ministers and community place such importance on the two families never marrying?"

"This conversation is inappropriate for dinner," Eliza mumbled.

"Well, when is a good time, Eliza? I guess I can wait. It's not like I have a lot going on in my life since I've taken a leave of absence from teaching to visit here, and I'm not seeing anyone."

Eliza said nothing and wouldn't meet her eyes. Ruth studied her. She'd definitely been crying. Ruth hurt for how much pain she was going through. But how much additional pain did she cause by her actions?

Ruth sat straighter in her chair. If she jogged their memories, maybe they could tell her something useful. Anything. "I remember hearing about a sister to Auntie Rose. Another great-aunt. She married an Ebersol, right?"

Dat's and Mamm's eyes met. Dat set his fork down. "Jah. That's correct."

"And they left the church?"

"Ruth." Mamm wiped the corner of her mouth with her napkin. "This sort of thing isn't what you want to record in the family history."

"Why not? 'Those who cannot remember the past are condemned to repeat it.' Isn't that what a philosopher said, and historians agree it's true?"

Dat chuckled. "Now, how would we know that? You're the scholar."

Ruth smiled at him. "How can the younger generation remember and learn from an important past if no one is willing to talk about it?"

Dat nodded. "Her name was Verna, and I think his was Omar. They divorced, Ruth. The Amish remained true to them before they divorced, trying to talk them out of it, trying to get them to accept help in repairing the marriage. They refused and were shunned. They left the Amish so that they could divorce and live however they chose. As far as I know, neither one has ever returned."

"So they had personal marital issues. Why the superstition that Bontragers and Ebersols in these parts were to never marry?"

"I'm not sure." Dat's brows furrowed and he looked deep in thought. "I remember my mamm and dat whispering about it a few different times, saying the power between the two, when married, was akin to witchcraft."

"What?" Ruth dropped her fork.

Mamm choked, coughing hard.

Witchcraft? Ruth looked at Eliza, but her sister stared at her plate as if she'd known their time travel would be considered witchcraft by some.

"Is that enough open talk about it for you?" Levi grinned.

Dat chuckled. "I didn't mean it *was* witchcraft or anything close. My grandmother referred to it as powwow remedies. Powwow medicine is sort of a mixture of faith and folklore. Our ancestors used their Bibles and a specific activity—perhaps fresh water from a certain nearby spring to heal a burn—to help boost their faith. Their intention was to draw closer to God through fervent prayer and some type of physical action."

"So . . ." Levi swallowed a bite of food. "You don't believe whatever happened had any chance of being connected to witchcraft?"

"Nee. I don't. Praying to God doesn't open up events to the likes of witchcraft. That'd be like planting corn and it grows a harvest of stones. Never gonna happen because that's not how God set things up to work. He is independent of time, and He moves in mysterious ways. That's all I know." He took a sip of water. "But old wives' tales say that when a Bontrager and Ebersol marry, it's a powerful union that causes a lot of trouble between them and for them. From what I've seen of those few marriages throughout my lifetime, it seems to be true. Hard to say since none of those couples remained in Calico Creek or even in Pennsylvania. I guess they were aiming to move on to greener pastures."

Eliza stood, glaring at Ruth. "I'm not feeling well. Please excuse me. Mamm, I'll help with cleanup later."

Ruth ignored her as she went upstairs. "But only Verna and Omar divorced, right?"

"Jah, as far as we know," Mamm said.

"When did they leave? I take it you met her? And maybe her husband?"

Dat took a long sip of his water. "Nee. Them leaving and

the divorce would've taken place in the late fifties, I think. So that happened a good ten years before I was born. I never met them."

Ruth had a lot of questions she'd like answered. "Auntie Rose died just a few years ago. I always assumed her older sister Verna was dead, but no one ever said it. Is there a chance that she's alive? Maybe I should look for her and interview her."

"Ruth." Dat reached across the table and put a hand over hers. "You can't make contact. Even if she is physically alive, as far as we are concerned, she's already dead. They both are."

Dat hadn't said Verna was dead. This meant her hunch could be correct—her great-aunt Verna was alive. Maybe she held the answers Ruth needed. Maybe she even had the quilt in this timeline.

"Just leave it alone, Ruth," Dat said.

Ruth didn't respond. She had no desire to lie to her father. But if she could change the timeline, he'd have his health back. The family would be prospering again. Ben would be alive. She didn't have an answer for her sister's broken heart or Jesse's over the difficult loss of Penelope. All she knew for sure was the price of erasing their marriage was too high. Just too high.

She had no idea how to go about finding Verna, and Ruth's two closest friends, Eliza and Andrew, were not on her side. She barely knew them anymore. Eliza might truly be a lost cause. Was Andrew? She hoped not. Still, she had to try to find Verna and discover as much truth as she could. Maybe she could do nothing with that truth, but she had to chase it.

Before Jesse entered the workshop, he heard the swish-swish of Dat at work, no doubt sanding the table and chairs he'd been commissioned to refinish. The scent of fresh-cut pine, old and new paint, and the metallic, smoky smell left over from earlier welding met him inside.

"Hey, Dat. Mamm said you were out here. She also says to come eat dinner."

"Jesse, good timing. Want to pick up a sander and help me out? Gotta finish this, then dinner."

"Mamm also says you'll be sorry if you wait too long and it gets eaten by the little fellas. It's beef and barley stew."

Dat looked up and frowned. "We better finish quick, then."

Jesse laughed and walked to Dat's cluttered workbench. He sorted through the pile of tools until he found another hand sander.

Getting to the table in a timely manner was always important. Jesse's twin twelve-year-old brothers were notorious for packing away food. There'd been a lot more food to spare since Jesse started working for Mulligan Builders and giving his parents part of his salary. It also helped that in the last eight years, he'd had four younger siblings marry. Would Jesse's one good salary be enough to help his mamm, dat, and siblings be comfortable, while at the same time supporting himself and Martha and their children? The thought nagged at him, but he'd figure it out. He always did.

Jesse put the sander to the table and applied even, steady strokes. This shop was so familiar. On the other side of this long building was his apartment, the one he and Dat finished building out. Jesse lived there when his current jobsite with Mulligan Builders was close enough to get to work from here.

When it wasn't, he found a cheap room to rent somewhere, preferably with the Amish because then, for a little bit of extra money, meals were included. Finishing a room for him hadn't been too difficult since Dat already had water running out here to his workshop.

Still sanding the table, Jesse moved closer. "I wanted a chance to talk to you, anyways."

"Uh-oh. Please tell me you're not getting cold feet about Martha. We love Martha."

He ran the sander over the opposite side of the table that his dad was working on. "No, I'm quite ready to get married. Surprisingly, I don't want to live in your shop forever. It smells bad when you weld, and you stay up too late working."

Dat let loose a huge laugh. "Well, it's not as loud as the main house with all the littles underfoot."

"The littles aren't so little anymore."

"Nope. It's about to be your turn to wrangle babies." Dat gave Jesse a wink.

Jesse shook his head, picking up his efforts on sanding. "Let me get married first."

"Then what'd you want to talk about?"

"Have you ever heard of someone having a strong intuition?"

"Intuition?"

"Maybe that's the wrong word, but have you ever touched someone and you saw . . . things?"

Dat stopped sanding, concern reflecting in his eyes. "What kind of things, Son?"

"Like memories, but you know those things never happened."

Dad stared at him for a while before he returned to his work. "Can you describe what you saw?"

Jesse focused on the table as he sanded it. "Eliza and me . . ."

"With Eliza? Son, you should not be close enough to touch her. When and why would you be?"

"I mentioned to you before that Moses Bontrager is working with me right now. Eliza is supervising him. It happened the other day when I shook her hand and then today when I touched her cheek."

"Whoa. This is disturbing. You're engaged. Why would you touch her cheek?"

"I don't know, Dat." Jesse seemed to lose all sense of proper boundaries where Eliza was concerned. "She was crying, and I was trying to comfort her. What does seeing things, like old memories, possibly mean?"

"It means you should stay away. Trust me. I know." Dat moved to a wooden box and opened it. He pulled out a file with a few papers in it. "This is a list of Ebersol and Bontrager marriages that your grandfather began. Not one couple was a half-decent union. Not one, Jesse. Every couple is supposed to support the community, be extra hands to help, another home to have church in, more people to pray and work together. But Ebersol and Bontrager couples do the opposite of good. The opposite of receiving God's blessings. Your great-uncle married a Bontrager woman, and they were miserable together. Worse, they ended up excommunicated from the church and from the lives of everyone who loved them."

"I thought he left the church because he got a divorce."

"That was certainly part of it. No one knows the full story, including any fly on the wall inside their home. The long and short of it is Omar and his wife, Verna, should've never married. They'd been warned, same as you."

Being excommunicated was never the goal of the church. The punishment of a shunning or ban was to bring the sinner back into the fold. Not to cast them out forever. "Was the excommunication . . . for having intuitions?" That didn't seem like a punishable offense. Jesse didn't see anything on purpose.

"No, not for that specifically, but rumor said they followed after those insights, doing bizarre things. Some called it witchcraft. Your grandfather said that his brother wasn't the kind to participate in such things. He also said that Omar claimed he and Verna had used some ancient cloth or blanket and prayer to change the past. They said they'd changed time more than once and wanted to repent of it. Omar said he could prove that he'd changed time by sharing visions with any Bontrager who was willing to shake his hand, so the Bontragers in the community lined up."

"Wait, people *believed* him?"

"Not so much believed him, but they gave him the benefit of the doubt. When Bontragers shook Omar's hand, according to your grandpa, only one saw something, although she was unsure what she'd seen. Same happened when Verna shook the hands of Ebersols. People were scared. That's why some called it witchcraft. When fear is stirred, people assume evil is at work. But faith and miracles go hand in hand—healings of all kinds and resurrections of the dead. God's power is scary. Can you imagine seeing a dead person resurrected or seeing water turned to wine? All of that aside, the bottom line is Omar and Verna were just like every other Ebersol-Bontrager marriage; they weren't good for each other or this community." Dat held up the papers. "Here's the proof."

Jesse took the old papers and read the list. It had wedding dates and listed all that had gone wrong for the couple or in the community because of the couple. "Doesn't every couple face their share of troubles on this planet?" Although in studying this page, Ebersol-Bontrager couples did seem more prone to tragedies. "I . . . I don't know what this means."

"It means you should stay away from Eliza." Dat's brows furrowed, concern in his sad eyes. "I know how close you two were and how deeply you mourned when she turned you down."

Dat knew. He and Jesse had talked about it as often as Jesse needed to, but few others knew. He had vented about it to his cousin Ben too. He missed Ben. *May he rest in peace.*

"Son, I'm sure it's hard to see her again and not think, *What if?* But you and Martha have a good thing going on. A godly engagement and an upcoming wedding. Just stay away from Eliza for another three weeks, and I promise, you'll be so grateful you did."

"I'll leave this alone. I wasn't thinking of her that way." Was he thinking of her that way? Had he ever really stopped thinking of Eliza that way? Even though she turned him down before they went on a single date.

"Gut. Focus on your wedding. On that sweet girl who wants to marry you and on your future."

Dat was right. What was he doing? None of this really mattered.

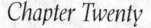

Chapter Twenty

Eliza clicked her tongue and tapped the reins on the horse's back, trying to get the old girl to move a little faster on the long, winding mountain driveway to the Ebersol house. The October sun hung low, casting pinks and purples across the sky. It'd be dark soon, and she pulled her thick, hand-made sweater tighter around her shoulders.

Staying busy was her only sanity of late. Remembering the past while watching Jesse build a new future was something she hadn't known to prepare herself for. But in truth, nothing could've prepared her for the loneliness she felt. She'd voluntarily given up her husband, her home, the life they'd built. Her decision had cost Ruth her love. Eliza swallowed hard and refocused her thoughts.

She had several quick-woven blankets and three scrap

blankets she'd made the past week while Moses worked. She also had the start of a quilt, but she was doubtful that it could be done before the wedding. Added to those, she had the quilts she'd already made to sell, which Aunt Bette had shipped to her. Eliza would complete more quick blankets later, but she wanted to at least give Jesse's mamm some proof of the work she was doing, an assurance that Eliza was decreasing her workload and stress about the upcoming wedding. Amanda Ebersol had ten children, including Jesse. The five younger ones were still at home. Helping with this was no issue, especially with all Jesse was doing for Moses. When Eliza and Jesse had married, she'd received so many lovely gifts she was still putting to good use as of a week ago, when she'd changed time.

Now he was marrying someone else in only three weeks. Could it really be? It still felt surreal. But it was what he needed. To spare him pain.

Finally Jesse's parents' house was in sight. It didn't look as bad as her parents' home. Perhaps the Ebersols hadn't been as affected by the change. That was a small comfort. As she got closer, she saw a man painting some of the home's clapboard siding. His movements were unmistakable. It was Jesse. What was he doing painting on a Saturday at nearly sunset? Her stomach churned with nerves. She'd thought he'd be out with Martha, and she was hoping to just give her work to his mamm. Now they'd have to talk for sure.

She pulled the rig to a stop next to the hitching posts. She couldn't turn around and try later—he'd already seen her. Best get this over with. She hopped out and fastened the horse to the post, giving his snout a rub.

"Eliza?" Jesse had set the paintbrush down and was walking toward her.

She was right—he'd stopped to talk to her. "Hello. Sorry to drop by. I just wanted to give your mamm these quilts, rugs, and blankets." She opened the door to the buggy wide so he could see.

He wiped his hands on a towel he'd pulled from his pocket, then touched the fabric, looking through the pieces. "Wow. When did you have time to make all of this?"

"Several of them came from my aunt's. I made three scrap blankets while Moses worked with you, and the rest I sewed on after getting home with Moses." It was almost impossible to sleep and sewing gave her something to do during the long nights.

He grinned at her. "You really have a gift. I forget how talented you are sometimes."

Her face felt hot as she steadied herself with a deep breath. "Denki. It's nothing, though. I . . . really appreciate you giving Moses this chance. And I'm really happy for you and Martha. I'm glad you're marrying her." It'd all be worth it—all this pain—if he could be happy. No more dead babies. No worries about whether or not he could have a family. Martha was healthy, energetic, and fun. She'd be wonderful to Jesse.

"Eliza." He took a step toward her, and she took a step backward. As if he sensed her nerves, he took a half step back, like he was giving her space. "I'm sorry. I know I said some really strange things at the jobsite. Inappropriate things. And I understand why you've been avoiding me again since then. I apologize. Can we try again on being friends?"

She drew a deep breath, trying to steady her emotions.

"I would appreciate that deeply." Regret for so many things twisted inside her. "Apparently I've handled years of things wrong between us. Please let me clarify again—that day at the creek all those years ago wasn't about your value as a marriage partner. I . . . I wanted to say yes." *I did say yes . . .*

His lips formed a sad smile. "It's okay, Eliza. You gave an answer, and that's how these things work. I accepted that long ago. What hurt the most, though, was how you left and never spoke to me again. You were my best friend. I guess you didn't see me that way." He sighed, looking away toward his parents' house. "There I go saying too much again. Years ago, I promised myself if I ever got another chance to speak to you, I would say what I needed to."

She almost grabbed his hand but then remembered what happened last time they touched. It'd been like her memories from the other timeline were contagious. She intertwined her fingers and rested her hands against her stomach. "No, it's not that we weren't the best of friends." *Don't say it! Don't you dare—* "I . . . loved you." Relief from that admission surged through her, going to her core. It was as if she were dying of thirst and honesty was a clear, cool glass of water, but she needed to shut up. Just shut up! But her lips parted and the words wouldn't listen to her commands. "I . . . I still love you," she whispered.

He faced her again, his eyes holding hurt and uncertainty. She'd undone him when she'd left. Deeply, completely undone him. She could see that plain as day. Why couldn't she have found a way of avoiding this pain for him when she'd changed the past? If she'd let him know her intentions years earlier, before their relationship had turned from friendship into love, maybe then she could've spared derailing his life. But even now she couldn't pinpoint another moment in the past that would allow her to redirect their paths without undoing both of them.

"Jesse, do you remember the warnings our parents used to give us about playing together? About—" she swallowed a lump—"the curse."

"I always told you to dismiss it as old people's superstitions."

If only. "I can't explain everything. And I'm terrified it counts as sacrilegious to even speak of it." If anyone knew what she'd done with the quilt, she'd be excommunicated for sure. "But bad things have happened every single time an Ebersol and Bontrager marry. Unexplainable bad things. More than anything, I wanted to say yes at the creek eight years ago. I relive that moment constantly." Along with all the memories from the years leading up to their wedding and the strength and beauty of who they'd been after.

"You relive when I proposed?" He looked taken aback. "I . . . assumed you didn't think of me after you left."

"I care for you to the depths of my soul. It's why I had to say no. It's why I had to stay away." Would knowing the truth help him? She hoped so.

But now . . . he was getting married in only three weeks. They could never be together after that. The door would be closed forever. With no threat of the curse anymore, and with her staying single for the rest of her life, could they return to being friends? Could it be enough? Maybe at least for a glimmer of hope in her life.

"My dat warned me of the same thing. You're right; maybe

we couldn't have married. But we could've worked that out together. You didn't have to leave."

"I wanted you to move on without my presence reminding you. But now I see how much I hurt you. Can you forgive me?"

He closed his eyes for a moment, like he was saying a prayer. "Jah, of course."

"You're marrying in three weeks. I . . . think we're safe to be friends again, don't you?"

Tears welled. "I'd like that."

Friends. Could she really have that with him? It hurt to be around him, knowing all she did while knowing he'd never get to experience those memories with her. But she'd been so lonely, so cold, even this burning ache in her core was better than the icy solitude without him.

Eliza smiled. "We could talk about old memories with Moses again, chat with Martha about your plans on your next projects. Maybe even you owning a future business?"

"My own business? That's just a dream. It takes a lot to launch one, and I don't come from a lot."

"But I *know* you can do it. You're so talented. You can build anything, even when you're just given castoffs."

"You're like that too, though. You made some beautiful rugs out of literal scraps. It's one of the reasons why I thought we—" He winced. "Never mind."

Staying away had hurt them both. She'd been wrong to do so. But this could do. She could spend time with him as his platonic friend. And as Martha's friend. She'd be like Auntie Rose. Everybody's friend and nobody's wife or mother.

Chapter Twenty-One

Andrew held the steering wheel and studied the road, looking at the numbers on each dilapidated mailbox he passed. A year ago he'd used student loan money to purchase this two-door Chevy with way over a hundred thousand miles on it. Had he ever expected to use it to return to Calico Creek? Maybe not, but he was on a half-hearted mission now and had a lot of things to take care of in this town over the next few days.

He looked at the stack of papers in the seat next to him and sighed. "What are you doing? Seriously, man. What?"

It'd taken him two hours to get to his hometown, and he'd yet to have a moment of peace about it.

Turn left in .3 miles. His GPS gave instructions to Ruth Bontrager's place, and despite his reservations, he continued to follow each direction given.

His gut twisted. "Still, she is a few bricks shy of a load, and you know it," he mumbled. But that one thing didn't define all of who she was any more than his grief and anger issues defined all of who he was. Her eyes reflected intelligence. Her inner person seemed to radiate that life was worth fighting for, even when believing she'd been dragged into a different time and may never figure out how to get back.

Why was he going to see her? He could accomplish his goals and leave this one part out. He'd done his due diligence in trying to reach her by phone, calling two times. Her mamm intercepted each voice mail, returned his calls, and told him to leave her daughter alone.

Turn left. His shoulders ached as he turned onto a rutty gravel driveway and eased his clunker up it.

A ramshackle house came into view with tattered sheets and blankets on the line, piles of unsplit logs here and there, and half-grown children everywhere. He could see why Ruth would choose to believe she wasn't living in the right time.

A middle-aged woman stepped onto the porch, wiping her hands on her black apron. She'd probably heard his car. The sound of a three-thousand-pound car on her driveway and a motor running would definitely stand out as different.

She stared at him, looking like a mama bear ready to protect her cub.

Andrew was ex-Amish, even though he'd never joined the church. Among the Amish, he would carry that title, that reputation of betrayal for the rest of his life. It meant many things, one of which was Ruth was forbidden from having casual, friendly contact of any kind with him, not that his own mamm had respected that line. Still, whatever Dorothy or Amos Bontrager felt toward him, he needed to apologize to their daughter. He shouldn't have been so blatant about her needing psychological help and then hung up on her.

He pressed the brakes, put the car in park, and turned the engine off. The woman came off the steps.

He got out. "Hello. I'm Andrew, and I'm here to see Ruth."

"Uh, jah. I didn't need some fancy college degree to know that." She glanced back at the house. "Please get in your car and leave. *All* we have is each other. Don't rip that from us. Please, just go."

He could certainly understand the woman's sentiments. To her, he looked like the embodiment of worldliness coming to snatch her daughter away. "I just need to apologize to her."

"No apology is worth—"

"Hey, Mamm." The front door opened, and Ruth stepped out, a book in one hand and a pen in the other. "Do you know what this is referring—?" She saw him and stopped cold.

He moved a couple of steps toward the porch. "Hi, Ruth. I'm just here to say a few things."

Ruth closed the book and nodded. But they just stood there, gazing at one another while her mamm and several siblings watched.

Dorothy made a tsk sound and passed him. "Not in my house, you won't, or on my porch." She clapped her hands. "Everyone else inside for a slice of bread with jam."

The yard cleared out and it sounded like horses were trampling up the wooden steps and into the house. Dorothy stopped once beside Ruth and said something. Ruth's eyes never left Andrew, but she nodded before leaving the porch and walking to him.

She stood a few feet in front of him, seemingly speechless.

He looked at the house, seeing her mother watching them from a window. A person's perspective was everything. To Dorothy, he was a disloyal, self-serving man who could do great harm to her family. To those in authority at Penn State who'd helped him navigate from Amish boy to college student, he was praiseworthy and stalwart in overcoming the odds.

He looked at Ruth. Who was he to her? A coward? A stubborn, disbelieving oaf? A savior from a time and place she longed to be free from?

Truth was, it didn't matter. He was here to do right by her because that's who he was, regardless of who thought what of him. It'd been hard breaking free of the Amish, harder still to let go of their negative opinions of who he was. It'd taken time and prayer, but he'd come to the conclusion that if he was following God and was also reasonably self-aware, his perspective of himself was all that really mattered.

Ruth clipped the pen on the bib of her apron. "How do you know where I live?"

The leather-bound book in her hand appeared to be really old, and he wondered where she'd gotten it.

He pulled from his thoughts and observations and focused on the young woman in front of him. "Ben's mamm, Lydia. Despite how the church feels about me, she and I talk a couple of times a month. She says it helps her cope with Ben's death. A few days ago, I asked her about you. Apparently you and Ben were playmates as children whenever his mamm was visiting her sister, which is Jesse's mamm, right?"

Ruth held the tattered book closer. "Jah, that's right."

"I guess I'd forgotten all the names he used to talk about from his visits with family on this side of town."

Ruth nodded. "It's understandable. You've been in a lot of tough battles. Losing Ben and leaving the Amish was probably just the start of losing parts of yourself. Then the fight to get caught up on your education so you could fight to be accepted into Penn State, and I'm sure keeping up your grades is another battle."

It seemed odd for someone who believed in time travel to talk with such a perfect grasp of his life journey. "I'm sorry I doubted you about Ben." *Say the rest! It's why you're here.* He cleared his throat. "When you offered me a chance to help people in Calico Creek, and I didn't even consider it, I later realized how very angry I'd become with the Amish. Consumed with anger, actually. Blinded by it. I said you needed psychological help, but what I didn't know at that moment was how much I needed to get help. I have an appointment to see a school-funded therapist later this week."

Her eyes narrowed just a bit as she tilted her head. "Wow," she whispered. "That was quite an apology. I accept. Denki."

Weight lifted off him. "Oh, and—" he held up a finger to her before reaching into his car and grabbing out a stack of papers—"I created a survey of health questions. I intend to go door-to-door, asking questions or passing out question-naires for people to mail in, whichever they prefer."

"You what?" Ruth took a stapled group of papers from him and read over it. She beamed. "Ach, denki, denki, denki!"

She danced a bit as she spun in a circle like an excited kid. After a few spins, she stopped and faced him again. "I have no words to express my gratitude."

"I think the jig said it all." He chuckled. "You could go with me." The words flew from his mouth, and he wasn't at all sure it was a good idea. They were from different worlds with no bridge between the two cultures. Also, they each needed to seek help for issues they were dealing with, although hers seemed far worse than his. Why would he ask for them to spend time together?

"You look unsure about asking me to go, and I don't blame you."

Again, how did someone with such wild ideas about time travel and crazy stories about their lives in a different dimension have such good insight and seem to be incredibly level-headed? It didn't add up, did it?

A horse and buggy came into sight and veered around Andrew's car. A young woman about Ruth's age seemed to take in what was happening.

She stopped the rig, got out, and strode toward Ruth. "No. No, no, no." She grabbed Ruth's hand, pulling her away from Andrew. "Andrew, get in your car and leave."

Did he know her? She and Ruth favored, except Ruth had fewer freckles and honey-colored highlights in her brown hair. But the way the woman spoke to him sounded as if they knew each other well.

"Eliza, let go." Ruth pulled free of her and walked toward Andrew.

"Don't do this, Ruth!" Eliza got between Ruth and Andrew. "Think! He's an Ebersol. You're a Bontrager." She turned, glancing at Andrew. "You saw it firsthand when I married Jesse." Her emotional whisper didn't keep Andrew from hearing what she'd said.

He remembered Ben telling him that Jesse had asked a neighboring girl to marry him. Wasn't the girl's name Eliza? And she'd said no and left home. That was a long time ago, like eight or so years, wasn't it? Besides that, Ben's mamm told him last week that Jesse was engaged and getting married soon. There was no way an Amish man had married twice unless he was a widower.

"Look," Eliza whispered, "we didn't turn our lives upside down to return to a time so that you can reconnect with an Ebersol."

"*We?*" Ruth's eyebrows rose high.

"Sh," Eliza said.

Ruth glanced at Andrew. "Okay." She lowered her voice. "Point is, I had nothing to do with changing our original timeline. There was no *we* part, just you."

If this was a normal situation, Andrew wouldn't eavesdrop, but it wasn't normal. Nothing about connecting with Ruth felt normal. Between reading her lips and overhearing a few words, Andrew was sure he caught most of what Ruth had said.

Eliza said several things he didn't hear, probably because she had a bit more control than when she first sprinted from the rig, yelling *no*.

"We can talk later, Eliza." Ruth pushed the book she was holding into Eliza's hands. "I'm going with Andrew. He has a health questionnaire printed so he can take a survey in the downtown Calico Creek area." She got in his car.

Eliza stared at him. "Again?" She backed away, shaking her head as if realizing what she'd said.

Why had she said *again*?

He got in his car, started it, and turned around in the driveway. "That's your sister."

"Jah." Ruth drew a deep breath and focused on the survey questions. "I need to clear my head for a minute. Okay?"

"Yeah, sure."

He pulled out of the driveway and drove down the mountain toward downtown, his head ringing with the conversation between the sisters. It was one thing for Ruth to somehow believe she'd traveled in time, but it seemed impossible for two sisters to believe the same delusion. Yet that's exactly how that conversation sounded, as if the sisters had experienced the same events.

"Ruth?"

What would happen if he touched her hand again? Until now, he hadn't wanted to know. But for two women to have the same delusion seemed too odd not to do a tad of investigating.

Ruth turned a page, studying it. "I think you left out one of the key questions."

"Hallo?"

She looked up.

"You said in the previous time, we went to an Ebersol family gathering. Tell me about it."

Her eyes widened for a moment before she shared several things, most of which he hadn't seen when they'd touched. "We were laughing about my lack of being able to roquet during croquet when the conversation became a bit more serious. You'd begun a conversation about how you felt toward me. I was going to tell you how I felt when Jesse interrupted us, saying Eliza needed me. I left, thinking I'd be back within the hour."

Andrew drew a breath. Parts of her recollection matched what he'd seen, but that was crazy. Wasn't it?

"Why'd you ask, Andrew? Do you have a memory of it?"

He shook his head, but in truth, he didn't know. All he knew for sure was he didn't want to talk about it. His mind zigged and zagged everywhere, and his heart raced.

Inside him somewhere, a part of him believed her. He couldn't wrap his head around it, but he kinda . . . sort of . . . maybe believed her.

Light from a gas heater lit the page as Eliza tapped the pen on the hard cover of her journal. When had she gone into labor with Penelope? She couldn't remember if it was three or four in the afternoon. Was it normal for that detail to become fuzzy? She remembered the first real contractions starting when she and Jesse had been laughing hard about who'd won the game of Uno earlier that afternoon.

The evening chill pressed in. The gas heater that sat on the porch beside her wasn't giving off enough heat to be comfortable outside, but she didn't want to miss seeing Ruth the moment she arrived home. John and Moses were out here with her, also worried. It was no small thing for Ruth to leave with an ex-Amish, and they didn't know nearly what Eliza did.

She'd tried to work on quilts, but the concern that her memories could fade pushed her to write the events in her journal. What if she forgot Penelope? Suddenly every scrap of memory regarding her was as precious as gold.

"Hey, 'Liza, look who's pulling back up." John snickered, pointing at the car lights coming toward them, up the long driveway. "Mamm's gonna give her an earful."

Moses flipped a page of his book. "I'm just glad I'm not number one on the getting-an-earful list right now. Ruth can have my spot."

Eliza stood, shoving the journal to the side. "I'm going to talk to her first. Don't follow me. Don't you two have somewhere to be? Inside?" She leveled a look at her brothers that she hoped signaled she meant business.

John laughed. "I think I remember I have some chores to do. Indoors. Come on, Mose."

Moses pushed himself to his feet, groaning. "I was just about to say it's getting chilly out here, better take it inside."

Eliza hurried toward the light. She had to reach Ruth and speak to her before someone in their huge family interrupted them. Ruth knew. She *knew* what it meant to leave with Andrew like this. It'd be a scandal when someone outside their family found out, and with so many here, it was only a matter of time before it leaked. And what was Andrew thinking? He understood the implications of this. Past that, Eliza had to make some headway concerning what it meant to be with an Ebersol. What the curse actually meant.

Andrew's old white car came around the bend in the driveway. Ruth locked eyes with Eliza from the passenger seat. If anyone in the community saw her in a car with Andrew . . .

Andrew stopped the car. Ruth said something to him, and he nodded back at her.

Ruth opened the passenger door and exited it, closing it hard behind her. "Yes, Eliza?"

Andrew backed the car up a few feet and turned the wheel. Probably a good idea to turn around and not pull all the way up to the house. If they were smarter, Ruth would've met him elsewhere, avoiding the driveway altogether. He drove away.

Eliza wanted to remain calm, but she shook with anger. "I don't even know where to start." But yelling at Ruth was unlikely to solve anything. Her sister knew how she felt. They'd argued on this same topic hours ago.

"Then don't. You made your choices. I'm making mine. Stay out of my business."

"Your business? Of all the selfish, ridiculous lines of thinking—"

Ruth crossed her arms. "You have no room to talk about selfish."

Eliza shook her head. Ruth didn't understand. "The decision I made was one to try to *spare* others pain, even at my own expense. I know it's caused unforeseen problems that I will get straight, but I don't see how it's selfish."

"Oh, it's selfish. And stupid. And impulsive. And life-ruining for many, many people. I would go on, but I really don't owe an explanation to you." Ruth walked toward the house. She turned. "Just know that I'm going to be doing my best to fix it. And if I can't, then I'm not throwing away my life with the man I love out of fear." She headed for the house again.

"Ruth, stop. We're not done talking. It wasn't out of fear! The curse is real. You *know* it's real. The reason we're dealing with all of this is to break the curse."

Ruth froze, then turned on her heels. "Eliza, I don't mean to come across as insensitive about Penelope's death. You know how devastated I was—I still am—about losing her. But listen to me: there are people all over the world who deal with genetic issues in their children. They don't throw their lives away and call it a curse. They don't ruin other people's lives and cause other people's deaths trying to undo it. They face it and deal with the pain that comes as a natural consequence of living on this planet."

How could she know? She'd never faced that pain. Eliza was trying to spare Ruth that pain! "You're saying other people deal with it better than I do? That's so hurtful I don't even know . . ." A bell went off inside her. "Wait, no one died. I prevented a death by changing time. I didn't cause one."

"You don't even realize the implications of what you've done." Ruth held her hands up, using them to punctuate each sentence. "You're so wrapped up in yourself, your pain. Have you noticed that Calico Creek *stinks*? How run-down and awful Dat looks? Andrew left the Amish before he could write his article that blew the lid off the plant's bad practices. There've been no repercussions to the plant's lack of safety regulations and all the toxins they've been spewing into our community's air. No medical bills have been paid. Dat wasn't reimbursed for any of the time he's missed work due to illness and no medical bills are covered. And people just get sicker and sicker."

The feed mill? How did the plant become her responsibility? "That's awful. Oh, that's why Andrew created a new survey. Clearly he's going to investigate it and set things right. The toxic issues won't go on much longer."

"Did you even ask yourself why Andrew left the Amish?" Ruth had dropped her voice to barely over a whisper.

She'd wondered, but . . . "It seems like a strange side effect of the change, but everyone is fighting a battle. Maybe he just succumbed to doubt here whereas he had strong faith before."

Ruth took a step closer. "He left because Ben died."

Ben—Jesse's cousin was dead? How and why? "Ben died?" Her breath came faster, like she'd been sprinting.

Ruth glared at her. "Since Jesse doesn't own a business, many of the young men in Calico Creek were forced to look for work elsewhere. Ben was one of them. He was working for an Englisch family and had a farm machinery accident. Andrew was by his side at the hospital when he died. Seeing that is why Andrew lost all his faith in the Amish and maybe some faith in God. I'm trying to help him, but I'm fighting an uphill battle. And it's all because of a stupid, rash decision you made."

Eliza's legs felt like wet noodles. She stumbled backward and sat down on the grass next to the gravel driveway. Ben, dead in an accident. Andrew, lost, his very soul at risk . . . "Ruth, I—I don't even know what to say."

"Do you get it yet? You're not sparing anyone pain. You're just doling it out differently. Have you been spared anything? It seems to me that you're carrying the grief from both worlds. What if that doesn't go away, Eliza?"

"But at least Jesse . . ." She looked away, unwilling to gaze in her sister's face. "At least Jesse has found some happiness with Martha. They'll have healthy children."

"Jesse doesn't look all that happy to me. He's marrying a woman he hardly knows. Have you looked in his eyes? I did when I saw him at church. I don't see any heartache removed. I see him still trying to make the best of the life he's been handed."

The weight of Ruth's words pressed in, and Eliza fought to breathe. "What do you want me to do, Ruth? You heard Mercy. She said when it's done, it's done. *This* is the world we live in now. *This* is all we have."

"I don't accept that. I'll move mountains to fix it and save everyone."

That sounded so familiar. "Not everyone, Ruth."

Ruth sat beside her. "Not everyone." She looped her arm through Eliza's. "Maybe there is no saving everyone."

Was that true?

Ruth sighed. "I want to return things to their rightful way."

Eliza held her head between her palms. "But what if this is the rightful way and it's all unfolding the way God wanted it? Us sort of stumbling on the old cabin while I had the quilt, me going back to change that one event?"

"You're wrong. You shouldn't have made decisions for everyone. It's wrong, and I'm going to fix it. Are you with me or not?"

"Ruth." She squeezed her sister's hand. "I just don't know what I could even do. I don't have the quilt anymore. I don't know who has it since Auntie Rose passed. If it does still exist, was it buried with her? How far are you willing to go for a plan that won't work according to the woman who actually knows about this stuff? If you keep associating with Andrew, you're going to get yourself excommunicated too."

"I told you I'd move mountains." Ruth stood. "If you aren't going to help me, then just stay out of my way." She all but ran toward their parents' house.

Ben was dead. People were in poverty. Her dat and other plant workers clearly had serious health issues.

Pain threatened to overwhelm her. Why had so much changed? And was it true? Would she always carry the grief of both worlds?

Had she spared Jesse any pain, or was her sister right—Eliza had only doled out the grief and pain differently?

Chapter Twenty-Two

With her sweater in hand, Ruth eased out the front door, hoping no one noticed her. Sunlight streamed through thick clouds. The coast looked clear. She slid into her thick black sweater and bundled it around her as she hurried down the gravel driveway. The weather always seemed to shift quickly once November hit, but she'd gladly deal with some chilly breezes rather than worry about her family's reaction to Andrew pulling up in front of her home. Sneaking around made guilt spiral inside her like snow during a winter storm. It didn't seem to matter to her conscience that being with Andrew was for the good of her entire family.

A gust of wind caused her to jog faster. Maybe if her heart rate went up, she'd feel warmer.

She and Andrew had interviewed residents, compiled and

compared their info with the health of others in the state and across the US. Basically, they'd worked like madmen all week. This part of Andrew remained the same no matter the timeline: once a fire was lit inside him, he was a workhorse. They must've talked with thirty different families between the two of them, usually in person, but sometimes by phone. Andrew even communicated with one man via text messages.

At last! She rounded the corner to the bottom of the mountain driveway and there was Andrew's white car.

She gave him a little wave as she jogged to the passenger side and hopped inside.

Heat welcomed her. "Thank goodness you have a heater running!" She held her chilled hands to the vent that was blowing warm air.

Andrew grinned at her. "There are perks to the evil Englischer lifestyle, even in the form of white, cheap, crappy cars."

She shivered. "I like it."

He chuckled. "Careful, I don't want to sway you to my wicked ways."

"Very funny."

They pulled away from the Bontrager family land. Had they been careful enough meeting like this? She'd been getting tsk-tsked by her mamm all week. There was no fooling her. If only Ruth could open up and tell Mamm and Dat everything. But if they believed her, and that was a huge *if*, no matter what they decided to do—keep it a secret or tell the church—it would put them at risk of getting into serious trouble. Her family had plenty of trouble in life without her adding to it. Ruth couldn't tell them. Hopefully, with a little time, she'd be able to put things right and fix Eliza's mistake.

Quiet music played on the car radio as they rode in silence. She was comfortable not talking, and she imagined he was too. It seemed like the song was made entirely of human voices, though they were making rhythmic sounds like instruments, with harmonies layered so Ruth couldn't even guess how many different notes there were.

Andrew gestured to the car radio. Had he noticed her attention to the song? "It's a student a cappella group, just like how the Amish sing at church and gatherings. Kind of nostalgic for me, and I hoped enjoyable for you and less irreverent than other music. Maybe."

Her heart rose at his thinking of her. "This sounds nothing like our singings, but it's nice. Thank you."

"I have a surprise for you."

She sat back in the seat and put her now-warm hands in her lap. "You do?"

"I visited Mr. Hannigan earlier today. He had an off day and was able to meet me. That's our final Calico Creek interview for now."

"You did? I thought you had class until two hours ago."

"I, uh, skipped it." He glanced at her. "Don't give me that look." He held a hand up between them as if to block her vision of his eyes. "This class is my second English credit, something almost every student has to take, called a core class. It's not difficult, and I'm caught up. I have absences to spare."

He was way more invested in the interview project than

she'd realized. "So you're saying my surprise is you're a delinquent class skipper?"

"Ha. No. Just a second, let me park." They pulled into Calico Creek's small downtown area, and within a few moments, Andrew had found an open spot.

Once the car was in park, Andrew turned to her. "My surprise for you is that Rick at the *County Times* called me before Mr. Hannigan's interview. Rick is now my contact at the newspaper."

"Jah, you mentioned him last week." She'd told Andrew of Rick's original involvement in Andrew's connection to the newspaper when she was on campus explaining their past to him. Did he remember? Had that helped Andrew know whom to reach out to? "He's supposed to keep in touch with you about the possibility of the paper running the story when it's completed."

Andrew nodded, a grin breaking across his face. "They're interested. Rick said the data we collected—even just the preliminary data—paints a clear picture of cover-ups by the feed mill corporation, and it'll shock the entire town. He's the one who wrote the original article with me . . . well, in the timeline before this one."

In that moment it sounded as if he believed her, but she knew that in another moment, he'd sound as if he didn't.

Andrew started to say something. He took her by the hands and stopped cold. He blinked, looking shaken and pale, then released her hands.

"Andrew, are you okay?"

He stared at her hands, unmoving.

"Andrew?"

After a moment, he drew a breath. *"Jah, Ich bin gut."*

Why was he speaking in Pennsylvania Dutch to tell her he was good?

"Awwer?" She waited for him to answer her one-word question of *but.*

He cleared his throat. "Sorry. I got distracted." He didn't sound distracted. He sounded distressed. "I . . . I'd like your help writing the article. We'll submit it together, under both of our names. Or with a pseudonym for you if you're worried about getting in trouble."

"I'd love to write it with you." She wanted to lean across the car console and hug him, but that seemed to assume too much. She'd needed his help, and despite the battle it caused within him, he'd done all he could to help her. Besides, what had that reaction of his been when he held her hands for a brief moment?

"Good."

All this work they'd done, would it be enough? Would authorities actually investigate the plant? At least she would probably sleep at night, knowing she'd done her best. "Did you want to get started right now?"

He adjusted a vent on the dashboard. "I, uh, thought we could do something fun while we discussed the important parts of the article. Since it's so cold outside, we could amble through the antique store, talking about the article, and then get some food? Then afterward, there's a dollar theater downtown."

"I'd like that. Mind if we swap the theater for the library?"

He chuckled. "I should've guessed you'd prefer that. Sure. I could recommend some fun books to you."

"That sounds nice, but I have some other research I'd like to do, and it'd be a good opportunity to do it since I'm downtown." Once they finished the article and submitted it, she'd be free to fully dig into researching everything she could about Mercy and that horrible quilt.

"Sure."

Time flew as they walked through the huge antique store, discussing what information should be in the beginning, middle, and ending of the article. They went to a café, took a corner booth, and ordered food. They quickly divvied up the work for the article, and she took good notes on what she needed to do.

Her stomach growled at the smell of the homestyle food. Theirs should be coming out any moment. Andrew had ordered tomato soup with a grilled cheese sandwich. She'd ordered chicken and dumplings, one of her favorites. It was an eclectic-looking place with string lights and walls covered in historical knickknacks. The items on the menu seemed like what would be served in someone's home kitchen.

Andrew stirred his ice water with the straw. "Now that we have planning the article out of the way, want to elaborate on what you intend to research at the library?"

"I figured you could deduce it yourself."

He nodded. "You want to find out how to change the timeline back."

"You believe me now?"

He shrugged. "Does it matter if I believe you or not? Pretty sure you're going to do what you're going to regardless."

That was true. But it did matter to her if he believed her.

"I'm going to look into finding my great-aunt Verna. I don't even know if she's still alive."

"How does she play into changing the timeline?"

"Verna and her ex-husband, Omar, left the Amish years ago. It's a huge skeleton in my family's closet. They divorced. At first, my parents got upset when I barely mentioned her name at dinner, and their leaving the Amish happened over fifty years ago."

He shook his head, brows furrowed. "It's hard to believe anyone Amish from fifty years ago would find the strength to divorce and leave everyone behind to accomplish it. It's almost unheard of even in today's time where there are pockets of ex-Amish a divorced person could take refuge with."

"Jah, I agree." They remained silent as a server put their food in front of them.

Ruth measured her breaths while unfolding her cloth napkin and silverware. She put the fork and spoon to one side and the napkin in her lap. "Verna is the sister of my great-auntie Rose, and Rose is the one who gave Eliza the quilt. Omar, the ex-husband, is distantly related to you. He's an Ebersol."

"So it's not just that I'm ex-Amish and a college boy that has your mom fired up against me. It's that we're an Ebersol and Bontrager."

"Jah."

"Did she have issues when Eliza and Jesse started seeing each other?"

Again he gave mixed signals about believing her, probably because he was still on the fence about most of it. But she appreciated that he listened to her and gave honest answers. That alone was him giving a lot of support in this type of situation. His questions were encouraging too.

She dipped her spoon into the thick broth of the chicken and dumplings. "My folks and the whole community were not pleased for a long time. Maybe that's some part of why they were willing to be engaged for five years." She continued stirring the soup, hoping the next part of the conversation went well too. "If I can just talk to Verna, maybe I can figure out how things work, and maybe she knows where the quilt is. I'm a Bontrager woman too. If what Mercy said was true, I can also rewrite an event in my life. And that means all I have to do is get time to go back to the day Jesse asked Eliza to marry her. Then, five years later, at Eliza's wedding, I need to prevent her from getting the quilt."

As she said the words, it dawned on her that the plan would only work if Eliza had no memory of any of the events, including time travel. If Ruth managed to return Eliza to that time, and Eliza still chose to turn down Jesse's proposal, Ruth's single chance at time travel would be wasted. Plus, how would she get to the wedding when time would return her to today? She really needed Eliza on board, wanting to set things back the way they were . . . if Ruth could find Verna and get enough answers to be able to change time.

They ate quietly for several minutes, Andrew seeming as lost in his thoughts as she was in hers.

"Ruth—" Andrew wiped his mouth with the cloth napkin—"even if you could change things back, should you?"

Ruth's heart jumped. "Of course I should! Are you kidding? Everything is so much worse here." The town, her family, and above all of that, Ben's death.

He studied her. "Would I even be myself anymore if you did? You'd be taking away my choice in the matter, just like what Eliza did to you. Wouldn't that mean you'd be the exact same as her?"

It was as if he'd slapped her. She wanted to scold him. She wasn't like that! All she was trying to do was undo what Eliza had done. That was different. Right? She bit her tongue and tried to temper her response.

Andrew pushed his unfinished soup and half-eaten sandwich away from him. "If what you're saying is accurate, you knew me when I stayed Amish. But my current life experiences make me who I am now, and that includes my choice in leaving. It was one of the defining moments of my life. I don't even know who I'd be if I'd remained Amish for the last three years, give or take a few months. That person seems like a stranger."

This was more complicated than she'd realized. It seemed so cut-and-dried before. Fix Eliza's change, go back to everyone being better off and happier. Go back to Ben being alive. Did Andrew really think he was better off in this time? Could she make that call for him and still be a decent person herself?

She couldn't do that to him, no matter how much she wanted to fix the timeline. Slowly she managed a nod. "I hear you. And I promise: I won't take your free will away."

Her heart felt like lead in her chest. Changing the timeline was an impossible choice. No matter what, someone would be hurt. But she could do what Eliza hadn't, give those affected by the change a choice.

But was Ruth really offering that? She was only asking Andrew. Maybe she was playing God just as much as Eliza had. Ruth rubbed her temples. How could she know what the right answer was?

Chapter Twenty-Three

From the next room, Jesse watched Martha in her mamm's kitchen, talking with her family.

Noise, a mixture of people talking and laughing, rolled through the Peight home in waves. That was to be expected with this many people inside a home. Martha was the fourth child of seven in her family. All her married siblings, their spouses, and their children were here this Friday evening, as well as the unmarried ones. In addition to her large family, several extended families from out of state had arrived to help prep for Thursday's wedding. More would arrive tomorrow. He understood the early arrivals. Families used the week before a wedding to enjoy visiting while working toward a very important goal—a well-planned wedding. An Amish wedding was an all-day event. Martha's and his would have almost four hundred guests, and the guests would have a formal, family-style meal, a lighter meal later in the day, and all the sandwiches, finger foods, desserts, and beverages they could possibly want.

Standing near the kitchen island, Martha waved at him before holding up a beige cape dress against the front of her. She looked down, studying the dress. It would be her wedding dress. Later it would be her best Sunday dress. He wondered if Eliza had made that too. Eliza was everywhere. In everything, including the quilts that were meant to be on his and Martha's bed. Clearly he hadn't thought through what it would mean for Eliza to make the quilts for him and Martha that by Amish tradition his mamm was meant to make for them.

Martha looked up from the wedding dress, grinning, and winked at him. He managed a feeble smile.

A wedding was a huge deal, meant to be a celebration that honored establishing another Amish family, another couple to help hold this lifestyle together through respect, love, and really hard work.

A group of men in the living room broke into laughter. A mass of women in the kitchen chattered loudly among themselves. Children ran around, playing games. Teens were huddled in groups in bedrooms and in the empty spaces of the long, wide hallway.

Jesse had one shoulder leaning against a bookcase, watching and trying to breathe.

Unable to walk away.

Unable to connect.

Six days until the wedding.

Six.

His heart pounded. In six days they would be husband and wife for the rest of their lives. Would thoughts of Eliza fade after he and Martha were married?

He'd worked for years to free his heart of Eliza, and all it took was her returning for a few weeks to renew the flame. It made no sense. Why was he still haunted by excruciating love for her? It was ridiculous. *He* was ridiculous.

Martha's dad, Paul, started for the back door. It was time to tend the horses.

Jesse stood straight. "I'll go to the stables and take care of the horses. You stay where it's warm and visit with your brothers." He was desperate for a bit of time alone to wrangle with himself, to cast down imaginations and bring every thought captive to the obedience of Christ.

Paul grinned. "Deal." He returned to the couch.

Jesse grabbed his coat and hat and went outside. He strode toward the stables. *What do you want?* The voice was calm and matter-of-fact, just as it had been for the last week. Was God nudging him? Or was the thought just his own?

How could he marry Martha?

How could he break up with her?

The no-win situation felt very familiar. When it came to Eliza, he'd been in a no-win situation since the get-go—couldn't get free of loving her and couldn't be in a relationship with her.

He heard someone running toward him.

"Hey there." Martha looped her arm through his. "Want some company?"

He smiled and nodded. Was this going to be who he was?

Someone who hid his thoughts, said what he didn't mean, and loved Martha far less than she deserved?

They walked through the huge barn doors. Martha reached into a bag of horse treats, pulling out a handful. She shoved them into her coat pocket. Jesse took out his pocket-knife, slit open a fifty-pound sack of feed, and emptied it into a wheelbarrow.

He pushed the wheelbarrow to the first stall, dipped out a scoop of feed, and went inside the stall. Drowning in dark, miserable thoughts, he repeated that pattern five times until he was entering the last stall to feed the last horse.

Martha was giving that horse a treat. "Mamm's pretty emotional that her baby girl will have or be expecting a baby by this time next year. I guess I hadn't thought of myself as her baby since I have three younger brothers."

This was what he'd wanted, wasn't it? A kind, loving wife and children? Then why did it feel as if Martha were handing down a prison sentence? Not just for him, but for her too.

After dumping the feed into the trough, he checked the fasteners on the horse's blanket, making sure they were secure. It'd be a cold night. A night could be comforting or miserable, depending on the contentment of the creature. How many long, miserable nights were ahead for him and Martha because he lacked contentment with her?

What do you want? The calm voice returned, as if God were giving Jesse permission to seek his heart's desire. The question wasn't about Eliza. God would never make Eliza go against her will for the sake of Jesse's happiness. The question was about living with integrity, being true to who God had made him, true to himself. In truth, Jesse would rather live out his days single than to marry one he loved a small amount while being madly in love with another. He'd grown up with severe lack, but standing here now, he realized there was a harder poverty to endure—a poverty of love in a marriage. That would be the hardest scarcity of all to endure.

He knew the answer to the question now, had probably known it for a week or more.

He left the stall. Martha's eyes met his.

He lowered his head, feeling sick to his stomach. "I'm sorry."

"Jah?" She sounded chipper. "What for?"

He looked at her and removed his hat. "You'll probably never know how very sorry I am for having to say this, but I can't marry you."

Martha's eyes grew wide and her body slumped against the wall. She stared at him. "You're serious?"

The confusion in her eyes sliced at him. He longed to fix the predicament for her. It was certainly within his power to fix it.

What do you want, Jesse?

He wanted Eliza, but that was never going to happen. What he wanted most of all was to be true to himself and not drag Martha into a shallow, empty marriage. Why had he let this relationship come this far? Hadn't he known all along that his love for her wasn't deep enough?

"I'm serious, Martha, and I'm truly sorry."

She stood straight, studying him. "You are serious." She shook her head. "I . . ." She laughed, a single sound that might be sarcasm. She put her hand on her chest. "I feel as if the weight of a horse just got off of me." She chuckled, lifting her arms and taking in a deep breath. "I can breathe."

"Jah?" Hope flickered and some guilt released him.

She nodded. "Jah."

He was pleasantly surprised that her first emotion was relief. That should tell her everything she needed to know as time passed. Her eyes narrowed, and he knew her secondary emotions were about to take over.

"Why wait until now?" She snatched the hat from his hand and used it to gesture toward her house. "Everyone knows we wed next week! I have family who've already traveled here!"

"I didn't know until now."

Martha scrunched the brim of his hat, shaking. "This is going to be the most humiliating thing that can happen. A week beforehand, Jesse Ebersol!"

Jesse closed the gap between them. "You are an amazing woman, Martha. Kind. Openhearted. Beautiful. You deserve a wonderful wedding with a man who adores you more than any other woman on earth. I fully agree that my timing stinks in realizing it, but I'm not that man."

She rubbed her forehead. "I guess the truth is better a week before we marry than a week after."

"I completely agree."

She straightened out the brim of his hat. "I know you're right. My sense of relief tells me that, but a broken engagement this close to a wedding day will humiliate my parents." Tears filled her eyes as she held out his hat.

"We can talk to them together." He took his hat from her. "Right now, if you want, and I'll let them know this is all my fault." He paused, giving her a minute to think. "I'll put a check in the mail later tonight and pay for everything, all the food, traveling expenses, cost of new clothes for the wedding. Everything."

She wiped at her tears. "Why now? I mean, I'm grateful you saw what I couldn't. But did I do something or say something that made you realize I wasn't the one?"

"Nee." He put on his hat while reaching deep within to speak the truth. "This is about me. My issues. My inability to love as I should."

She studied him before moving to the half-open door of a stall. She pulled treats from her pocket and fed them to the horse while patting his jowl. After several minutes, she sighed. "It's shocking news." Her voice was calm. "It'll be embarrassing for a while." She turned toward him. "I don't understand my sense of relief, and I'm sure I'll cry a lot at some point, but now that I think about it, I realize—" she used her hands to shrug—"I've been having cold feet too. There's almost a decade between us, and you're so settled in your calm ways and know everything about everything. When I laugh with Moses about stupid stuff, I think, *This is what I need.* When I know stuff he doesn't, I feel needed, like an important part of the relationship."

Jesse chuckled. "Good for you, Martha. This means we both know ourselves, at least enough to realize we shouldn't marry."

She nodded. "I guess it does. But I gotta ask . . . Eliza?"

He moved to pat a horse, giving himself a moment. "Seeing her again made me realize that my love for you isn't nearly what it should be. But she's dead set on staying single, so this isn't about having a life with her." In comparison, his love for Martha was a thimbleful, but she didn't need to know that.

"There is something undeniable about those Bontragers, jah?"

"Apparently."

She moved in close and fidgeted with his coat collar. "You're a good man, and I'll miss you."

"Jah, maybe until you get your first kiss from Moses," he teased.

"That long?" She chuckled and pushed him away. "I have no idea what to tell my family."

"Romantic relationships are very private matters, and you don't owe anyone the exactness of what took place."

"It feels wicked to not be completely honest with my parents."

There were times, like now, when he realized anew just how young she was.

He brushed her cheek with his finger. "It's not wicked to want privacy. You could also just say, 'We've called the wedding off' or 'We decided to not marry,' and leave it at that until you're ready to say more."

She sighed. "You're right. You're always right. I need me a man who is wrong some of the time."

He laughed. "Do you want me to go in with you?"

"Nee. I got this." She hugged him. "Bye, Jesse."

He held her, knowing he'd likely die a single man with no children, and yet he'd done the right thing for both of them.

Chapter Twenty-Four

The sound and smell of the library always felt familiar and reassuring to Andrew. It had since he was a little boy. Being here with Ruth felt familiar too, more familiar than just their time here over the last few weeks. Their time at the antique store brainstorming on the article and their time at lunch talking about time travel was behind them, but they had much they still hoped to accomplish today.

He squinted as he tried to focus on the digitally scanned old newspaper. He could already tell by a quick skim that this article didn't involve the Bontrager woman that Ruth was looking for. This Annie Bontrager wasn't Amish—Verna wasn't still Amish either, but based on a fragment of a sentence, this Annie woman had grown up in New York.

He closed the computer window and glanced at Ruth a

few seats away. She was intently staring at her screen, typing in hesitant keystrokes. He could practically see her brain working behind those beautiful eyes, a mind more powerful than any computer in its complexity. If he'd known Ruth before Ben had died—if they'd been dating—would he have remained Amish? These kinds of what-if questions were usually pointless, but not anymore. Not since Ruth had found him. What would be different about him if he'd never left Calico Creek?

Andrew pushed his plastic chair back a few inches. "Hey, I'm going to get a breath of fresh air."

She hit Enter, then turned to him and gave him a sad smile. "Wait. First, I want to show you what I've been working on. Just finished."

"You found some clues as to where Verna is?"

"Ah, no. I was working on something else. It's a letter."

Andrew went to her, leaned over, and looked at her screen. Microsoft Word was open, and she'd typed a full page. "It's addressed to me." He read it, realizing it was intended to inform him of his options if she managed to change time back to the original timeline. He was impressed with all she'd covered. If reading this didn't make him pause and consider getting an education, nothing would. "I'm not sure what to say."

"I understand. You can see my goal. No matter what changes or what doesn't, I'm hoping you'll have knowledge of your options." She swallowed. "Feel free to add anything you can think of that would open your mind and heart to leaving the Amish and getting an education. I'll write one to myself too."

"If you find a way to change the timeline back, would it even be possible to take the letter with you?"

"I think so. I had put a leaf in my apron pocket before Eliza changed time, and it was still in my pocket in this time, so if I can figure out how to go back, I'm pretty sure the letter can go with me."

Changing timelines. Ben would be alive. But Andrew would be someone different. Apparently he'd been someone different once before too. "That's good thinking. Thank you, Ruth. I'll get it from the printer and while I'm outside getting fresh air, I'll read over it to see if it needs to say anything different." He grabbed his coat off the back of the chair. When he picked up the letter from the printer, he folded it in half and slid it into his pant pocket.

One moment he believed her and the next he felt crazy for even considering her story as possibly viable. Desperate for air, he continued toward the library exit.

His mind moved to the flash of a thought he'd caught when he'd held her hands earlier. It'd felt like a memory—Andrew, dressed in Amish garb, his arm casually slung across Ruth's shoulders. Her adorable laughter. And Ben, alive, telling them all about a funny prank Moses had pulled on Jesse at work that day.

People tended to have strong imaginations, but whatever those thoughts were, they made him feel welcomed and loved in a life that didn't exist. Even if it had existed, he wasn't at all sure he'd choose it over what he had right now.

He went through the automated library doors, stepping outside. The cool evening air was refreshing. Maybe the change of setting could help him wrap his brain around what to do. He sat on the stone bench next to the book drop box, wishing he could discuss this with someone unbiased.

For the sake of arguing with himself, he decided to think about this as if all she said was true. If so, what was he so hesitant to give up in his current life? He'd accrued thousands of dollars in student debt already, and he would have plenty more before he graduated as a lawyer in another four to six years. *If* he graduated. He wasn't guaranteed to get into law school. So much of the song and dance of the university eluded him. He didn't fit in with the other students. Didn't care to attend parties, didn't want anything to do with 90 percent of the daily activities of his peers. The thing he kept chasing was fulfillment. Would he be fulfilled five years from now? Ten? Had he felt fulfilled in those snapshot memory-thoughts he had when he touched Ruth?

He pulled out his phone. Maybe Anh wouldn't mind a good hypothetical. He'd always told Andrew to call him if he ever needed anything.

He opened his short list of contacts and touched Anh's number. This was weird. He should hang up. Anh wouldn't want to be bothered with this. Before Andrew could talk himself out of the call, the line connected.

"Hello, Andrew. This is a first."

"Uh, hi, Anh."

"Good to hear from you. How's that cute Amish girlfriend?"

"You're funny. You know she'd never be allowed to date me. But I've been with her all afternoon. We got good news: we heard from the *County Times* about the potential article and they're interested in printing it."

"Nice! That's awesome."

"Thanks. You busy? I have a strange hypothetical for you."

"Oh? Coming from you, I'm intrigued. Yeah, I'm free." He heard running water in the background cut off. "I'm just cleaning up after making dinner with my girlfriend. I've got all the time you need."

Was he really going to open up about this? "This is gonna sound dumb."

Anh chuckled. "Try me. You know from class I love a debate."

"Okay." Better plunge into the conversation before his embarrassment could take over. "Imagine someone could rewrite time. One event. If I went back in time, changing who I am today, it would save someone's life, someone really important to me. My best friend from growing up. But I'd be stuck at home. Amish, that is. I'd never have left the little town I grew up in, never got an education."

"But your friend would be alive."

"If we did it right, I believe he would be. But there are no guarantees I'd retain my mind, remain myself."

"In this scenario, would you have to stay Amish forever?"

Andrew touched the folded paper in his pocket. "I'm not sure. It's possible a letter explaining things could travel with the person altering time. Even so, would I believe the information in the letter? Doubtful. I fought with myself to get to a place where I understood that I had the right and the strength and the coping skills to leave everyone behind and do what no one I'd ever known agreed with. I broke my parents' hearts, disappointed my community. I only managed to stagger away because I was so disillusioned with the Amish faith after Ben's death. His death broke my faith in the Old Ways. But no event could break the DNA ties or give me a new family or new friends I'd grown up with." He'd been racking his brain at the memory flash, trying to get inside the other Andrew's head. He remembered only feeling joy and peace. But that couldn't be all the time.

"How much about human development have you studied so far?"

"Just what they forced me to learn in introductory biology."

"Got it. Not a lot. Behavioral scientists say that most of a person's personality is set when they're three years old. Is the thing you're changing happening when you're a toddler or younger?"

"No. The part of the change that affects me would take place three years ago."

"You really think that Amish-you from three years ago is *that* ignorant?"

"I was pretty ignorant. My friend dying changed me."

"But when you were living Amish, you still wanted to learn. You still sought out knowledge, going to the library endlessly. You've told me all you did to try to be a local journalist before you came to Penn State. That part would remain the same."

"Yeah, that's true."

"Were you planning on having forty-two children or something?"

"*No.* I was sure I never wanted to get married, much less have kids. But then, apparently, Ruth happened."

Anh said nothing.

The connection Andrew felt with Ruth in the memory shone so bright. It was as if he'd finally found the missing piece of his life . . . of himself. But what did that mean for living Englisch? He cared about Ruth. A lot. If the timeline was redone, he and Ruth might marry, especially with Ben alive again and if Andrew didn't believe the letter. But if they married, they'd have to obey the Ordnung. They'd have to try for a large family, even if there were no resources to go around or if it was too much for the sake of his mental health. But Ruth didn't want a houseful of children either. She wanted the same things he did—to learn, to grow, to be herself. If he stayed Amish and married Ruth, could they be faithful to the Amish ways and also to themselves? Hadn't some of the couples in the community used a natural family planning method to limit their family size?

"Anh, you still there?"

"I'm here, just getting deeper in the mindset to continue role-playing as if this were actually happening to you. I think I'm ready now. I have several realistic questions to ask, and you answer by digging deep into who you are. Don't insert any 'if this were real' type thinking or responses."

"Yeah, okay." Andrew appreciated the freedom to hash this out so openly.

"Is your angst because you're not sure what reality to choose?"

"No. I don't think I'll get a choice. I want to help Ruth, and I want to scream at her to leave my life alone."

"Yeah, I can understand that. It seems to me that you're looking for peace. Since I've known you, you've been in search of that, but I think it can be found in either world."

"There's no peace if I lose myself."

"True enough, but you found your way to you once. You can do it again."

"According to Ruth, I've found my way twice, actually." He'd remained Amish in the previous life, but he'd accomplished more of his heart's desire through journalism than he had at this university. Yet being here was a different way of finding his direction to higher learning.

"Finding your way twice gives you even better odds of finding yourself again, Andrew. Are you bogged down in believing the lies about prestige and moneymaking? Because that stuff never matters in the long run. I gotta tell you, from what I've seen, you've been more alive in the past few weeks since you got your Amish girlfriend."

"What most scares me is I *don't* have a choice."

"Yeah, I hear you. A lack of self-determination is always hard for us to sort through."

Did Anh see right through this role-playing game to the heart of the matter? "I have to save Ben or at least try to, even if that means I lose my education."

"What are you afraid of losing? You think the Amish are the only ones who choose to shut out higher knowledge? *Most* of us choose to be ignorant in one way or another. All we can hope for is gaining a tiny fraction of understanding of the universe, of ourselves, throughout our entire lifetime. No one has it all figured out. If you have a desire to learn, you'll learn, no matter where you're planted."

This rang true. What *was* he so afraid of losing? His freedom. But what freedoms had living Englisch really brought him? A lot of stress and debt. A struggle to pay bills. What was it he was so angry with the Amish about? If Ben dying could be changed with something so simple, maybe it wasn't the fault of their lack of education, but rather just bad circumstances.

"And, Andrew . . ."

"Yeah?"

"Breaking my own rules here, but if this time travel was real, it would say something significant about who you are that Ruth was in both timelines, drawing out the best in you. Sometimes it's the things we never expected that end up the most important to us."

He wanted to lean in to Anh's words and find comfort, but they bothered him. It was as if Anh was saying a woman was reason enough to accept not finding himself or living as his true self. Neither men nor women should lose themselves for the sake of a relationship, should they? Shouldn't a person find themselves and then find a person to share a life with? Was Andrew thinking about life and love all wrong? As usual, he'd need time to sort this out, only right now, there wasn't a lot of time. He preferred to take years to think about a thing before calling it settled in his mind and heart. Still, Andrew's path had felt very dark, and his friend had handed him a lit candle. Andrew had direction and light. What more could a man need to guide him? "You've been really helpful. Thanks."

"Anytime, man. I always enjoy our conversations. They make me reflect on life differently."

"I appreciate your thinking this through with me, Anh, but I need to go. See ya."

"Bye."

He hung up the phone. The minutes ticked by as he let

his mind absorb the memories, and he knew what he wanted. Now he needed to come clean to Ruth. Let her know what he'd seen in the visions. Let her know what he'd decided.

"Andrew!" Ruth came rushing out of the library, a big smile on her face.

It must've been something good.

"Sorry to interrupt. But I found her. I *know* it's her."

He stood, her excitement infectious. "Show me."

They walked back inside the now-near-empty building. The library kept late hours for students, but with it being a Friday night, the place was about empty.

Ruth seemed to almost skip as she hurried in, going toward the computers. "It was in the search you'd made in the old newspapers. Two towns over, there's a charity that's similar to a homeless shelter. They let down-on-their-luck people stay for weeks, clean their clothes, give them haircuts, and find them leads on jobs. It's called Phoebe's House." She sat in front of the computer. "The name Bontrager was hidden in the article about its city council approval. The founder and owner is a V. Bontrager. But the article clarifies that it's a woman-owned business, and the head of the charity is named Phoebe. Verna Bontrager's initials are VB, and that sounds an awful lot like Phoebe. I think it's her. She wouldn't have wanted her real name on it. A new name would've been a fresh start for her."

"Wow. That's quite the theory." He leaned over to see her computer screen. The scanned article was from 1985. *Phoebe's House* was written on a hand-painted sign outside a huge Cape Cod–style house. "Is this place still in business? This article is from a few decades ago."

"Look." She gestured to the computer next to the one she was sitting in front of. "I searched for it. It's still open." She pointed to a spot on the computer. "Here's the address. The town is Freeport, about three hours from here."

Andrew pulled out his phone and typed the address into the maps application. "That's not a bad drive. My weekend needs to be devoted to compiling data and writing that info in a way that really hits home with the average citizen as well as the authorities, and I need to do it while everything is fresh in my thinking. You need to get your parts done too. But we could head there first thing Monday morning."

"You'd do that for me?"

Andrew wanted a more secluded place for them to talk. He spotted a private study room. "Kumm." He stepped into the smallest room, the one with blinds on the door and windows. Once Ruth entered, he closed the door. The lights flickered off and back on, usually a warning that the library would close in ten minutes. But it must've been an electric surge or something because it wasn't time for the library to close yet.

Andrew focused on Ruth. "I need you to know that I'm all in."

She stared, looking every bit as shocked as she did pleased.

He chuckled. "I have a confession to make."

"Okay."

"When we touch, I see fragments of who we were."

"What?"

"I wasn't ready for you to know that until now. But the first time it happened was on campus, when you were asking me to hear you out. I was trying to go around your outstretched arm. When I brushed against your hand, I saw us. We were playing croquet. It's happened twice more since then, but I wasn't sure what was happening or what I was seeing. Besides that, I felt torn, unsure that I wanted to believe you, unsure what would happen to the life I've carved out if I got on board and helped you fix the time issue."

"I understand that you want the life you've carved out in this timeline."

"I'm putting my desires about my life on hold. All that matters right now is trying to undo what Eliza did. I want Ben alive. I want your family out of poverty. I want the previous life back in place, and I'll figure out my life from there."

A beautiful smile graced her mouth as tears filled her eyes, but her head barely shook, as if she couldn't believe his words. "Denki, Andrew. I didn't want to pressure you, but I knew if I didn't have your help, I may never be able to change the timeline."

He took her by the hand, seeing nothing this time. "I choose to stop worrying about my life and to focus on what you need, Ruth. It's the only way to get Ben back."

Her body seemed to waver, and Andrew pulled a chair out for her. She sat, still shaking her head as he held her hand. "Denki," she whispered again, and he realized how important it was to her that he get on board to help.

Maybe when they changed things back, he'd get a flash of today: Ruth in a café eating chicken and dumplings. Ruth and him in the library as he wrestled with what he believed and what he wanted. "Let's go over the facts of what we do know about the timeline being changed."

"Eliza was—"

There was a knock on the door, and a woman opened it. "Excuse me," she said. "I'm sorry to interrupt. We're closing up early." The librarian, a woman in her early forties, stood there with her purse on her shoulder and keys in her hands. "There's been an accident at the feed mill."

"Your dad," Andrew said.

"He worked an early shift." Ruth stood. "But we're both likely to know other Amish who were on this shift. How bad?"

"Several serious injuries. One confirmed fatality, possibly more. The firemen are clearing the entire block for easier access."

"Thank you. We'll leave right now."

She nodded and hurried off, probably checking the library for any other patrons.

Ruth's joy from moments ago had disappeared from her face, seeming in the distant past. "We were too late. I'm sure it was that ancient, not-maintained boiler. Before, the authorities made them fix it."

They hurried out the door and got in Andrew's car. Sirens were going off nearby. He started the car, backed out of the parking spot, and pulled up to the main road, turning right to head away from the direction of the plant.

An accident bad enough to clear the entire block? It couldn't be good. What could he even say? "It'll be okay."

She turned worried eyes from the direction of the sirens back to him. "Andrew, when we get to a good place to stop, will you pray with me? I know you and God haven't been on close terms since Ben's accident, but those people in the plant . . . It could've been some of the families we met while doing the door-to-door survey."

"Yes, of course I will." He turned right again, then left into a gas station.

He hadn't prayed much over the last two years, mostly for guidance here and there. He certainly hadn't prayed for an injured person since Ben died. What would it feel like? Could he even still do it?

He pulled into a parking spot off to the left of the row of gas pumps and put the car in park. He could try for Ruth.

He took a deep breath and closed his eyes.

"Heavenly Father, we ask for Your comfort, not for ourselves, but for those involved in this accident. Swiftness and steady hands to those giving medical aid. Healing for those who are hurt."

He felt Ruth's hand over his on the steering wheel. Again, there were no memories flashing in his mind.

He continued. "Bring peace to the families affected, no matter what the outcomes."

A wave of serenity hit him, washing from head to toe, and the high amount of tension in Andrew's body left him. He hadn't realized he'd been holding it in—probably for years.

How could he wonder if he could still talk to God about every matter that arose? He was being silly—of course he could. God had never left him this whole time.

Silence fell over the small, humble space of the tiny car. But it didn't matter where Andrew was—here, in what his family considered a worldly, forbidden machine, or at a service in the most upstanding of church members' home. God was the same God, and He was everywhere. Talking to Him was the easiest thing in the world.

It felt like coming home.

Chapter Twenty-Five

Ruth turned her family's front doorknob slowly, feeling the familiar click of the mechanism as she pushed in slightly before easing it open. All the siblings had eventually learned to open the door "the quiet way." But surely Mamm and Dat had been asleep a while since it was past eleven.

"Ruth."

She jolted so hard her feet left the floor. Her mother's voice was *not* what she wanted to hear right now.

Ruth turned to face her, holding a hand up. "I'm sorry it's so late. I was at the library and got caught in a mess due to an accident at the plant."

Mamm moved in closer, almost pinning Ruth between the door and herself. "Jah, we got a call about the accident, but that's not what this is about. You've been getting in a car with Andrew Ebersol. Don't think I've been blind to what's going on right under my own nose."

It made no sense to argue with her mother. Ruth wouldn't be sneaking out if she hadn't been flung into this time when so many things needed to be set right. If it wasn't for the time shift, they wouldn't be having this conversation. Where she was from, dating Andrew was easy and accepted. And she was twenty-four, for goodness' sake! Was she supposed to argue with her mother about this as if she were a teen?

"Mamm. Have I ever given you a reason not to trust me?"

"Since you've come for an extended visit from Ohio? Jah. Absolutely. I don't know what's changed about you and Eliza, but something is off. Something big. You're both hiding something."

Her mind spun as she considered her options. What was the best possible thing to happen if she told her mother? Assuming Mamm believed Ruth, Mamm might relax a bit about her leaving with Andrew, but then again, she might not—even knowing Andrew had stayed Amish in the other time. What was the worst possible thing to come of her telling? Mamm could panic, thinking their actions were somehow connected to witchcraft. She could call the bishop and put a stop to Ruth's efforts to set things right. Option one was the only safe option.

"I'm sorry. I know how this looks. I do, but I need you to trust me, okay?"

"I can't." Mamm stayed in place, keeping Ruth near the door as if refusing to welcome her daughter any farther into her home. "You're blind where Andrew is concerned, which makes no sense. As far as I know, you barely knew the man before a few weeks ago. Just the fact that he's an Ebersol from Calico Creek should cause you to avoid him. Make this make sense to me, please."

"When Eliza and I came home last month, I went to see Andrew at Penn State. I'm not fully sure what I'd hoped to accomplish, but I needed to explain some problems going on in my life." She shrugged. "I guess it made no logical sense for me to beeline it to him, but he politely listened."

"What kind of problems?"

Ruth shook her head. "I can't. I'm sorry." She shrugged. "But the conversation caused us to start working on the pollution coming from the plant. We're working on an article that will hopefully be printed in the newspaper, but as important as that is, I think I was hoping against hope that he'd see me and want to return home."

"You love him." Mamm stared at her, concern deepening. "How? I mean . . ." She sighed. "It doesn't matter. From what I've seen, he's doing a much better job leading you astray than you are leading him home."

Was that true? Ruth had no desire to live in the Englisch world. Everything was fast and harsh. Even the "humor," like what she'd experienced from the fraternity boys in front of the journalism building, was mean. "No, that's not what's happening."

Her heart belonged to the Amish. From every possible viewpoint she had, Amish life won out over anything else this country had to offer. But would Mamm hear her even if she told her that?

"Ruth, you're riding in a car with an ex-Amish man. That's forbidden, and yet you're doing it. You're working on an article for an Englisch paper as if you're a part of *that* world. You've always been a free spirit, and I've never wanted to smother that, but I'm afraid for you."

Someone let out a racking cough from another room. Mamm's eyes cut toward the sound, then back to Ruth.

Dat.

Ruth had heard him cough like that so many times since she'd come to this timeline. There had been blood on one of his handkerchiefs when she was doing laundry the other day. Was that from him coughing? The fear of what it might mean turned her stomach.

"Andrew and I have been talking to people who live in town about the plant smell. Many of them work there, like Dat. I know the toxicity from the plant exceeds the legal amount, and it's our goal to make the plant clean up. That's what the article is about. We both want to help Calico Creek."

"There are some things that need to be left in God's hands while we, *you*, stay where a young, single daughter should. Do you hear me?"

"Mamm, you're the one not hearing—"

The front door opened, running into Ruth's back. She almost fell over. Who was coming home this late?

"Oops, 'm sorry, Sis." Moses reached like he was trying to catch her from falling, but he came nowhere close.

"Moses? What are you doing?" Then the smell hit Ruth. Alcohol. Strong, coming off his clothes and breath. That would explain the slurred speech and delayed reaction.

Moses seemed to notice Mamm. He tried to stand up straight but didn't quite succeed. "Uhh, what're you two doing up at this hour? I'z just taking a walk." He closed the door a bit too hard, shaking its frame.

Mamm looked from Moses to Ruth and shook her head, tears brimming. "Both of you, go to bed. If you care about this family, neither of you will leave this house for the rest of the night. We'll talk in the morning. I need to pray." She kept her head up as she walked toward her and Dat's bedroom at the back of the house, toward the sound of his awful cough.

How could Moses do this? Ruth wanted to scream at him. "You've been drinking."

"Ya might wanna look at yourself in the mirror before you accuse me of anything. You've been sneaking out with your Englisch boyfriend. Worse, he's ex-Amish. I was walking by myself. I'm not hurtin' no one."

"Not hurting anyone? Did you see Mamm's face?" Her voice rose at the end of the sentence. She needed to keep it down or she'd wake the whole house.

Too late. She heard footsteps upstairs. She went to the bottom of the steps, ready to intercept any little sibling who might be looking for Mamm. The last thing Mamm needed now was questions from a little one.

Eliza. She held a kerosene lantern as she peered down the stairs.

Good. She was awake. She needed to see the consequences of what she'd done.

"Ruth? What's wrong?"

"Come downstairs and ask Moses."

Eliza hurried down the stairs, nightdress flowing. "Moses?" She stopped in front of him, holding the lantern so she could see him better.

Moses looked away. "Ruth is overreacting."

"Moses . . . there's alcohol on your breath." Eliza's brows knit, her eyes watering.

"Look. Don't you join 'n too. It's not a big deal. I just wanna escape from my own head a bit. Turn the worried part of my brain down. I havva secret stash. I go off in the woods, and I just relax. Don't need to involve no one else. It's not gonna affect m'job. I'll be back to myself long before Monday morning."

Ruth pointed at Eliza. "You'd moved off, although within easy walking distance, but I lived with Moses in the previous time. He wasn't like this at all." She didn't care if Moses thought she'd lost her mind. He probably wouldn't remember anyway. "Whatever you did to 'fix' it—" she put the word in air quotes—"didn't work. This timeline is broken."

Eliza winced and turned away. "I realize that not everything may work the same, but—"

Ruth stepped around, making Eliza look her in the eyes. "No. No buts. It's *broken*. There was an accident at the feed mill today. Serious injuries. At least one death, maybe more. All because *you* changed the past and Andrew's article was never written, so the authorities never cleaned up the plant. He and I have been busting our backsides trying to replicate the research for the article. But whatever we manage to accomplish, we were too late to stop the boiler explosion. What families are missing their loved ones because of this accident? Just like Ben died. Who's going to be next?"

Moses blinked, held up his hands, backing away. "I dunno

what you two have going on, but I'm gonna go." He shook his head and slunk off toward the stairs.

"Eliza." Ruth crossed her arms. "We need to fix it."

Eliza turned and took a step away. "I . . . don't know. I think those lives are gone forever. We just need to accept—"

"I refuse. I'm not going to just drop this. I'll never stop fighting for our family. For Ben. For Andrew."

Eliza put her palms over her eyes. "It's not that easy! Mercy said that time is gone!"

"I'm not saying it'll be easy. Is that what you're looking for, easy? I'm asking you to help me. Do you have any ideas where the quilt is?"

"I don't know. I really don't. Since I didn't get married, Auntie Rose didn't give it to me."

"I think I've found Verna. First thing Monday, Andrew is taking me to see if it's her."

Eliza didn't budge.

"Whoa." Moses staggered toward them. Clearly he hadn't gone upstairs. He made a slow movement, waving his hand through the air. "That could get you shunned."

Ruth looked at Eliza. "I don't care. But I need help. *Please*, Eliza. I don't think Andrew and I can do this alone! We need you."

Eliza walked to the front window, putting her palms on the sill and looking outside into the dark night. "I need to tell Jesse."

"Yes. Thank you."

"When . . . we touch . . . Jesse gets flashes of our old lives. Of our marriage. Of Penelope." Eliza swallowed after saying her name.

Ruth went to her sister and put a hand on Eliza's back. "Andrew gets those too. I think it's a sign that the other time isn't gone."

Eliza leaned her head against the glass. "Jah. Maybe so." She drew a deep breath. "He's going to hate me when he finds out what I've done. Just like you do."

There was her sister. *There* was Eliza. Her grief had been blinding her, Ruth knew it, but until now, she couldn't reach inside the thick dark cloud. "No, Eliza. I *love* you."

"But after all I've done . . . Ruth, I'm so, so sorry. Dear God, please help those people. My arrogance, thinking I knew right . . ." Eliza turned, facing Ruth. "I'm so sorry."

Ruth pulled her into a hug, letting her sister sob into her shoulder. "I forgive you."

Saying that phrase seemed to fan the flames of fresh rage inside her. She didn't know why, but she had to forgive Eliza regardless of how this mess turned out. Her sister hadn't known what she was doing when she changed the timeline. Not really.

But would she ever be able to look at her the same if Eliza was right and the old timeline was gone?

Chapter Twenty-Six

Eliza's eyes burned as she stumbled out her front door. They were so swollen that blinking felt weird. Sleep had been hard to come by throughout the night, and the little she had was fretful. How many people had died because of her? How many more would? It rolled around in her head all night. Reminding her. Haunting her.

She buttoned her black coat as she stepped into the windy, gray Saturday morning. Even though it was a little past ten, the cloudiness and patches of fog made the world seem dim.

How dare she think that her grief over losing Penelope was the only pain that mattered? How had she let herself get to a place of wearing horse blinders? How must Ben's mamm feel? How would her own mamm feel once Moses' path toward alcoholism met its inevitable end?

Eliza had been selfish. So unbelievably selfish. Ruth's explanation about the butterfly effect was true and made sense. How had it never occurred to Eliza before she'd changed the past? She'd thought if she just got Moses a job with Jesse . . . but it wasn't the same, was it? In this timeline, Moses had three formative years to get his drinking habit ingrained into him. Jesse wasn't in Moses' life at the time Moses needed.

Her thoughts shifted to the quilt and the power she had been given. She was unworthy of that kind of power. Why had it been offered to her? Had God answered her prayers and allowed her to make this mess?

Brown leaves crunched under her shoes and anxiety rolled through her with each step. She used to walk this path to the Ebersol property nearly every day when she was younger.

Tell him. The words echoed inside her while a part of her cringed, begging her to go the other way.

She kept moving forward. She owed it to him—to everyone, really. Jesse would believe her. Even after all these years apart, he was that insightful, able to see into what was true despite how crazy it felt or sounded. When she'd arrived in this new time, she'd wanted to hide from him who they'd once been, hoping he'd believe they'd never been more than friends and believe even that had been long ago. But in no time, he knew something was up. Whether he knew through his own inner compass or because of the memories he saw when he touched her, he understood there was far more between them than an old friendship she'd abandoned eight years ago. It wouldn't be difficult to convince him about the time travel. In some ways, it would be a relief to him to understand why she refused to marry him and disappeared, to make sense of what he felt between them.

A shudder ran through her. He would believe her and finally have answers to the questions that haunted him, but he'd be angry too. How angry? Angry enough to hate her? Want to be free of her? Regret he ever loved her and trusted her in the first place?

Footsteps echoed and she looked up. A figure walked toward her. She squinted against the patch of fog.

Not just a figure—Jesse. She could recognize even the cadence of his hiking in the woods. She wasn't ready for this conversation! She was supposed to have more time to think as she walked. It would've been helpful if she'd been given time to sit on a log at the edge of the woods near his home for a bit before knocking on his door.

Jesse must've noticed her too, as he picked up his pace, closing the distance between them. He smiled. He wouldn't be smiling once he knew what she'd done. "Good morning, Eliza."

She fought her urge to flee. Clearly, in one way or another, she'd done that entirely too much of late. "Hi."

He angled his head. "Something's wrong."

She nodded and swallowed hard. "I . . . need to tell you something." How to even begin? "Last night, there was an accident at the feed mill. Dat wasn't involved."

"Jah, I'd heard. It's a bad situation. Three people died, and I think about five more were injured."

Three dead! Five injured! Three more deaths directly caused by her actions. Just like Ben's death had been. She took a few deep breaths, trying to quell the nausea.

"You have a good heart, Eliza."

No, she didn't, but she had no voice to tell him that. She looked around, trying to place herself in the woods. *Her* tree wasn't far.

He started to reach for her, but he stopped short and put his hand in his pocket. "I was coming to your home because I wanted to tell you something, before you heard it from someone else. Martha and I ended our relationship."

What?

He chuckled. "Don't look so shocked. We weren't a good match. I'm sure you could see it. I was too old for her, and honestly, I barely knew her. While other people can build strong marriages from short courtships, that wasn't going to work for me. I was so desperate to feel put-together. I'm twenty-nine years old and single, for goodness' sake. But I realized nothing was going to put me together, not while I was missing the biggest piece of my life."

What was he missing? What else had gone wrong?

"You look confused." He smiled, taking her hands gently into his, warming her cold fingers in his gloved hands. "It's you, Eliza. I was missing you. It was like being without a limb. You're my inspiration, my muse. You're humble, hard-working, and resourceful. When I'm with you, I feel like we can do anything together."

He wouldn't feel that way about her once he learned what she'd done. She was going to have to tell him everything no matter what. She tried to find her voice. Tears stung her sore eyes. "I love you, Jesse. To depths I can't describe."

Disbelief, maybe shock, reflected in his eyes and covered his face. They stood there, her heart pounding like mad.

The surprise faded and a slight smile emerged. "Jah?" he whispered.

She longed to melt into his arms, to be held and treasured like she had in a lifetime that no longer existed, embraced by the one man she'd always loved. He reached out to her, but she backed away. He waited, his eyes peering into hers.

Say it, Eliza. Tell him the truth! Go ahead, break his heart once again. She was such a fool! Again, she longed to know how she had let grief blind her so completely.

"Jesse." Her voice cracked.

"It's okay, Eliza. Whatever it is, we'll figure out a way around it."

She shook her head. There was no way around it. No way around the truth of what she'd done. No way around the truth of their genetic makeup that merged together to create a baby, then maimed and killed it. She cleared her throat, begging the tears to stay in hiding. "I need you to listen to me. Please, hear me out."

"Of course." His smile fell, replaced by a look of concern.

She walked toward her tree, and he ambled beside her. Once he found out what she'd done, he was going to be so angry. Anyone would, especially since she might not be able to fix it. In fact, all evidence pointed to how *this* was the only reality now. Ruth wanted to believe they could do something so badly, and Eliza would try, but . . .

She gestured to one of the tree's largest roots, forming something of a seat. She'd been here with Jesse many times. "I know it's cold, but can we sit?"

"You're cold." He put an arm around her as they sat

together. His warmth felt amazing. Was this the last time she'd feel it? "Tell me what's on your mind."

Her heart raced. This was it. "You say you know about the curse. But there's more. So much more. I'm scared to tell you."

"You can tell me anything. I don't care what it is, Eliza. We'll face it together."

She nodded. How should she explain it? Then she knew . . . "There was a young man and a young woman. They lived next door to each other. Their parents didn't want them to, but they became best friends, inseparable."

He stroked little circles on the small of her back through her thick coat. "Go on."

"When they were old enough, the young man asked the young woman for her hand in marriage, and she joyfully accepted, because she'd always loved him, even before she knew what that meant."

A tear formed in the corner of her eye. She rubbed it away before continuing.

"After five years of waiting and hard work while they built a new business, they married and made a life together. Built their own home on a beautiful creekbank. Using his skills, he gave jobs to other hardworking men in the community, including both of their fathers and several of their brothers. But in their happiness, they'd been ignoring one thing the entire time. The families had a curse, lurking inside their bodies. When they conceived children, every child was affected by it, and in three years' time, three of their babies died."

She stole a glance at his face. He was looking away, staring through the trees. Did he understand what she was trying to tell him?

"There was a secret the young woman held on to. She'd been given a family heirloom with seemingly magical properties. If a woman in the family experienced a tragedy, she could use the heirloom—a quilt—to go back and rewrite an event of the past. When her third baby died, a full-term, beautiful girl named Penelope, the woman was overcome with grief, desperate for any relief from the unrelenting pain. Desperate to spare her husband of the shame that his wife couldn't bear him children and the grief that they'd never have children."

Eliza swallowed back a sob. She *had* to finish. He deserved to know everything.

"She wasn't herself. In her despair, she made a stupid, impulsive decision to go back in time and undo their marriage, thinking it would make things better for her husband to not be bound to such loss. When she came to the new timeline, the quilt was gone. And everything was different."

Her words hung in the chilled air. He didn't remove his arm. He didn't move at all. Silence hung between them for at least a minute. What was he thinking of all of this? Did he believe her?

"Jesse, I—"

"It's for real, isn't it? It's us."

She nodded. "You believe me?"

"I do. As impossible as it sounds, everything makes sense now." He stood and took a few steps away, facing the woods.

"I'm so, so sorry." Her head swam and her legs felt too weak for her to stand, so she stayed put. "I couldn't see up from down. I feel like I'm barely coming out the fog. I have a hard time recognizing myself in the actions I took. Now . . . your cousin Ben died because he was working a dangerous farm job instead of working for you. Moses didn't get clean from alcohol. Dat works at that awful feed mill, still. In the other time, your second cousin Andrew published an article that made the plant clean up. Here, three people died. It's all my fault. I didn't mean to—I only wanted to spare Penelope. To spare you. And me."

He turned abruptly, catching her eyes with his. "How do we undo it?"

She shook her head. "We can't. The woman named Mercy—something of a guardian angel—told me once it's done, it's done."

He turned away again, taking several deep breaths. "You had no right." He faced her, looking down as she remained sitting. "You made this decision for me. You didn't ask me. If you did, I would've told you *no*. How could you think you had the right to do this? You're not God!"

"I know." She pulled her knees up and put her face in the crook of her elbow. "I know."

"Do you have any idea of what the last eight years have been like for me? To love someone the way I love you but to have you separated from me? You weren't dead—you were right here on this earth, but I couldn't get to you. It made no sense. It's been torment." He shook his head. "I need a walk. Some space and a breather." His face was pale now. His hands trembled. Grief and anger owned him, and all he asked for himself was for time to walk and think. He pointed at her. "Don't go home. We're not done."

"Okay." She scooted closer to the huge tree and leaned her

back against the rough bark. She wasn't going anywhere—there was no home for her anymore.

He was her home, and she'd destroyed him.

Jesse strode faster and faster away from where Eliza was, until he was almost running. Every piece had clicked into place. It was an impossible story, and yet it was the only thing that made sense of the last eight years of his life.

He wasn't even on a trail, stumbling through the woods. A quilt that could change time. How could such a thing exist? Nevertheless, he believed her every word. All those pieces of memories he'd seen when he'd touched Eliza . . . they *were* real. He'd had those events in another life. He'd had her as his *wife*.

And she'd cast it all aside, on purpose. This felt worse than being turned down at the creek all those years ago. Worse than her running from him, hiding for years. She'd known him intimately, body and soul, and *still* decided to reject him. He slowed, rubbing his aching chest. This pain was unbearable.

And there, as he exited the tree line, was the creek and his favorite creekbank. Their home in another life? Ugh. He'd have to move. Leave Calico Creek forever. But no, that wouldn't be enough. Even if he ran his entire life, she would still haunt his every waking hour, every dream.

Eliza. He could never stop loving her. Even when she'd done something unthinkable. Even when she'd caused death and pain for untold numbers of people, although she'd not done those things intentionally. He walked to the clearing, trying to remember the pieces of their cabin that he'd seen in flashes. The grass still had bits of green mixed with the brown. Soon winter would arrive and the whole mountain would be brown, life asleep for months.

What should he do now? Leaving Calico Creek, leaving Eliza, wasn't an option.

He let his brain drift into building mode. If he were creating a home here, he'd level this section of dirt and build up the sloping part. A strong, good foundation made the difference between a construction that lasted multiple lifetimes and one that was bulldozed in a few decades.

Like the most beautiful home in his current subdivision. The first thing he'd done was to tear the entire thing down—it was filled with mold and rot after being abandoned to the elements for so many years. But the foundation was good. As they cleared the debris, he could see the future of the home, filled with love, filled with family. He'd rebuilt it from the solid foundation up. Then it became the jewel of the neighborhood. For a while it was the model home. All the families that decided to move to that neighborhood had done so because of that previously rotted, destroyed house that was remade into something beautiful.

His and Eliza's relationship had a strong foundation, built while they were only children. Rebuilding it was going to be really difficult, wasn't it? Tedious. Painful. And yet wasn't that home his most beautiful work? Eliza . . . she was worth it. She made him want to be better. Apparently, when together, they'd changed a lot of lives for the better. That life was the one they needed to get back to.

Maybe she was wrong about her ability to go back in time

again. He had memories of the other time too. If they found that quilt, maybe *he* could use it and reset everything.

But even if they couldn't, even if here was all they had, with her dat sick and Moses' drinking issues and Ben's death and all the other things that changed for the worse in this time, his life with Eliza was worth rebuilding.

He raced toward the woods, toward Eliza sitting under that tree. It was important to them; he could feel it. To their daughter. He had a daughter! He wanted to see it all.

"Jesse." She stood, wiping tears from her face.

He pulled his gloves off and tossed them aside. "I want to see her. Please."

She nodded and offered her bare hand. He grabbed her icy fingers in his own, which were warmed by gloves and jogging.

Penelope. And there she was, wet from the womb. A head of dark hair, button nose, scrunched-up, tiny face, and the most beautiful cry in the world. The utter joy he'd felt in seeing her, in holding her. They only had moments with her. It wasn't enough. But a lifetime wouldn't have been enough.

A sob escaped him as he pulled Eliza tightly against his body. "I forgive you."

She sobbed. "How? I'm not worthy. Anyone would hate me for what I've done."

"I could *never*. I love you. You're my wife, and I'm your husband. I'd love you across any lifetime."

He drew back, cupped her tear-soaked face in his hands, and kissed her. The world melted away, blending and swirling into the pictures that sprang into his mind. Their wedding! Reuniting in the driveway after he'd returned—late for their wedding. How he'd pushed to get home, to get to her. She was worth it, all the effort. Their five years of work, facing down the negativity of their families.

And she was worth this.

Then he felt something else. Her sadness—it was like he could see into her soul, feel the endless ache. The embarrassment of failing him. The near insanity. The desperation to do *something*, anything to ease the suffering of losing a being so precious, so perfect as Penelope was.

He pressed his forehead into hers. "I see you, Eliza. I see your heart. And I forgive you. You are worth lifetimes of pain, if I can just have any amount of time with you."

"I'm not."

He wiped both sides of her face with his hands. "You are, my love. You are."

"What do we do? I don't have the quilt here. And even if I did, Mercy told me I couldn't use it again. Once it's done, it's done."

He sat down where she'd been before on the tree root, pulling her into his lap, wrapping his arms around her body. "But I remember. Doesn't that mean there's hope?"

"Ruth thinks so too."

"Ruth knows?"

She nodded. "She was walking with me in Hunters' Woods when we saw smoke from the cabin. Mercy was inside, and we went in together, so I accidentally involved her. That's how she knows I ruined everything between her and Andrew. I had a quilt with me for the sake of comfort that was a wedding gift from Auntie Rose. Mercy explained some things about the quilt and being able to go back and change one event. Then I broke a stitch and restitched the quilt, wanting to change time. That happened on the day of the Ebersol family gathering, only minutes before I ran into you and Martha at the creek."

"You were at the Ebersol family gathering, the one last month. Then you changed time, and yet you landed back on the same day, with a life completely different?"

"Jah."

"My sweet Eliza, no wonder your eyes radiated a brokenness that didn't make sense to me." He kissed her forehead. "Tell me more."

"I didn't know what would end up happening. I didn't know I'd find the old cabin in Hunters' Woods or that what I was thinking was real. It felt like a dream at the time."

"It would feel surreal, wouldn't it?" He gazed into her eyes. "Grief has a way of making everything feel too real and yet completely unreal at the same time."

"It does. Ruth is grieving now too, and she's pretty mad at me. She's forgiven me, and yet she's trapped in anger because of my decision, so I understand, but it hurts. I didn't know that forgiving is separate from letting go of anger, did you? I thought whenever I still felt angry about something that I hadn't forgiven."

"I think that forgiving is a decision, like making a vow is a decision. Anger is an emotion that will need time to yield to her decision. It seems that forgiveness says, 'I hold no vengeance against you. You're human, like me, and we all need forgiveness.' But emotions say, 'You really hurt me, and that hurt hasn't gone away yet.'"

"Then I need to find ways to help her stop hurting. But what if I can't?"

He leaned in and kissed her forehead again. "Love and time can accomplish a lot. Trust in that."

"And you. It's not like she's the only one I've hurt. And the community. And—"

"Breathe, Eliza." He inhaled, inviting her to do so too. She couldn't make up for everything the day she began to see what her choices had done to others. No one could. "So in the original time, your sister and Andrew Ebersol, my second cousin from Calico Creek Glen? I've never spent much time with him, but you're saying he stayed Amish and took your sister to the family gathering?"

"Jah. In this time, she's reconnected with him, and he's helping her search for answers, researching various things. They may have found my great-aunt Verna."

More people working on the problem was a good thing. "The four of us should talk about it. I'm with Ruth. If we can all remember a life we once had, then the other time isn't gone." It couldn't be. Right now, that life felt more real to him than them going to their parents' homes to live separately.

"Jesse, what do you want to do now? Try to meet with them?"

"Later. First, I want to hold you. I want to see everything."

He pulled her against him and kissed her lips. The warmth of their shared lives washed over him, in all its bliss and pain.

Chapter Twenty-Seven

After a three-hour drive from Calico Creek, Andrew put his car in park as his mapping app announced in a pleasant voice, *"You have arrived at your destination."*

Through the gray November mist, he saw a painted, hand-carved sign in front of the beige-and-brown structure. It read, *Phoebe's House.* He looked the building over. It appeared to have been the home of someone wealthy long ago. A historic construction, with white filigreed pillars holding up a wide front porch that could use a coat of fresh paint. The upstairs windows had blue diamond-patterned stained glass on the top panel.

"Not bad timing after all." Ruth smiled and took the last bite of her burger from the drive-through they'd hit about twenty minutes back. Andrew had long since finished his food.

He turned the car off and removed the keys from the ignition. "You ready for this?"

"Oh yeah. Chomping at the bit." She winked and wiped her hands and mouth on a napkin.

"Nice horse joke. Think of how long it would've taken us to ride here from Calico Creek via buggy."

"I have a suspicion that's why Verna relocated all this way out." She put the food wrappers back in the bag they came in. "*If* it's her."

"It's her. I've got a feeling."

Honestly, he did too. Excitement hung in the air. The possibility of answers. Andrew reached over and took Ruth's hand, then closed his eyes and said a quick, silent prayer for guidance. So many people's lives were riding on them figuring this out. He squeezed her hand and nodded at her. "Let's go."

They stepped out of their respective sides of the car and closed the doors. The thuds echoed across the otherwise-silent parking lot. Someone had paved extra space in the old house's front yard to allow for more cars. How many people lived here?

They walked through the gray mist and onto the porch with the pillars. The double front doors were made mostly of frosted glass with red-stained wood around the edges. Ruth knocked on the wood. Andrew could see a bunch of people inside, working at a large table. Maybe a craft?

"Come on in!" someone yelled. Female, with the lower timbre that comes with age. Could it be Verna?

Ruth's eyes met his before she turned the knob and opened the door.

The place smelled of fresh cinnamon, with the under-tones of the slight musty smell that always seemed to linger in an old house.

A woman who looked to be in her mideighties walked from the table, wiping her hands on her red flower-print apron. She had long silver hair, pinned back into a loose ponytail with a few wisps escaping. "Can I help you?" Her eyes fixed on Ruth's Amish garb, and she froze.

"Auntie Rose," Ruth murmured under her breath.

Andrew studied the old woman. She *did* have the same eye shape as Ruth and her sister. Family resemblance, no doubt. "Are you Verna Bontrager?"

The woman's smile disappeared, and she shivered from head to foot. A moment later, her smile, looking genuine and peaceful, returned. "I prefer Phoebe. Some of my friends here call me Miss Fee." She gestured behind her to the people at the table. There were small piles of colored wool at each place setting, and each person used a needle and foam pad to shape the wool into what looked like felted Christmas ornaments. "Who am I speaking with?"

"Um, I'm Ruth."

Andrew considered whether he should put a steadying arm under Ruth's elbow, but he decided against it. Her face indicated that she was quickly recovering from whatever shock had overcome her.

Ruth extended her hand to the woman. "I think you're my great-aunt. Could you please spare a few moments to speak to me?"

The woman shook her hand, then glanced back at the table. "Yes. Let me tell my friends. One of my long-term guests, Carol, can help them with the craft while I'm away. We're making ornaments to sell to raise money. Let me just give her some instructions."

Andrew looked around the space while he and Ruth waited by the doors. The walls he could see were painted in colorful shades, unlike any Amish home would be. While the house might have been old, the style inside wasn't. It reminded him of the dorm room of an art student he'd once studied with, creative and eclectic. Framed paintings done by people of various skills took up most of the wall space, along with some shelves holding sculptures and even some trophies. String lights zigzagged back and forth over the stairs. The chattering of voices and occasional bursts of laughter came from the craft table, in what was once the home's formal dining room.

Phoebe returned, sans her apron. "Follow me. We'll go somewhere quiet."

They followed a few steps behind her, passing the group at the table, the ancient wood floors creaking under their feet. Phoebe pulled a set of silver keys from her pant pocket and unlocked a door. "This leads to my personal apartment. I've lived here now almost thirty-five years. This place was a dump when I bought it."

"I read about Phoebe's House online. It's amazing how many people you've helped find their footing over the years," Ruth piped in as Phoebe held the door for her.

"Thank you. *They* let you use a computer?"

Ruth didn't answer as they walked into a small kitchen with its only light coming from a little square stained-glass window. Houseplants hung from kitchen cabinets and the window ledge.

Ruth paused next to an eat-in table. "Well . . . no. Some Amish people are allowed to use a computer if it's absolutely necessary for their business. But I went to the library. I don't think the bishop realizes the things I can do there. And I'm breaking the rules—the Ordnung—a bit by being here."

"Yes. I know you are." Phoebe motioned for Ruth and Andrew to sit at the small, round wooden table with two metal sculpted chairs. They sat on the crocheted chair cushions.

Phoebe pulled up a stool to the table, perched slightly higher than Andrew and Ruth. She searched Ruth's face for a moment. What was she looking for? "And your friend is Englisch?" Verna studied Andrew, looking as if she knew something was a bit askew about him. He'd spoken to her, and according to his college friends, his accent, with its slight hint of a German lilt, said something was a bit unusual about him. Verna could probably place the accent as clearly "Amish," a distinct inflection that came from being raised in a small community that spoke Pennsylvania Dutch as its first language. Like most Amish, he'd entered the one-room Amish school in first grade before he began to learn to speak English.

"This is Andrew, and jah, he is." Ruth's eyes locked on his, like they were questioning that. He had much soul-searching to do. What was he? He didn't feel Amish anymore. But yet living Englisch hadn't made him feel any more fulfilled or at home. So much he had to figure out . . . after they fixed the timeline. That was the only thing worth focusing on now.

Andrew angled himself toward Phoebe. "It's nice to meet you. Thanks for talking to us. We're looking for a Bontrager family heirloom. A quilt."

There. A subtle cringe. Phoebe smoothed the expression on her face almost instantly, but he'd seen it. "Afraid I can't help you. You are correct I used to be Amish. And Bontrager is my family name. But I left a *lifetime* ago."

He opened his mouth to speak again, but Ruth's sharp look in his direction made him stop. He'd asked too quickly. He should've known better. But Phoebe wasn't throwing them out, so that was good.

"Um, Phoebe, you're the sister to my great-aunt Rose Bontrager, right?"

"Rose was my little sister. I loved her dearly."

"I'm sorry for your loss. Auntie Rose was special to me too."

"She was one of a kind. I was banned from the community, but I managed stealthy visits to Rose on occasion. She visited me too. I'm grateful for the time we had not long before she passed." Phoebe stood, pointing to a brass kettle sitting on a two-top stove. "Let me brew us some tea. Then you can tell me the real reason you came." She moved to the stove, turned on the gas burner, then removed a flower-print tin and a large glass teapot from the cabinet above the stove. She dumped a few scoops of the black tea leaves into the teapot.

"*Sorry,*" Andrew mouthed to Ruth.

She smiled and nodded. "*It's okay,*" she mouthed back.

He took in the surroundings of this apartment. It was homey, with a flower and plant theme, rather than mismatched like the front of the house. There was a rose embroidered on a large hoop hanging on the wall next to him. Beside it, a shadow-box frame held a fabric square of quilt. She'd lived here for almost thirty-five years? Starting and keeping up a charity of this magnitude was quite an accomplishment for anyone, even more so a woman in her eighties. But she didn't appear to be slowing down.

After a moment, the kettle started singing. Phoebe switched off the stove, poured hot water into the glass teapot, and the fragrant, rich smell of black tea filled the kitchen.

She carried the now-full pot of tea to the table, setting it on a wood trivet at the center. She placed a teacup at each of their places and brought a glass jar of sugar cubes and a small spoon, setting them next to the brewing tea. "Either of you need creamer?"

"No thanks, black is fine with me," Ruth said.

"Me too."

Ruth breathed deeply, closing her eyes. "That tea . . . is so familiar."

Phoebe sat on her stool again. "It's my favorite."

Ruth opened her eyes. "Mercy's tea. At the cabin."

Phoebe's head angled slightly as she studied Ruth, looking warm and wary at the same time. After a moment, she nodded, a solemn look on her face. "I searched for years to find a brand that approximated the kind she'd given me."

Ruth leaned forward, palms on the table. "Who is she? A . . . guardian angel? Or is she something more sinister?"

Phoebe shook her head. "That's a smart question for one so young, but there's no way of fully knowing. I've wondered the same thing many times. I think she's an echo."

"An echo? You mean a ghost, then?"

"No, I don't think so. An echo. Like screaming into a cave or canyon. The noise that bounces back isn't from a ghost or a person yelling back to us. It's an echo that we put in motion. Maybe she's an echo of our prayers, our greatest hopes, or our strongest determinations to change what is. It's more likely that she's a guardian angel, but I really don't know. How did she appear to you?"

"She looked a lot like you and Auntie Rose. In her forties maybe?"

"In my memories, she looked just like you."

A chill went down Andrew's spine. The logical part of his brain wanted to reject all this. It was too crazy. *Could* it all be true?

Phoebe held a hand up. "Maybe she looked a decade older than you are now. But it's been many, many years since I've seen her." She picked up the glass teapot and poured three cups, starting with Ruth's, then his, then her own.

"You also returned to the cabin in Hunters' Woods and changed an event in your life?" Andrew asked. "And you saw the same woman decades earlier than Ruth did?"

"Yes," Phoebe whispered. "I saw Mercy about sixty-five years ago. I was so young, probably years younger than Ruth is."

He couldn't move his eyes from Phoebe, as if her eyes or face could tell him more than her words. "No matter how I try to wrap my head around it, it's difficult to believe."

Ruth reached for his fingers on the table, brushing them gently. "Andrew, haven't you seen enough proof that this is real when you touch my hand?"

She was right, and he was embarrassed for still looking for confirmation. He nodded. "I know enough."

Phoebe pointed at him. "He's an Ebersol, isn't he? An ex-Amish Ebersol."

Andrew nodded. "Jah, that's right."

"Before time was changed, were you two together?"

Ruth nodded. "Dating, not married, but he was Amish."

Phoebe sighed. "The families really need to move, separate by a few states so you kids aren't dealing with the same issues we had."

Ruth squeezed his hand. "We know about the curse. Please, we really need any help you can offer. Do you have the quilt? Or know who might have it?"

Phoebe tilted her head. "So what did you change?"

Ruth shook her head. "I . . . I didn't. My sister did."

Phoebe rose and went to the sink. She turned on the faucet, filled her cupped hand with water, and placed it against her lips. She remained there, repeating that several times before using a hand towel to dry her mouth. She turned. "You're the little sister caught in what the older sister has done. It's so familiar, I feel sick for you and her."

Ruth rubbed her forehead. "Me too."

Phoebe returned to her stool and brushed a long, silvery wisp of hair away from her face. "So your sister . . ."

"Eliza."

"Eliza's the one who wanted to change the past."

Ruth put a hand over her heart. "Jah. She went back in time and undid her marriage to an Ebersol man. She had three babies that died in our original time. You know, from the curse."

"What?" Phoebe tapped her short nails on the table.

"I looked it up at the library recently. It's a genetic disease, a form of dwarfism that's often lethal. It's recessive. Eliza and Jesse were caught in the hereditary curse that our families forewarned all of us about so many times. It's why my family and Jesse's family didn't want them to be together."

Deep pain reflected in Phoebe's eyes. "My child, that's not the curse."

Ruth flinched, jolting back. "What? It has to be." She looked at Andrew before regaining some composure. "Then what is?"

"The curse is the time travel."

"What?" Ruth stood, unintentionally hitting the table with her legs. Some of her tea spilled onto the table.

The curse was time travel? Andrew's shock at this revelation was nothing compared to Ruth's. Her mouth was open. Her head shook a steady *no*.

"What?" she whispered again as she slowly sank to the chair.

Phoebe drew a breath. "I'm sorry, child, but the curse *is* the time travel."

Ruth grabbed several napkins from their holder and placed them over the spilled tea. "The curse is Bontrager women can time travel?"

"Only a few Bontrager women can time travel. There are many Bontrager women, but only a handful can tap into the power of the quilt—those who are direct descendants of Ayla Bontrager, have been given the quilt, and have been told the secret of time travel." Phoebe pointed at Andrew. "Ebersol men who are direct descendants of Bytzel Ebersol have the power to time travel too, although they are very limited in the ability to be aware of it. The reasons for that are simple. The quilt belongs to the Bontrager women. It takes a Bontrager woman to pass it down and share how to time travel, just as I assume your great-aunt Rose did with Eliza."

"Jah, Auntie Rose gave the quilt to Eliza on the day of her wedding. But Eliza had to marry to be able to time travel."

"No. Once Eliza had the quilt and knew how to use it, she could've used it once to change an event before or after marriage. My dat's sister wasn't married to an Ebersol when she used it to go back in time and change one event, thus saving my future dat from being killed in a logging accident."

"I'm confused." Ruth rubbed her forehead. "If marrying doesn't cause the curse, then why are Bontragers and Ebersols not supposed to marry?"

"The other Amish don't know that the issue in an Ebersol and Bontrager marriage is time travel. Even when Omar and I tried to explain it and be forgiven, they couldn't wrap their heads around what we were saying, so they believed what made sense to them. For centuries each generation was told that a marriage between the two families drives the man and woman to madness and to be in open rebellion against each other."

The room was silent as they took a minute to breathe while drinking the tea.

Ruth tapped the table lightly. "There's more to this folklore about Bontragers and Ebersols, isn't there?"

Phoebe set down her teacup. "Can't you feel it?" She looked from Andrew to Ruth. "Time changed, everything changed, and yet you found each other again. Did you not?"

Andrew nodded. "She came looking for me."

"You felt it, didn't you? That inexplicable magnetic pull to this woman."

"I tried not to." Andrew shrugged. "But yes, I definitely did."

She turned to Ruth. "Apparently, against all sane thinking, he believed you because you're both here." She took a sip of her tea. "When things line up just right, a Bontrager and Ebersol have a unique power to change things, and I don't just mean time. I'm sure you've seen it at work."

"Jah, my sister and Jesse changed the entire economic structure for our Amish community. Whenever Andrew and I connected, we brainstormed and stumbled on answers that led us to uncover the toxicity at the feed mill, which changed the quality of life for about ten thousand people in downtown Calico Creek, not to mention all the employees. My sister and Jesse, Andrew and me—we instinctively knew what our next step needed to be in order to change something for the better, and that step often took us beyond what an Amish education could. But I didn't really think about it like you're saying because it took a lot of hard work and patience too."

"Did you notice an abundance of bad things?"

Ruth shook her head. "Not until Eliza changed time, trying to free Jesse from their marriage."

"Once a Bontrager woman is married to an Ebersol man, they can travel numerous times, although I don't know how many. There's more power in the marriage union than when someone is single. I think of it as the Amish version of what Englischers call a *power couple* . . . until the time travel curse enters and every good thing they've accomplished is undone."

Phoebe stared into her teacup. "The power between the two can be used for good, but when selfishness enters, things go awry. I have to tell you that even now, I don't fully understand how the time travel works other than knowing that the more you change time, the worse everything gets. I'm reminded of the verse in 1 Corinthians chapter 10. The one that says something along the lines of 'All things are lawful, but not all things are helpful.' I'm reminded of other events written about in the Bible, like when Israel asked God to give them a king. He knew that wasn't best for them, but they kept asking, and He agreed to it, knowing they would regret the consequences for many, many generations. Sometimes God allows the things we ask for, but they are not His best way. Omar and I broke apart our lives and all the ones around us. Changing time never makes things better."

"Never?" Ruth whispered.

Phoebe put a sugar cube into her teacup and swirled it with the small spoon. "It's an odd thing. The quilt had many strong, faith-filled women crying out to God as they pieced it and sewed it. Maybe it took years to sew. Maybe a decade. We don't know, but the power of all those fervent prayers said over the quilt seems to come alive again under the right circumstances with certain people. Perhaps Mercy is an echo of their faith. But here's the truth—maybe not for our ancestors, but for the past few generations: what we think the quilt promises and what actually takes place are not the same."

Andrew studied Phoebe, trying to hear what she wasn't saying. "Earlier you said your aunt saved your father before you were conceived, but now you're saying that time travel never makes things better."

Phoebe cleared her throat. "I was born a year after that event, so I only know what I was told some twenty years after she saved his life. Once my aunt told me what happened, I asked several questions. The look in her eyes held pain and her face clouded every time I asked. She refused to say any more on the topic. Looking back, I think she was haunted by other events that took place when she changed that one event. Maybe that's not what was going on, but I stick to what I believe—changing an event makes things different, never better. You see, I'm afraid I can't help you, unless you want a listening ear, which I'm happy to provide. I can tell you some of what has helped me over the years."

All right! This was something Andrew could understand—gaining information to analyze. It seemed clear that the time-worn quilt was somehow connected to being able to time travel. But Phoebe didn't have it, or if she did, it sounded like she wouldn't give it to them. She'd also used it herself, multiple times, which was good news for them that Ruth hadn't seemed to hear. Changing time more than once was possible. But then there was Phoebe's warning that time travel itself was the curse.

Did he and Ruth really know better than this wise, experienced woman who'd lived a full life dealing with the aftermath of the time travel?

Chapter Twenty-Eight

Time travel is the curse. Ruth breathed in for five counts, then back out the same way. Changing an event never made things better?

We both can do it. She and Andrew. She'd come to the full knowledge through the back way rather than an elder sharing the information directly with her, but still, she and Andrew fit the criteria of being direct descendants who'd been told the secret of the prayer power in the quilt, so they could time travel too . . . if they could find the quilt. That was what she wanted to hear, wasn't it? That it was possible to change time again. That Eliza wasn't the only one with the power to change the past. Ruth could use the power. Andrew could too. Even Jesse had the ability to—if they could get him on board.

Time travel *was* the curse. But she had no other option, did she? If she went back to the day that Eliza and Jesse were first engaged, could she convince Eliza to say yes when Jesse proposed?

If Ruth convinced her sister to say yes, or somehow made her say yes, would that change something else for the worse—and Ruth would be the cause of it? Would it be enough if she went back to the day they'd stumbled on the cabin, and somehow, she kept Eliza from going inside, maybe convinced her to leave or maybe knocked her out cold? Was it possible she could simply return to the wedding and intercept the quilt from Eliza, and destroy it without Eliza ever realizing its power?

Maybe Phoebe would know the right answer. "Tell me how, Phoebe. *Please.* People are dead here that were alive before the change. My parents are miserably poor. Dat . . . I'm afraid he's really sick. In the other time, he was working a different job, one that didn't continue damaging his lungs over the past three years. I don't want anything for me. I don't want money or success or any of the temptations this power might give others. I just want to save those I love. Please."

Andrew put a hand on her knee under the table. His supportive presence was full of comfort, but it didn't seem like he had any answers either.

Phoebe closed her eyes and released a deep sigh. "Oh, honey. I'm sorry. It sounds like she undid a pivotal event in your family and community." She took a sip of her tea. "Let me try to explain things better. Let's use a quilt metaphor since we're so familiar with it." She set the cup down and traced a square on the table. "The problem comes with how every event is interconnected. You can't see all those connections, all those threads, until you pull one. When that thread breaks, a piece of the quilt becomes loose. Then you go in and pull a different thread in order to get a chance to sew the loose patch in. That loosens something totally different. The more you try to fix, the more you undo, until the whole quilt of your lives ends up unraveling. Have you ever tried to stay warm with one tiny patch of quilt?"

Andrew rubbed the back of his neck. "Ruth and I have seen it in action. A lot of people call it the butterfly effect. But we don't want to go back and fix the repercussions of Eliza's change. We want to undo the original thing she changed."

"But by experiencing what you have, this change has already become a part of your lives. There are so many factors. You might think you're covering your tracks when you go back, accounting for all the little changes, but it's impossible."

"You recommend doing *nothing*?" Ruth asked. "Andrew's cousin Ben is dead because of the change Eliza made. The boiler at the feed mill exploded, killing three people and injuring others. In the previous time, Andrew changed that. Toxins from the plant continue to ruin people's health in town and the plant workers. All of Calico Creek, the ridge and the glen, are much worse off."

Phoebe folded her hands in front of her teacup. "I'm certainly in no position to tell anyone what to do. But going back may be impossible now."

"Why?"

A door creaked open, and then a screen door bumped

closed. "Honey?" an elderly man's voice called through the apartment. "You have company?"

"I do, but come on in," Phoebe answered.

Footsteps, then a man carrying a large paper bag walked into the kitchen. It was probably groceries, since a head of romaine lettuce stuck out the top.

"Hello." Ruth smiled at the man. He was completely bald with no beard or even a shadow of a beard, wearing what could almost be called Amish men's clothing: a white button-down shirt, black trousers, and suspenders.

"Hi there." He set the bags on the kitchen counter and turned to face their table. "Oh. I see."

Phoebe nodded. "Yep. These two are Ruth Bontrager and Andrew Ebersol. Ruth knew Rose."

It couldn't be a coincidence that he was dressed in what was pretty much Amish clothing. And why would Phoebe mention their last names? This man had to be . . .

"Are you Omar?" She glanced at Andrew to see his reaction.

He blinked, looking stunned, before he smiled back at her.

The older man laughed. "That's my name, don't wear it out. I didn't get a fancy new moniker like V. here."

"You're still together? I thought you left the Amish so you could divorce."

Phoebe smiled. "We left for that reason, and we did divorce. But we found our way back to each other. You know what they say: God works in mysterious ways."

Omar pulled the head of lettuce out of the grocery bag and put it in the small, old-looking refrigerator. "That He does. We lived separate lives for thirty years. Even remarried and had children with our spouses."

"When I left the Amish, I legally changed my last name back to my maiden name, Bontrager, and refuse to change it again. I moved far enough away that I wouldn't run into anyone who used to know me. I went to work as a nanny, then married when I was thirty and we had two great kids. But through the years, this place was my big dream, a safe place to land for anyone who is down on their luck or forcibly kicked from their family. Not long after Jerry died, my husband of twenty-three years, I bought this place. Two years later, I ran into Omar. Turns out he'd been a widower for numerous years and had just moved to Freeport. He had no idea I was living here. What were the odds?"

Omar removed a half-gallon of whole milk from the bag, then put it in the fridge too. "We started meeting weekly over tea, just to catch up, and turns out we still liked each other. A lot." He closed the refrigerator door and walked to Phoebe.

Phoebe beamed as he rested a hand on her shoulder, putting her hand over his. "The blessing of the Ebersol and Bontrager union is a love that isn't experienced very often. I imagine your sister's husband is very much in love with her no matter what she broke through changing an event."

Eliza had returned much later on Saturday, eyes puffy from crying, but a smile on her face, and seeming lighter than she had since Penelope died. She'd shared the amazing things Jesse had said, and then Ruth had cried. They'd embraced, holding on to hope that Ruth could find answers here. Would Verna . . . Phoebe . . . give any?

"He is. She told him two days ago how she'd erased their marriage, and yet he forgave her."

"Then I'd bet they'll find a way to be together here also. Maybe they needed to experience all of this to ultimately bring them closer."

Ruth shook her head. "You don't seem to understand. I *need* to be able to go back. You two did it multiple times. Please, help me and Andrew do that."

Omar touched the top of his head. "Do you know what melanoma is?"

Andrew nodded. "Skin cancer. Treatable if caught early, deadly if caught too late."

Omar rubbed his bald scalp. "I had a spot on the top of my head—which used to have a lot more hair, mind you— that I didn't notice. It grew for years before my doc pointed it out. I had other symptoms too that I blew off as just from being . . . shall we say *well-seasoned*."

Was Omar sick too?

"Malignant melanoma. Stage 4. That's the deadly stage. Now, since Verna and I can use the time travel power, do you two think we should go back and, I don't know, make me wear sunscreen? Maybe stay Amish, so I'd always wear a hat? Or go to the doctor earlier and get the spot cut off?"

Ruth tilted her head. Was this a trick question?

Verna stood, holding Omar's hand. "No. As much as I want Omar to live with me as long as possible, if I, or he, or both of us, went back in time to try to fix it, we could end up messing it up to where we never connected again. We could ruin our respective marriages while our spouses were still alive, and that would remove our children with those spouses from this earth, and our grandchildren. That's only the basic concept of what and who is unraveled due to changing an event."

Omar nodded. "All we have is this moment. That's all any of us have. Not one day in the future is guaranteed. My cancer is at bay for now. I've got a lot of smart doctors watching over me. But since it's the spreading kind, it's going to show up somewhere else one day. My time here on earth will end. I can't focus on that day. Not when I've got today." He kissed Phoebe on the cheek.

Ruth needed a moment. She took a sip of the delicious now-cooled black tea, hoping to steady herself. "But all that you've lost . . . all those years you could've been together. All the time you missed."

"You can't think like that, child," Phoebe said. "That sort of thinking is what messed us up. We only live in and appreciate the moment, and we try to give back to others wherever we can. We thank God for each day. My advice to you both? Acceptance. That's how you break the curse. Give up on fixing anything. Live like you only have this one moment, because it's all you truly have. And trust that God knows more than we do. Humans aren't meant to be able to time travel. We're meant to experience life linearly."

Andrew fidgeted with the teacup. "You speak like a learned woman."

Phoebe waggled her eyebrows. "I went to school starting at thirty-five and whittled away at it until I got a PhD in philosophy. I'm sorry to disappoint you both, but I can't in good conscience tell you how to change time, especially since it wasn't you who made the changes you're dealing with." She reached out and put Ruth's hand over Andrew's. "Go back. Live your authentic lives, whatever that may look like. Your memories of the other time may never completely fade. But whether that's true or not, you accept what is and move forward from here."

Ruth's heart sank. She'd failed and there were no answers to be found here. What would she tell Eliza?

Chapter Twenty-Nine

Cold, mid-November air surrounded Eliza as she stirred mostly spent embers in the metal firepit. She blew air onto the sputtering, tiny flames and added a few twigs. Smoke wafted in her face as the wind shifted. She stood, staring at it. This spot at the far reaches of her parents' backyard where grass met a patch of woods felt so familiar. Yet nothing felt normal. What had she done?

Jesse wrapped his arms around her from behind, their bulky coats between them. "Hm. Not sure we're going to be able to keep this thing going since it's so damp out here. I'd say go get some newspaper and dry kindling from inside your home, but . . ." He tugged on her hand, and they moved to a simple wooden bench beside the firepit. He pulled her closer. "I don't want you to get caught up in the needs of homelife, unable to come back out. I don't want us to waste a moment."

She nodded, feeling the same need, except deep desires were only part of what she carried. Guilt, heavy guilt, ate at her. She wouldn't voice it because he couldn't remove it from her, although he would try. It was her fault they were in this predicament, and she'd never be free of that part.

She watched the smoke spiral heavenward while reflecting on the last two days. Yesterday had been a between Sunday, which helped a lot. Since there was no church service, it meant Jesse didn't have to face hundreds of angry or curious people wanting to know why he wasn't getting married later this week. Any man who asked a woman to marry him and then broke it off was a scoundrel. To do so less than a week before the wedding was absolutely unheard of. It didn't matter that Martha said the breakup was mutual. She was eight years his junior, and the community felt he should've known himself better than to have asked her to marry him.

Again, it was her fault his reputation was suffering, would continue to suffer for years if time couldn't be changed again. Yet here he was, right beside her, loving her despite everything. Apparently she had a lot to learn about steadfast love.

They'd spent most of the between Sunday by the creek, out of eyesight, talking endlessly over thermoses of hot coffee and a small fire.

This morning, Jesse and Moses had gone to the construction jobsite. Jesse had been clear—he couldn't abandon his work responsibilities. That would put unfair stress on Frank Mulligan today, even if Eliza could change life back to the original timeline tomorrow or next week.

With the Sabbath behind her, Eliza had plunged into searching for the quilt Auntie Rose had given her the day she and Jesse wed. Eliza scoured her home first. Then she went to the home Auntie Rose had purchased as a young woman and still lived in when she passed. Auntie Rose had sold that place to distant Amish relatives of Eliza's, so Eliza knocked on their door and asked if there might be boxes in the house somewhere that once belonged to Auntie Rose. She said she was looking for a specific quilt Auntie Rose gave her when she was twenty-three, which was very true. She explained that she'd somehow misplaced it. They welcomed her and gave her access to search the attic, a storage room, and an old outbuilding, assuring her they'd put anything of Rose's in one of those spaces.

Eliza searched diligently, but she found nothing close to resembling that particular quilt.

Now they were here waiting, hoping, for good news from Ruth and Andrew. Would the trip to find Verna prove fruitful?

This afternoon Jesse had dropped Moses off, driven his rig home, and then walked here to covertly meet up with Eliza at the back of her property, just inside the edge of the woods where this firepit was. They longed to be together every moment. Still, they had to be cautious for everyone's sake. Jesse and Martha broke up three days ago. Their wedding should be taking place three days from now. Jesse's and Martha's families, the ministers from each district, and both communities were a hornet's nest of emotions. Had any other Amish couple ever broken an engagement—especially that close to the wedding date?

Eliza carried the guilt and shame for that too. Apparently once she broke with faith in order to time travel, she'd caused others to break faith with their commitments too—like Moses to sobriety, Andrew to exposing the feed mill, and Jesse to Martha . . . to mention a few.

"Eliza." Jesse's calm, loving tone interrupted her thoughts. She faced him.

He lifted her chin. "I love you."

She nodded, tears threatening. He knew the weight she carried. He couldn't remove her remorse, only lighten the load by loving her as she walked through it.

The sun had recently dipped below the mountain, and the evening was darkening quickly. Eliza had to accept what she'd done and forgive herself. What else could she do—keep dragging around her toxic guilt and unintentionally poisoning the innocent loved ones around her? But it would take her some time to get free of it. Until then, Jesse deserved a less mopey long-lost friend.

She wiped her eyes and smiled at him. "The fire is pitiful. You going to keep me warm instead?"

"Well, if you insist." He pulled her from the bench and onto his lap, putting his nose against her cheek. "Show me more, Eliza. I have eight years to catch up on."

She should stand up, put some distance between them in case anyone got close enough to see Jesse despite the trees and underbrush. But being held by him felt so right. She'd missed this closeness throughout her entire being.

Jesse brushed his lips against her cheekbone and her breath caught. The touch was so intimate, so natural. And yet if someone saw them . . .

He kissed her neck, and she pressed her palms against his chest, pushing them apart. "Jesse." She was breathless as if she'd been running. How often since arriving in this time had she imagined, dreamed of being with him? "If someone spotted us, it'd be a scandal." In truth, he'd likely be shunned. Maybe her too, which would hurt and embarrass her parents.

"A scandal for kissing my own wife? I remember taking those vows, clear as day."

"No one else here does. Well, besides Ruth."

"And I intend to change that. Either we fix the timeline, or I marry you again." He leaned forward and brushed his lips against hers. "As soon as possible."

That sounded so easy, as if the ministers would allow them to get married whenever they wanted to. It wouldn't work that way. "But—"

He silenced her protests with a finger on her lips. "Eliza, I have longed for you to the depths of my soul for the past eight years. As I said before, I don't intend to miss any more time."

But there was another issue. One they'd been avoiding. He just didn't want to see it.

She stood, reluctantly pulling from his arms. "I . . . I need you to hear me. Can you do that?"

"Always."

"What about the problem that caused me to want to set you free of our marriage? I might not be able to give you children."

"But you already have. Penelope is my beautiful daughter who I'm proud of. We're just as much parents as anyone with a healthy child."

Hearing his heartfelt love for Penelope simultaneously made her eyes water and her heart swell. But their daughter didn't exist here. "The world won't see us that way, whether we're able to fix the timeline or not. I might never be able to give birth to a healthy baby. Are you sure?"

He tilted his head, confusion plain on his face. "About us being together? I—"

Footsteps crunched through the leaves, approaching them.

"Eliza?" Ruth called.

Thank goodness it was just Ruth. "Jah, here by the fire."

Ruth came into view, frowning. Andrew right behind her.

Ruth pointed at the embers. "That's not much of a fire."

But it'd been plenty warm out here.

If only they could visit their cabin, have Ruth and Andrew over to talk in the privacy of their own home, then go to sleep in their own bed . . .

Eliza eyed her sister. "It wasn't good news."

Ruth shook her head. Andrew's expression appeared to agree with Ruth's assessment. He plucked a twig from the ground and leaned against a tree.

Ruth walked to the bench and sat down on the opposite end from Jesse. "We learned a lot. But Phoebe—uh, Verna—gave strong reasons why we shouldn't try to fix anything. She talked to us for a while, offering a lot of insights about time travel, but when I asked if she had the quilt or knew where it was, she never answered me."

"I spent the day searching through our home and Auntie Rose's former home for the quilt. It's not in either place."

Ruth nodded. "That tells us more than we knew this morning."

"So what did Verna say?" Eliza asked.

As Ruth and Andrew filled her in about the hours-long conversation, Eliza felt revelations hit like hailstones. The Ebersols could change time too. Verna and Omar had gone back more than once. They'd lived entire lives apart from each other after doing so. Then found their way back to each other. Verna, now going by Phoebe, considered time travel to be the curse. How could that be?

Eliza stood and paced, thinking. "The quilt has to still exist, and we have to get it back. I don't even know how we'd attempt changing time without it."

Ruth glanced up at Andrew, who was still leaning against a tree. Then she looked to Eliza and Jesse. "Are we in agreement? The four of us. Do we all agree we should go back, despite Phoebe's warnings?"

Andrew nodded. "I'm in. For Ben. And for the town."

Jesse clasped Eliza's hand between both of his. "I'm in. For our marriage. And for our daughter . . . actually, for our children, all of them."

Eliza took in the three of them, all so affected by her decision. They were caught in a difficult life because of her. This couldn't be how things ended. "I have to set right the choices I stole from everyone."

Ruth's lips twitched in a small smile. "Gut."

But how? Eliza paced around the firepit. Maybe walking would jar some ideas from her mind. "The quilt is still our only clue on how to do this. Verna told you that each of us could time travel. But what does that even mean? It's not like I could *will* everything to be fixed or it would already be." She paused, staring at the ground. "I'm the one at fault—"

"Eliza." Jesse stood and pulled her close. "No more beating yourself up. You were blinded by grief."

"But—"

"I know. I understand, but I also know you. You won't give up. You'll do all you can to make it right. We will do our best together."

"Eliza?" Dat called.

Eliza jerked from Jesse's embrace.

"Is that you?" Her dat approached from the side of the house. Only a few trees and mostly barren underbrush stood between the firepit area and their home. How had they not been paying enough attention to hear his footfalls?

Eliza wiped her eyes with the back of her hand. "It's just us, talking."

He stopped once they were in full view, looking at each one. "What's going on?" He sounded concerned.

Eliza wanted to hug him and assure him everything was fine. But it wasn't, and no one knew that more than the four gathered around the firepit. "We're just talking," she repeated.

"All of you." Mamm seemed to show up out of nowhere, glaring at them. "Inside the house. Now." She pointed, fully expecting them to do as she'd said. "I've had enough of this sneaking around."

Andrew took a step back. "I should go."

"You too, Andrew Ebersol." She pointed again. "In the house."

Mamm spun on her heels, heading toward the house

ahead of the others. Dat followed after his wife, moving a lot slower.

Did Mamm really expect them to obey her as if they were teens caught dallying? Even in this timeline, they were independent adults with jobs and their own places to live, for goodness' sake! Well, more or less their own places. Ruth and she lived with Aunt Bette. But Jesse was almost thirty! He shrugged and motioned for the group to follow Mamm and Dat.

"It's okay, Andrew," Ruth said. "You can go. I understand."

"No." He shook his head. "If your mom wants me to hear her out, I will respect that."

They followed Dat and soon they were each stepping into the house. If the other siblings were still awake, they'd been smart enough to make themselves scarce.

"Sit." Mamm gestured at the kitchen chairs.

The four of them sat, but Mamm and Dat remained standing.

"I don't know what you're thinking, not any of you!" Mamm flailed her arms. "Jesse, you were engaged five minutes ago, and one minute ago you're out back, around a campfire with my daughter."

Jesse intertwined his fingers, resting his hands on the table. "I know how this looks."

"Nee, I don't think you do. And you, Andrew Ebersol, you left the Amish. Is your goal to talk my Ruth into leaving with you?"

"No, ma'am."

"Don't *ma'am* me. I'm not Englisch. I want whatever is going on to stop. Do you hear me? There's rumblings in the community saying Eliza is the reason Jesse called off his wedding. I thought to myself, no one has any reason to think such a thing, and then I find you two together!"

Eliza glanced at Ruth. They'd never seen Mamm livid before.

Mamm pointed at a window. "Rumors about both of you girls have reached the bishop, and he dropped by here earlier today, asking questions I couldn't answer." She smacked the table. "If Aunt Mary hears about any of this . . ."

"Wait." Ruth held up her hand as if she were a student in a classroom. "What does Dat's oldest sister have to do with anything?"

Dat coughed hard, covering his mouth with one hand and grabbing on to the back of a chair with the other.

Mamm grabbed a glass and filled it with water. She passed it to him and rubbed his back. "I can't believe you would stress your father like this."

Chills ran up Eliza's spine. How many times had she heard Dat cough like this since coming to this time? He hadn't sounded like that before. He was always in bed resting when he wasn't at work. Mamm's worry . . . all the pieces clicked into place. She looked at her sister. When their eyes met, she knew Ruth had pieced together far more than Eliza had. Still, her sister's worry was clear.

Eliza got up and moved a few feet from Mamm. "He's sick. *Really* sick, isn't he?"

Pain twisted across Mamm's face. "Jah."

Dear God, please don't let my actions have caused this too! Eliza stepped toward Dat and touched his elbow. "From . . . the plant?"

He shook his head, setting the glass of water on the table. "There's no way of knowing. Doc just gave me the results a few days ago. Lung cancer. But don't you all worry. Your mamm and I have a plan."

Ruth put her arm around Mamm's shoulders and squeezed. "I'm so sorry." She moved to their dad and hugged him. "Dat, I hate this."

He held her. "I know. We all feel that way, but beyond the shock and pain of today and tomorrow, we must choose to trust God in all things."

Eliza's guilt pressed in again. Dat let go of Ruth and held his arms open to Eliza. She rested her head on his chest, remembering how safe his arms had always felt.

"I'm so sorry." Eliza's voice cracked. If he knew she was the reason he was going through this now, would he still hug her like this? She couldn't watch Dat die. Not when he was healthy in the other time.

"This isn't what I wanted to talk about tonight, but I suppose I needed to tell you two soon anyways since you're the oldest. The plan is for us to move in with Aunt Mary, which is why you two need to behave. If there's too much trouble, she won't welcome us. She's a stickler about righteous behavior."

"Why do we need to move in with her?"

"The cancer treatment is expensive, but God dropped an opportunity in our lap to be able to pay for it." Mamm looked at Jesse and nodded. "We're selling all our land to a developer, Beckford Construction. Seems that Calico Creek is finally starting to appeal to builders, and they'll be building an entire subdivision on our property, hundreds of homes.

The land may not pay for all of Dat's treatments, but if we don't own any land and we use all the money for medical bills, there's some sort of medical emergency assistance program we can tap into."

"Sell the land?" Eliza sputtered. But the cabin where Mercy showed up was here. "We're moving out of Calico Creek?"

Mamm put a hand on her shoulder. "I think, given the temptations you and Ruth have faced since returning home, that the two of you should move back in with Aunt Bette. Eliza, you were doing well with your crafting and running the store for Aunt Bette. Ruth was teaching. As much as I love having the two of you here, I want both of you on the right path." She looked at Andrew and Jesse. "Each of you need to steer clear of my girls, for everyone's sake." She plunked into a chair. "Please, I'm begging you."

No, no, no, this was all wrong. "How much time do we have?" Eliza asked.

"We signed the papers last Friday. We go to closing in a few weeks, but they have our permission to start moving their machinery onto the property at will."

"Why would you agree to that?" Ruth asked. "Who allows work to begin on a property before closing?"

"Because we *are* going to closing, no way around it, so why not?"

Eliza stared at the table, unable to lift her eyes to meet Jesse's. What had she done? Was there a way out of this?

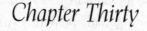

Chapter Thirty

After learning the Bontragers were selling their land, Jesse's night had been a long one. He breathed in the morning air and buttoned his coat as he continued walking. The sound of footfalls caused him to turn. Eliza was coming toward him, trudging through the foggy woods toward their agreed-upon destination. There was no path to where they were going, but he knew the spot. He waited, watching Eliza. She was so beautiful. His wife. Well, she *should* be his wife; he had the memories back now, and the love in his heart, but so many things made it impossible here.

"Eliza."

She looked up and her face broke into a smile as their eyes met. "Hi there."

He pulled her into a tight embrace. "Ruth's not with you?"

"She'll meet us at the cabin shortly."

He let go of the hug and held her hand. "Let's go see it." The mystery cabin that had apparently ruined his life.

The woods were quiet, with only their footsteps crunching through the leaves.

Finally Jesse asked, "How did Moses take the news that he couldn't go to work today?"

"Concerned he'd done something. But I assured him you weren't working today, so he couldn't either."

"I'll speak to him later today and assure him he hasn't done anything wrong. This week was going to be odd for him anyway. Under normal circumstances, I would be off starting tomorrow and for the next ten days. But as it's turned out, I should go to work after today, and he should too."

Eliza's eyes grew wide. "Oh, you were scheduled to be off because you were supposed to marry."

This revelation seemed to be something else to weigh on her. "It's not a problem, Eliza. If I'm there, I'll get work done this week they hadn't planned on, and if I'm off, it was planned far in advance, so it's okay."

She nodded and began walking again. Something new in the forest caught his attention. A freshly clear-cut path?

"Ach! Nee!" Eliza sprinted forward. "No, no, no, no!"

Adrenaline spiked in him. What was wrong? He followed her and it immediately came into view. Site prep had begun. A silt fence was installed. A yellow front-end loader sat on already-cleared ground.

Why did the Bontragers have to sell to Beckford Construction? If they'd sold to Mulligan Builders, Jesse would at least have some sway.

They kept hurrying toward the cabin site. A wide path had been cleared for the construction entrance, although no temporary stone base had yet been brought to the site. Trees were toppled, and underbrush had been uprooted, pushed into huge piles here and there.

They picked up their speed. Eliza stopped short, and Jesse almost crashed into her. "No!"

He moved to her side and chills ran down his spine. Through the foggy mist it became clear.

The cabin was gone. Only the chimney remained in place.

Despite the brown, sandy soil that now covered the floor of the former wooded area, he could see a few rocks strewn around the site, and some rocks had been pushed into the woods that hadn't yet been cleared. The cleared area took up about three acres worth of land and, with the exception of the chimney, had been flattened. Why? What terrible luck dictated that the developers would start *here* of all places? His construction experience jumped in and he knew why— road frontage access was closest here. Although no one on the paved road could've seen the old cabin due to trees and underbrush, the road was only three hundred feet from this spot. He imagined they'd left the chimney standing because it'd become part of the entryway to the subdivision and an attractive drawing point for potential buyers. It was a shame they didn't feel that way about the cabin itself.

He and Eliza moved in closer. The four walls of the cabin as well as the four stone pillars of the cabin's foundation had been dismantled and scattered. Some of the stones were buried, but a few larger pieces jutted out from under the freshly turned dirt.

"Jesse." Eliza's voice wavered.

"Maybe the cabin won't matter."

She picked up a flat stone the size of her hand and studied it. "And maybe it does. It's like one setback after another, and I have the awful feeling that this cabin being intact matters a lot."

Through the fog that surrounded them, he searched what he could see of the outer perimeter of the cleared space. A burn pit! Someone had used a machine to already dig a hole to burn trees and underbrush. He hurried to the spot, no more than fifty feet from where he was standing.

The logs! They were under and on top of uprooted underbrush and felled trees.

"Eliza, look." He pointed at the pit. "It's the logs, and they appear to be in decent shape." It didn't look as if whoever did this was trying to break the logs before moving them to the pit. Maybe the cabin could be rebuilt. "Wood roof shingles are in there too. I guess everything that was in or part of the cabin is in this pit."

She walked to where he was, silently staring at the hole.

"There's good news, Eliza. The logs appear whole, and no one started a fire. They probably didn't have a burn permit yet." He put his arm around her waist. "We're going to get through this one step at a time, the way we always have."

While he was counting the number of logs he could see, she grabbed his arm. "Jesse."

He looked up and followed her gaze.

A couple walked toward them through the fog. He blinked. Were they real? That was crazy thinking, but since time travel sounded crazy too, his thought seemed less irrational. As the

couple drew closer, he could see their faces. The woman—
the shape of her eyes and nose strongly resembled Eliza's,
though she was at least eighty years old, probably more. The
man looked like Jesse's own father, whom everyone had told
him he resembled. Was this . . . Mercy? Or another supernatural being? Or perhaps a glimpse of Eliza and himself in
the distant future.

They were wearing modern clothes, Englisch ones. The
man could nearly be Amish in his open black coat and
black pants with suspenders, but he didn't have a beard. The
woman had on a purple trench coat. She wore her silver hair
in a low side ponytail, with a black wool hat.

The couple watched their footing as they walked, but
when they came to the clearing, where trees had been felled
and dirt was upturned, the woman stopped and looked up.
"Oh, my," she gasped. "The cabin . . . what happened?"

Jesse steadied Eliza as she took a step forward over several
clods of dirt. The woman seemed to notice them for the first
time.

"Hi." Eliza nodded. "We were just as shocked as you are,
but my family signed papers Friday to sell this land to developers. The construction company has an oral agreement with
my folks to begin clearing."

The woman studied Eliza, looking her up and down as if
very curious about her. "Are you Ruth's sister? The one who
messed with the quilt?"

"Jah." Eliza's voice was raspy, her face constricted. "I'm
Eliza. This is Jesse."

The woman grinned at the man walking with her. "That's
your great-nephew, no doubt. Same nose."

The man laughed. "Nice to meet you. I'm Omar and this is Phoebe, V., or Verna, or whatever she feels like going by this day."

Verna elbowed him in the ribs. "We met your sister and Andrew yesterday."

Jesse's mind flew in so many directions. This couple had to have a good reason to come here. Weren't they excommunicated, given a lifetime ban? Not that he would enforce such a thing. He and Eliza had no room to talk about what was proper.

Jesse extended his hand to Omar, not something an Amish in good standing did for someone excommunicated, although Jesse's position of *Amish in good standing* was teetering since he called off his wedding four days ago. A handshake was Jesse's way of saying all that needed to be said in this moment. Omar smiled and shook his hand. Jesse then offered his hand to Verna, who also shook it. "It's very nice to meet you." He put an arm around Eliza's shoulders. "We have so many questions."

Verna looked at Omar and nodded. "I doubt we'll be able to answer them all. But we'll try. First, I want to give Eliza something." She reached into the pocket of her trench coat before passing a small thing to Eliza.

Eliza unfolded the piece of fabric. It was a patchwork piece, a little larger than the size of Jesse's hand when splayed. It had a brilliant star pattern on the square.

Eliza's face looked as if she'd just watched a puppy die. Hope seemed to drain from her eyes. "Mercy's quilt."

Verna hugged her. "I'm so sorry, child." She put her hand over the piece of quilt in Eliza's hands. "When Rose gave it to me right before she passed, I thought the kindest thing I could do for the world would be to destroy it. I wanted to destroy all of it, but part of me wanted to keep a reminder to accept what is and lean on God for what isn't, so I cut out this piece. Then I burned the rest and had my own funeral for my dear sister Rose and for that part of my life. I didn't know—I couldn't have known—that you'd used the quilt in another time. I should've given this piece to Ruth when she came, but I was afraid it might still have power in it. Omar and I came to this spot to mull over what to do with this scrap. Since you and Jesse are here, I believe you're meant to have it. Besides that, it wouldn't be fair to let you all keep obsessively searching for the quilt for the rest of your lives."

Eliza turned to Jesse, tears brimming. "It's my fault, and I can't fix it. I . . . I changed time thinking I could make things better, that I could fix whatever else was wrong, and I can't."

He pulled her to his chest as she sobbed. What would they do now? First the cabin, now the quilt was destroyed. Why did so many things keep going wrong?

Eliza took a few deep breaths and a few steps back. He knew she was digging deep within to find strength.

He looked to Verna. "How did you go back more than once?" They needed answers. No more avoiding this conversation.

Verna's eyes held sadness as she looked to Omar. She moved to a nearby fallen tree and sat. "Let me tell you both our story. We met because our families lived next door. And like you, I'm sure, we were told not to be friends, not to mingle, and certainly not to date. But you know, young hearts."

"I was fascinated with V. from when we both were kids. It only made sense that we would be together. Or try to. When we were only eighteen, we were engaged."

"Omar's business was cabinetmaking." Verna picked up the next sentence like they were in sync. "Now, mind you, this is back in the fifties. We didn't have the ability to advertise online like people nowadays do. And in a little mountain town like Calico Creek, opportunities were few. There was this man, Hyram, who offered an apprenticeship to young men in town from time to time. My older brother tried to work with him, and Hyram stole several hundred dollars' worth of materials and left him with nothing."

"You have to remember how desperate I was to make some money, to be able to provide for myself and her. When Hyram approached me at a craftsman show, I was all in. I gave him the money I had on the spot, and I planned to move to his town, even though it would mean Verna and I would miss that year's wedding season."

"I was so angry that Omar would do this without listening to me about what I *knew* to be true about Hyram. Omar had used all the money we'd saved for getting married. Our rent and food money. Each of us were oldest siblings who shared rooms with younger siblings, so we couldn't move in with our folks. But I was worried that during our time apart, he'd find someone else. My mamm had gifted me the quilt as an engagement gift and told me the story. I thought, *Here's my chance to fix things.* I took the quilt to Mercy's cabin. I went back to that craft show, just a few days prior, and made sure to intercept Hyram, telling him to leave and making sure he'd never speak to Omar. Amazingly, it worked. Time snapped back to the present, and the wedding was still on. We married that season, and I was happy."

Omar nodded. "But it'd been a hard year for us as a couple, although I couldn't put my finger on why. When Hyram came to town the following year, he made sure to look me up and tell me how V. told him to get lost. I realized the opportunity I'd missed, and I was angry. I resented her. And most of all, I wondered how she even knew that he wanted to come speak to *me* and offer the apprenticeship. During that year, I'd been getting these flashes of where I could've been—working with Hyram, learning new things, training in my craft, making decent money."

"So I told him. He believed me immediately—the flashes of memories helped, of course. I showed him the quilt, told him how Mercy said it was a one-and-done sort of deal. But he wanted to try to fix it. We brought the quilt here and went into the cabin. But Mercy wasn't inside. Just us. I found the swath of cloth holding the needles and scissors, and then I showed Omar how I'd pulled a string after Mercy had asked me what event I wanted to undo."

"And suddenly we both were back at the craft show. I handled it differently this time, running forward, excitedly telling Hyram how I wanted the apprenticeship. He grinned and accepted me on the spot. Of course, taking my money."

"Then time snapped back to the present," Verna said. "We were married, which I was relieved for, but we didn't live in Calico Creek Ridge anymore. We lived in downtown Calico Creek with Hyram. And then I realized the new timeline had an awful event. Rose had been in a buggy accident a few months back and was severely injured. It seemed it happened during a day she was supposed to be at *my* house in the previous timeline, but I'd just left."

Omar nodded. "And the good flashes of memories I'd had with Hyram? They didn't happen after we made the change. He took advantage of me, just like V. was afraid of. All I could figure was that it was because I'd sounded so desperate rushing up to him at the show. I had a shop, but it was struggling."

"We returned to Calico Creek Ridge as soon as we could. Rose wasn't going to be able to walk properly again, and it would probably prevent her from having children. But she'd met a great guy and soon was engaged. Omar and I decided we needed to try to use the quilt again and make sure that we were visiting Calico Creek on the day of the accident, since being with me kept Rose safe originally. We made the change, and I kept her out of the buggy."

"Then time snapped back to the present, and my business was gone. Turns out on the day of Rose's accident, there was a fire at my shop because I wasn't there. We now were both living with V.'s parents. I had no prospects. My reputation was tarnished because of the bad deals promised by Hyram."

"And Rose wasn't engaged. I don't know how she and her fiancé got together, but it must have been inadvertently because of her accident. Now with that erased, she was single. And I was spiraling. I was so mad at myself, mad at Omar. He didn't feel like the man I married anymore, and I didn't want to be his wife anymore."

Omar shrugged. "At that point, I didn't know what to do. I took the problem to the church elders and confessed everything."

Verna looked in the direction of the paved road and shook her head. "They didn't know what to do either. I believe this was outside of anything they'd ever expected to run into. Needless to say, they panicked. They accused us, but mostly me, of witchcraft. They wanted us to confess everything publicly. And they demanded we return to living as husband and wife. I said no. I wouldn't make my family continue to bear the brunt of my mistakes, and I wouldn't be ordered back into marriage."

"You always did have a mind of your own," Omar said.

"I know, dear. That's why you love me." Verna smiled at Eliza, but her eyes looked sad. "Your sister probably told you: The family curse between the Bontragers and the Ebersols *is* the time travel. Each time we use it, it unravels more and more of our lives. But I can't make that decision for you. I don't know if that little piece of the quilt will be enough. But I owe it to you to let you try."

Jesse considered all the instances Verna had mentioned. "It doesn't seem like you ever tried to put anything *back*, even though you changed events a bunch of times."

"Jah." Verna nodded. "That's a fair assessment. We kept thinking we could fix it to be better and avoid the pain caused by each set of circumstances."

"Jesse and I don't want to avoid the pain," Eliza said. "He never did, and I get that now. I so get it. We know what will happen if we can go back to the original time, and I embrace all of it."

Jesse lifted her hand to his lips and kissed it. "We know we'll lose the three babies we've already lost, including our full-term daughter. We know we may never have a healthy baby. All we want to do is return to the mix of joy and sorrow that was our lives together."

"To return to the life we had carved out and be truly thankful for that gift." Eliza wiped a tear.

Omar put his hands in his coat pockets. "I hope you're able to do so. Will you get married in this time?"

"I wish we could," Jesse said.

"We can't, not anytime soon," Eliza said. "He was engaged to be married the day after tomorrow."

"Oh." Verna's eyes grew wide, concern evident. "In all my years, I've never heard of an engagement being broken, and that close to your wedding day? You're in the doghouse with ministers and Amish everywhere, aren't you, young man?"

He nodded. "It's a storm we'll weather. If we can't get back to the previous timeline, we'll bide our time and start a business like I had before. We waited five years to marry the first time."

"What?" Omar gaped, unmoving for a moment. "I've never heard of that among the Amish either. You two are unique all the way to the top of a silo, aren't you?"

"Verna," Eliza said softly. "If you traveled without Mercy in the cabin, do you think it's possible to travel without the cabin and with only a square of the quilt?"

"I have no way of knowing the answer to that. Anything you do from here out will be through trial and error. What I do know is the cabin was built much like the quilt was sewn—in faith and unity between Bontragers and Ebersols as they prayed every step of the way."

Verna stood and stretched for a moment before slowly walking closer to where the cabin had stood. Jesse put his arm under hers, steadying her amid the clumps of dirt and roots. Eliza and Omar made their way to the same area.

Verna studied the area. "I don't know what to tell you, child." She turned to Omar. "I'm cold and achy, and you need some rest."

"Jah."

"I wish I knew more to say, but if you can't fix the past, we hope you can accept your lives now. Here's my business card with my number." Verna passed Jesse a small paper card with *Phoebe's House* written on it in bold black letters, followed by a phone number. "Call me if you ever need anything. As you know, I don't have all the answers, but I'll do my best. And no matter where you land, keep in touch. It's a terrible burden that we've had to carry. We might as well stick together."

"Hallo," Ruth called loudly as she and Andrew walked in from the road area rather than from the side of the land the rest of them had walked. Once closer, Ruth pointed at the smashed cabin remnants, her breath quickening. "No! What happened?"

"Early construction," Jesse said. "By the looks of it, this will be the main entrance for the upcoming construction to build a subdivision."

Ruth looked around, jolting when she saw Verna and Omar.

Verna smiled. "Well, hallo. It's good to see you again, and

I hate to leave this soon after you arrived, but it's cold out here with no comforts for old folks. Your sister and Jesse can tell you all about why we were here." Verna winked at Jesse and Eliza. "Call us if you need."

Hand in hand, Verna and Omar retreated back into the mist.

"Did they know we were all meeting here?" Ruth asked.

"I don't think so. But, Ruth, Verna brought me this . . ." Eliza held out the patch of quilt to her.

"No." Ruth covered her mouth, looking horrified. "I can't believe this."

Andrew gestured at the piece. "I saw that on Phoebe's wall, but I didn't think it might be from part of *the* quilt."

"So the quilt *and* the cabin are gone?" Ruth asked.

"The logs are in a burn pit." Jesse pointed. "They appear to be in decent condition."

Andrew bent down to touch one of the scattered foundation stones. "Are you thinking the cabin could be rebuilt?"

Eliza ran her hands over the piece of quilt. "I hate it, but I think we already have our answer about time travel under these circumstances. What remains of the quilt *is* at the cabin site. I could sense an eeriness to this area when I changed time. I don't sense anything now."

All four were silent for several heartbeats.

"Let me see it, Eliza. I'm a Bontrager woman, and I've never used the quilt, but you have. Maybe if I pluck a thread."

Eliza passed the piece of quilt to Ruth. She broke a thread and closed her eyes, but nothing seemed to happen.

"Do you see anything, Ruth?"

"No." She opened her eyes. "I see what you see. A missing cabin, a few scattered stones, and a lot of shattered hopes."

"I won't accept this as finality in the matter." Eliza started pacing around the site. "If the cabin and quilt were built by Ebersols and Bontragers as they prayed to God in faith and hope, that's what we need to do." She stopped in front of Jesse and met his gaze. "Isn't it?"

There. Jesse could sense what was happening. Her inner fire had relit in her beautiful brown eyes. He was sure it was fragile and would be for a while, but it'd been dormant for so long, both here and in his memories from the other time, ever since Penelope had died.

"Jesse, you're a builder. I'm a quilt maker. We've used these gifts in each lifetime. Maybe there's a reason we have these particular gifts. Our ancestors originally built this cabin using those logs. You can do that. I know you can. Moses needs to help you because he's a Bontrager. I can sew. I think we need to search for the oldest fabrics we can find to sew a quilt while praying fervently. You can rebuild the foundation stones and log cabin."

His heart swelled, not only because of the hope changing her, but because he believed her. Yes! Together they could accomplish the impossible.

Jesse pointed at Andrew. "How are your building skills?"

"Uh . . . I'm a writer."

"True." Jesse removed his black felt hat, staring at the mess. They needed to search for the missing stones and put them back as close to their original stacking as possible. Maybe parts of the log walls were still intact down in that huge burn pit hole in the ground. Could he use heavy machinery to get the logs back in place? That would be very helpful, but would using modern machinery be too dissimilar to how the original cabin was built? What parts of this effort needed to be as close to the original Old Ways as possible? He needed help, but he couldn't pull just anyone in on this. There would be no way to explain why he was doing what he was doing, especially since it would all be torn down again by the same construction company. Maybe if he told his brothers he needed their help in rebuilding the cabin as part of his way of finding his God-intended life since breaking off the wedding to Martha. They might be willing to help him do that. He would need all the help he could get. Those logs were incredibly heavy. "Still, Andrew, if you're willing, I need your help."

"Jesse," Ruth said. "He lives two hours from here, and he has daily classes. He can't throw in the towel on the life he's built that may be the only life there is for forever. He can't afford to fail a class that student loans won't pay for him to retake."

Jesse's heart pounded, physically shaking his chest. Her words stirred dozens of opposing thoughts and overwrought emotions. Was this the life they'd live out—with Eliza's dat dying, the community bound to poverty, families of the workers who died at the feed mill grieving, Ben dead? His Eliza had made an error in judgment during a time when she couldn't see anything but her pain. How could she live under the weight of this timeline?

A list of obstacles tugged at him, but soon he had several answers.

He put his hat on, ready to get to work. "Jah, I understand.

I'll get Moses to come here to work for sure. Maybe some others too." He turned to face the others. "We have something in our favor—because of the former wedding plans, I'm scheduled to be off work starting tomorrow and for the next ten days. I'll go ahead and take those days off."

"That's gut," Ruth said. "Very helpful."

Jesse studied the cleared land. "We need a way to make sure Beckford Construction doesn't return to do more demolition work. I'll reach out to my boss, Frank Mulligan. He knows all the owners of every construction company in these parts. If he has a good relationship with Beckford Construction, he can simply reason with them."

"I agree," Andrew said. "Since the Bontragers still own this land, and everything Beckford Construction is doing is based on an oral agreement, Frank should be able to get them to hold off until they go to closing based on a cautionary tale of legal logic. I wish I could step in and be of more help since I'm studying law, but an ex-Amish like me better steer clear for all of your sakes."

"I totally agree," Jesse said.

Eliza's studious face had a smile tugging at her lips. "You know . . ." A huge smile filled her face and lit his heart. "While you and Moses and maybe some of your brothers and mine rebuild the cabin, Ruth and I will take this quilt piece to our home and get Mamm and our teen sisters to help us remake it. The Amish family living in Auntie Rose's old house has a small stash of vintage fabrics stored away in boxes in their attic. Aunt Bette sent me some vintage fabrics for Jesse's wedding quilts, and I used some, but I still have a bit left."

"Why vintage fabric?" Andrew asked.

"I hesitate to use new fabric for this project. I think it's going to need remnants that hold meaning to our families who came here in the 1740s. I don't know that any of the pieces go back that far, but I think that the older we can get, the better."

Andrew rubbed the back of his neck. "For reasons I can't put my finger on, I seem to remember that my folks have a cedar chest of fabric in our attic. Some of the scraps are really old. But I don't recall going through anything in our attic—"

"You did," Ruth said. "You and Ben went through your attic for me. I was grieving the loss of Penelope, and you wanted to do something kind to lift my spirits. Since my thing in the previous time was old journals, letters, and anything with Amish history, you and Ben went digging in your attic, spent a day on it. You found a lovely treasure, a diary containing two decades of weather and gardening from your great-great-great-grandfather."

Andrew's eyes held confusion, but he nodded. "I believe you, but I can't just barge in. I haven't been home in forever. How will I justify entering their home while still in college? They'd have to answer to the bishop for that. And, uh, oh yeah, on top of visiting, I want to go through your attic and then leave?"

Ruth lifted one finger. "I have an idea." She grabbed Andrew by the coat collar. "Let's go, college boy. I need a lift to Calico Creek Glen." She pulled him a few feet before stopping and releasing him. "After he drops me off, I'll go to see his mom on my own and hire a driver to bring me back home. You two keep thinking and making plans. I'll be home in a few hours, and we'll get started on the quilt."

Eliza hugged her. "You're the best sister."

Ruth held her. "We'll get this fixed. Two Bontrager women and two Ebersol men—we can get back to the right time."

Ruth and Andrew hurried off toward the paved road.

Eliza watched them until they were out of sight.

Jesse closed the gap and put his arms around Eliza. He gazed into her eyes, faint memories of her as his wife sweeping through him. He lowered his lips to hers, and the fire in his soul ignited.

"What is going on here!" The bishop's voice thundered through the clearing.

Jesse and Eliza put distance between them, as if that would help anything.

The bishop pointed. "You were to marry Martha Peight in two days. Two days! But you're here, in the arms of someone else?" His face was beet red. "You'll answer for this, both of you."

Pressure settled in on Jesse's shoulders. Why was the bishop even here? First Beckford Construction chose this spot out of forty acres to begin their demolition. Then Omar and Verna came here to think. Now the bishop was here?

Had this spot become a magnet, drawing people to it?

If so, would others feel that same draw, and would that be another obstacle to overcome?

Chapter Thirty-One

Andrew clutched the steering wheel and checked his rearview mirror for the umpteenth time, knowing he was pushing the speed limit. He kept half expecting to see blue lights in his rearview mirror at any minute.

His cell phone rang. He glanced at the screen. Aunt Lydia. Before earlier today, Ben's mom had never called him. She'd always waited for Andrew to call her. Since Ben died, he'd called regularly, hoping to help her navigate her grief.

With his earbuds in place, he swiped his finger across the screen. *"Hallo, Aenti Lydia. Wie bischt Sache?"* He heard static, and he waited to hear a response to his question of *How are things?*

She was the reason he was heading to Calico Creek. He'd been in class when she'd called him to say that the bishop had called an evaluation meeting with Jesse, Eliza, and Ruth, which made him sick to his stomach. Evaluation meetings were very serious, often leading to embarrassing and unyielding discipline.

"Aenti Lydia?"

"Jah, Andrew . . ."

She spoke fast, and he hung on her every word as she answered.

His heart palpitated. "The meeting's already begun?" The two hours between Penn State and Calico Creek grated on his nerves of late, especially today.

"Jah. All the ministers are at David Lapp's house."

"Already at the bishop's house? Man alive!" He pulled into a stranger's driveway and backed out, going the other direction. "That changes my plans. I won't come by your place first."

He'd intended to go to his aunt Lydia's, change into Amish clothes, and borrow a horse and buggy, causing him to go to the meeting in a respectable way. Now he'd show up in blue jeans and driving a car.

"I was told a few minutes ago that the bishop caught Jesse and Eliza in each other's arms, making out, day before yesterday."

Andrew groaned, knowing what this could mean.

"The community is outraged, Andrew. I've never seen anything like this among the Amish. Our people are vibrating with anger. Have Jesse and Eliza lost their minds? They know how our People feel about respect toward another— a widow or widower is asked to wait a minimum of a year before courting, let alone remarrying, unless circumstances with little ones or finances dictate otherwise. When a young man and young woman break up, even if it wasn't serious, neither should date anyone else for at least a month. Here we are, Martha and Jesse should've gotten married today, and he and Eliza were seen kissing two days ago! The only thing the bishop can do is an evaluation meeting, insisting they answer for disgraceful, disrespectful behavior. I've never understood Eliza, leaving her folks the way she did eight years ago, never coming home on a church Sunday. But I thought Jesse was a good, decent man."

"Listen, it sounds bad. It looks even worse, but please don't join the community in their backlash." He came to a two-way stop, grateful the back road intersection was empty. His aunt was wound up, clearly upset at what was happening and needing to talk. "I appreciate your calling me earlier to let me know what's happening."

"Well, when we talked three weeks ago, you asked a few questions about Ruth, sort of checking on who she was and any rumors about her mental health. You've never asked about any Amish girl before, so when I heard she was being beckoned to an evaluation meeting with the ministers, I knew I had to call you right away and let you know. I was worried I'd interrupt a class."

"You did the right thing to call, Aunt Lydia."

"Maybe." She sighed. "Do your parents know?"

"No." How could they? He'd been keeping everything to himself until he knew his mind and heart on the matter. "But I need to be the one to tell them. I'll go see them just as soon as the meeting is over."

"I won't say a word, but we can only hope they don't hear the gossip before then."

"*Jah, Mich aa,*" Andrew agreed. Was he crazy? He was putting all of who he was on a line of trusting what seemed impossible and believing what he felt to be true. What he felt to be true? How solid could a feeling be?

Ruth.

Good thoughts about her flooded him. She was absolutely one of a kind. Maybe love had blinded him, but he was willing to lay down his life on the chance that what he felt and thought he knew was worth it.

He pulled onto the bishop's gravel driveway, stopped in front of his home, and turned off his car. Hopefully they would allow him inside. Just inside the barn stood four carriages with blanketed horses still hitched. That meant the bishop didn't expect the meeting to last long.

He climbed the steps to the back door and tapped. He could hear voices.

A moment later, the bishop's wife opened the door, concern reflecting in her eyes.

"I need to be here, please."

She hesitated before opening the door wider and pointing at a small bench near the back door.

He could easily see the long, oak kitchen table where everyone except the bishop's wife was seated—Eliza, Ruth, and their parents, Jesse and his parents, the bishop, the preacher, and the deacon. No one seemed to notice that he'd come in.

The bishop had his hands folded on his open Bible. "We've read numerous Scriptures this evening, and we need to keep those in mind as we move forward. Jesse—" the bishop touched the pages of his Bible—"I expected to read very different Scripture to you on this day, your wedding day."

David's voice was soft as he spoke, but Andrew knew this man well. He was a good man, trying to temper his mounting anger. "How is it that a man as dedicated to keeping the Amish ways as you've always been, one who was engaged to a pure Amish woman last week, is sitting here today, giving an answer for being in the arms of Eliza Bontrager on what should be his wedding day to Martha Peight?" David banged his hand on the table. "You're not a teen. You're almost thirty, and in all your years as an adult, I've known you to be responsible and upright." He turned to look at Eliza, who sat across the table from Jesse. "Unfortunately, that causes me to look at you."

"Nee," Jesse said. "No reason to focus on Eliza. The open display of affection is my fault." He looked as unruffled and steady as one of the homes he built. "All of it."

"Fine. Let's look at you. I saw an elderly couple leaving Hunters' Woods, and I spoke to them, introducing myself and learning who they were. Our history tells us that Omar and Verna Ebersol are nothing but bad news for any Amish in good standing. No one should be having contact with them, so why did I see them coming out of the very woods I found you in only minutes later?"

Jesse nodded. "That one's easy. Eliza and I had never met them before or had contact with them. They came to that spot to think, and we were there, shocked that the construction owners who are buying Bontrager land had already started moving dirt and tearing down the old cabin of our ancestors in Hunters' Woods."

The bishop turned to Eliza. "You'd not seen them before two days ago?"

"No." She shook her head.

Andrew's heart raced, ready to jump to Ruth's defense if the bishop turned his questions to her, but he simply nodded. "Okay. Good Amish folk have told me of other times when one or both were seen going in or out of Hunters' Woods, so your explanation seems possible." He took a sip of water. "I'm certainly not going to reach out to them to get their version of things." He picked up a pencil and struck through the first question on the lined school paper.

No one spoke as he tapped the eraser on the page. "What were you doing alone with Eliza in Hunters' Woods? Are you trying to hurt and embarrass poor Martha? Because that's exactly how it looks, as if you and Eliza decided that ending the engagement that close to the wedding day wasn't enough cruelty for Martha." The bishop sounded as if he was preaching now, raising and lowering his voice to make points, barely taking a breath when on a roll. "I don't know what Martha did to anger you, Jesse, but I assure you ending the wedding was enough punishment."

Jesse shook his head. "Martha didn't do anything wrong. Not one thing. That was my fault too."

"Her parents have appealed to the ministers in Brush Hollow, pleading with their bishop, preacher, and deacon that your ministers in Calico Creek bring justice down on your head. I can't imagine how many years it will take to build goodwill between the two districts. I can assure you one thing: they feel the ministers in Calico Creek have done a poor job with our flock."

Ruth rubbed her forehead. "Perhaps Jesse and Eliza are guilty of indiscretion—"

"Perhaps?" The bishop thrust his hands forward. "Perhaps?" He spoke even louder the second time.

Andrew stood, ready to defend Ruth. Her eyes met his, and she barely shook her head as if telling him to leave without drawing attention to him. He wasn't leaving. He wasn't sure what all she'd need to answer for, but Aunt Lydia told him one issue would be riding in the car of an ex-Amish. Nope, he wasn't leaving. But he took a seat before anyone else noticed him.

"Eliza Bontrager," the bishop said, "explain to me why you returned from your home in Ohio to Calico Creek mere weeks before Jesse was to wed? How is it that you finagled your way into being on the jobsite with Jesse every workday since you arrived?" He jabbed the table with his index finger. "Is it true that you sewed items for the wedding and that you delivered them while Jesse was home and took that opportunity to also spend time with him?"

Jesse leaned forward. "Look, here's the deal: before she moved to Ohio eight years ago, I asked Eliza to marry me."

"What?" Eliza's mamm whispered, staring at Eliza.

"I've always loved her," Jesse continued, "but the past six months, I convinced myself it was time to find a wife and start a family. Eliza didn't seduce me or conjure up opportunities to get close to me, although I understand how it could look that way. She wanted me to marry Martha."

Jesse's dat sighed. His mamm scoffed. "Not likely."

The bishop didn't respond to the restlessness in the room. He fidgeted with the edges of several pages in the Bible. "I appreciate your honesty about your feelings toward Eliza. It makes a lot of things add up for me. I couldn't understand why someone who's been such a steady, good man all these years would end things with Martha and be in Eliza's arms within days of that." The bishop closed the Bible. "Now I understand. I hate to say this, Jesse, but you need to hear me: Eliza has you buffaloed."

Eliza stared at the floor, looking overcome with embarrassment.

Jesse stood. "That's not what's going on here."

"Sit down, please." The bishop waited.

Jesse's face was red with frustration, but he sat. He motioned at Eliza, catching her eyes. "We—" he gestured from her to himself—"know the truth. That's all that matters."

"You're wrong about that! It matters to hundreds of people in three districts—Calico Creek Ridge, Calico Creek Glen, and Brush Hollow—and all of Martha's family." The bishop spoke through gritted teeth before gaining composure. "Moving on." He cleared his throat. "I've done my due diligence on this topic, talking to Martha and her family. What I described is exactly what has happened, Jesse, whether you can see it or not. Let's go through the steps. Twenty-one days passed between when Eliza showed up at the creek where you and Martha were on the day of the Ebersol family gathering and when you broke up with Martha. Eliza doesn't live in this state, but she came here to stay for weeks, something she has not done since she moved to Ohio, apparently after you proposed to her. I think that she was fine with you being single all those years, but when she caught wind of your plans to marry, she set out to do exactly what she's done—ruin things between you and Martha, using any method possible."

Eliza's lips were pursed, tears trailing her face. "I'm so sorry, Jesse."

Jesse shook his head. "She's not apologizing for things she didn't do. Her apology is about the timing of everything."

"Maybe so." The bishop sighed. "It brings me no pleasure to give an edict concerning Eliza, but the ministers and our People from all three districts insist on justice. With this much outrage from our People and this much clear wrong-doing, I feel it's fair—"

"Wait." Ruth's eyes said she'd just realized something. She tilted her head, watching the bishop. "You've been doing interviews. Were they seen together any other time than in Hunters' Woods two days ago?"

He shook his head. "His parents saw them outside their home when Eliza was delivering quilts for the wedding, but other than that, not that I know of. Maybe they were—" he looked to Ruth's mamm and dat—"and no one I spoke to was willing to say anything."

Ruth fidgeted with a string to her prayer Kapp. "If they were in Hunters' Woods all alone except for you showing up, how is it that everyone knows they were together, kissing?"

The back of the bishop's neck turned red. "Look, I'm not the one answering to an evaluation meeting. I can agree that the indecency of seeing them like that got the best of me, and I spoke of it too loudly while sharing it with our preacher and deacon. But I wouldn't have needed to talk to anyone about it if Eliza hadn't been determined to end Jesse's wedding to Martha."

Andrew wasn't surprised that the woman in the relationship

would be singled out as the sinful party. Unless Jesse was willing to leave the Amish and break his and Eliza's families' hearts, he couldn't do much about what was heading Eliza's way.

The bishop scooted his chair toward the kitchen table. "Speaking of a Bontrager and Ebersol being seen together, I understand that you, Ruth, have ignored the Ordnung about riding in a car with an ex-Amish and that you and Andrew have been seen together numerous times."

Andrew stood. "If I may . . ."

The bishop turned, his eyes wide. He got up and went to a window and peered out. "Jah, that's the car I saw the two of you in. You need to go. This doesn't concern you, Andrew."

"It does, David. Ruth rode in my car on several occasions, but only because she has a good heart."

The bishop narrowed his eyes. "What are you saying?"

Andrew moved closer to the table. "When Ben Mast died, I lost my faith in living Amish. No amount of rules or him keeping those rules had saved him. I felt if he hadn't been Amish, he wouldn't have had that accident. Seemed that everyone tried to comfort me with words that sliced my faith into shreds. Most Amish feel that his death was planned by God, and I . . . I just lost my ability to believe the way our People do."

David put a hand on Andrew's shoulder. "It doesn't matter whether God planned it or He allowed it—we must remember that this world is temporary, and we must continue steadfast in love and acceptance."

"Jah, I agree. I really do . . . now. But it took Ruth being my friend and showing me what's worth fighting for and what's worth accepting." He pulled the keys out of his pocket. "I'll sell my car this week. I've already quit school."

Ruth's chair scraped against the floor as she stood. "Andrew." Her beautiful brown eyes bored into him.

He smiled. "I choose you, Ruth. This evaluation meeting caused me to come here today to say what I was going to tell you tomorrow, after I moved back home and sold my car."

"You choose Ruth?" Bishop David asked.

Many Amish men stayed because they fell in love, and the bishop knew it. Andrew was sure he didn't mind. "I choose to go through instruction when it's offered this spring and join the church. I choose to be faithful to the Old Ways, even when my faith staggers. But above all that, I choose Ruth."

The bishop moved to the window to look out again, maybe to gather his thoughts.

Andrew smiled at Ruth. "As a trusted friend once said to me, it says something significant about who I am that you were in two lifetimes, drawing out the best in me."

Ruth stared into his eyes.

"Two lifetimes?" The bishop turned to look at Andrew.

"It's an expression we use."

The bishop nodded. "You move back home. After you bring me a receipt of the sale of your car, you and Ruth will spend Friday evenings here, reading the Word with me, for at least a month. Then we'll revisit the plan."

Andrew wanted to hug Ruth. He lowered his hand to his side so it could brush hers.

The bishop's eyes caught the movement of their hands, and Andrew knew the next several months of proving himself would be very strict ones. Unless they could fix the timeline.

The bishop pointed to an empty chair on the opposite side of the table where the men were sitting. Andrew squeezed Ruth's pinkie before going to the other side.

"Jesse—" the bishop returned to his chair—"for six months you will not be alone with Eliza. No buggy rides. No walks in the woods."

"You're asking too much. I've waited eight years."

"Push me on this, and I'll put far stricter restrictions on your life." The bishop turned to Eliza. "You will be under the ban for six months. You will not sit at the table during a mealtime if others are eating there. You will not join any of the women's work frolics or quilting bees. No dishes or laundry or groceries will pass from your hands to anyone, not a sibling or a parent or anyone else, and nothing from anyone's hands to yours. And you will not, under any circumstances, go to the jobsite where Jesse works. Do you understand?"

Eliza nodded, looking too burdened with guilt to even look at Jesse.

Andrew's heart sank. How could the four of them do all they needed to do in order to try to change time back with this many restrictions?

Chapter Thirty-Two

Rays of early morning light poured into the room as Eliza smoothed the center piece of what would become the new quilt. The home vibrated with an abundance of noise since it was Saturday, and her school-age siblings were home today. She studied her mamm's table and all that was on it. The patchwork piece Verna had given her as well as a few other freshly sewn pieces and lots of cut fabric were spread out on the Bontrager family's massive kitchen table. Her heart was heavy from the unnecessary grief she'd caused Jesse, Martha, and their families, but if she could change time back, it would help tremendously.

It'd been four days since Verna brought the one patch-work piece, and Eliza had been working diligently every spare minute, gathering vintage fabric and sewing individual patchwork pieces.

Mamm walked by with a broom and dustpan, shooting her a hurt look. Despite Eliza's best effort, she and Mamm had argued more than once since Thursday's evaluation meeting. Mamm had learned things in that meeting that a parent shouldn't ever have to know, at least not without the framework of information that would explain Eliza's behavior. Jesse's revelation to the group that he loved Eliza, that he'd asked her to marry him eight years ago, had only made it worse for Mamm. In Mamm's eyes, Eliza had turned Jesse down eight years ago, disappeared, and then was in his arms two days before he should've been wed. Mamm was rattled to the core of her being, and there was nothing Eliza could say or do to console her.

Eliza counted quilt squares and stacked them according to color.

Also four days ago, Ruth had bravely gone to Andrew's home without him and asked his mom if she could rummage around the attic. She'd told his mom that she was in need of vintage material for a very important quilt and that Andrew had suggested she ask his mom. Ruth said the woman was very surprised Andrew mentioned her attic, but she was incredibly welcoming. His mamm and dat both helped Ruth move boxes and dig through the attic. Either in this timeline or the one they all longed to return to, Eliza felt sure that Ruth would have a wonderful mother-in-law one day. Jesse's parents had been great in-laws to Eliza, but in this timeline, they had no respect for her at all, not that she blamed them.

That night when Ruth returned with vintage fabric, she and Eliza gently prewashed it by hand. They did the same for the vintage fabric Eliza had managed to find. They hung it overnight on the backs of kitchen chairs near the fireplace. The next day, Eliza spent hours heating the black cast-iron pressing iron on the wood-burning stove and then using it to work out the wrinkles from the fabric. Apparently really old material was a magnet for crumples that did not want to yield to an iron. But their ancestors would've treated the fabric in the original quilt with great care, and Eliza would do the same, including constant, fervent prayers that God would grant His generosity and bless their efforts to make things right.

Although Thursday's evaluation meeting had been rough on Eliza, it had some beautiful perks for Ruth. After the meeting, Andrew drove his car to a used dealership and sold it. Ruth drove a rig to the car dealership and picked him up. Then together they went to see his parents to tell them he was dropping out of college and moving back home. Ruth said his folks were beside themselves with relief and excitement. Andrew would be watched closely, but that's all the trouble he'd be in with the ministers since he'd never joined the faith, and now he'd put his worldly ways behind him and returned to the fold.

Once home from all of that, Ruth had helped Eliza endlessly with the quilt. Since eighteen-year-old Annie and sixteen-year-old Naomi weren't working at the bakeshop in town today, her teen sisters were pitching in too, which was great as Eliza and Ruth aimed to be done as soon as possible.

"Eliza, this is beautiful." Naomi tilted her head as she regarded it. "Who is this quilt for again?"

"It's for all of us." She pointed at the beautiful piece from Mercy's quilt. "This piece is from a very old quilt that belonged to Auntie Rose. I want to remake the quilt. All of the quilt-top pieces will be created from vintage fabric from various Amish attics. The backing will be too, but I'm not sure I have enough vintage fabric for the binding. My goal is to match this quilt pattern the best I can to the one Auntie Rose had, from memory." She recalled spreading out the quilt for a picnic with Jesse on their riverbank. Wrapping it around her shoulders as she ran to meet him on their wedding day. Lying on it over Penelope's grave.

Naomi put the piece back in place on the table. "I miss Auntie Rose."

Eliza smiled at her sister. "Me too."

"You sure you want me sewing on any of this?" Annie asked. "I'm not nearly as good with a needle as you and Ruth."

"Me either," Naomi chimed in.

Ruth stood and squeezed Naomi's shoulders. "Jah. It's a family project."

"Becca will help!" Five-year-old Becca pushed Eliza in order to stand behind her on the chair.

"Ugh, third person." Naomi sighed, shaking her head at Becca.

"Come 'ere, you little stinker." Ruth scooped her up and set her feet down away from the table. "You're more likely to create chaos."

"Wait," Becca protested. She folded her arms and pouted, not budging or saying anything else. Eliza understood Ruth's sentiments, but how could they have every Bontrager sister working on the quilt and leave out the youngest girl? It wouldn't be nice, even if she was only five.

"It's okay." Eliza put an arm around Becca's waist and moved her to stand on a chair. "She can help too."

"Enough." Mamm put a hand on the table. "I've tried to be patient, Eliza, giving you some space about wanting to sew a new quilt, but then I turned around and you had pulled in Ruth. Today you do the same with Annie and Naomi. And now Becca? No. Do you hear me? *No.* You can't ask this of them. No one in this house will work on anything with Eliza. She's shunned."

"Shunned?" Becca asked. "What's that? You sick?"

"Nee. I'm gut." That answer was a stretch. Eliza had had an ongoing headache for days and had been nauseated since the evaluation meeting, but no one needed to know that. The circumstances that caused the stress were her own fault.

She set Becca on her bottom in the chair. "I've been careful, Mamm, even when it was just Ruth and me. Nothing has passed from my hands to theirs or from theirs to mine. This morning I set up a smaller table for me to sit separate. They can work at this table sewing individual patchwork squares, and I'll work on my squares over at this little table." She pointed to the corner of the dining room where she'd put a kitchen chair under a beat-up old nightstand where a kerosene lantern sat each evening, giving off light.

Mamm scowled. "You're not taking the spirit of the consequence seriously."

"Mamm . . . you said weeks ago how worried you were about me. I'm working on something that's bringing me a bit of peace, a purpose, and a goal, and yes, that involves eventually marrying Jesse. Can't you see all of those things matter more than the social rules? We're not going against anything in the Bible."

"You were smooching with Jesse when, by all godly rights, he should've been with Martha. You need a chapter and verse in the Bible to tell you that's wrong?"

Eliza closed her eyes. Dat was no happier with her than Mamm.

"Listen to me, Eliza," Mamm spat. "If the bishop, or *anyone* connected to the church stops by and sees you girls working together on that quilt, your dat and I could be shunned. For what? So you could play childish games with Jesse by running from him and then breaking up him and Martha? So you can now play house with your sisters and all of you sew on a quilt? I won't stand for it!"

"Mamm, please." Ruth tried to meet Mamm's eyes. "None of our friends or relatives are out to get us. They love us."

Mamm huffed and went back to her sweeping. Eliza hated this predicament, the one she'd caused. It couldn't come at a worse time for her precious mamm. She was under so much stress due to Dat's sickness and Moses' drinking, and now all the problems her eldest daughter caused. Eliza couldn't be mad at her, but she also couldn't explain.

Dat walked through the dining room, coughing into a handkerchief. He caught his breath and gestured. "I heard some of what was said. What's going on?" He eyed Eliza. "Are you making things more difficult for your mother? She's got a lot on her right now."

"I'm sorry, Dat." Eliza truly meant it. It was completely unfair for her parents to get caught in the middle of all of this. *Please work,* she pleaded to the pieces of quilt.

Dat tilted his head, regarding her. "Why have you pulled in your sisters' help on this new quilting project of yours? The bishop gave an edict, and so now you've decided that your siblings must help you? It's as if you feel you must defy the bishop and other ministers for some ungodly reason."

Eliza needed every pair of hands helping to get this quilt done as soon as possible. Well, she could work faster without Becca's help, but little ones deserved respect and patience no matter what rush the adults were in. Besides the need for many hands to help the project go faster, they needed many hands in unity and prayer to try to replicate the first quilt.

Unity? There was far more angst and anger than unity.

Jesse and some of his younger brothers as well as Moses and Levi were dragging logs from the burn pit and finding stones at a surprising speed. Eliza needed this quilt done as soon as they were finished. She looked from her dat to her mamm. Would telling them a little something help at all? Or would it cause them to panic the way Omar's bishop had all those years ago?

Talk to him.

To just Dat? That seemed odd. And tell him what? She couldn't imagine how to explain any part of this in a way that would bring him peace or cause him to want to get on board.

Trusting her gut, she took a step toward her father. "Dat, can I talk to you in private?"

He nodded and motioned toward the front porch for Eliza to go first. As she walked, she could hear Ruth giving instructions to her sisters to start sewing. Good. Ruth was wasting no time.

He closed the door behind them. "Eliza, what's really going on?"

Memories of him tucking her in at night flooded her. He took that time as he tucked his daughters in bed to recite Hebrews 11:1-11. They called it his *By Faith* outlook.

"Dat, by faith Abel, by faith Enoch, by faith Noah, by faith Abraham, by faith Sarah, by faith many others." She didn't fill in all each one did by faith. Dat knew, and it was too many words for right now. "By faith, Dat. You taught me to trust God and you by faith. Remember?"

He nodded, looking unsure.

"I'm asking you to trust me by faith. I know my life looks sinful and rebellious. But I need to get the quilt made by many loving hands as we pray over it. Can you trust me by faith, regardless of how my life looks?"

Dat lifted her chin and stared into her eyes, examining her soul as he had on occasion with each of his children. His brows furrowed. "Tell me again."

"By faith, Dat. No lies or trickery. No seducing of a man who was to wed another. What appears to be is not what is. We are walking in earnest."

He held her chin firm, still looking in her eyes. "We?"

"Jesse and me." She stared into his familiar eyes, seeing love and deep concern. "Dat, what appears to be is not what is," she repeated. He'd repeated that saying hundreds of times in her life, but it was her first time to say it to him. "Trust me. I'm begging you to trust me."

"How is Jesse connected to you and your sisters sewing a quilt?"

"He's not. He's at the old cabin in Hunters' Woods. It

was destroyed by machinery, and since it's Saturday, all six of his brothers, two of mine, and Andrew are trying to rebuild the cabin."

He lowered his hand. "Why?"

"I think it's best explained by Jesse's own words. He told his brothers rebuilding the cabin is his healing, his only way back to himself, and they are helping him . . . in faith that rebuilding the cabin will do what Jesse hopes it will." Jesse wasn't lying. It was his way back to himself, to the life he'd built before she changed time.

"Eliza, your actions and his make no sense whatsoever. There's more going on here than you're saying."

She nodded. "But me saying more will not give you the answers you're seeking."

His shoulders slumped. "What are you doing?" he whispered.

She took a moment to ponder his question. "What I can."

He would understand her answer. He'd brought them up teaching that when life put them between a rock and a hard place, when life told them what couldn't be done, they were to ask themselves, what *can* be done?—and they were to do that with all their might.

He took her in. "By faith?"

"Jah. I give you my word, Dat."

His brows relaxed and he drew a deep breath. Slowly a smile formed on his lips. "Then I will not stand against you."

Relief surged through her and tears stung her eyes. "Gut!" she whispered, hugging his neck. He held her, rubbing her upper back. A moment later, they both took a step back.

"Tell me, Daughter, what do you need from me? Should I go to Hunters' Woods to help Jesse?"

"Well . . . I think your health will hinder you from doing much lifting. What I really need is for you to talk to Mamm. Try to help her understand the importance of what I'm doing, even if she'd never believe in me as you do."

"I'll certainly do my best." He opened the front door while Eliza waited on the porch. "Dottie?"

Mamm set a dishcloth on a countertop and approached them, suspicion on her face. She walked onto the porch, closing the door behind her.

Dat put his hands on her shoulders and rubbed them. "My love, you once promised you'd always trust me."

"Jah?" Mamm narrowed her eyes, looking as if she was waiting for him to share really bad news.

"We are going to do our best to help Eliza with the quilt and stop hindering her efforts. Jesse and several men, including Andrew, Moses, and Levi, are at Hunters' Woods, trying to rebuild the cabin that Beckford Construction tore apart."

Mamm's eyes grew large. "The quilt," she whispered. "The cabin in Hunters' Woods?" She looked at Eliza. "All of this is about the folklore between Ebersols and Bontragers." She stared at them for what seemed like five minutes. "The folklore?"

"By faith, my love. Eliza is asking us to believe in her, and I do."

Mamm blinked, shaking her head. "This isn't about faith! This is somehow connected to us giving our oldest girls to Ebersol men, and I will *not* participate."

"My sweet Dottie. Please, as a favor to me, let them do

as they need unhindered. If I don't have much longer on this planet, help me lean in to our family, supporting our daughters, as well as Jesse and Andrew."

"What? Nee, I can't."

"I believe you can. I am. By faith."

Dat paused. His faith was contagious, and Mamm seemed to be catching it.

"Dottie, trust that this is where faith is the hardest, where you can't see or feel confidence in what I'm asking, in what Eliza is asking. I've seen you do incredible things in the face of difficult reality for many long years at a time. We close on the property in two weeks. It's just for two weeks. Then we'll sell the land, move, and deal with whatever comes next."

Mamm stared at Eliza and then returned her attention to Dat. Her face softened. "Our girls to Ebersol men?"

"What is the one thing you've wanted for our daughters their entire lives, the one thing you've prayed for them above all else?"

She looked at Eliza. "That they would marry good men who loved them above all else on this earth." She sighed. "I guess Jesse and Andrew have proven that for sure."

He nodded. "Jah. They have."

"Okay. For that reason and for you, Amos." She gave Eliza a half smile. "And for my oldest, usually most levelheaded daughter, I can give some allowances."

Eliza grinned at her. "Denki. I love you both so much."

Mamm rolled her eyes. "Says any child who is getting exactly what they wanted."

Eliza chuckled. "True. But you know I mean it, jah?"

Mamm nodded and hugged her. "I know you do."

"I'll head to the site." But Dat opened the back door for them to enter, and then he followed them into the kitchen.

"Girls." Mamm snapped her fingers. "Let's get moving on this quilt." She put a hand on her hip. "You—" she pointed at Dat—"will absolutely *not* go into Hunters' Woods to build anything."

He waved her off. "Don't worry. The only thing I'll build are some sandwiches. They're gonna need some lunch."

Mamm sighed. "Dear Gott, help me. This family is trying to drive me crazy."

"Trying?" Annie asked. "Or succeeding?"

All of Mamm's girls broke into laughter.

She joined them and picked up a sewing needle. "What's the plan?"

Chapter Thirty-Three

Ruth took a sip of her warmed-up coffee as she paused over the sink, looking out the window. The late afternoon was already darkening. How had another day almost passed? Her back ached, her eyes were tired, her hands sore. With the exception of church four days ago, they'd hardly taken a break. They'd been working on the quilt all day—all *week* long.

She could hear the voices of Eliza and Mamm, still at work at the table.

"Eliza, does this binding match what you remember?"

"It does. There's no way of knowing the exact colors, of course, just like on the rest of it. But it sure *feels* close to the off-white binding I remember."

"Gut. I need to fix dinner; then I'll work on it with you. Kumm, Annie, Naomi, Becca. You can help me."

Mamm had been a lot of help. Ruth woke one night to find her quietly shedding tears as she murmured prayers while working on the quilt. Their precious mamm was terrified for her daughters, not understanding what was going on, but clearly she'd chosen to set aside any arguments over legalistic things, and she'd chosen to work with them and pray fervently. Ruth knew Mamm's prayers would add much to hers and Eliza's.

They were close to finishing the actual quilting. The process of hand-sewing through all the layers—the pieced top, batting, and backing—was typically deeply gratifying. But by this point, they were tired and anxious and just ready to be done. When the quilting was finished, all they had to do was fix the binding around the completed quilt. If they pushed, they could be done tonight!

As her mamm and younger sisters walked into the kitchen, she heard the front door open and the sound of several male voices—Andrew, Dat, Jesse, and Moses.

Ruth set her coffee cup beside the sink and walked to the front door. Eliza and Mamm had moved to meet the guys there too.

"Hi." Andrew smiled as he gave a little wave to her. He looked so handsome in his Amish clothes. Even though what they were doing had a high chance of getting them all excommunicated, his clothes told Ruth that he was true to what he'd said at the meeting—he chose her. No matter what happened.

"Eliza . . ." Jesse walked to her sister, reaching to touch her shoulder but stopping before embracing her. "We're done.

The cabin is complete, and we rebuilt a smaller kitchen table from the broken pieces we could find."

Dat coughed. "Each foundation stone, log, and most of the wood shingles for the roof are back in place as close to the original as any of us could recall. I spent so much time playing in those woods and in that dilapidated cabin as a boy, I was glad I could offer a little help, even though I couldn't actually build anything."

It was complete! This meant as soon as they finished their quilt . . .

"I don't fully get why any of this means so much to you all." Moses hung his black coat on the rack by the door. "We go to closing next week, and then we move. I can only hope Jesse found his way back to himself, since that seems to be why we did all that work."

"Moses—" Mamm crossed her arms—"how about you go help your brothers haul in wood for the night and add more wood to the furnace in the basement. It's going to be a cold one."

"Uh, sure."

Mamm nodded at Ruth and Eliza; then she and Dat moved to the kitchen.

Eliza and Jesse went to the living room. Ruth paused, enjoying a quiet moment just between her and Andrew before they followed her sister and Jesse.

Eliza and Jesse were standing in the middle of the room. Ruth grabbed Andrew's hand and pulled him toward the nearest couch. "We need to make a plan."

"Jah," Eliza said. "We're very close to finishing the quilt.

I can't believe it, but we only need about three more hours of sewing time."

Jesse grasped her hand. "That's fantastic. Are we trying tonight?"

Eliza shrugged, giving him a small smile. "I don't see a reason to wait. Nor do I think I could sleep without knowing if all of our efforts will come to fruition . . . or be nothing but a false hope."

There was no way of knowing. Ruth could sense her sister's apprehension.

"Who's going to go?" Jesse asked.

"To the cabin site?" Ruth asked. "All four of us, I would think."

Andrew winked at her. "I think he meant who's restitching the quilt in hopes of traveling."

Eliza eased into a love seat near the fireplace, staring into the flames. "I feel like I should fix it, because I'm the one that messed everything up." She looked up at Jesse. "But based on what Mercy and Verna said, I don't think I can return to that moment again. I've been trying to think of another time I could use to set things right, and I can't find a clear time. Jesse was gone from Calico Creek most weeks and weekends. What if I landed somewhere unfamiliar and couldn't find you? What if I found you, but nothing I said in those few minutes made sense to you, so nothing would be changed? Going back only allows for a few minutes to alter one decision before the traveler is pulled back to now."

"I agree." Ruth nodded. "Maybe I should be the one to go. I could return to your wedding, intercept the quilt once Auntie Rose gives it to you, and I'll just destroy the quilt."

Jesse sat next to Eliza. "From all Andrew's told me, that kind of move is risking the butterfly effect. Our wedding day had so many moving parts, and if anything goes slightly wrong, you won't get to burn it before you get pulled back to now." He rubbed his chin. "I hate to disagree with the two of you, but I think it has to be me, and I have to return to the creek when I proposed."

Ruth shuddered. So much was riding on what a person could accomplish during a brief time travel. "But I know where Eliza put the quilt once you showed up to the wedding, and we had fifty-five-gallon drums set up, ready to start fires for the cleanup after the wedding. I know I could get the quilt, start the fire, and accomplish the task."

Jesse rubbed his forehead, clearly thinking. "We don't know if our wedding exists in the past since we're living in the time that Eliza changed. I think our best chance is me returning to the day I proposed at the creek. It's an event that both time-lines share, so it's probably our best chance to change what is."

"My head hurts from thinking." Andrew rubbed a temple. "How do we go about traveling anyway? The cabin is rebuilt. We'll go there as soon as the quilt is finished. Then what?"

Good question. Ruth fidgeted with a string to her prayer Kapp, trying to imagine how it should go. "Before Beckford Construction uprooted trees, there was a clearing between the woods and the cabin. We should go to that same area, although it looks very different now, and hopefully we'll see smoke coming from the chimney. I think we wait there for Mercy to open the cabin door and invite us in. Whoever is going to travel back needs to be the one carrying the quilt into the cabin."

Eliza cleared her throat in a way that said she was on the verge of tears. "When I traveled, I thought of where I wanted to go before I cut the thread. When it was time to resew that spot, I had plenty of thread already attached to the quilt to work with. It just showed up, long and beautiful, as if I hadn't just snipped that same thread from a tightly sewn quilt."

"Okay, so once we're in the cabin with Mercy, the normal laws of life and physics are altered for more than just time traveling." Andrew shifted, still looking deep in thought. "I'm sorry, Ruth, but I have to agree with Jesse. His plan makes the most sense for all the reasons he said. Based on all we know, he should be able to change Eliza's change."

Ruth tried to breathe. The word *should* had never been a frightening one before now. She leaned forward. "I understand why you all feel Jesse should try, but we don't know what Eliza he'll meet—the teen girl who's in love with him or his grieving wife who is determined to set him free. How would he change *grieving* Eliza's decision? I was with her that day she and Mercy changed time, and there was no talking her out of her decision."

Jesse looked into Eliza's eyes. "You were my best friend even before we got engaged. I'll convince you to marry me, whether I meet young Eliza or grieving Eliza at the creek."

Eliza shook her head. "I'm not sure you can change the mind of grieving me, not if I have no memories of the fallout changing time caused. All I felt was a need to free you."

"I'll meet you there, armed with information and lots of prayers. If our engagement plays out with you saying yes, I think that will fix the timeline."

Eliza smiled, but it looked more sad than anything else. "We have a plan, and I pray it works."

Jesse held up his kerosene lantern, lighting the path for him and Eliza. He carried the newly finished quilt in the crook of his other arm, holding it as carefully as one would a newborn baby.

Andrew and Ruth walked behind them, carrying lanterns of their own. The night was dark—no moon, and the trees obscured any stars in the sky. Jesse's anxiety had risen with each minute that the women completed the quilt. After finishing up dinner around seven, the women had worked for about three hours on the quilt, and he'd prayed the whole time. Another prayer now couldn't hurt. *Please, God. Let us be able to go home. Let us return to our lives.*

Eliza's parents knew the four of them were together, finished quilt in hand as they came to the cabin. The looks on their faces spoke of deep concern, and yet they chose to trust what they could not condone or understand. All his life he'd known them to be people of faith, but this was nothing short of remarkable, and it had changed him.

Eliza tripped over a root, and without dropping the quilt, he caught her elbow, stabilizing her. A small smile graced her lips, the lantern light casting shadows across her face, accentuating her knit brows. She was just as nervous as he was—probably more so. He knew how much burden she carried over actions they might not be able to undo. They continued walking.

"I thought we'd see smoke by now."

Please, God, for Eliza's sake most of all. "Maybe the night is too dark to see it."

They walked onward. The cabin came into sight.

Eliza stopped walking. It sounded as if Andrew and Ruth stopped right behind them. Jesse held his breath. They stared at the cabin. No smoke. They waited, hoping Mercy would open the door.

Jesse silently prayed again. He took a few steps forward.

Nothing special or different about the cabin. Just the silhouette of the freshly rebuilt structure and stack-stone chimney. The door didn't open. His heart pounded. It was all he could do to not drop to his knees in despair.

Eliza took the quilt from Jesse. "Maybe drape it over your shoulders. That's how I was wearing the quilt the first time."

"Jah, that's right. She was." Ruth gingerly helped Eliza unfold the quilt and put it over Jesse's shoulders. The sisters closed their eyes, then opened them again. "Nothing," Ruth whispered. She shook her head. "Maybe we should knock on the door or just go inside."

Eliza held up her hand like a stop sign. "There's no smoke coming from the chimney, Ruth. If Mercy were there now, we'd see smoke. Be patient."

Ten minutes passed. Andrew's face was drawn as he barely shook his head, his eyes meeting Jesse's. Despite all their effort to unearth the scattered stones and the wood shingles for the roof and the logs out of the burn pit, this wasn't working.

"Come here, Eliza." Ruth motioned. "Let's put the quilt around your shoulders and approach the cabin like we did the first time."

Jesse put the quilt around Eliza. He then stepped back

with Andrew as they watched the sisters move away from the cabin and then walk toward it, apparently as they had when the cabin first appeared. Over and over they tried. One holding the quilt, then the other holding it; then they both held it. Jesse and Andrew joined walking with them, using every combination of people holding the quilt.

After what seemed like hours, all four sat on a felled tree, the same one Verna and Omar had sat on nine days ago.

The heavy mood seemed every bit as dark as the silent night surrounding them. No bugs or tree frogs chirped. Just weighty silence in the cold, dark of night on a ridge in the Appalachian Mountains.

"Eliza?" Ruth's voice broke the silence. "What do you want to do?" She stumbled on the last word.

"I . . ." Eliza shrugged, seeming unable to find her voice.

Jesse put his arm around her, and she leaned in, resting her head on his chest. She probably couldn't feel much warmth radiating from him through his heavy coat, but he longed to wrap her in every kind of warmth this earth had to offer.

She stood straight. "Let's go into the cabin." She motioned and they followed her up the two steps and inside.

The kerosene lanterns they carried cast shifting light. Eliza put the quilt on the table Jesse had rebuilt. This table was smaller and more beat-up than the one Jesse remembered being in here from his childhood. Eliza passed him a pair of old scissors from her coat pocket.

His hands were trembling. "Did you bring a needle?"

She pulled one from the fabric on the bib of her apron, but she didn't pass it to him.

He lifted the scissors. "Should we try?"

Eliza studied the room. "Let's wait for a bit. It doesn't feel right. It feels empty, like four outsiders who stumbled on some old cabin."

They waited. Jesse was sure each one was silently praying as another thirty minutes passed.

"I . . . I think we should go home." Ruth's voice was uncharacteristically quiet. "It doesn't mean I'm giving up. But whatever we thought was going to happen tonight clearly isn't. We can return first thing in the morning, when we're not having to search for our footing by the light of a kerosene lantern. Okay? Maybe . . . part of the problem is when we came here. If we return at twilight—like when Eliza and I first found it—maybe Mercy will show up. Or maybe it'll feel right to cut the thread without her. But nothing feels as it should."

"She's right," Eliza whispered.

Jesse nodded at her. "Maybe so. Maybe the time of day matters."

Andrew reached for Ruth's hand and guided her as they left the cabin. He moved his lantern to light the path as they walked back toward the Bontrager house.

Eliza crossed her arms, looking away. Jesse would wait all night with her here if it would help. Sleep didn't matter anymore. This was their only goal, their only purpose.

Jesse gestured up the path, waving on Andrew and Ruth. "Go on without us. We'll be back in a bit."

They soon disappeared into the night.

"Denki," Eliza whispered to him.

"What would you like to do?"

Her eyes held tears. "Let's go to my tree. Penelope's tree. I want to pray."

Chapter Thirty-Four

Eliza closed her eyes as she touched the rough bark of the ancient oak, feeling the texture under her fingertips. This tree, this living thing, existed in both timelines, always the same. Despite the passage of time and the choices of humans, it was the same. *God, You are the same, no matter where I go in this life.* And no matter what happened.

She opened her eyes. "Let's spread the quilt out like we used to and both talk to God. Maybe He would be willing to guide our path."

Standing behind her, Jesse kissed her cheek, then took the quilt from her arms. He passed the lantern to her. The thick fabric made a satisfying swoop sound as he shook it out and spread it across a blanket of fallen leaves. It was the middle of the night. No bishops, parents, or anyone else would disturb them.

He took the lantern and set it beside the quilt.

She knelt on the blanket, facing the tree, then fidgeted with the soft fabric. They'd put so much love and care into creating it. And prayers. It *looked* very much like Mercy's quilt, as far as Eliza and Ruth could remember. Why hadn't Mercy appeared? Maybe she didn't have to be there, but if that were true, why had going into the cabin or having the scissors ready to cut a thread and a needle ready to sew felt completely empty, as if nothing they'd done had any power behind it?

Jesse knelt beside her. "It feels blurred here. Does it to you?"

"What do you mean?"

"I mean, both timelines feel just as real. Marrying you. Building a life together. It feels like we should be able to stand up and just *walk* home."

"Jah. It does."

She closed her eyes and prayed from her heart. *God, please. Forgive my mistake that I made in grief. I should've had better, deeper faith. I want to go home. I want all of it—the pain and the happiness. I want to mourn Penelope in a time and place where she did exist.*

I choose to trust You, God, and where I falter in it, I choose to learn from my mistakes. I believe You want good things for us. Pain is an inevitable part of the journey on this mess of a planet, and yet Your way of taking care of the ones we've lost is a victory. A huge one.

Jesse reached for her hands. "God, I confess and believe that You have ordained marriage to be a union between one man and one wife, and a blessed marriage is in accordance with the way we have been taught."

Those words . . . they were from their marriage vows.

She smiled at him. "I do too."

Jesse nodded. "I have confidence that You, Lord, have provided me with Eliza as a marriage partner. The only one for me, no matter what."

"And I have confidence that Jesse is my husband, whatever path life takes us."

He caressed her cheek with his thumb. "In weakness, sickness, and in health."

"In love, forbearance, and patience."

His eyes held her gaze. "Until God separates us in death, I promise."

"And I promise."

Jesse closed the space between them, kissing her on the lips. His lips were as warm and loving as his words. They hadn't kissed like this in their real ceremony in front of the crowd, but here, with only God as their witness, it was right.

He broke the kiss and clasped her hands tight in his. "There, Eliza. No matter what timeline we live in, I make those vows. And I'll make them again if I need to. I love you. I love our daughter and the little ones we lost before her."

"I love you. I accept our lives together. Wherever they are. I'm with you."

Maybe Verna was right. Maybe this was where they were supposed to be. As much as it hurt.

A flutter of white caught Eliza's eye. She turned and picked up a small, white petal from the quilt. A daisy petal.

"Do . . . you see this?"

"Jah." Jesse looked around. "Flower petals in late November?"

Eliza nodded. "They're just like the ones I laid at this tree. Before Penelope died. Daisies." She looked around the grove, seeing a few more petals, almost like in a trail. "Jesse."

"I see them." He stood and offered a hand to help her up.

She stepped off the quilt, following the tiny petals through the forest floor of fallen leaves.

Behind her, she could hear Jesse shake out the quilt as he lifted it from the ground and followed her.

The petals would be nearly impossible to see on a night this dark if not for the stark whiteness of their color and the light of the lantern in Jesse's hand. Just a few, here and there, but it was enough to keep going. She walked faster and faster, until she was almost jogging, her heart pounding.

A swirl of petals tumbled into the clearing and kept going.

Something caught Eliza's eye. She came to a stop and took in the view. "Jesse," she whispered.

He was right behind her, carrying the quilt and kerosene lantern.

Chills running amok, she breathed, "Smoke."

Holding the lantern in front of him, Jesse guided Eliza toward the cabin. Smoke poured from the chimney. He realized the white petals were on the steps, leading to the door. Was this real and not some dream he was having while sitting on the quilt with Eliza? But no, the quilt was in his arms.

"I don't think Mercy will meet us." Eliza looped her arm through his, her body trembling. "I believe it's going to be up to us."

"We can do it. We can do anything together." He put his

arm around her shoulder and squeezed, his heart thudding like mad as hope and anxiety spun inside him.

They approached the wooden steps. Eliza paused. "If you go back, you're going to have to convince me to say yes. What if you can't?"

"I'll convince you." He smiled with confidence he didn't have.

She opened the door. The place was empty, save for one wooden table and two chairs at the center of the single room. No fire in the hearth. It looked like a shell of a home. They walked inside, and Jesse set the lantern on the edge of the table, leaving room for the quilt, its flame casting eerie shadows around them.

Eliza's hands were shaking as she handed Jesse the scissors and sewing needle.

"This will work," he offered with all the encouragement he could muster. He sat down in one of the chairs. "What do I do now?"

"Concentrate on the day at the creek, over eight years ago, then break a thread on the quilt, thread the needle with the broken thread, and restitch it."

He paused, focusing. "I remember every moment of that day. From both timelines. But they're so intertwined to me. How do I get to the right one?"

"I don't know." Eliza shook her head. "Jesse, look." She pointed at the quilt. A thread was glowing. "There's your thread. Break it. Then sew a new one."

Jesse touched the glowing thread. The creek. He picked up the scissors and cut it.

Eliza held out a needle. Jesse took it and clumsily threaded it with the shimmering string still attached to the quilt. Before jabbing the quilt with the needle, he looked at Eliza. She nodded, looking confident in his ability to do this right. He poked the needle into the gap he'd made when he cut the thread.

The world spun, lighting up. Suddenly he was surrounded by a summer evening. The crickets and cicadas chirped. Cool water ran over his bare feet. And Eliza . . .

She was standing in the creek with him. Her face was young—still a teen. And yet . . . her eyes contained deep sadness. He was back in time, no doubt. The time where she'd turned him down. His time here was limited, and he couldn't afford to return to the former time without convincing her to marry him. How should he go at it? There wasn't time to deal with it head-on by telling her the truth of his own time travel or trying to explain how badly she longed for the life they once had.

"Eliza, sit on the riverbank with me."

She looked as if she was about to be sick to her stomach. "Sure."

He cleared his throat, trying to remember the words he'd said. "I think a cabin would go well right over there." He pointed to where their home would go. *Please let us be able to go home!* "Then we wouldn't have to walk far from the creek to be home."

She licked her dry lips. "You should build a cabin there for you and your future family."

"Eliza, I have so many ideas I want to share with you. About the business I want to build. How I want to help our community. It's going to take work and perseverance and *waiting.* Goodness, the waiting is going to be hard. But it's worth it. Us together is worth everything."

She looked confused at his words, like they were wrong. No doubt they were different from what she'd remembered. "You should build it. Your business, your home. But you'll have to choose someone compatible with you to build that life with."

"You're grieving, and you're hurting over something that hasn't happened yet. I am so, so sorry. Grief will be a part of our journey. There's no escaping it."

Her face drained of color. "Wait." She studied him but seemed to shake off her concerns. "Listen to me, Jesse: you don't have to walk that path with me. You can have happiness and *children* with someone else—"

"I *want* to walk that path with you. Only you. I'd choose the pain every time if it means getting to wake up beside you. To go on the journey with you. Eliza, I know it seems bleak now, but I promise, joy comes in the morning. Just like the Bible teaches us. We just have to get to the morning, and we haven't yet. But I promise to be there for you as we walk through the darkness of night. Let me in. Trust me. Let *me* make that choice you came here intending to remove from me."

Tears ran down her cheeks. "Jesse, you don't understand what will happen if we marry."

"Yes, I do. Look at me. I *do*. I'm here to tell you that. I'm going in with my eyes as wide-open as my heart. I want a life with you."

Her eyes went wide, and her breath caught. She must've fully realized now. "The quilt . . ." Her words were barely over a whisper.

"Please hear my words and trust them, trust me. I'm talking to both young Eliza and grieving Eliza. You're the most important person in the world to me—past, present, and future. I know you in all of them."

"You can't want this pain. Not if we can avoid it. I'm trying to set you free, Jesse."

He shook his head. "We can't avoid pain. It can only be doled out differently. We're human. Yes, we grieve . . . hard. But that grief is born out of love."

"I love you too much to doom you. I . . . don't think I'll ever feel better."

"The thing about grief is while we're in the midst of it, the dark seems endless. But I've seen it. You'll find yourself again. Trust me. Trust God."

"But it's hard. Penelope . . ."

"She's in her heavenly Father's arms. Her life was short, but it was important. All of our lives are short compared to eternity. But we're all precious to Him."

"What should I do?"

"Trust God. And trust in my love for you. Marry me."

Her mouth opened to reply, but the world dimmed to darkness before he heard her answer.

Chapter Thirty-Five

Consciousness slowly roused in Eliza's mind. She pushed against white sheets and the edge of a thick quilt. Her bed. Which bed? Her eyes struggled to adjust to the early morning light. She thrust her right hand out to the space next to her, grasping, hoping . . .

The pillow was cold. Rubbing her eyes, she sat up. This was the bedroom she shared with Jesse. Pine walls and a quilt she'd made on their bed. But where was he? She looked around for any clues. His clothes weren't hanging from the wall rack. None of his shoes were on the shoe rack.

Dread shrouded her. What had happened? A cold sweat crept down her neck and back. The time travel—it was so difficult to tell what would change. Their home existed. But why wasn't Jesse here?

She threw the covers off and jumped to her feet. "Jesse?" She spotted the quilt hanging on a quilt rack at the foot of the bed. Something needed to be done with that—perhaps she should give it to a museum to use as part of their early American history section. She wasn't sure yet, but she'd never, ever use it again or pass it down to someone else.

She ran out of their bedroom, through the hall, and to the kitchen. It was still dim, quiet. No coffee or breakfast greeted her, the way he used to sneak awake during her pregnancy to fix her food to stave off morning sickness.

She leaned against her table, breathing hard. *Think.* This was a different time than the one she'd been in before last night—their house was here again, after all. Shouldn't she have memories of what happened?

She caught sight of the tree wall hanging she'd sewn before they were married. Yes, they were married here. That was a relief. She walked to it and examined it. Penelope's name was written on the first branch of the tree, along with her birth and death date: September 22.

A wave of relief washed over Eliza. Her daughter existed. The memories of Penelope's birth were as strong as ever. She'd never have to worry about forgetting meeting her. How strange to feel grateful to have carried her for nine months and held her for a few precious moments rather than only feel the grief of the difficult loss.

But Eliza couldn't relax yet, not without Jesse. Maybe someone else would know. Dat! Was he sick in this time? Were he and Mamm still selling their land? She rushed back to her room and dressed quickly, adding a warm coat over her dress. It didn't matter how early in the morning it was, she had to know, had to find out if everyone was okay. She'd ride and find out—and find Jesse!

Eliza rushed out the front door, not bothering to lock it. She hurried to the barn and saddled her horse just as quickly, hands shaking, but not with cold. She led the mare out of her stall and out of the small barn to the mounting block, where she climbed onto the saddle.

Jesse, where are you? As her horse trotted toward her parents' home, she tried to pull up any memories she could. What had happened at the creek? She remembered time traveling, turning Jesse down, but things were so . . . muddled. He'd met her there! The him from the future. An understanding washed over her. She'd said yes!

Her parents' house came into view. The relief at the sight of it nearly made her fall off her horse. It was fixed up with fresh paint. Dat was standing on the porch, a hot cup of coffee in hand. He waved at her. "Mornin', Eliza. Everything okay?"

She dismounted her mare. "Jah, I think so. Have you seen Jesse?"

"Was I supposed to?"

She fumbled with the reins as she secured her horse to the hitching post. "I . . . don't know. How are you feeling, Dat?"

"Me?" He tilted his head. "I'm good."

She ran to him and hugged him tight, making his coffee slosh. He wasn't sick. She wouldn't see him die in the next few months.

He chuckled. "Hm. Bad dream, perhaps?"

Had he seen anything? Would he get visions of the other times like Jesse had? She nodded. "You could say that."

He smiled. "You look good, Daughter, better than I've seen you look in months."

She returned his smile. "I'm better, Dat." Her grief wasn't gone. It was still a strong part of her, would be for a while yet, but she carried it differently now—with some perspective and a whisper of gratefulness for what she and Jesse had together, however briefly. "Where's Ruth?"

"Probably getting ready for work."

"Her work at the school?"

"Um, are you okay? Did you need Ruth for something?"

She nodded quickly. "I'm fine. I just need to get my bearings."

Ruth came barging out the front door. "Eliza! I heard your voice." Ruth grabbed her and hugged her tight. "You did it!"

Well, Ruth certainly thought they were back in the right timeline. Eliza stepped back, looking in her sister's eyes. "Jesse did it. He's the one that went back. Have you seen him yet? Or Andrew?"

"Not yet." She gestured toward Dat with her head, grinning. "But I've had a bit of time with Dat, and he's good. And Moses!"

Dat raised an eyebrow and took a sip of his coffee. "Is there something going on I should know about?"

Ruth scratched her head. "Um, nah. We've just been busy setting things right in our little corner of life."

Dat laughed. "Well, if that's all."

Ruth giggled, looking at Eliza. "I think I need to call a substitute teacher for today. I can't stay in a one-room school teaching on a day like today. We need to live this day right!" Ruth was one very happy woman.

Eliza couldn't match her sister's excitement, although she was relieved by what she did know about this time.

Dat chuckled and headed inside.

"To the phone shanty," Ruth said.

Eliza walked across the yard with her. "Tell them I need you today. It's not a lie. They'll understand." She wasn't shunned here—the community didn't hate her for breaking up Jesse's marriage to Martha. Here people admired her for helping Jesse build a business that made life better for the Amish in these parts, a difference that would matter for generations to come.

"Of course." Ruth went into the phone shanty. "Just a minute."

As Ruth made her call, Eliza tried again to remember exactly what had happened. She'd told Jesse yes. From that day on, after accepting his proposal at the creek, she hadn't remembered changing time or telling Jesse no, not until today. She'd been living her life as she would have without time travel or memory of it . . . until she woke this morning. She'd told him yes at the creek, and her resolve to marry him never wavered. They'd waited five years to marry, just like the first time. And the memories from her wedding day were very clear: Jesse running late, receiving the quilt from Auntie Rose, running outside to meet him as he arrived. If that was all the same, where was he today?

She'd still lost two babies early in pregnancy, and she'd carried and given birth to Penelope with Jesse at her side. Penelope was still affected by the genetic disease. Mercy had said nothing could change that.

What had she been doing for the past month—the month

she'd spent in the other time, inadvertently breaking up Martha and Jesse and coping with all the havoc she'd caused in people's lives when she'd changed time?

She remembered now: praying, grieving, healing. That'd taken place in this time. Taking care of her mind and body. Ruth had returned to work with Eliza's blessing. Jesse too, going back to the job that was so important to their entire community.

The sound of trotting hooves on the gravel made her look up.

Jesse! Her heart went wild.

A memory came to her. Yesterday he'd gone on his first overnight trip since they lost Penelope.

He nudged his horse faster at the sight of her, closing the distance, then easing it to a stop.

He dismounted, holding the reins in one hand. "Eliza, I'm so sorry. Apparently I was out of town last night of all nights. When I woke around two in the morning . . . after, you know what, I realized I needed to get back to you so you didn't think the worst. I just came from our house and you weren't there, so I figured you were here."

She laughed and cried at the same time. She cupped his bearded face with both her hands. "You're home now. We're home."

He pressed his forehead to hers. "We are. We did it. I'm so proud of you. You were so brave."

"Me? I'm the one that messed everything up to begin with. You went back—you met me at my weakest point and convinced me."

He shook his head, smiling through tears of his own.

"That strength had to come from you. You've always had it in you. You bring out the best in me, in everyone in your life. You've always been a pillar and didn't even realize it."

He kissed her and the feeling of rightness—of being home—engulfed her entire being.

She hugged him tight. "I love you. I love you so much. I promise to never doubt that God brought us together."

From behind her, Ruth chuckled. "Boy, am I glad to see you, Brother-in-Law! But not as glad as Eliza is."

Jesse put an arm around Eliza's shoulders as she turned to face Ruth. "The way things happened, we didn't have time to even think about getting you." He shrugged.

"Whatever you did, I'm just glad it worked. But we need to find Andrew. And Ben."

Jesse smiled. "Ben was on the trip with me. He's alive and well. Snoring peacefully last I saw him. He's coming back later this morning. But I woke in the wee hours of the morning, impatient and needing to see my wife."

Ben's alive. Eliza felt fresh relief at those words. She knew they were true because she remembered Ben working with Jesse all these years.

Eliza nodded at her sister. "Go find Andrew. If you feel like it, bring him to our house. I'll make us a cake or something."

Ruth grinned. "A welcome-back-to-the-right-timeline cake. Who knew? A whole new occasion to celebrate!" She gestured toward the barn. "I'll leave you two and go hitch a horse to a carriage."

"I'm still focused on the 'our house' part," Jesse said. "Care to go there now, my dear wife?"

Eliza laughed, leaning into Jesse's warm chest. Home. She was home.

Ruth grabbed the rig's hefty tack off the barn wall, getting ready to hitch a horse to a buggy. A familiar sound of carriage wheels caught her attention, and she went to the barn door to look out. A rig came toward her home, but she couldn't make out the driver. Her parents came out onto the porch, each carrying a cup of coffee. Mamm smiled and waved at her, looking so much healthier and content than in yesterday's time.

The driver of the rig came into view. Andrew! She hurried toward him, nearly jumping for joy. Each inch that the wheels rolled brought him closer to her. She'd missed the Andrew who knew her like this Andrew did, the one who spent years getting to know her, falling in deep like with her, maybe even going so far as falling in love. She ran to him, not caring how crazy she looked to her folks.

He slowed his rig until coming to a stop, and she met him at the driver's door. No more little white car rolling up to the house. She liked this much better.

"Hey there." He grinned and got out of the buggy in one big step, then lifted her, spinning her in a circle. He lowered her feet to the ground and hugged her tight. "Ruth."

"You remember, right?"

His brows furrowed. "I remember you should be at school teaching, but you're not, and I remember you clearly looking thrilled to see me just now."

Her heart seemed to jolt to a stop.

He chuckled, holding up his hands in surrender. "I'm sorry. I remember everything. Well, I think I do. How would I know if it's not *everything*?"

She pushed his shoulder, laughing. "You're full of energy to burn, aren't you?"

"I am. I woke in my home with research papers spread out over a table in my bedroom for an article I'm working on for the *County Times*, and all I wanted to do was rush here to see you . . . in this timeline."

"I know!" She held her hands up and did a little jig. "I'm so happy." More so than she could ever put into words. "I called a sub to cover me at the school. I couldn't see working, not today. I wouldn't be able to stand it, wouldn't be able to pay attention. It's a celebration day."

"It is that. I went to the phone shanty to call Aunt Lydia's house, hoping Ben was there, but she hadn't seen him. He'd been on a trip. I left a message for him to meet up with me as soon as possible. I'm so ready to see him. But until then, would you care to take a ride with me?"

She smiled. "Jah, please."

She waved to her mamm and dat. Mamm nodded at her, looking very pleased.

Andrew seemed to notice her folks for the first time.

Mamm smiled, waving at Andrew. *"Guder Marye, Andrew."*

He waved back. "It is a good morning. Same to you." He followed Ruth to the passenger side, holding the door open. "I think she likes me a little better in this time."

Ruth nodded. "Just a wee bit."

He got in on his side, and they rode down the long, familiar path of her driveway, slowly leaving the ridge and entering the glen, continuing toward town.

Their chatter filled the cab of the buggy with talk of their relief at being home, hopes for the future, hypotheses of why the time travel worked and where it came from. Should they try to find Verna and Omar here? Why did they have memories when it was Eliza and Jesse who found the cabin and went back? Would the memories they'd made in the alternate time ever fade? About thirty minutes later, Andrew stopped the rig at the Calico Creek Public Library.

Ruth laughed. "What are we researching now? Whatever it is, we may have to wait. I don't think they're open yet. They don't open until eleven on Fridays."

Andrew grinned at her as he brought his horse to a stop. "It seemed like the most appropriate place."

"For what?"

"Hold on, you have to move your feet so I can get to something."

He had something he wanted to show her?

She turned her body, pulling her knees in as she moved completely onto the bench seat.

Andrew moved a blanket aside and removed a large package, about the size of Ruth's torso and a hand-length thick, wrapped in brown paper with a twine bow.

How had he found time to get her a gift?

She ran her hands over the stiff brown paper. "What did you do?"

"Something I've thought long and hard about. In both

timelines, actually. Open it. You may not like it, and you may not be ready for this."

Ruth pulled on the twine to release the bow, then carefully removed the paper.

It was a wall clock with beautiful mahogany wood, a shining gold face, and a golden pendulum under filigreed glass. A wall-hanging grandfather clock.

She ran her fingers over the carved wood. "A beautiful antique reminder of the value of time."

"It's certainly a great reminder of time and all that means to us, but this isn't about that."

She looked up, meeting his eyes. "It's an engagement ring?" she teased.

Andrew fidgeted with the reins as they sat still in the library parking lot. "I don't know why I'm nervous, 'cause I think I've made myself pretty clear in that awful evaluation meeting we attended in the other time."

Her heart ran wild. This handsome, smart man she adored wanted to marry her.

He reached over and put his hand on hers. "Ruth, you're the one I want to be with, and if this experience taught me anything, it's that no matter where I go or what I want out of life, you eclipse all else for me. Will you marry me?"

"Jah! Many times over, jah." She couldn't reply fast enough.

He grinned. "Good. Phew. I remember back when you didn't want to marry."

"You didn't want a spouse either. Something changed that."

"Someone snatched my heart and every thought." His eyes met hers.

He wanted to marry her! Her heart palpitated. "We'll have to both go through instruction and wait almost a year from now before the next wedding season."

"I know. I wish we'd gone through instructions last spring."

She touched the smooth wood of the beautiful timepiece. "You spent too much on this!"

"Actually, I didn't. It's an antique. I found it in the attic about two months ago. You remember when I was looking around in there for something to cheer you up after Penelope died. I knew it would mean more to you than something brand-new. I had a clockmaker fix up the mechanism, and apparently during this timeline, somewhere between the Ebersol family gathering and last week, I asked Jesse's dad to polish and refinish the wood. I have memories of doing it."

This was just like Andrew—he thought long and hard about each one of his actions, taking his time. And when he acted, he had no regrets, no wavering on his decisions. She loved that about him.

But she had to be sure about one more thing.

"Andrew, the whole reason for the crazy journey we went on was that Eliza and Jesse are carriers for a deadly disease. We each could be too. I know this, and I accept the risks. Are you . . . ?" How could she ask the question?

"I already know about the genetic disease and our risks. Somehow my brain retained a good bit of that college education. I wonder if a side effect of that trip will be that I keep the knowledge. I know that we, just like Jesse and Eliza, could face a one-in-four risk for each of our children. I trust

God, and I trust that you're the partner I want in life, whatever path that brings. I'd never want to change it. As far as children go, we could have as many or as few as you want. I know the Old Ways don't allow for birth control, but we could use natural family planning."

That was a relief to hear. "Jah. I agree, and we'll figure it all out as we go."

"Ruth." He caressed her face. "May I kiss you?"

"You may." Ruth leaned forward, and they kissed over the clock. Her first kiss. Butterflies seemed to be floating through her body. A clock—it was a magnificent gift. It meant engagement. But he was also giving her time, a timeline they could build together. An amazing blessing that they'd never second-guess.

"Wow," he whispered as their kiss broke.

A silver car pulled up beside their buggy, making them look. Did they think the people in the Amish rig sitting outside a closed library needed help?

The back passenger door opened. A familiar Amish young man got out.

"Ben!" she squealed.

Andrew met Ruth's eyes, grinning even bigger. He nodded to her, and she gently set the clock on the bench seat of the buggy, scooting over to exit through the driver's side with Andrew.

Ben had barely shut the car door when Ruth and Andrew grabbed him, hugging him tightly, one on each side.

"Uh, guys? You okay?"

Ruth squeezed him tighter. "We're just really glad to see you!"

After a moment, Andrew clapped him on the shoulder as they released him. "So glad."

Ben laughed as he fixed his hat and rumpled shirt. "Guess I should go out of town more often."

Ruth crossed her arms, looking at the silver car leaving, obviously a hired driver. "How'd you know to find us here?"

"It's nothing magical. I had a driver taking me home after Jesse left *very* early this morning—not sure what was up with that—and as I was riding through town, I saw Andrew's rig pulled up to the library." He nodded at Andrew. "Did ya give her the . . . you know?"

"He did. I said yes." Ruth beamed. "Of course I said yes—in this time or any other. We'll go through instruction, then marry in the fall." She pointed at him. "I'm going to be on the lookout for the perfect young woman to pair you with on our wedding day."

"You do that, Ruth." Ben straightened his hat. "Maybe you'll find me a wife."

"Oh, I asked Mamm about a Martha Peight," Andrew said. "She's single, still living at home in Brush Hollow. We need to finagle a connection between her and Moses. Jah?"

Ruth looped her arm through Andrew's. "I love how you think."

They'd face whatever the future brought, together.

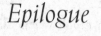

Epilogue

A YEAR LATER

Eliza squeezed Jesse's hand, turning both their hands pale. The pain was blinding, threatening to overtake her, but she'd done this before. *Breathe. Take it slow. It'll pass. It always does.* The wave subsided, and Eliza stared at the ceiling of their cabin, so grateful to be inside the home Jesse had built for them.

"She's crowning," Leah's steady voice encouraged. "Breathe through it, Eliza. Not too fast."

She. They knew their baby was a she already; they'd seen her thanks to modern medicine and two ultrasounds.

Another tightening racked Eliza's body. *I can do this.* It was almost like she was a bystander in the process of childbirth, her body taking on a mind of its own. *Don't get injured,* she told it. *That way you can take care of your family.*

Jesse wiped her forehead with a cool washcloth. "So close. She'll be with us soon."

They'd worried so much when Eliza came up pregnant again. Even after all they'd been through to get there. Even though they trusted God. How could they not feel angst? Trust and faith didn't erase human emotion. Jesus wept even when He knew He'd raise Lazarus from the grave. Overwhelming emotions weren't a reflection of whether someone had faith or not.

Eliza reached up and grasped Jesse's arm. She made herself take a mental step back. Set everything aside and just *trust*.

"There's the head! One more push!"

A great relief flooded Eliza as the tiny body separated from hers.

"Beautiful job, Eliza!"

Eliza closed her eyes, breathing easier. The pain had completely subsided. Then . . . a warmth on her chest, in her arms. Her baby! Faith's dark eyes met Eliza's instantly. How strange—it felt like she'd always been here.

Faith cried, the volume shocking for her tiny size. On instinct, Eliza started to shush her, then remembered and chuckled to herself. Crying was *supposed* to happen with newborns. Tears obscured her vision, and she tried to wipe them with her shoulder. Jesse wiped them for her, then kissed her deeply.

He put his hand on their baby's still-wet head, murmuring softly, and she realized he was praying.

Jesse reached into the soft towel that wrapped Faith and pulled her two little fists out. Eliza needed to see this too. Her mind tallied the number of digits. Five fingers on each hand. *Thank You, thank You, God.*

They would've loved her just as fiercely if she'd had six on one of her perfect hands, as they still loved Penelope. She was a big sister in heaven now. Did she know about Faith? Could Penelope see her family from heaven? So many unknowns. So many things Eliza wouldn't get to know. But what she knew was enough.

Leah changed the pad beneath Eliza, then tucked in the covers around her legs. "No injuries. Can I examine baby Faith now?"

How long had they been staring at her? It was like time had ceased to exist. She'd hardly noticed what Leah or her own body had been doing. She and Jesse were totally focused on the miracle they were staring at. Eliza nodded at her midwife, then passed Faith, still wrapped in her towel, to Jesse.

Jesse cradled her like she was the most precious thing in the world, kissing her soft forehead. He moved carefully to Leah, who'd set out some examination items on a towel at the end of their bed. Eliza sat up a bit to watch them.

Leah unwrapped Faith, and the newborn started wailing again. "That's what I like to hear. Look." She pointed at Faith's chest, smiling. Memories of that dreaded moment with Penelope came crashing back: the moment Eliza and Jesse realized Penelope couldn't stay with them. But that wasn't what was happening today. Faith's chest *wasn't* hourglass-shaped. Her cries were strong and robust.

Leah clamped the baby's umbilical cord and handed the scissors to Jesse for him to cut it.

Eliza watched Jesse assist Leah in weighing, diapering, and

rewrapping Faith in a fresh receiving blanket. Her pain—all that had happened—had led them to this moment. And here there was peace, happiness, even . . . wow. After Penelope died, Eliza had felt she'd never love another baby that fiercely, that doubt even creeping in during her pregnancy. But love wasn't a finite resource. She loved Penelope just as strongly as she always had *and* loved Faith the same.

Jesse brought Faith, now clean and swaddled, to Eliza's arms.

A knock sounded on the door to their bedroom. "Eliza?" Ruth's voice was brimming with anticipation. She and Andrew had been waiting in the living room.

Eliza opened her mouth to respond, but Leah pointed at her. "Quick visit. Mamm and Bobbeli need to nurse. Did I say it right? I've done so many Amish births, I figure I should work on my Pennsylvania Dutch." Leah winked at her.

Mamm. Eliza breathed it in. She was a mamm. She'd been one for a long time, but now a healthy baby was in her arms.

"Jah, Ruth. Come in. You both can; I'm decent."

Ruth burst through the door, a huge grin on her face. She carried a tin pitcher of daisies. "Hi." She placed the daisies on Eliza's dresser, then ran to her side. "So happy for you." Ruth gave her a tight hug across her shoulders, being careful of the baby in her arms.

"Meet your niece." Jesse put a hand on Faith's swaddled chest. The little girl had settled into a contented sleep. Must be big work being born.

"Aww!" Tears were in Ruth's eyes. "Little Faith!"

Eliza had shared Faith's name—and medical status—with Ruth while she was still pregnant. Since she and Jesse had known about their one-in-four chance of having a baby with Ellis-Van Creveld, they qualified for some additional prenatal care, including ultrasounds. They'd never again have a pregnancy where they were blindsided by a sick baby at birth. They'd known from twelve weeks along and again at twenty weeks into the pregnancy that Faith was healthy.

"She's beautiful, brother." Andrew shook Jesse's hand before pulling him into a hug.

"Denki." Jesse's face was absolutely alight with how big he was smiling.

As Ruth gushed over Faith's tiny and adorable features, Eliza took in her sister. She was going to be the best aunt. She already was. And one day perhaps a mother herself. She and Andrew were taking their time with their engagement, enjoying each other while preparing to be wed in just a few weeks.

"Out with you both." Leah winked at Ruth and Andrew, shooing them out.

Soon Eliza settled into nursing her new and precious gift.

An hour later, Ruth was back with her, this time bringing a big glass of orange juice and a bowl of beef stew.

Jesse sat in the high-back chair next to the bed and held little Faith, who was now swaddled and sleeping.

"I'm not sure if this is the best time to tell you, but I finally got my results in."

Eliza didn't need to ask which results those were. Three months ago, Ruth and Andrew had tests run for a full genetics panel, just to have a chance of knowing what they would face when they tried to grow their family after marriage.

"We don't carry the genetic issue you and Jesse do."

Eliza squealed and reached for Ruth. "Jah!" She held her tight. "I'm thrilled for you."

"I know you're as thrilled about it as we are." Ruth gave another squeeze before releasing her sister.

Eliza's and Jesse's eyes met. They had a burden to carry in that area, but through ultrasounds, they would learn the fate of each child early on. They'd use that time to prepare themselves, knowing they'd have to lean in to the pain, sit with it, accept it, and release it, remembering to be grateful for all they did have.

Ruth sat on the edge of the bed. "Guess what? Despite the obstacles we've faced trying to get Moses and Martha to meet, he . . . by happenstance . . . or rather by God's steps, ran into her in the grocery store earlier today."

"How?" Eliza laughed. "They live in different towns and don't go to the same stores."

Ruth shrugged. "Who in this world knows? After all our failed efforts, they met on their own, and she invited him to attend a Brush Hollow singing."

Everyone in the room cheered.

"Finally!" Eliza clapped before sinking back onto the bed and closing her eyes.

Her heart was so full, so very grateful for being given a second chance at this life with its flaws and blessings. Dat was healthy and whole. Mamm was so proud of Eliza and Ruth, not remembering the poverty or shame Eliza had brought back into their lives. Jesse's and Eliza's brothers and so many young and older Amish men had good jobs through Ebersol Cabins.

Verna and Omar were doing well. They weren't welcome

in the community, but the four of them—Jesse, Eliza, Ruth, and Andrew—visited every few months, and they intended to continue doing so. They were good people who missed having Amish family. Eliza and the others couldn't fix that, but they could ease their pain.

The quilt hung in a museum hundreds of miles away. The curator had been thrilled to have this piece of Americana. To onlookers, it would conjure up matronly women of faith sewing as they crossed the ocean and began life in this new land. It was so much more, but like most objects—or people—that survived time, no one knew most of the history.

Cradling Faith in his arms, Jesse moved to the edge of the bed. "Look at what we've done, Eliza." His smile warmed her heart.

Eliza drew a cleansing breath. "Denki for loving me through my worst, for forgiving me, for helping me to set things right again." She looked at Ruth. "The same is true of you, Sister." Eliza longed to live worthy of such love. She never could, but she'd spend her life enjoying the blessing of trying.

A Note from the Authors

Hello, dear readers! Erin and I appreciate you so very much, and we felt you might enjoy knowing a little about why we wrote this Amish time travel story.

In January 2016, I lost an unborn granddaughter to an incredibly rare and, in this case, fatal form of dwarfism called Ellis-Van Creveld syndrome or EVC. Erin was halfway through her pregnancy at twenty weeks. During this difficult time, I began texting Erin in a different manner than we'd done before. We could share our grief in great fullness through texting because we were free of trying to control our tears, our trembling voices, and the emotion on our faces. We were also free of needing to respond immediately, like people often do when face-to-face.

Soon, through the deeper bond we were experiencing, I had a new thought spring up—what if Erin wrote some chapters for and with me on a novella I was writing? Later, when I asked her via a text, she really liked the idea of refocusing her thoughts into something creative for a few hours each day. We knew it wouldn't end the grief, and we weren't looking for it to do that. Grief is a difficult season that all of us will experience one day, but to get past the most difficult parts of it in a healthy way, we have to allow it whatever time it needs.

Erin once expressed her thoughts on my blog: *Suddenly and unexpectedly, my husband and I faced grief unlike anything we had experienced. When someone you love dies, especially so out of turn as losing a child, the grief of such loss feels as if a hole has been ripped in your lives and the former quilt of your family is frayed beyond recognition. How do we face the fact that there will always be a child missing in our family?*

After this loss—their second loss—Adam and Erin had each side of the family, grandparents included, give blood for genetic testing. One grandparent on each side was a carrier of EVC. I was the carrier on Adam's side. In a striking coincidence, Ellis-Van Creveld is seen mostly among the Amish, though it occurs sporadically throughout the world. Based on the genetic testing, it appears that neither Adam nor Erin has any Amish ancestors, nor relation to the other, and although the syndrome is still called Ellis-Van Creveld, the version we carry is on a different gene than the version seen among the Amish. Yet with my being an Amish fiction author, this coincidence was too great to ignore.

All of those things—shared heartache, genetic information, and new writing partnership—created rich soil for brainstorming on a story of loss, grief, and the often-distraught desire to go back in time and change one event. We shared many conversations and took many notes for years before we were ready to write this story.

If you've ever wondered what it might be like to go back in time and change one event, you've come to the right place, dear readers. Erin and I would love to hear from you at cindy@cindywoodsmall.com.

Thank you for suspending your disbelief to read this fiction story! We enjoyed adding the supernatural element, even though (thankfully for us!) time travel remains purely in the imagination.

Gross Sege (Many blessings),
Cindy and Erin

Discussion Questions

1. Eliza and Jesse choose to have a long engagement, which is not something Amish typically do. Andrew and Ruth also take an unusually long path to get to know each other. Do you feel the characters were justified in their choices, or should they have followed Amish tradition?

2. Eliza carries guilt as well as grief after her repeated pregnancy losses, yet she never blames her husband. If Eliza were your friend, how would you comfort her if she came to you with this self-blame? Are there any Bible passages you'd recommend she read? Do you think society tends to hold women more responsible for infertility or pregnancy losses than men?

3. When Ruth is stuck in the mess Eliza created, she's justifiably angry with her sister. Do you feel Ruth's interactions with Eliza directly after the timeline adjustment are too harsh, not harsh enough, or have an appropriate amount of anger? If the changes couldn't be undone and you were mediating the two

sisters through their arguments, what might you suggest they do to mend their relationship?

4. A theme throughout the book is how one tiny change can affect an untold number of other things. Is there another event in Eliza's life you'd suggest changing to get a better outcome? What one event in your life would you be most tempted to change, if given the chance? What do you imagine the ripple effects might be?

5. Many people, like Andrew, go through a deconstruction and reconstruction of their faith when they're young adults. What are some tips or resources you'd recommend to a person like Andrew? What do you think Andrew's future would've been like if he'd remained estranged from the Amish?

6. Were you surprised by what Verna reveals as the true curse? Do you feel that her advice to Ruth and Andrew is fair? If you were Ruth and could ask Verna an additional question, what would it be?

7. After Jesse ends his engagement to Martha, he and Eliza face the bishop's fury and their own families' confusion and disappointment. Could they have handled the situation better? If yes, how so?

8. Once the timeline changed, if Eliza and Jesse had decided to sneak off and marry, they would have had to face the outrage of their community and the consequences of such a rash decision. How would that have affected your view of them?

9. Despite the warnings and setbacks they face, Eliza and the others are determined to undo the time change through rebuilding the cabin and remaking the quilt. Why do you think their efforts were unsuccessful? How do you discern when obstacles should be pushed through and when they're meant to keep you from a certain path? What do you think the characters learn in the end about our own efforts versus God's grace?

10. How did you expect this story to end—with a return to the original timeline or with our characters in the new timeline permanently? If you were writing this book, which ending would you have chosen? Why?

Acknowledgments

To Dr. Jeff Bizon, Dr. Alexander Allaire, Dr. Ravinder Dhallan, and all the kind medical practitioners who helped me, Erin, through the genetic testing process I went through in 2016. The knowledge you shared with me was invaluable both to my medical needs and also in this story's creation.

To Jan Stob and Sarah Rische with Tyndale House Publishers, thank you for your encouragement and support. You've been inspiring and uplifting during every step of this journey, and we appreciate it deeply.

To Wes Yoder, we came to you with a unique idea for this genre, and you supported us. You also answered some unusual questions about how the Amish might handle certain aspects of the time travel. Thank you!

To our husbands, Tommy and Adam, as always, thank you for your ears, sharing your areas of expertise, and offering cherished opinions.

To my friends and family who supported me through listening to ideas, babysitting, moral support, and more—thank you! —Erin

To my friends and family who supported me in the same

ways as Erin's supported her—minus the need for child-care!—but often in the form of sharing meals—thank you!
—Cindy

We'd like to encourage anyone who feels led to donate to helping Amish families dealing with genetic disease to consider the Clinic for Special Children. They provide genetic counseling and testing, physician home visits, and palliative care visits for Amish children and families dealing with genetic disease. You can find them at clinicforspecialchildren.org.

About the Authors

CINDY WOODSMALL is a *New York Times* and CBA best-selling author of twenty-five works of fiction and one nonfiction book. Coverage of Cindy's writing has been featured on ABC's *Nightline* and the front page of the *Wall Street Journal*. She lives in the foothills of the north Georgia mountains with her husband, just a short distance from two of her three sons and her six grandchildren.

ERIN WOODSMALL is a writer, musician, wife, and mom of four. She has edited, brainstormed, and researched books with Cindy for almost a decade. More recently she and Cindy have coauthored five books, one of which was a winner of the prestigious Christy Award.

TYNDALE HOUSE PUBLISHERS IS CRAZY4FICTION!

Fiction that entertains and inspires

Get to know us! Become a member of the Crazy4Fiction community. Whether you read our blog, like us on Facebook, follow us on Twitter, or receive our e-newsletter, you're sure to get the latest news on the best in Christian fiction. You might even win something along the way!

JOIN IN THE FUN TODAY.

 crazy4fiction.com

 Crazy4Fiction

 crazy4fiction

 @Crazy4Fiction

By purchasing this book from Tyndale, you have
helped us meet the spiritual and physical needs of
people all around the world.